The Break-Up Clause

Niamh Hargan is a writer and lawyer. *The Break-Up Clause* is her second novel. Her first, *Twelve Days in May*, was shortlisted for the Katie Fforde RNA Debut Romantic Novel Award.

Born and raised in Northern Ireland, Niamh is now based primarily in Scotland. She has no husband, no children, no dogs, and no cats.

Also by Niamh Hargan

Twelve Days in May

The
Break-Up
Clause

NIAMH HARGAN

HarperCollins*Publishers*

HarperCollins*Publishers* Ltd
1 London Bridge Street,
London SE1 9GF

www.harpercollins.co.uk

HarperCollins*Publishers*
Macken House,
39/40 Mayor Street Upper,
Dublin 1
D01 C9W8
Ireland

First published by HarperCollins*Publishers* 2023
2

A catalogue record for this book is available from the British Library

ISBN: 978-0-00-851891-2

Set in Birka by Palimpsest Book Production Limited, Falkirk, Stirlingshire

Printed and bound in the UK using 100% Renewable Electricity by CPI Group (UK) Ltd

*To my sister, Caitriona: solving all my problems – creative,
sartorial and otherwise – since 1989. How did I get so lucky?*

WEEK ONE

Chapter One

On the rooftop of Zelnick, O'Leary and Abbott – 'Manhattan's largest mid-size law firm' – a speech has been going on for at least fifteen minutes. And Fia Callaghan has barely heard a word of it.

She caught the first bit.

'I'm thrilled to welcome this year's cohort of summer associates,' one of the partners said. To his left, twenty or so handpicked law students – all now blending into one large mass – nodded along eagerly.

'We're so pleased to have you with us, to learn from us *and* to teach us. You are the future of our profession. Over the next ten weeks, I can promise that you'll have the chance to get real, hands-on legal experience. Each of you will share an office with a dedicated "attorney mentor" from our firm. And, as ever, we'll also be inviting you to take part in our dynamic programme of networking and social events. I make no apologies for the fact that, here at Zelnick, O'Leary and Abbott – or "ZOLA", as we affectionately call it – we're especially known for our corporate and commercial expertise. But it's not *just* about the deal. We place an absolute premium on the mental wellbeing of our staff . . .'

It was probably somewhere around this point that Fia zoned out. By now, she's attended so many seminars on the firm's theoretical position on mental wellbeing that she could practically deliver one herself. In essence, there is a sunrise yoga class right here on this roof terrace on Tuesdays – which lawyers are welcome to attend if they book sufficiently far in advance to secure a spot – but those whose burnout necessitates more than two weeks off work should still fully expect to be fired.

Fia can't imagine that this reality is likely to feature in the partner's inspirational speech. But no matter. Even for her, it's hard to remain too much of a cynic on a morning like this one. Over in the far corner of the terrace, an impressive array of fruit and pastries has been laid out, with a waiter serving breakfast cocktails and coffees. And, against the clear blue sky, New York's familiar landmarks look practically computer-generated.

Fia lets herself gaze out at the Chrysler Building just ahead, as the partner chats away about *sharing expertise* and *strengthening bonds*. There are very few moments like this, whereupon Fia stops to think that she has made it here, in this city so far from home. Or, at the very least, she's *making* it. Starting today – starting with this year's summer associates' programme – she feels more firmly on course than ever before to meet her goals. Professionally speaking, that is.

Personally speaking, Fia doesn't honestly have any particular goals – although she has, in the very recent past and following a certain milestone birthday, begun to consider drumming up a few. It has occurred to her that, perhaps, at a minimum, she should set about developing some grown-up skills –

maybe unearth some sort of a latent passion, even. This seemed to be the thing about ageing, in the year 2023: you couldn't just let it happen, the way your mother and grandmother did before you. No. You had to be *getting better and better*. You had to be grasping at opportunities to *really get to know yourself*, etc.

What could Fia say for herself so far, aged 30 years and six weeks old?

I like to run the length and breadth of Manhattan with my headphones in. I like to drink overpriced cocktails with my friends. I am extremely good at getting red wine out of things, even very pale carpets – by the time I'm finished, you'd never know there'd been a spill at all. I can always keep my balance on a moving subway without needing to touch anything gross.

These are all true things, and they don't feel insubstantial when Fia is doing them – not one bit, actually. But she suspects the day might arrive when they'll feel extremely insubstantial in the retelling. She's not sure that they quite constitute the sort of fulfilment and well-roundedness she should probably be aiming for within this new decade.

In any event, of course, none of that matters here, in this skyscraper on Madison and 49th Street. Here, she wears a suit and bills for her time in six-minute increments, and people increasingly seem to think she knows what she is doing.

By the time the partner's speech ends and everyone has begun milling about (and/or wondering when they might politely sneak back to their desks), Fia can't help it: she's feeling veritably *peppy*. She's chatting idly with some of her co-workers when Celia – equity partner Celia – approaches.

'Hey, Fia, let's go find your new roomie, huh?' she suggests, and, right away, Fia looks suitably alert.

'Of course!' She finds a surface on which to deposit her empty mimosa glass. What a disappointment that had been, many years ago now, to learn that the American mimosa was no more than an Irish Buck's Fizz. 'Can't wait to meet her!'

'Meet *him*, you mean,' Celia returns. She leads them both through a few clusters of people, until she's reaching up to tap someone on the shoulder.

Very much a 'him' then, Fia thinks. This guy – apparently her mentee – must be nearing six feet tall. She pictures the desk that, just last week, had been wedged into the corner of her little office, practically forming a right angle with her own desk. That she might be sharing such close quarters with a *boy* had, for some reason, not even occurred to her before now. The small space is shrinking by the minute in her mind. She only hopes she's managed to conceal her dismay by the time this stranger in his navy-blue suit turns around to look at Celia.

And then, as he does, dismay suddenly becomes the least of it. All at once, Fia feels the breath sucked from her body, every last bit of her sunny disposition stolen within seconds.

Dark hair, dark eyes, the beginnings of a summer tan. It looks like him.

And yet . . . *no*, she thinks. It can't be.

Can it?

Her mind races, tries to find the glitch in the system here, the flaw in her own faculties. Is this an error of perception or of memory? It has to be one or the other – and, suddenly, she finds herself paralysingly unsure of which. It's been such a long time, after all – years, by now, since the two of them last laid eyes on one another.

'Benjamin, let me introduce you to Fia Callaghan,' Celia says then, her voice as brisk and bright as ever. 'She'll be your mentor for the summer. Fia, meet Benjamin Lowry.'

This serves not so much as an introduction but as an utterly dismal, dreaded confirmation. It *is* him. Really and truly.

'Oh my God!' Fia exclaims. The words fly out of her mouth before she can stop them, in direct contravention of her long-held and unfailingly successful policy: no displays of emotion in the office. She feels like her accent gets about 30 per cent more Irish than usual, to boot.

Celia looks very surprised – because overall it probably *is* a very surprising outburst – and Fia chokes out a little half-cough.

'Sorry. I, uh . . . hi,' she manages then, her voice sounding slightly more normal. Still, though, could she be having a stroke right now? Does someone in the vicinity need to act F.A.S.T.? In what could well be the last few seconds of full mobility she has left, she watches her own hand reaching out in greeting, as though it belongs to someone else entirely.

'I'm Fia,' she hears herself say.

And then, for what feels like a very long time (though in reality may be very little), he just *looks* at her. Benjamin does. Benjamin Lowry. Here, at her place of work. *Benjamin Lowry.*

Fia finds her breath hitching in her chest as she waits for whatever is to come next. An exclamation, a revelation . . . an apology, maybe? Needless to say, she wouldn't mind one of those, though given the choice, she'd very much prefer to receive it without an audience.

'. . . Hi,' he replies eventually.

That, apparently, is the height of it. That's all he has to say. He reaches out to meet her handshake, his fingers closing around hers, and what he looks, more than anything, is confused. *Confounded*, even. He looks pretty close to how she feels. Immediately, it is obvious to Fia that this is not some sort of plan on his part. It's not a trap, not a trick. He was no more expecting to see her today than she was expecting to see him.

Meanwhile, Celia appears happy as a clam. 'Fia's part of our private client team,' she swoops in easily. 'Which – I may be biased, but I have to say – I think is secretly the best one in the whole place. And Fia's one of our brightest associates – soon to be senior associates.'

Is there a little bit of a wink in her tone as she says that last bit, Fia wonders? A promise hidden underneath the quick smile tossed in her direction? It's extremely fortunate that Celia Hannity, of all the partners at ZOLA, happens to be Fia's direct boss – the head of the private client department. Right from the beginning, she has always seemed to be on Fia's side. Fia can't claim to be entirely sure why. That Celia was born, apparently, into a family of proudly blue-collar Irish Americans maybe hadn't hurt. 'We Irish girls have to stick together,' she has been known to proclaim, on more than one occasion.

Right now, though, she's turned her attention back to Benjamin. 'So, like we said in your final interview, you'll be assigned work from all our departments,' she's telling him, 'and from time to time you might relocate to be closer to different teams as the work demands. Fia's office is going to be your home base, though. She's here to point you in the right direction with assignments, answer any questions you might have . . . just think of her as your big sister for the summer.'

At this suggestion, an expression settles on Benjamin's face that, in other circumstances, Fia might actually somewhat enjoy. Bug-eyed and horrified, he looks like a guy in a hostage video. It could pass for nerves, though – probably.

'Got it,' he says, and Celia smiles warmly.

'All right, well, great! I'll be rounding everyone up soon, but there's a little bit of time before we have to head downstairs, so I'll leave you guys to get acquainted,' she replies.

With that, she disappears – off, no doubt, to make another introduction – and Fia and Benjamin just stare at one another.

In the silence that follows, it feels as though children could be born and raised. They could graduate and get married, take a cruise and die of old age. And yet, somehow, Fia Callaghan and Benjamin Lowry are still standing here, on a rooftop in Midtown Manhattan, astonishment pulsing silently between them.

'So, how've you been?' Benjamin asks eventually, ever the wisecracker.

Fia scowls, feeling in absolutely no mood for comedy. Instinctively, her eyes dart around, looking for somewhere they might escape listening ears. Save for off the side of the building (which seems extreme), the only option is inside, to the little vestibule that houses the lifts. Of course, it's glass fronted – at ZOLA, all the doors and walls are made of glass to the maximum extent permitted by modern engineering. There is really no such thing as privacy in this place. But it's as good as they're going to get right now.

She yanks her head in that direction and, wordlessly, Benjamin follows her as she marches over to the vestibule.

'*How've I been?*' she hisses in return, once they're inside it. 'Ben! What the fuck?! What are you *doing* here?'

'What are *you* doing here?' he counters, and he sounds every single bit as agitated as her now. He still, she notes, has that very slight hint of a North Carolina drawl.

'I work here, *obviously*.'

He shakes his head, as though in nothing less than disgust. 'I can see that,' he says icily.

Fia offers no reply. Her blood is pumping urgently through her veins, making her feel panicked, out of control. In such a context, words seem to fail her. What she wants, ideally, is to be able to let out an almighty screech, even if just for her own sense of release. Of course, she can't do that. The walls are only so soundproof. And, in fact, there has perhaps been a little too much gesticulating – on both their parts – already. Even the way they are standing probably seems more like two people about to begin a fencing match than two new co-workers getting to know one another, buoyed by a mutual love for American jurisprudence.

She forces herself to take a few deep breaths. She paces the perimeter of the small space, consciously willing her body to relax.

'Look, you can't be here,' she says, as soon as she feels able to speak once more. 'That's just the bottom line. I'm sorry. You're going to have to quit.'

What is blatantly obvious to her seems not remotely so to Benjamin – though that, she supposes, is nothing new.

'Are you kidding me?' he replies, quick as a flash. 'Do you know what I had to go through to get this gig? I would've had an easier time getting into fucking NASA for the summer.'

As it happens, Fia actually knows this to be true. In the US legal market, the summer associateship – coming as it does between the penultimate and final years of law school – is viewed as a vital step towards securing one's job prospects as a fully fledged attorney. Landing a position isn't easy, especially not at the larger commercial law firms. Now that she thinks about it, she's more than a little surprised that Benjamin Lowry, of all people, has evidently made it to the other side of that particular obstacle course.

Probably, she realizes, his parents know a guy. Plenty of that goes on, too.

'Well, we're going to have to get you reassigned, at least,' she says, thinking on her feet. 'Having you at the firm for the summer might be one thing, but having you in *my office* is . . . another.'

He shrugs. 'Cool with me.'

And isn't that so like him? No initiative, no follow-through. Just that same *laissez-faire* attitude she suddenly remembers perfectly. It restokes in Fia a very particular kind of exasperation. Nothing irritates her more than people who describe themselves as *chill* – as though that makes any kind of grammatical sense, as though it is a good thing. Don't they realize the inherent selfishness of that? Don't they realize the burden it puts on others?

Her eyes drift back outside to the terrace, and she can see that the summer associates are being corralled now in preparation for their tour of the building. They'll be heading this way, Celia Hannity at the helm, any minute.

Benjamin lets his gaze follow hers deliberately. 'So. I guess you can't exactly kick me out for no reason, right? Do you wanna tell the partners about our . . . situation?' he asks. 'Or shall I?'

That's when Fia realizes. He has her over a barrel here. What's more, he fucking knows it.

She very, very much does not want *anyone* to be telling the partners about their *situation*. That is true even setting aside her promotion prospects and thinking only of her professional standing and general personal dignity.

She inhales deeply through her nose and exhales just as deeply, the way Adriene does in yoga. It's nowhere near as cleansing as she might have hoped. But perhaps it does bring a certain clarity, an acceptance of the inescapable.

'All right, Benjamin. You know what? Fine. Fine!' She is unable to prevent her voice rising slightly, in a fashion she's sure he would term hysterical. 'It's ten weeks. If you have to be here, then you have to be here. I suppose we're just going to have to get through it.'

She glances outside once again, clocks the herd in motion. Within ten seconds, she knows, they will come through the vestibule doors, and Benjamin will be swept up into their midst. Nonetheless, she's not done here. And the thing – the one key thing – she has to say to him, she knows she can say fast.

She turns back towards him, her eyes narrowing to a squint. 'But I really think we should go ahead and get divorced, don't you?'

Chapter Two

Fia doesn't wait for the lifts. She can't bear to cram into one alongside Benjamin – or alongside anyone else, for that matter. Instead, the moment the vestibule begins to fill with people, she slips into the back stairwell. As fast as her high heels can carry her, she skips down the stairs, taking them two at a time, three at a time.

She must have gone down ten floors already when she trips, her ankle seizing painfully. She's a runner – she knows enough to feel confident that there's nothing seriously wrong – but it makes her stop all the same, a curse hissed instinctively into the silence. It's then she realizes that she's breathless, that her head is spinning madly.

She clutches at the banister and waits for this dizziness to subside, attempting to somehow gather herself. Of course, a bomb (in the form of a human being) has just detonated right in front of her. She can hardly blame her body for noticing it. Nevertheless, it wouldn't do for anyone to see her like this. She operates in a certain way at ZOLA, after all: a place for everything, and everything in its place. That goes for her own emotions every bit as much as for all those hard-copy documents the firm insists she retain in duplicate.

She will go down to the lobby, she decides, giving her head a little shake. Logic, problem-solving, objectivity – those are the parts of herself she needs to reach for, now more than ever. She begins to walk again, making herself breathe evenly, all the way down fifty more flights of stairs. This time, she moves slowly. She allows herself at least that brief respite, at least these few stolen moments of solitude.

Once she's reached the lobby, though, bodies zipping around her in all directions, there is nothing else for it. No matter that the anonymity of Madison Avenue seems to call to her – no matter the urge to just *run*, her sore ankle be damned – she has no choice but to take the lift all the way back up to her little office on the fifty-eighth floor and try to recommence some semblance of a morning.

Apparently, the summer associates will be occupied with welcome and training sessions for the entire remainder of the day. And so, that's something. What it turns out to provide for Fia, more than anything else, is plenty of lovely time to stare out the window, questioning all the choices she's ever made in her life and where they've got her.

By noon, she hasn't done a tap of work. Instead, she sips absently at her coffee, gazing out at Manhattan in the June sunshine, at the endless windows of other office buildings just like her own. Her mind just won't stop racing as she tries, yet again, to devise a way out of this thing.

She could say that she's reassessed her workload, realized that she simply doesn't have the capacity to take on a summer associate this year after all.

Immediately, though, the flaw in that thinking is evident to her. Absolutely *everyone* at ZOLA is busy, all the time. Complaining about this unchangeable reality has a way of making people look not so much overworked as under-efficient. And what was it Celia said back in the spring? She said that Fia needed some formal experience of supervising others before the firm could promote her. The type of thing she already does with the paralegals is good, but it doesn't quite tick the box.

The prospect of said box being left unticked, maybe for a whole 'nother year, does not exactly fill Fia with joy. At this point, she is quite keen to begin doing, on an official basis, the job she has actually already been doing for some time now, albeit with none of the accompanying benefits: senior associate. The bumped up title and pay grade feel tantalizingly close.

Some sort of exchange, then, perhaps. Might there be any way to make that happen without, as Benjamin had implied earlier, having to spill all the mortifying details of their history? Without having to publicly out herself, to all her bosses and co-workers, as a total moron? If there is, Fia can't think of it. How can she go to Celia Hannity and say: 'about the summer associates. I want one, I just don't want *that* one?'

She can't, really. An explanation would inevitably be required.

She's draining the last of her coffee, every drop like liquid hopelessness, when, in the atrium outside her office, a kerfuffle catches her attention.

Around the perimeter of the fifty-eighth floor, all the lawyers' doors and walls are made, needless to say, of glass – and beyond, in the open-plan area, sit two dozen paralegals and secretaries. There is absolutely nothing Fia can do inside her little cubby – as a matter of fact, she'd wager there is nothing she *does* do – without being observed by at least one of them. But then, that works both ways. Sitting up a bit straighter at her desk now, craning her neck a little, she can see a horde of people lingering by the printers.

It's the summer associates, she realizes, presumably being in some way instructed or inducted. She finds Benjamin amid the group fairly easily, now that she knows enough to look for him. The morning's events, then, were not some sort of psychological break on her part, some horrendous dissociation with reality. He's actually here.

For no other reason than that the opportunity presents itself, Fia studies him for a moment. It is, first of all, entirely bizarre to see him in a suit. In her mind, he exists in shorts and T-shirts, perhaps jeans and a button-down at a push. She would once have imagined he'd look utterly ridiculous in more formal attire. He doesn't, though – she has to admit that, as she takes in every inch of him, from his dark brown hair all the way down to his fancy leather dress shoes. Of course, he's one of the older people in the bunch – maybe even the oldest. But that is not necessarily any bad thing. So many of the other summer associates just have that *look*, like kids dressed up in their parents' clothes. Benjamin – again, honesty compels Fia to admit it – wears his extra few years well.

Weirdly, the whole exercise makes her wonder what *she* looks like today – or rather, what she looked like when he first set eyes on her earlier.

This is weird because, of all the topics that Fia's brain is known to rewind and review on a loop, her own physical appearance is very rarely among them.

Of course, there was a short while, in adolescence, when she fretted over this or that, when she was convinced that her future success and happiness – both with the opposite sex and in general – was linked to making herself look a certain way.

However, she had realized earlier than most that what society valued in women, much more so than great beauty, was simply thinness. If thinness was combined with any sort of non-threatening aesthetic, then of course a woman's life was not necessarily going to be a bed of roses, but her appearance was not going to be a thing making it any more difficult. She could get a job, get a man, get an outfit, all without undue hassle.

Fia happens to be thin – wiry, she'd probably say, herself – and she seems destined always to be so. And honestly, that has taken a lot of the pressure off, looks-wise. She does not think she could develop Kardashian curves if she tried, and she suspects she might not be the most elegant walker in heels – but she has long legs, lean arms, and she enjoys the sense of herself as being somehow a little scrappy. She feels capable inside her own body. In this regard, as in most others, she is pragmatic.

Still, she finds herself taking out a little compact mirror from her handbag, peering into it discreetly at her desk.

She's not sure what she was expecting to see, really. It's just her face: pale skin, blue eyes, red hair that, blessedly, remains mostly contained within its bun at the nape of her neck. Left to its own devices, Fia's hair is a bird's nest of curls reaching halfway down her back. There's a way to wrangle it – to make it look much more like a statement than a surrender. On the occasions over the years when she has committed herself to a multistage process of combing, diffusing and seruming, she's actually received some very effusive compliments about it, mainly from drunk strangers in public bathrooms. At work, though, for lack of the time or energy to do much else, she always goes for the bun.

'You look stunning,' comes a voice then, and Fia freezes instantly. This time, she doesn't even need to look up to know exactly who it is.

Chapter Three

'As ever,' Benjamin continues drolly, looking right at her as he speaks. It doesn't feel like a compliment, though – not really.

Fia just scowls in response, every bit of the loathing she feels for this man reflected right back at her in his expression.

She snaps her little mirror closed decisively, pushing it into a desk drawer. How maddening to have been caught looking at herself, by him. How – she hates this word but there is no other – how *disempowering*, somehow.

Stepping into the office now, the door swinging closed behind him, Benjamin stares over at the desk intended to be his. He makes no move to sit down at it, though. Instead, he stays at the perimeter, leaning his weight against the glass wall. There's a ZOLA-branded ring binder in his hand, together with a ZOLA-branded pen, and he brandishes them.

'So, I have to go around and fill in some information about a bunch of people in different practice areas within the firm. Starting with you, as my . . . mentor,' he says, as though the term tastes like bile on his tongue. 'It's like a get-to-know-you thing.'

'What?' Fia asks.

Benjamin huffs impatiently. 'It's an exercise to help the summer associates get to know—'

'No, I understood you,' she interrupts. 'I just . . .'

Fia finds herself trailing off with a mirthless, disbelieving little laugh. Then, she begins again, more purpose in her voice this time. 'First of all, we already know each other, Ben – more's the pity. And, second of all, do you really think that should be our priority here? Your fucking *worksheet*?'

He shrugs, the gesture somehow detached and defiant at once. 'What would you rather talk about?'

'Hmm,' she replies, affecting rumination. 'Well, let's review. You might remember I agreed – out of the sheer goodness of my heart, I might add – to do you a favour, and—'

'Oh yeah, sure looks like that's what's happened here,' he interjects, glancing pointedly around the office. 'Somebody's done *somebody* a favour all right, Fia. Jesus *Christ*.'

Fia cannot remotely fathom what he's trying to get at with that one. It's the least of her concerns, though. By now, there have been several hours of build-up towards saying her piece on this subject, and she's keen to get back to saying it.

'—and I put off dealing with the divorce,' she continues heatedly, 'like you asked. And where did it get me? Oh, that's right. Emailing your *Hotmail account* over and over again, like some kind of teenage headcase. Having five hundred conversations with your voicemail service. Tell me you aren't going to pretend all that somehow failed to reach you.'

'It reached me all right,' he replies gruffly.

Fia barely hears him, barely pauses for breath. 'Meanwhile, from you . . . tumbleweed! Crickets!'

'Oh, say more metaphors, *please*,' is his only reply, and this time, Fia makes herself stop to take it in. When she does, she's unable even to summon a response. She exhales a slow, shaky breath of some emotion she cannot exactly name.

Whatever it is, though, the strangest thing is that she's fairly sure it's not actually about him. Or at least, it is not *only* about him. It's about the reflection of him on her. The physical manifestation of Benjamin Lowry – the biggest mistake she's ever made in her life – turns out to be so much worse than the mere thought of him, not least in terms of the impact on her own self-esteem. How had she ever got herself into this situation? How has she failed, even after all this time, to get herself back out of it? She thinks of all her little lists, all the emails she sends on a daily basis: *just following up on the below; I note it has been twenty-one days since our last correspondence; regrettably my client has been left with no option but to escalate this matter.* Somehow, the efforts she makes as other people's lawyer, all the ways she tries so hard to stay efficient, stay on-track, don't seem to have extended into her own life – or, into this part of it, at least.

When she speaks again, her voice is quieter. 'Look, we had our . . . ups and downs,' she says, and she decides to ignore the *I'll say* expression that leaps to his face. 'But, believe it or not, I really never thought you were a fundamentally terrible person, Benjamin. And maybe more fool me. 'Cause the fact of the matter is, I haven't heard one single word from you in . . .' She counts backwards in her head, hardly able to believe the number when she reaches it. 'Nearly eight years. *Not one single word*,' she repeats slowly. 'And now here you are, invading my life. I think you could at least have the *decency* to apologize.'

It's the most sincere thing she's said to him – certainly so far today, and perhaps ever. With it, she seems to take a bit of the wind out of his sails. He stands a little straighter, as if, at last, some part of what she's said is beginning to register.

For what feels like a very long moment, he just stares at her, the muscles in his jaw tensing visibly. His dark eyes are as intense as they have ever been. Fia looks right back at him, her gaze unwavering. If this is a competition, it is – as ever – one she's determined to win.

'. . . You're right,' he replies eventually, and there's a satisfying sort of simplicity to the admission. 'I'm sorry.'

Fia's mouth falls open slightly. She has never once heard those two words from Benjamin Lowry's lips, and she'd have bet her bottom dollar that she never would. They're so wholly unprecedented that she doesn't quite know how to process them.

'I . . . should have reached out to you,' he continues uneasily. 'I guess I just . . . got busy.'

And, with *those* two words, any hope of detente vanishes as quickly as it began to flicker. Just like that, Fia finds herself incensed once more.

'You *got busy?*' she repeats.

That she is still managing to keep any sort of a lid on her emotions – to restrict herself to a hissed, sitcom-esque shriek – is evidence only of her practice in this regard. There is, after all, a very particular ecosystem to a big international law firm, with all its gloss and glass. Fia has had to train herself into – and out of – a lot in order to succeed here.

'Busy doing *what?*' she barks out, when no further reply from Benjamin seems forthcoming.

Still, he says nothing – or, at least, he says nothing within the three seconds she allocates for his response.

'*Seriously*,' she continues, her voice rising a little in sarcasm. 'If you're going to be here, we should probably at least get caught up, don't you think? What have you been spending your precious time on, Benjamin? When you haven't been stonewalling me, obviously.'

She leans back slightly in her chair, crossing one leg over the other deliberately, as though she's settling in for a saga. Unabashed now in her inspection of him, she keeps her eyes fixed on his.

For a moment, he just stares back at her. It's not a matter of whether he'll engage with this line of questioning – Fia knows that instinctively. It's a matter of *how*. He's weighing her, somehow, weighing his options. And then his response, when it finally comes, is as mild as if they were two strangers discussing the weather.

'Video games, mainly,' he says.

She blinks. 'What?'

'I was working as a developer and tester for a video games company.'

From this, the absolute bare minimum of information, Fia conjures the impression of a very insubstantial endeavour, but one that might be associated with a lot of perks and personal autonomy. It seems, in short, like the perfect job for him.

'Okay. And so, what? One day – *poof* – you decided you wanted to be a lawyer?'

Although she would deny it convincingly, she can't help but find herself a smidge intrigued by this career change – surely a fairly unusual one for anyone and all the more so for a guy like him.

Once again, Benjamin lets his gaze drift around the space. 'I mean, not really *this* kind of lawyer . . .'

He trails off, and Fia pounces. 'What's that supposed to mean?'

'Well – how can I put it?' he says, and the vaguely superior expression on his face drives her crazy. 'That – uh, I don't even know what we'd call it – *cornucopia* of mini muffins in the break room looked nice and all, but it's not exactly why I'm going to law school – you know what I'm saying?'

Even Fia herself would not have expected that this – *this* – would be the bridge too far, bearing in mind all the other bridges that Benjamin has blazed past today already. It's true that there are always a *lot* of free mini muffins in the break room. And Fia loves them. She eats at least three a day, on account of their being so mini and her days often being so long. She cannot have them insulted.

'*Oh my God!* So, then, why are you even here?!' she just about explodes. 'If you'd rather go and fight the power in some shitty Portakabin somewhere, now would be a great time to do it!'

As far as Fia can see, that would solve everyone's problems – or at least the one most obviously confronting them right now. Benjamin, however, seems wholly unmoved by the suggestion.

'My mother wanted me to do a summer in corporate law, just to rule it out,' he says. 'So, here I am. Ruling it out.'

Subconsciously, Fia shakes her head a little in response. *Unbelievable*. And yet, so entirely believable. 'Wow. And how old are you again now, Ben?' she murmurs, although of course she knows perfectly well. He is one year younger than her: 29. 'When do you reckon you might stop letting your mam brush your hair?'

At this, she watches a shadow of what might be embarrassment cross his features. *Good*, she thinks. By this stage of her

23

life, she has met one too many men who seem like overgrown babies, men who are all about start-ups and idealism and 'disrupting' things, and who are always – *always* – funded by someone else.

'You know what? Screw you, Fia,' he replies.

A playground sort of insult, really, but the way in which he delivers it – spits the words out at her – somehow feels weighty. It feels cutting, and ugly.

He flips open his ring binder, pen poised. 'Just answer these stupid questions so I can get out of here,' he continues, his voice flat as he stares at the sheet in front of him. 'Number one: "What does your role at ZOLA involve?". Feel free to be extremely brief.'

Fia lets the question hang in the air for a second. Not deliberately – it's just that she's struck anew by the grim reality of their situation. They are really doing this, she realizes. This is the first of many occasions, over the next ten weeks, on which she and Benjamin Lowry will have to pretend. They'll have to keep their shared secret, play their respective roles as best they can. She takes a deep breath in and out, feeling as though she is steeling herself not just for the present task but for all the ones that are to come.

'Well, it sounds like you've figured out that we deal with rich people here,' she offers eventually. 'And rich companies. I'd have thought you'd feel right at home.' She smiles snarkily at him, but his expression remains unmoved. Thus, she continues. 'Most of our business is generated from corporate work – mergers and acquisitions, commercial real estate, and so on. But we also have a small private client department, because you know what sometimes happens to rich people?'

Benjamin offers no response, just stares back at her expectantly.

'They die,' Fia continues plainly. 'And we don't want all those billable hours winding up in some other law firm, now, do we? No. Sorry if that offends your delicate sensibilities, Benjamin, but we don't. That's where I come in. I deal with private tax planning for our high-value clients: their trusts and estates, their wills and probate. Other . . . family matters.'

What precisely such matters tend to be, Fia finds herself disinclined to get into right now. And Benjamin, evidently sorely lacking in lawyerly curiosity, doesn't ask.

'Fine,' he says, scribbling away in his file. 'Question two: "How did you get here?"' At this, he looks up at her, his eyes flashing. 'Well, I guess I pretty much know the answer to that one,' he continues, all rancour. 'But don't worry, I won't write it on the form.'

Chapter Four

How did she get here?

*H*ow did she get here?
The question rings in Fia's ears long after Benjamin hightails it out of her office. Of course, she knows that so far as his induction exercise was concerned, he'd been supposed to enquire in a purely professional sense. What dominates her thoughts, now, though . . . that's undeniably of a much more *personal* nature.

The truth is that, most of the time, in life, human beings behave predictably. Not always perfectly, not without a few false starts or wrong turns or long ways around – but there is, generally, some sense of a natural evolution, of one thing leading logically to another.

Other times, more rarely, people do things that don't make any sense, things for which there is simply no explanation. If they happened on a television drama, fans would take to Twitter and criticize the writing. *That was just so out of character,* they'd say. *It stretches credibility – it's a bolt from the blue. I don't buy it.*

Getting married to Benjamin Lowry was, for Fia Callaghan, one of those things.

She is analytical by nature, though. She cannot help but try to come up with *some* sort of rationalization.

First of all, they were in Las Vegas.

Looking back on the whole thing, Fia actually blames the city of Las Vegas for most of it.

After all, before that summer, her life had been proceeding very normally. At the very least, no legally binding commitments had worked their way into the mix.

Having freshly completed her final year of university, Fia spent most of the summer in question working as a camp counsellor. Quite how she'd even landed the position was unclear to her – certainly, she hadn't needed to demonstrate any particular talent or experience with children. One single form, filled out at a careers fair with the free pen provided, and the rest seemed to do itself. Before she knew it, she was jetting out of Dublin airport and heading to north-west Oregon, a place to which she had never previously given one single moment's thought in her life.

Camp Birchwood turned out to be all tall trees and wide lakes, the nearest town an hour's drive away. In other words, it was a *make your own fun* sort of situation. And Benjamin Lowry certainly liked to make his own fun. Hailing from somewhere in North Carolina, he'd travelled all the way across the country to arrive in Oregon, but no one would have guessed it. Within thirty minutes, Benjamin's laugh was ringing out constantly across Camp Birchwood; his name seemed to be on everyone's lips, as though he had never lived a day anywhere else.

Although he was only very slightly younger than her and employed in an identical role, it soon became clear to Fia that working alongside Benjamin was like having another child in tow – another person all too ready to play a prank, pick a fight, ask her *why* seven times.

'I say let's just wing it,' he was known to proclaim at regular intervals. Or, sometimes, 'It'll all work itself out.' Or, quite often, as the weeks wore on, 'I swear to fucking Christ, Fia, if you say *one more word* . . .'

It was quite a remarkable feat, really, that whatever Benjamin Lowry's opinion over the course of summer 2015, Fia tended to have the very opposite view. And neither of them were shy about expressing themselves. At times, Benjamin seemed, in fact, to almost *enjoy* swearing that what Fia called black was truly white. For her own part, Fia certainly didn't seek out this antagonism; she hadn't experienced anything like it with class-mates or colleagues past. She really wasn't, in her own view, a particularly confrontational sort of person. But there was just something about Benjamin. Their relationship seemed to come with frustration, with a kind of tension, built into it.

That Benjamin was very evidently a rich-boy hadn't helped matters. Fia had an instinctive, dearly held dislike of rich-boys. More so even than dislike, it was a matter of distrust. She didn't trust Benjamin's rich-boy hair or his rich-boy sporting abilities, his rich-boy enthusiasm and joviality. Everyone else might have eaten it up (everyone else absolutely *did* eat it up), but not her. She could see that he was fundamentally cocky, careless, insincere. Meanwhile, she couldn't have ventured to guess at her own core deficiencies – but, whatever they were, Benjamin Lowry seemed uniquely placed to perceive them.

All in all, it made for an interesting summer, to say the least. The situation was unbelievably aggravating, at times confusing, but inherently temporary, of course – and certainly never boring.

By mid-August, the children were dispatched back to their parents, and Camp Birchwood's dozen or so counsellors arranged a long weekend away to mark the end of their time together. The summer had flown past; soon, Fia would be back in Dublin, taking her first steps into the legal profession. The Vegas weekend was a last blowout before everyone returned to their respective lives, and in hindsight, this – the very theme of the trip – was perhaps never going to make for top-class decision-making from anyone involved.

Immediately upon arrival, Las Vegas seemed weird to Fia. There were escalators and moving walkways dotted along the Strip for maximum convenience – yes, right there on the street, in the *open air*. Slap bang in the middle of all the action, hordes of tourists were queuing excitedly to climb a replica of the Eiffel Tower. Per a wholehearted recommendation from their hotel concierge, the gang from Camp Birchwood spent an entire afternoon cruising the elaborate 'Venice canals' – which, in fact, were housed inside a shopping mall, complete with imitation gondolas and a painted blue sky above them.

Afterwards, as their little group wandered the streets, taking in the sights and sounds of the place, even the mountains in the distance somehow looked to Fia like they must be part of a film set. Everywhere, people were drinking, and everywhere, people were dressed in all manner of costumes – some for what seemed like professional reasons and some for what seemed like no reason at all. It was all very kitschy, very carnivalesque. The normal rules of life simply did not seem to apply here.

In short, even stone cold sober, there was an overwhelming sense of the surreal.

And, on the night it all went down, Fia was so, so far from stone cold sober.

Vast quantities of alcohol were consumed by her, by Benjamin, and by everyone else besides. This was not, at least on her end, because she was masking a secret pain, or because she needed the sambuca in order to feel confident, or because she was in some masochistic way intent on self-sabotage. It was because she was 22 years old and, for the first time in ten weeks, there were no American children for whom she was directly responsible. Presented with the chance to let loose in a way she hadn't felt able to all summer, Fia was inclined to take it.

Furthermore, the drinks were free. That was a critical point, actually. All the casinos, in an effort to retain custom and encourage gambling, gave out endless drinks to college kids *for free*. The most cursory glance at their IDs (some of which were not even especially good fakes) was all it seemed to take.

Hours passed, that night, in a blur of neon lights and palm trees, games machines and card tables. At some point, a very sweet Texan named Brittany was seized with the sudden impulse to get a tattoo. Things everyone had previously known about Brittany included that she was studying to become a diabetes nurse, and that she was wholeheartedly convinced she would ultimately give birth to triplets, or at least twins, because they ran in her family – probably, she thought, this would happen within the next five years; she wanted to be a young mother. It was with some surprise, then, that Fia watched as the words *Yaaas Queen* were printed in bold black ink on this girl's upper arm. But nonetheless, Fia whooped and hollered her support right alongside the rest of the gang.

She can remember, after that, standing in a huddle on the Strip, everyone rowdy and buzzed. The night air was dry and thick, as though heat were being pumped out by some unseen generator. Fia would not have been a bit surprised to find that it *was*. More fakery.

'Oh my God, you guys!' a slurred voice offered then. 'You know what we should do? For real . . . ? Someone should get married!'

Much surrounding giddiness ensued, with the general consensus being that, yes, this was an excellent idea. It made only good sense. When in Rome, and so on.

'It should be you guys!' someone else piped up, pointing at Fia and Benjamin.

'Oh my God, can you imagine?! They'd kill each other!'

'I don't know! You guys already argue like an old married couple sometimes!'

Through all this laughter and noise, Fia glanced across at Benjamin.

'Nah,' he said quietly, and even in his drunken state, he managed – with the quick rise of his eyebrows, the focus of his stare – to achieve what must surely have been the desired effect. 'Far too sensible, aren't you, Irish?'

She looked right back at him, undaunted. 'Let's just say I'm not sure you're husband material, Benjamin.'

That was all it took, thankfully, for the idea to be dropped – exchanged, instead, for more drinking, more dancing, more spectacle and silliness into the wee hours. It must have been nearly 3 a.m. by the time Fia was standing at that craps table, watching as some stranger rolled the dice. She was hammered by then, well and truly, and glad of a solid surface to lean against, when a familiar voice emerged from behind her.

'To think, we could be man and wife already,' Benjamin said, low and scratchy, the words murmured right into her ear.

He lingered there for a moment, and she could feel his breath against her skin, could smell the mixture of alcohol and something else. The sensation sent a peculiar shiver through her.

Following his gaze, Fia looked over to the very far end of the casino. She could make out the words WEDDING CHAPEL written above an archway. She snorted out a laugh, twisting herself around just enough to see him properly.

'Oh yeah, right,' she said. 'You wouldn't have done it.'

'*You* wouldn't have done it,' he countered, his face inches from hers.

More so than anything that came before or afterwards, it was the one moment of the whole cursed night that – even years later – Fia would remember with shocking clarity: she and Benjamin Lowry looking at one another as if that crowded casino were some sort of hunting ground and they were the only two creatures there – as if they had been trying for the entire summer to outrun each other and still had no clear consensus as to who was the pursuer and who was the prey.

It was a moment, between the pair of them, of utter madness. Not of frenzy, but of madness nonetheless.

Almost a decade later, Fia sits in the office of her fancy New York law firm, allegedly all grown up now. And still, her memories after that point are patchy – they come back only in fragments, like flashes from a nightmare. What she can seem to access, more so than any verb or adjective, is a *sensation*. The feeling of knowing that Benjamin Lowry expected her to back out of this thing and knowing that she absolutely wasn't going to – knowing that in fact *he'd* be the one to back out, even though, somehow, he hadn't, not yet . . .

She remembers that same, overwhelming sense of the surreal – the utterly laughable and ludicrous – that she'd felt everywhere else in Las Vegas. They were in a room dressed up to look like a sort of church, but it wasn't one really. The officiant was playing at being Dolly Parton, and Fia was playacting too. This was all a lark, the last in a long line of times she and Benjamin had fought to get the last word.

Fia remembers all of that, and then she remembers realizing, in a hazy sort of way, that the whole thing was – maybe – over? At that point in her life, she had never attended a wedding ceremony that had lasted any less than ninety minutes at a bare minimum. Without all the hymns and the readings and the other God bits, though, it turned out that Dolly Parton could really crack on with things.

Chapter Five

By the time that Fia steps off the subway, after day one of Benjamin's summer associateship, it's past 9 p.m. She had a lot of catching up to do, work-wise, in the afternoon, and as the time wore on, she let herself get lost in it. She found herself, on this one occasion, actually almost *appreciating* the all-consuming, endless nature of it.

Even on ordinary days, Fia is often in the office long after her contracted hours. A certain level of stress has come to feel normal. And there are certainly, she reminds herself at regular intervals, worse ways to earn a living. She's *lucky* to have her job. Absolutely no one would have ever predicted she'd end up working on the fifty-eighth floor of a building in Midtown Manhattan – least of all her. There are, after all, a whole lot of lawyers out there in the world. Very early on in her career, she divided them in her own mind into three broad categories:

Firstly, there were those who liked the notion of power and prestige. Often, it turned out that these people's fathers had also been lawyers – or judges, sometimes.

Then, there were those who had watched *Erin Brockovich* at a formative age or who had perhaps gone through some horrendous personal ordeal or who had otherwise come to genuinely care a lot about, like, *justice*.

And, finally, there were the people who had simply been good at school, but in more of a words sort of way than a numbers sort of way. This last group accounted, in Fia's experience, for a huge proportion of the legal profession, and she had always considered herself very definitely among it.

When she first began as a trainee solicitor at ZOLA's Dublin branch, there had been nothing much to suggest that she was special, that she might one day find herself parachuted out of there – and to America, at that. Back then, the London office was the carrot. That was the place to which unsatisfied employees might legitimately hope to be transferred or sent on secondment. But to the New York office? The San Francisco office? They were so patently out of reach as not even to be weaponized for purposes of recruitment and retention. It would have been borderline unethical.

And then, on one wholly unremarkable day when Fia was 26 years old, an opportunity arose. Six months, leaving in three days' time, just to help out on the contentious administration of one huge Manhattan estate. Just – as it eventually turned out – to work almost literally day and night sorting through boxes of documents, while still being paid her Dublin salary. Maybe other people in the Dublin office saw that reality coming. One way or another, it turned out that Fia was in the right spot. Everyone younger than her was deemed ineligible for the transfer on the grounds of inexperience. Most of the people her age or older self-selected out: they had bought a house within commuting distance of Dublin already; they had a child, perhaps, whose nursery school place had been hard won.

In the end, only three other solicitors were both sufficiently qualified for the role in New York and interested in taking it. As luck had it, all three of these people were also total dicks – not even the sort who were commonly liked by their male superiors, but the sort who were disliked wholesale. And so, armed with one single suitcase and the fervent hope it weighed less than twenty kilos, off Fia went.

All that was four years ago now. Somehow or other, once she arrived, Fia had just never left. Six months became a year, and she found an apartment, joined a bunch of social groups in the city, like an overeager fresher. A year became two, and she found a different, better apartment, managed to extract herself from the social groups she couldn't bear any longer. Along the way, of course, she met George, settled into the sense of belonging that a relationship like that could bring. Eventually, the solidity, the (at least semi-) permanence of the situation began to dawn on her. She kind of seemed to . . . *live here*.

More than that, to this day, she really *likes* living here. Even when she feels depleted, the renewable energy of this city just seems to have a way of filling her up – or at least, most of the time it does.

This evening, she's bonetired as she climbs back up to ground level at 77th Street station. On the street, busy people whoosh past her; crosswalks and hot-dog vendors and bodegas sprawl out in all directions, but she hardly notices any of it as she makes her way north, then east. She trudges past the ever-present scaffolding, past the forest-green awnings announcing the number of each building, towards home.

This neighbourhood, the Upper East Side, is not generally considered a cool one in which to live. In fact, contrary to what *Gossip Girl* had very clearly implied in the late noughties, it is generally considered the very opposite of cool. It's considered *boring*. There is no black box theatre up here and only a handful of plant-based restaurants, and almost none of the local residents appear to consider dressing for the day to be a form of performance art.

Of course, a person can absolutely still get a trendily baked Brussel sprout if they so choose. There are plenty of good coffee places, and Central Park is close by. It is by no means a wasteland. It's just that a critical mass of music conservatories and medical establishments have created, overall, a certain impression of sedateness – at least relative to other parts of the city.

This is all fine by Fia. She doesn't mind that, were she ever seized with the desire to watch a moustachioed man play ping-pong over a craft beer, she would need to hop on the subway to do it. What the Upper East Side provides her, instead, is the ability to afford a very nice, remarkably spacious – albeit shared – apartment, within a short commute of her office.

Approaching said apartment now, Fia squints up at it from the street. Back in Dublin, some of her old friends have been buying houses – not her single friends, obviously, but the ones in couples. With two salaries or parental help, it seems to be just about possible to find a fixer-upper somewhere in the city or close to it. A few people she knows have even moved deep into the countryside, begun intimidating-looking building projects, become experts on the merits and demerits of different types of sinks.

When Fia thinks about that, it's very hard to look up at her apartment – to think about the small fortune she haemorrhages every month, renting alongside two other people – and feel like it's the wisest way to spend her money. But then, that's probably just the day she's had. Too much self-reflection, she is convinced, can be extremely bad for a person.

Crossing the building's lobby with a nod to her doorman, she hops in the lift, tries to pull herself together. And when she turns the key in her front door, hearing *The Daily* podcast on in the background, familiar chatter over the top of it, a wave of genuine gratitude overwhelms her.

By now, she's been in enough different living situations to know that this is rare: the feeling of walking into her apartment after a bad day and actually being glad to see the other people who happen to be there. Annie and Kavita might not be George – even now, such a long way down the line, Fia still misses George more than she'd ever let on – but finding genuinely, truly good roommates is no small feat. It's as hard as trying to find a good boss or a good boyfriend. That Fia has ended up with two out of those three boxes ticked is, she reminds herself, really nothing to be sniffed at.

She lets herself flop down on the sofa dramatically, lifting the back of her hand to her brow like a woman in a painting.

On the adjacent chair, her legs slung over the arm of it, Annie exhales a little laugh. 'Rough day?'

Fia just groans in response. 'Kav, what are you making over there?' she calls out, weakly.

From their strip of a kitchen along the back wall, Kavita cranes her neck to look around. 'Sort of a . . . risotto, I guess. Or a paella. I just got home myself, so I'm improvising. You want me to toss in some more veggies, stretch it out a little?'

'Yes please.'

'I mean, it won't be, like, super good or anything,' Kavita

clarifies needlessly. At this point, their roles are pretty well established. Annie is the cook of the apartment, Kavita, not so much, but Fia – more practised in ordering and reheating than anything else – always allocates generous points for trying.

'That's fine. Anything's fine – thank you so much.'

'So, what happened?' Annie asks absently, one eye still on her phone. And, for a minute, Fia thinks about telling her roommates everything, the whole sorry tale. In the end, though, she finds she just cannot face it. There has been about enough drama for one day, she decides. It's probably unnecessary to add yet more into the mix. After all, Benjamin won't even be her husband much longer. Fia plans to start looking for a divorce lawyer this very night.

'Nothing,' she mumbles. 'It was just . . . you know. Work.'

Chapter Six

The following morning, Benjamin arrives at the office at 9 a.m. on the dot, and Fia makes a great show of looking at her watch. She has been at her desk for almost two hours already.

Benjamin, in turn, creates quite the performance of rolling his eyes in response, but otherwise he says nothing, stepping over a neat stack of her files in order to get to his desk.

Fia feels something inside her constrict. The mere sight of him there – turning on his computer, setting down his Thermos cup – just has such a sense of permanence to it. And they really are so very *close* to one another in here. He's positioned adjacent to her, his side profile in her direct line of vision now. From her seat, Fia could practically reach out and high five him if she wanted to (which of course she does not). She can *smell his cologne*. How can she be expected to tolerate this for ten whole weeks?

Meanwhile, Benjamin has taken off his jacket and is staring resolutely at his screen, his mouth a tight line, his hand clutching at the mouse. Tension seems to radiate from every inch of him.

Fia waits for one minute.

Two.

Three.

'Well, good morning to you, too,' she says then, purely out of a desire to say something – and to say something arsey, at that. He just seems to bring it out in her.

'Hi,' he replies sourly, barely glancing in her direction.

And somehow – perhaps very masochistically – it's his reluctance that makes her suddenly determined to pursue this communication.

'Beautiful day,' she adds blithely.

'Mmm.'

'Don't you just love New York in the sunshine?'

This time, he looks up at her. 'More than words,' he answers, everything about him thoroughly unamused. Something in Fia perceives it as a tiny victory.

'It's not like you to be so quiet, Benjamin,' she continues, and she takes a quick glance over at the door to make sure it's properly closed. 'Back at Camp Birchwood, sometimes it seemed like the only thing I heard was your voice, all day long, from morning 'til night.'

'Well, admittedly, it was pretty difficult to drown you out,' he snaps back, 'but I had to try – for the *sake of the children*.'

Fia rolls her eyes hard. Just like that, her victory isn't tasting quite as sweet.

'Are we done here?' he asks, sounding about as exhausted and put-upon as a person could possibly be. 'Or you wanna talk about the weather some more?'

She affects an affronted expression. 'I was just trying to be friendly, Benjamin. It can be very scary starting a new job, especially when it turns out you've royally fucked over the one person who might be most available to help you.' She leans into a forced smile. 'You'll be sure to let me know if you need anything today, won't you? I'm your "big sister for the summer", after all.'

'I won't,' he says shortly, and then, after a second, he clarifies, 'be needing anything from you. Not today, not at any point. You can go ahead and take that as a given right now.'

And sure enough, Fia can tell from the look on his face that Benjamin Lowry would rather die than ask her for so much as a Wi-Fi password.

She shrugs. 'Fine.'

He just stares at her in response, one eyebrow arching the slightest bit. 'Fine.'

And she shouldn't say it. She really shouldn't – there's just no need at all.

Of course, she says it.

'*Fine.*'

With that, Fia reaches for a few files from the top of her pile on the floor, plonking them on her desk with an unnecessary thud. It is, she thinks, going to be an incredibly long summer.

That afternoon, Benjamin *knocks over* her pile of files with his big stupid feet. He lets out a long-suffering sigh, as though the fault lies with the files themselves, or – more likely – with Fia.

'Don't!' she says sharply, as he bends down on his hunkers, begins to gather them up. 'I'll do it. They were in an order.'

Benjamin studies the files, taking in the yellow, pink or green Post-its that are stuck to each one of them.

'Oh wow, *colour coding*,' he says, every word mean and

exaggerated. He stands up again, backing away. 'You knock yourself out, Fia. I'm sure the only thing better than getting to organize that shit once is getting to do it twice, right?'

On Wednesday, it's more of the same: more silence, more sniping, absolutely no mentorship on matters of the law.

By the time Thursday rolls around, Fia feels like she is hanging on by a thread. Already, she has ceased to be able to think in terms of their whole summer together. Instead, it has become a question of getting through the days – sometimes even the hours.

Benjamin's very presence in the office is oppressive, unignorable. Even the fact that he appears *also* to be incredibly unhappy about the whole arrangement is of cold comfort.

Rather, it actually irritates her all the more, the way he often behaves as though he is somehow the wronged party here – as though his right to be pissed off is equal to, if not even greater than, hers.

He does, at least, appear to have accrued plenty of work to be getting on with. There's been some satisfaction in witnessing that, if nothing else. She'd swear she's even seen a few flashes of panic here and there, as the reality of a big boy job makes itself clear to him.

Files are mounting up on his desk now, and if he has put in place any sort of system by which to deal with them, Fia cannot ascertain it. In fact, his whole corner of the room looks increasingly like it belongs either to some sort of mad genius or to a woefully disorganized teenager. Fia knows which one she thinks is the more apt comparison. There are papers on practically every available surface, plus all manner of other miscellany – a coffee cup here, a stapler there. *Her* stapler, as it happens.

It's midmorning when Brett Sallinger – a junior partner in Mergers and Acquisitions – swings by. He gives the doorframe a perfunctory little knock.

'Benjamin,' he says, 'can I grab those disclosure schedules from you, buddy?'

Fia looks up to offer Brett a nod of greeting, and out of the corner of her eye, she can sense a bit of a scramble. Excellent. *This*, she thinks to herself triumphantly, *is what happens when you don't have a system*.

'You mean the ones from the, uh, the Sonex merger?' Benjamin asks, amid much rustling of papers.

'No. The Goldsberry merger,' Brett corrects, a tiny furrow appearing in his forehead. 'Didn't we talk about you taking first pass at the mark-ups?'

'Right, I remember now,' Benjamin replies, sounding much more at ease than Fia can remember feeling in her entire first year at the firm, never mind her first week. 'Any chance I could get 'em to you this afternoon? I'm just a little, uh . . . under the gun right now.'

He offers a self-effacing little chuckle, and in response, Fia senses her own silent intake of breath. Her body tenses vicariously for the dressing down that will now surely follow.

Except, it doesn't. After a few seconds' pause, Brett just smiles. 'I get it,' he replies. 'End of day'll be fine. Let me know if you want to bounce anything off me, 'kay?'

And as he strides down the corridor away from them, it takes everything in Fia to bite back some choice commentary.

She supposes she kind of understands Brett's response. Kind of. The odd thing about the summer associates is that they are here to be tested and wooed, at once. The point is not only for the firm to suss out every detail of the professional and personal capabilities of their prospective hires; it is also to give the prospective hires – many of whom will soon have their pick of job offers – an impression of the life they could expect to lead as a fully fledged lawyer at ZOLA. And everyone knows that there are larger firms out there: firms with higher salaries, more secondment opportunities, a dry cleaner in the building. What ZOLA must offer, instead, is the sense of a slightly better work-life balance. It is important, therefore, that the summer associates leave at the end of August feeling that the expectations here are reasonable, that support is available, that the partners are human.

Still, Fia can't help but think that Benjamin's just been let off the hook pretty damn easily. And it is so frustratingly familiar – hadn't he always been able to gloss over his own shortcomings, pull something out of the bag when forced to, wangle things exactly how he wanted them? Brett might as well have said *sure thing, champ*. Would he have done the same with a female summer associate? Fia doesn't know. Logic tells her that not every positive interaction between men in this office is evidence of the boys' club, alive and well – but neither does it do much to disprove that possibility.

All this circles in her brain as she drafts an unrelated email – one she knows she'll have to reread when she's done, to ensure that none of her internal rage has somehow crept in. She's at *warmest regards* when she senses the force of Benjamin's stare, and she glances up to meet it.

They blink at one another.

'Oh no, please,' he says, all sarcasm. 'Type louder, Fia – really. There might be someone up on the fifty-ninth floor who can't hear you.'

Fia bristles immediately. 'I'm sorry,' she fires back. 'Am I disturbing you in *my* office?'

She supposes she tees him up to contradict her there, and contradict her he does. He has always been, if nothing else, reliable in that way.

'*Our* office,' he replies, and she hisses out a sigh in response, not caring that she sounds – even to her own ears – like a petulant teenager.

'Oh my God, you're such a melter,' she mutters, halfway under her breath.

'What was that?'

For a moment, Fia says nothing. She'd sincerely been talking mostly to herself – just an instinctive urge to let off some steam. But since he's asked . . .

'A *melter*,' she replies, each syllable enunciated deliberately. 'Alternatively, a *head-melt* – someone who is so incredibly annoying that they make you feel like your brain is actually starting to *melt*.'

He takes in the explanation, before barking out a grim laugh. 'Well, back at you, Irish.'

And, for reasons Fia could never quite explain to anyone, that final word out of his mouth is *it*. Her very last nerve, well and truly stricken. She thought she'd be able to handle this whole thing with Benjamin very much on a solo basis. Why reveal to her friends or family the doing of something that is ultimately going to be undone? That has been her thinking for most of the past decade and certainly for the past few days.

However, she can see now that such a strategy just isn't going to work any longer. It cannot – not when she has to look at Benjamin's face every minute of the day. She will explode.

She cannot help but wonder what George would make of all this. George is, after all, the one person in her life to whom

Fia has ever confessed everything that happened in Las Vegas – the one person she might have readily turned to, this past week, for wisdom or for comfort.

Of course, that's a fool's game, though. Asking George is not an option anymore.

Instead, she reaches for her phone, opening her group chat with Annie and Kavita.

Are you both home tonight? she texts. **Or can you be? I will need ALL the wine.**

Chapter Seven

They order in Thai food, and it doesn't feel like she can say anything before the delivery arrives. It's just not the right time.

Then the food comes, and they're busy unpacking everything from containers, divvying up items and topping up their glasses of wine. This doesn't feel like the right time either. Annie's had a first date earlier in the week, and she's recounting all the details as they eat together around their kitchen table, spring rolls and Thai ribs being passed between plates. It's delicious food, accompanied by a delicious topic of conversation, and Fia is suddenly loath to so thoroughly change the shape of the evening.

After all, it's not like the three of them do this nightly – or even necessarily weekly. They all moved into this apartment on 81st Street at different times, each having responded to an online ad posted by the outgoing roommate. In other words, they did not choose one another. They did not arrive here with a shared history, a pre-existing sense of sisterhood. Each of them have jobs and friends and interests outside the apartment – things that make their respective schedules ebb and flow. Their lives are not always perfectly in sync. But, gradually, there has developed a certain loose, pleasantly overlapping shape to things between them. It's nice.

Fia waits for a break in conversation, and then – before she can change her mind – she bites the bullet.

'So, you know how I said I was getting a summer associate?' she begins. 'At work, I mean?'

'Mmm, yeah,' Annie replies, her mouth half-full of prawn satay. 'How's that going? Did you get a guy or a girl?'

'Guy,' Fia says, her trepidation kicking up a notch even with this small acknowledgement.

Annie's eyes seem to brighten in the way that only the friends of a single woman do. 'Ooh, *interesting*. I'm imagining, like, young-Barack-Obama vibes?'

Fia can't help but snort out a laugh at the very notion. 'Maybe if Barack had been richer, lazier, less smart but *much* more of a smartass . . .'

'Ugh. That bad, huh?

'Yeah. Also, this – the summer programme, I mean – it isn't our first time meeting. I'm sort of . . . I don't know how to say this' – she physically tenses, as though bracing for a blast – 'sort of married to him.'

Annie seems to splutter and inhale at once – and, being mid-bite, it's not a winning combination.

Fia rushes to pat her on the back before she chokes entirely, shoving a glass of wine into her hands merely for its liquid properties.

'What?!' Annie yelps, once she's had a sip, her eyes still little watery. 'Oh my God! You're *married*?! How did this happen? And when? And—'

'All right, just . . . take a breath,' Fia interrupts, and she reaches for her own glass of wine, mostly to have something to occupy her hands. 'I'm not *married* married. It's . . . well, it's complicated.'

'Kavita, are you *hearing this?*' Annie says, turning to the other girl. Fia looks in Kavita's direction now, too. She's uncharacteristically calm. If Fia had been asked to predict who would get loud in response to her news and who would get quiet, she'd have been proven wrong right off the bat.

'I'm hearing it,' Kavita replies slowly, a little frown appearing between her brows. 'I'm just not . . . understanding it. I mean, what do you mean you're not *married* married? I kinda think you are or you aren't, no?'

With both her roommates staring at her now, almost literally with bated breath, Fia finds herself faltering, unsure of where to start. Once again, she wishes she didn't have to tell them all this. She wishes she could just fast forward to the part where they already know. Alas, that's not an option. And, in fact, what she probably needs to do here is the very opposite thing. She needs to rewind.

'Did I ever tell you I was a camp counsellor when I was younger?' she asks, and although she knows very well what their answers will be, she waits for them to shake their heads anyway. Buying time. 'Well, I was. And there was this guy there.'

Across the table, Annie lets out a barely audible little sound, somewhere between a squeak and a sigh. She has an expectant sort of expression on her face, almost as though she is settling in to hear one for the ages – some grand tale of romance and angst. This, Fia thinks, will not do.

'And just bear in mind through all this,' she adds, 'we're talking about someone who's now invaded my place of work, and whom I desperately want to be rid of, 'kay?'

'Got it,' Kavita says, apparently on behalf of both her and Annie.

With that, Fia takes a deep breath and begins at the beginning.

The actual wedding itself, when she comes to recounting it, is a weird one. Some substantial part of her feels like she will never be able to give an adequate account of it. Equally, though, there turns out to be some extent to which even the most basic details suffice:

Twenty-two years old.

Steaming drunk.

Las Vegas.

Was there, in retrospect, something a little desperate about that whole night? Had everyone in their gang seen *The Hangover*, been determined, collectively, to tick off this life experience? Not just a night out in Vegas, but a *wild* night out in Vegas – a story they could tell later?

Fia doesn't get much pleasure out of telling the story now, but Annie and Kavita do seem to follow along without any great difficulty. It's afterwards that the confusion begins in earnest.

'You live in an apartment with two roommates, Fia,' Kavita says plainly. 'You go on *dates* – I mean, not as many as I think you should, but that's another story. You do go on *some*. Having *been married* is one thing . . . how can you *still* be *married*, though?'

Again, Fia winces. This is, indeed, the worst bit of it all, the hardest bit to explain.

* * *

The morning after her . . . *wedding*, she woke up in a hotel room on top of a clean white duvet cover. Overall, the surroundings were actually a big improvement on, say, a student house in Dublin's Rathmines, but the sensations were fairly similar.

By that point in her life, Fia had been drunk and hungover a normal amount – which was to say, quite a lot. She knew what it was to greet the day with her throat feeling like sandpaper, wondering whether everyone liked her less now than they had before, and if indeed they ever really had to begin with.

She had never, however, woken up quite like this – with what seemed to be huge black holes in her recollection of the night before. It was actually a little frightening. She dreaded to imagine what the photographs would be like when they were put on Facebook. De-tagging oneself always seemed a bit of a hostile move, but sometimes, it was the only thing to be done.

Looking down at her own body, she realized she'd taken one leg out of her jeans but not quite managed the other. Worse than that, when she rolled over, beside her in the bed – albeit actually under the covers – lay Benjamin Lowry. Fia almost shuddered at the proximity. With gargantuan effort, she managed to haul herself upwards to sort out her trousers and to survey the situation more generally. Dotted around on the floor, on makeshift beds comprised of spare hotel linen, lay three friends.

Two of them remained out for the count, but Michelle – who simply never seemed to suffer the consequences of anything she put her body through – was wide awake.

'Crazy night,' Fia said, her voice coming out thick and dry.

Michelle nodded, looking somewhat startled to hear from her. 'How do you feel?'

Fia winced. 'Do you know where Lourdes is?'

'. . . No?'

'Would you know what I meant if I told you I felt as sick as a plane to Lourdes?'

'I guess I'd get the idea,' Michelle replied, and she sounded sort of . . . dazed. Amazed? Fia wasn't all that interested in investigating. She just let herself flop back down on the bed, curling into the foetal position.

'No, Fia,' Michelle continued, more urgency in her voice now. 'I mean, like, how do you *feel*? About last night?'

'What about it?'

'Well, about the . . . the wedding.'

Fia snorted a laugh. 'Whose wedding?'

There followed a strange, slightly drawn-out silence between them. From somewhere in the far corner of the room, a gentle snore continued rhythmically.

'You're kidding, right?' Michelle said then, and more than her words, it was the nervous, disbelieving little laugh that followed – that was what planted the first seed of panic in the pit of Fia's stomach.

It made her tug herself upwards again in bed. Confused, she stared across at her friend for another long moment until, beside Michelle on the floor, it sounded like another body was stirring.

'Um, Clay, you took pictures, didn't you?' Michelle chirped, her discomfort entirely unmistakable now. When Clayton provided only an extravagant grunt in response, she huffed out an exhale. 'We get it, dude – you're hungover, it's tragic. Just gimme your phone.'

The next thing Fia knew, the other girl was clambering up beside her, phone in her outstretched hand. Fia took it, looking down at the screen.

'Oh Jesus Christ,' she breathed out, her mouth falling open.

The photograph before her was small and low quality, but nonetheless, it made the basic situation clear enough. Standing in front of a vaguely familiar-looking altar, there was a pretty good Dolly Parton impersonator.

And there was Benjamin Lowry.

And – could it really be true? – there was Fia.

Beside her, Michelle's voice seemed to warp, the details of the room falling away. Fia had no idea how long she spent just staring, as though she'd been plunged headfirst into a tunnel – just her and this photograph, remnants of recollection beginning to come at her like a gruesome hallucination.

Then, at some point, her eyes began darting around frantically. It was as though she'd realized, suddenly, that she was trapped – that she'd wasted vital minutes already, that she should have been looking for an escape all this time. Quickly, her gaze landed, as luck (or lack thereof) would have it, on the mahogany dresser a few feet away from the bed. A document seemed to have been abandoned right there, beside a few half-finished bottles of Blue Moon. Fia stumbled towards it instinctively. The heading read: CLARK COUNTY, NEVADA. Below that, in slightly smaller lettering, it said: CERTIFIED ABSTRACT OF MARRIAGE.

In a split second, something in Fia's body took over from her brain. She strode over to Benjamin, still sleeping like a baby, and began shaking him violently.

'Get up! Benjamin! Ben!' She was shouting like a woman possessed. 'Get up right now!'

He awoke, bleary-eyed, his hair sticking up at odd angles, and Fia gave him no catch-up time whatsoever before she thrust the piece of paper into his hand.

He took one look at it – his eyes widening, his brain engaging – before he ran to the bathroom and vomited right into the sink.

Because of all this vomiting (him) and screaming (her), it was at least another hour before they made it downstairs for breakfast. In the dining room, the others in their group looked greasy and ashen-faced. Nonetheless, galvanized by coffee and one another, they soon summoned the energy to review recent events.

Questions, sympathetic arm rubs, more than a little laughter, and – horrifyingly – the occasional additional photograph all hurtled relentlessly towards Fia. More memories were still coming back to her in fragments, and by now she wasn't sure if she was trying to grasp for them inside her own mind or actively repel them.

Nodding along with the barrage of advice from everyone around her, she had the undeniable impression that a lot of these people would categorize the present situation as some exclamation-mark *drama!* rather than as a full-stop crisis. One by one, they inspected the wedding certificate, as though it were a suspicious-looking mole and they each were competing medical experts. Everyone agreed that it was utterly impossible that the document before them could be genuine, could have any real-world effects. Surely it was essentially a souvenir? A printout from the internet, like the certificates handed out liberally on school sports days?

'I don't even remember there being vows,' someone said. 'I'm pretty sure there was some kind of, like, *aquarium* in that place. I fed some leftover bar snacks to a Siamese fighting fish. There's just no way you can go from that to any type of . . . actual legal shit.'

Over by the pancake station, Brittany the future diabetes nurse was in floods of tears. 'At least they can get divorced!' Fia could just about hear her telling Michelle. 'Big deal! People get divorced all the time!' She pointed at the inflamed, objectively terrible tattoo on her arm. 'I'm going to have this for the *rest of my life*!'

Benjamin, meanwhile, was positioned about as far away from Fia at the breakfast table as it was possible to be. Perhaps it was on account of this distance that the two of them were presently managing to maintain any level of civility. Perhaps the other people in the dining room were now functioning as something of a diluting agent – or, more likely, both Fia and Benjamin simply found themselves lacking the fortitude for any more fights. Fury, confusion, and lots and lots of blame – all that had already been mutually expressed back in the hotel bedroom, in the moments when Benjamin's head was not in the toilet bowl. Fia couldn't help but think that his whole handling of the matter, digestively speaking, had been markedly inconsiderate. After all, she herself had been feeling so ill as to be almost unable to function. The last thing a person in that condition needed was the nearby scent of someone else's sick.

In any case, their predicament was such that they couldn't stay apart for long. After breakfast, they marched grimly to the hotel's business suite, armed with their sheet of paper and determined to ascertain its veracity once and for all. They studied it. They googled it. Mortifyingly, they *asked at reception*. The woman there barely batted an eyelid. She just pushed a plastic binder towards them, stuffed full of attorneys' business cards.

'Ten per cent discount if you quote the name of the hotel,' she said, and finally Fia and Benjamin flopped down onto a leather sofa in the lobby, exhausted and hideously hungover and – apparently – legally wed.

It was just the two of them now, and while, of course, Fia couldn't say she relished his company, she found she was glad to be free of the group. The hysteria, the analysis by committee, hadn't been helping matters one bit. And could it be that Benjamin, too, seemed a little relieved, somehow? Back in the dining room, with everyone else, he'd managed to resurrect a bit of his usual humour and horseplay. However, it had seemed much more half-hearted than usual, at least in Fia's estimation.

'Why is your name spelled like that?' he asked then, looking at their wedding certificate with a little frown. Fia followed his gaze, staring down at her own name in its official form: *Fiadh*.

'Oh. It's Irish. That's just how it's spelled,' she replied, a new wave of nausea and exhaustion washing over her. In the circumstances, she found she lacked even the energy to roast him over his ignorance. Something about the question just seemed to throw the reality of their situation into ever more stark relief. She and Benjamin Lowry had spent one summer together, mostly in large groups of other people, mostly trading inconsequential barbs. They had failed to gather even the most basic facts about one another. Yet now here they were: husband and wife.

For another few moments, they just sat together in the lobby, neither of them saying anything. Inexplicably, all around them, other hotel guests appeared to be going about their days as normal. Over in the corner, there was a tour guide in a baseball cap, rallying her group for a trip to the Pinball Hall of Fame. It was true what people said: there really was nothing to do in Las Vegas in the daytime.

'Well.' Fia sighed eventually, flipping through all the business cards before her. 'That's it, then. I suppose we'll just get divorced.

Or annulled or whatever.' The precise terminology didn't much matter to her, so long as the upshot was the same.

'Right,' Benjamin agreed – until a moment later, as though the reality of this was now hitting him anew, too, he winced.

'What?' she asked, her voice rising. 'You want to make a go of it? Have a couple of kids? Yeah, cool.' She put a sarcastic smile on her face. 'You'd probably really like Dublin once you got used to it.'

Uncharacteristically, though, he didn't rise to the bait, didn't try to best her. 'It's just, I . . . sorta have this situation right now,' he said. 'With my mom.'

'What kind of situation?' Fia replied, trepidation creeping in. Her first thought, honestly, was that his mother must be critically ill. It was hard to put her finger on what exactly the difference was in him – some small shift in the tone of his voice or his body language maybe – but one way or another, throughout the summer, she'd never seen Benjamin quite the way he suddenly seemed now: unsure of himself. It would sort of make sense, she thought, if this was the moment he'd choose to reveal his secret pain, bare his sensitive soul.

In fact, he did not do that at all.

'She's running for AG of North Carolina,' he said. 'Attorney General. That's like—'

'I know what it is!' Fia interrupted. This was a lot less on account of having just recently completed a law degree herself and a lot more thanks to having watched scores of American law shows on television. From these, she had gathered that the Attorney General was the top prosecutor in each US state and that the position was an elected one, voted for by the public in the same fashion as a political office.

'If this gets out,' Benjamin said, gesturing vaguely between the two of them, 'it could seriously hurt her campaign. Even kill it, maybe.'

Fia was sceptical. 'Do people really care that much about her kid's . . .' She trailed off, unsure how to finish the sentence. Horrendously, the phrase 'love life' came to mind, which did not seem quite appropriate in the circumstances. '. . . Well, about this type of thing?'

'Anything that's distracting is good news for her opponents, basically. When she ran for District Attorney, they spent six months debating some stupid paper she wrote in undergrad about fossil fuels. "Candidate's son in drunken Vegas wedding"?' he tossed out. '"Candidate's son in quickie divorce shocker"? Yeah. That's a lot more interesting than fossil fuels.'

Fia didn't know what to say to that, so she said nothing at all.

'It's just kind of a . . . high-octane vibe in the Lowry house right now is what I'm saying,' Benjamin continued. 'This is really not the time for me to come home with more drama. If we could just . . . wait.'

'*Wait?*' Fia repeated sharply.

'I just don't want to do anything that could jeopardize her chances. She's already . . . well, it's already a tough race in North Carolina, let's put it that way. And it's really hard to get elected for anything as a woman.'

Fia paused, let that sink in. Then, she cocked an eyebrow wryly. 'So, hang on, you're saying I have to stay married to you for . . . feminism?'

He rolled his eyes. 'Not forever, obviously. Believe me, I want to be done with this as much as you do. Just for . . . a while.'

'How long?' Fia asked, and it was only once the words were out that she realized: she must actually be considering this.

Benjamin thought for a second. 'A year? She'll be in office by then – or, y'know, *not* in office. One of the two.'

It was Fia's turn to pause, to try to weigh up the ramifications of his proposal. Truthfully, she was broke. She was, in two short weeks, supposed to be moving into a new flat-share in Dublin and starting her professional legal training at a fancy firm called Zelnick, O'Leary and Abbott. *More* administrative and financial burdens were the last things she needed right now.

A little bit of time to cool down from the heat of this *utter bin fire*, to research some options, save up some money . . . she had to admit, none of that necessarily sounded like it would be such a terrible idea. That way, she and Benjamin could deal with the matter discreetly, with a nice big ocean in between them – and without the need to involve anyone's parents, her own included.

She squinted over at him. 'One year?'

'Yes. In fact, look . . .'

She watched as he produced a pen from his rucksack and reached for one of the tourist leaflets piled at the far end of the coffee table in front of them. This one suggested they *Visit the Grand Canyon* and was accompanied by a glossy photograph of a helicopter from which Fia could well imagine plummeting to her death. Benjamin turned the leaflet over, scribbling away for a moment on the expanse of white, before handing it to her.

August 15, 2016 – get divorced, he'd written, with his signature down below.

She raised an eyebrow. She'd give him points for brevity, if not elegance, of expression.

'Now, you sign it,' he said expectantly.

And, somehow, taking the pen he offered her, Fia found herself doing just that.

'There,' he said, once she was finished. 'Now, we have a contract.'

'Hardly,' she replied sceptically. She hadn't paid huge amounts of attention in her contract law class, but phrases were suddenly dislodging themselves from the back of her mind: offer and acceptance, consideration, Carlill versus the Carbolic Smoke Ball Company.

She said none of this aloud and, in any event, Benjamin seemed typically unconcerned by specifics. The constituent elements of a claim, the relevant case law – none of that would mean anything to him.

'Sure we do,' he countered. 'Haven't you heard about people being held to, like, agreements they made on the back of a beermat?'

And, truthfully, Fia was pretty sure she *had* heard of such cases. Whether for that or for some other reason, she elected not to question him any further on the matter. Instead, she just looked down at the piece of paper before them, as though it might suddenly combust.

'So, what?' she asked. 'Will we write out another one, or do you want to *Parent Trap* this thing or what?'

Benjamin smiled, and it was undeniably the smallest bit pleasing – the unspoken way that he seemed to get the reference.

'It's okay,' he said, handing the leaflet to her. 'You just hold on to this. I will contact you, Fia, exactly one year from today.'

And something about it – about the evenness in his voice, the steadiness of his gaze – felt like a promise.

But it wasn't one he kept.

Chapter Eight

Around the kitchen table in her apartment, Fia feels as though she has been talking for a very long time. At last, she takes a big breath in and out and shrugs, the sign she's reached the end of this particular anti-fairy tale.

'I mean, obviously I contacted *him*,' she concludes. 'Repeatedly. Once the year had passed, I sent emails, I called – the whole shebang. And . . . nothing.'

'Oh my God! What an asshole!' Annie exclaims. 'I mean, I try to give people the benefit of the doubt, but that is just . . . it's *inexcusable*. Do you still have the contract? Or, y'know, the leaflet.'

Fia hesitates. 'Mmm, I don't know, maybe somewhere,' she says vaguely.

'The whole thing is so insane,' Kavita jumps in. 'I can't believe you've had to deal with it by yourself all these years.'

This time, Fia says nothing. She's been *not* dealing with it more than anything else, if truth be told. That slight twinge inside her – the same jagged twist of guilt and shame that she felt flare up when she first laid eyes on Benjamin – makes itself known again. Her zeal to make contact with him had lasted . . . she doesn't remember exactly . . . somewhere between nine and eighteen months, maybe?

In the years since then, of course she's *thought* about renewing her efforts, here and there – but in much the same way as she sometimes thought, for instance, that she should take out income protection insurance or start making some regular charitable donations.

Under her bed in this very apartment, there is a shoe box – and in that box, among various other documents, is a leaflet with a photo of the Grand Canyon on one side and her and Benjamin Lowry's signatures on the back. Fia, in truth, has always known exactly where that leaflet is. She's held on to it, carted it across the Atlantic. Keeping the box closed, though, keeping it well out of her own view, never mind anyone else's . . . that's actually proved surprisingly easy. Over the last few years, especially, she's thought about it only very rarely.

Of course, rarely is not quite never. And on the occasions when the matter *has* darted, uninvited, into her brain, it has always been such a source of discomfort, on both a practical and an emotional level. For all this time, there has been an item on Fia's to-do list that has gone undone. Worse than that, there has been lingering feeling that, ultimately, she let Benjamin Lowry walk all over her – *let* him leave her merrily in his wake, like acceptable collateral damage.

But then, she tells herself, she's been busy: moving countries, building a career – the months and years seem, in retrospect, to have flown by, just the way old people always said they did. It is little wonder that a single drunken night when she was 22 years old has not always occupied prime real estate inside Fia's head.

And, really, what more could she actually have done? What she's just told Annie and Kavita is true. She *did* email and call and text. Benjamin was the only person she knew who had never got involved with Facebook, so that was a no go. What else was there? Short of hiring a private investigator, she found herself fresh out of options.

She decides – once and for all, right here in this kitchen – to absolve herself of any blame. *He* was the one who left her high and dry. *He* was the one who had evidently never planned to clean up the mess that was their marriage unless and until it especially suited him to do so. Fia should at least, now, get to feel a bit sorry for herself. She should at least get to properly bask in her friends' sympathy.

'So, what happens next – you just serve him with divorce papers?' Annie asks. 'I mean, I guess if there's an upside to this whole thing, it's that you definitely know where to find him at this point.'

Fia supposes that's true.

'*And* you know the whole legal process and whatever. That has to help. I guess you can't do your own divorce, though, right?'

'No. I've been trying to find someone who can handle it,' Fia says. 'The thing is, I can't have this getting out at work – it's just not a good look, you know? Who wants a lawyer who can't even keep her *own* life in order? So, it can't be anyone I've ever been on the other side of on a case or whatever. Equally, obviously, I want it to be someone who isn't totally incompetent. There's this one woman I emailed today, actually, who might be good, if she gets back to me.'

'Well, there you have it,' Annie replies warmly. 'This will all be behind you in no time.'

And Fia nods along, but still, she feels glum. Perhaps she looks it, too, because suddenly, Kavita hops up from her seat.

'I think we should see what Pema says about this whole thing,' she proclaims, all energy.

Fia frowns in confusion. 'But it's not the morning,' she counters.

On their kitchen windowsill, alongside the dead fern and the washing-up liquid, is a little book. *The Pocket Pema Chödrön*, it's called, each page containing a pithy inspirational quote. It was Kavita's contribution to the household; before Kavita moved in eighteen months ago, Fia had never so much as heard of this particular Buddhist teacher. Now, however, on the occasions that all three roommates overlap in the kitchen in the mornings, sometimes they pause for a little communal intake of wisdom.

'Okay. Let's see,' Kavita says, once she's back. She is not a Buddhist herself. She isn't anything. Rather, she simply purchased this book on a celebrity's recommendation and seemed to consider it akin to a Magic 8 Ball. As ever, she lets it fall open at a random page, and clears her throat.

'"Nothing ever goes away until it has taught us what we need to know",' Kavita reads out, and even as she utters the phrase, her face falls, as though it is clear to her that this, in the situation at hand, does not exactly hit the bull's-eye.

'What? No! That's not what I want! Go again,' Fia orders.

Her roommate duly repeats the exercise. '"Rather than letting our negativity get the better of us, we could acknowledge that right now we feel like a piece of shit and not be squeamish about taking a good look",' she quotes solemnly.

Fia groans. 'Eugh. Has she got anything that says "the past is in the past, and it's completely fine to just ignore it"?'

'I don't think that's really Pema's vibe, hon,' Annie replies, with a sympathetic chuckle.

'No, I suppose not. Anyway, I *do* feel like shit,' Fia continues. 'She's dead on with that one.'

'Poor Fi,' Kavita murmurs.

'Honestly, I just want to go home,' Fia continues, and nobody even questions what she means. That's the thing about a flat-share. Very often, all the people in it have some other place that feels equally, or more so, like home. For Annie, that's California. For Kavita, it's Texas. In Fia's case, of course, it's Dublin.

'Well, not long to wait, right?' Annie says encouragingly.

And that's true. Every July, lawyers from ZOLA's four branches come together in one location to look at some PowerPoints, do some team-building activities, and get a bit drunk. The Summer Summit, they call it. This year – extremely fortuitously, as far as Fia is concerned – it is Dublin's turn. In exactly four weeks from today, she'll be on a plane.

'Or, hang on, do the summer associates go on that, too?' Annie continues.

Fia shakes her head. Of all the nice things about Ireland, suddenly none are as appealing as the simple fact of Benjamin Lowry's absence.

'Perfect!' Kavita says. 'Something to look forward to is exactly what you need. Not to mention you'll get to see Hot Irish Guy.'

Fia's brain is so frazzled that it takes her a second to decode that. 'Who?' she asks, before she realizes. 'Oh! Ryan Sieman.'

She met Ryan at the Summer Summit three years ago – it was held, that year, right here in New York City. Ryan had newly joined the firm's Dublin branch by that stage, and he was fun – attractive, available, easy company. Since then, no matter the location, none of ZOLA's annual conferences have ended any other way than with her and Ryan Sieman in a hotel room together, naked. Has she seen him on a few other nights as well, when she's returned home to Dublin for Christmas and the like? And did they occasionally email back and forth, just the two of them, trading one-liners in response to a company-wide chain? Yes, all of that might be true. One way or another, Ryan can generally be relied upon to provide some welcome escapism.

Now, though, at the thought of him, Fia can manage only a wan smile. She casts her eyes across the spread on the kitchen table: the plastic containers of food are well picked over by this stage, the bottle of wine empty but for a last dribble no one has wanted to claim. She can sense Kavita and Annie following her gaze, can feel the way the entire mood of the evening seems to have flattened.

'You wanna go out? I feel like we should go out,' Kavita proclaims then, with every bit of her usual decisiveness.

Surprised, Fia looks down at herself. She's in her comfy clothes already. 'Out where?'

'Wherever. Some kind of alcohol emporium.'

'I'm down for that,' Annie chimes in.

But still, Fia hesitates. It's been a long day, preceded by a very long week, and she still has Friday to endure with Benjamin tomorrow.

'Oh, come on!' Kavita says, and then a wicked grin spreads across her face. 'We could think of it as your belated bach-elorette party!'

Even as Fia rolls her eyes, she can't help but laugh. 'How is this my life?' she moans dramatically, but she lets herself be tugged up from the dining table, going along with it as they all get ready to leave. They'll just walk to Antonio's around the corner, they decide – have a few casual margs, perhaps fashion an effigy of Benjamin Lowry from tortilla chips and guacamole. Jeans are pulled on in place of tracksuit bottoms, shoes are located, and then they're out the door.

'But, so, I really don't think I get this guy,' Annie starts, as they make their way down the hall and into the lift. Quite a lot of Annie's sentences start that way, as though they are all already part of the conversation she's been having in her own head. 'Benjamin. Is he, like, a happy, dumb Labrador kind of guy?'

'Right!' Kavita jumps in. 'Or is he, like, a *bro*?'

'That's what I was thinking,' Annie continues. 'Like, just your basic Brad-slash-Chad douchebag?'

'But, then, there's this weird, holier-than-thou, "I wouldn't even consider working a corporate job in Midtown Manhattan, even though I've literally chosen to work a corporate job in Midtown Manhattan" thing. Superiority complex?'

'Or an *inferiority* complex, and he's trying to mask it?'

Fia has no answers. Benjamin Lowry could be any of the people her friends have described. She would acknowledge that he probably can't be *all* of them, one personality surely having the capacity to contain only a certain amount within it. In any event, though, she doesn't feel any great need to try to work him out.

'Whatever which way, he's going to be right there in front of my face for another *nine* weeks,' she replies.

'Well, hey,' Kavita says then, as the lift doors open out onto their building's lobby. 'Now you have a prime opportunity for a little revenge, right? Okay, he's a dick, and it's a bad situation in a lot of ways – I get that. But there's got to be at least some enjoyment to be had here. You're finally going to be able to pin him down for a divorce, and in the meantime, you have the power to basically make his life a misery. Can't you just rope him into doing all the stuff for your clients that you don't want to do?'

Fia thinks about that one. She can say with some confidence that she's done a stellar job of aggravating Benjamin this past week – sometimes when she hasn't even been trying to, and sometimes when she very much has. As far as actually assigning tasks to him, though, actually inviting him further into the weeds of her working life . . . that seems a bit counterproductive to her. After all, she doesn't want any more involvement with him than she absolutely needs to have – never mind all the ways in which he might screw things up and leave her with the fallout when he goes.

'I don't know,' she replies dubiously. 'Not to be a bitch, but I just have no idea how he even got onto the programme at ZOLA in the first place. I mean, obviously his mother is probably pretty well-connected, but even when the firm hires people's god-children and whatnot, there's normally a certain standard. This is a guy who once argued with me for maybe ten full minutes about whether the phrase was "for all *intensive* purposes".'

'Wait, are you saying it's not?' Annie asks, and she doesn't have to wait too long for Fia's horrified expression. 'Kidding! I'm kidding!'

She pushes open the building's main door, all three of them laughing as they head out onto 81st Street, falling easily into step with one another. The smell and the sound of the city is all-encompassing, immediately, but – at least on these Uptown streets – Fia no longer finds it overwhelming. She actually finds it comforting, familiar – like a cocoon.

'And you said he's been doing *what* since undergrad?' Kavita continues. 'Being a *gamer*?'

Maybe that's not exactly factual, and Fia couldn't say for certain that the inaccuracy originates with her roommate. Nonetheless, she finds herself disinclined to issue a correction right now.

'Something like that,' she says. 'Whatever it was, it doesn't seem to have left him too keen to exert himself, anyway. Waltzes in at nine every morning, doesn't stay a second after five thirty.'

'Right. If you ask me, you should basically go full Miranda Priestly on his ass. If you don't trust him with anything significant, then just give him a ton of really annoying, menial tasks. This moron's not going to know what's hit him.'

Fia just laughs, feeling suddenly glad that they decided to come on this little jaunt tonight. It's good for a person, she thinks, the way that New York City seems to make it impossible to stew, to stagnate, for too long.

'Well, I'll bear it in mind,' she replies merrily. Perhaps, now that she thinks about it, she *does* have some admin that needs to be completed on a fairly urgent basis. Perhaps there are some ancient boxes of trust deeds that simply aren't going to sort themselves. And – she finds ever more enthusiasm building inside her – there's just something about a shop-bought coffee, isn't there? Even the fancy aluminium machines at ZOLA don't seem to quite hit the spot in the same way as that place down on Madison and 44th. In short, there are bound to be all sorts of ways she can fill Benjamin's day – tasks with which she can occupy and exhaust him, while still staying well within the limits of his intellectual capabilities.

The very next day, in the break room, one of the paralegals tells Fia that Benjamin Lowry is currently third in his class at Columbia Law.

She just about chokes on her mini muffin.

WEEK TWO

Chapter Nine

'As requested,' Benjamin says flatly, plonking a hefty bundle of documents on Fia's desk, all freshly photocopied. Five copies per page, she asked for. One never could tell when they might need extras.

'Thanks,' she says. 'Did you paginate them?'

'Sure did!' he replies, injecting a plainly false brightness into his voice as he sits down at his own desk.

Fia just nods, feeling the wind taken out of her sails a little bit. He had forgotten to, last time. She isn't above admitting that she had a bit of fun with that, with the sheer frustration that was written across his face as she sent him right back out to the reprographics station.

More than halfway through their second week in captivity now, it's turned out that Kavita was right: it *has* been somewhat satisfying, finding opportunities to have Benjamin Lowry chase his tail for her. At this point, though, she's in danger of running out of tasks, even semi-bullshit ones. And if he starts to get better at them? If it becomes merely a process of him easily providing things for which she must then express gratitude? That doesn't seem quite what she's after. It's bad enough knowing that he's allegedly a boy genius. How can that *be*?

In any event, over the past day or two, it's actually become somewhat difficult to nab him. Benjamin has begun spending what seems to Fia more time than must strictly be necessary up on the fifty-ninth floor, assisting on some big merger thing. Needless to say, there are ways in which this suits her just fine. The less time she has to deal with the sight and the sound and the *scent* of him, the better. However, at least right now, she's grateful to have some overlap in their little office. There are certain communications that just do not belong on a company server.

'How're things upstairs?' she enquires, attempting civility.

His only response, though, is an indistinct mumble. Already, he's engrossed in reading something, his brow furrowed slightly in concentration. Fia watches as – amid the carnage that continues to be his workspace – he reaches blindly for some other document. After more than a little kerfuffle, he unearths it from under a mug, a block of Post-its, a *stapler*.

'That's my stapler, by the way,' she tosses out. For some reason, having restrained herself for over a week, she just cannot resist it in this moment.

He pauses, looks up at her. 'It's not,' he says, 'but whatever.'

'It *is*,' she insists, and then she mimics his tone of voice, 'but whatever.'

He takes a deep breath in and out, as though to make very clear the extent to which his patience is being tried. 'Well, how about this, Fia? You call it, and then *I'll* call it, and we'll see which one of us it comes to.'

Fia just glowers in response. It's the strangest thing, though – the sensation that in other circumstances, she might have laughed out loud at that. She moves to bury it – and swiftly.

'So, I found someone who can help us with our situation,' she says.

Benjamin, reabsorbed in his task, looks up at her once more, a blank expression on his face.

'A divorce lawyer, Ben,' she says plainly. 'I found a divorce lawyer.'

Their office door is wide open, the atrium populated as usual by all the paralegals and admin staff at their desks, plus passing pedestrians. Benjamin lets his gaze travel out there deliberately, a half-smile pulling at his lips.

'What's that, Fia?' he says, raising his voice a little. 'You found us a *divorce lawyer?*'

And it's just a joke, really. He's not loud enough to genuinely attract attention. From outside, nobody even glances in their direction. Nonetheless, this time around, Fia cannot remotely see the funny side – not even secretly.

'Yes!' she replies, her own voice lowering to a hiss. 'Her name is Susan Followill. She said she could squeeze us in next Monday at lunchtime – assuming you can fit that into your, uh . . . busy schedule.'

It's perhaps a little unnecessarily caustic, the way she says that, given that he actually *does* appear to have a pretty busy schedule at this point. Alongside his genuine work assignments, plus the various jobs she's been manifesting for him, he's also expected to attend all manner of seminars, training sessions and 'opportunities to get to know one another in a less formal setting'. She's heard on the grapevine that, last night, a bunch of summer associates, including one Benjamin

Lowry, were invited to the theatre with all the real estate partners. Fia cannot personally imagine any faster way to ruin
Dear Evan Hansen than the insertion of what amounted to a
mini job interview over Chardonnay at the interval, but that
is neither here nor there.

'There's a workshop on client management, I think,'
Benjamin replies. 'But I can probably skip it.'

'Great,' she says shortly, considering the matter dealt with.
When she turns back to the lengthy agreement on her screen,
though, there's some sense of lingering discomfort. She can
still feel his eyes on her. She looks at him once more, and it
prompts him to speak again.

'I guess I'm still trying to figure out why the hell you
would even want . . .' He trails off then, reroutes – perhaps
because of what Fia can only imagine to be the perplexed
expression on her face. 'Whatever. Your funeral. So, that's how
you want to do this, huh?'

Still, Fia does not follow.

'As in, together,' he clarifies. 'One lawyer for both of us. Can
one lawyer even do that? Wouldn't that be a conflict of interest?'

Fia sighs deeply, deliberately. 'Family law not quite your
speciality, eh?' she asks. An unprofessional response, perhaps,
but then, the same could be said of the face Benjamin makes
right back at her.

'There are two kinds of divorces,' she continues briskly.
'Courtroom divorces, and conference room divorces. If you end
up in a courtroom, you need a lawyer for each party. But if
you can just reach a settlement via mediation, one person can
handle that – they're called an attorney mediator.'

Fia pauses for breath. Before she agreed to become a mentor
this summer, she'd wondered whether she really had sufficient

expertise for the role. Celia assured her she did, and Fia was comforted. *Yes*, she told herself staunchly. *I know things. I could pass along some wisdom.*

She had not anticipated that it would be in quite this context.

'Anyway, basically, I think let's just get one person to handle it fast and split the cost,' she continues. 'Unless you plan on gunning for 50 per cent of my . . .' She pauses, struggling even to come up with a hypothetical asset to her name. 'I don't know . . . *clothes*, I think we should be good. I mean, this is essentially an administrative matter, right?'

'Right,' he agrees. 'Still, though, I'm not so sure how I feel about having your buddy as our mutual divorce lawyer. Or our . . . attorney mediator.'

'What? Susan's not my *buddy*,' Fia replies, and the word – which had sounded perfectly normal in his accent – sounds faintly ludicrous in hers. 'I found her on the internet.'

How aggravating, that she has done all the legwork on this thing, that she has spent the past ten days relentlessly emailing suitable-seeming strangers, *praying* they would get back to her, all to have him wilfully assume the worst of her.

Over at his desk, Benjamin says nothing for a moment, before offering a nonchalant shrug.

'Well, I'll think about it,' he replies, and it's enough to get Fia's blood boiling – just the notion that, somehow, he still feels like the control ultimately rests with him.

'You'll *think about it*?' she repeats.

'Yeah. I'll think about it. I'll *keep it under advisement*,' he says loftily.

In a flash, Fia is truly a new level of livid. Before she has time to say anything further, though, a figure appears in her doorway, stooped but dapper as ever.

'Mr Zelnick!' she says, pasting on a pleasant expression. 'Hi!'

'Top o' the morning to ya, Fia!' he replies, as he very often does. If this man were not pushing eighty and a dote and, technically speaking, her Big Boss, Fia would have a lot less time for it. As things are, her smile doesn't waver.

'What can I do for you?'

'Got a case for you! Olivia Chestnut's the name. She's from your neck of woods, so naturally I thought of you.'

Fia's expression shifts a little in surprise. 'She's Irish?'

Mr Zelnick hesitates. 'Well . . . close enough. Anyhow, she's a client up in corporate – she's one of these online business-women – I don't know, I just handle the taxes. Seemingly things aren't going so well on the home front, though.'

'Oh?'

'Thought I'd send the divorce your way if you can squeeze it in? The husband's already filed, *and* he wants custody of the son. I have to say, he sounds like a real piece of work – the husband, I mean. I can't say I know much about the son!' Mr Zelnick twinkles at his own little joke, and Fia fights the urge to wince.

Quite why, she couldn't exactly explain. There is, after all, nothing inherently unusual about what Mr Zelnick seems to be requesting of her. On an ordinary day, she would probably have considered it good news to have even crossed his radar.

This is not an ordinary day, though, and instead Fia finds her whole body suddenly seized with tension. It must, she knows, be on account of Benjamin.

The instinctive desire she feels to bring an end to this inter-action can *only* be on account of Benjamin – the very definite sense she has of him, three feet away and suddenly vastly more curious about her work than he's ever been before.

'Um, okay,' she hears herself offer disjointedly. 'I just . . . I'm not sure if I have capacity at the moment. Maybe Jeff or Soo-Yin could—'

'Ah, hogwash!' Mr Zelnick interjects, all cheerfulness. 'Surely you wouldn't turn an old man down, Fia? You wanna know the *real* reason I thought of you for this case?'

At this juncture, Fia isn't all that sure she *does* want to know. But nonetheless, it seems very much like Mr Zelnick is going to tell her.

'I went to Celia Hannity,' he continues, 'and I said, "who's my best bet?" – and you know what she told me?'

'What?' Fia asks, her voice coming out laced with something like dread. She's just so acutely aware of Benjamin's presence, of the completeness of his attention now.

'She said that when it comes to divorce cases, there's no one like you. She said you're forensic, ferocious . . . a "total shark", I believe was the phrase.'

And, again, in usual circumstances, Fia would have no trouble taking this as the compliment it is intended to be. As things are, she finds herself with absolutely no idea of what to do with her face, much less what to actually say in response.

Across the room, she'd swear she can hear Benjamin *breathing*, the sound of it seeming to magnify in the silence. Seconds stretch out before his input arrives at last, his voice coming out soft – but all the more loaded for that, all the more dangerous. 'Is that so?' he asks.

Chapter Ten

'Uh, Mr Zelnick, this is Benjamin Lowry,' Fia swoops in, attempting to regain some sort of control of the conversation. 'He's a summer associate. Benjamin, I'm sure Mr Zelnick needs no introduction . . .'

This man's name is, after all, on the stationery, his late father having been the OG 'Zelnick' in Zelnick, O'Leary and Abbott. These days, it is commonly accepted that he practises very little law and often none at all – yet he could not be prevailed upon to leave the firm. Even the retirement party thrown for him last year hadn't worked. He'd disappeared for what amounted to a long holiday and then, suddenly, there he was, back again every morning in his suit and bow tie. Fia has never once heard anyone, no matter their own seniority, refer to him on a first-name basis.

For a few minutes, Fia waits it out, lets Benjamin and Mr Zelnick exchange the pleasantries that must be exchanged, paying only vague attention. At a certain point in proceedings, though, her ears prick back up.

'So, Benjamin,' Mr Zelnick is saying loftily, 'let's talk turkey. They teaching you anything about divorce over there at Columbia?'

Benjamin shoots Fia a sidelong glance, and she's sure he deliberately takes his time before replying. She's sure he wants her to sweat a bit. She *does* sweat a bit. For the very first time, it occurs to her that she is involved not just in concealing her personal history with Benjamin: she has also concealed the fact of their ongoing, sadly not-at-all-historical, spousal relationship. She's let him join the firm, let herself become his mentor, without mentioning that – at least on paper, at least as far as Human Resources will be concerned – he is her *husband*. Failure to disclose something like that . . .

Suddenly, it occurs to Fia that embarrassment over a youthful mistake made public, the thought of her character being called into question, the prospect of a delayed promotion . . . all these things should be the least of her worries. What she's involved in now, the degree of deception involved . . . it's a fireable offence, surely.

In Ireland, of course, there is a whole process. Employees have to be given chances, and quite a lot of them at that – it seems to be pretty difficult to get shot of even the most incompetent staff members. In the US, though, things are different. You can be there one day and quite literally gone the next. Fia's seen it happen in the New York office with her own eyes.

And, given the look on Benjamin's face right now, she would not be at all surprised if this were the moment that he decided to drop her in it, the impact on his own future prospects be damned. The frightening thing is: he's contrary enough to do it.

In the end, however, he gives a little shake of his head.

'Not so far,' he replies. 'Though interestingly enough, Fia here was just giving me the benefit of her . . . *experience*.'

He looks over at her properly as he says that last bit, holding her gaze, and Fia averts her eyes. She doesn't know why she hasn't mentioned this particular aspect of her legal practice to Benjamin before now. Maybe it just felt a bit too close to the bone – like something he would surely find a way to twist or mock or make all about him.

Meanwhile, across the room, Mr Zelnick is nothing but delighted. 'Well, how 'bout that!' he exclaims. 'Y'know, it's funny – as an attorney, you gotta be able to turn your hand to anything. Me, I'm a corporate tax lawyer, really, but you wanna guess how many times I been down at the Metropolitan Correctional Facility bailing people out of jail? More times than I can count! We're a *full-service* law firm here at ZOLA, that's for sure!'

Both Fia and Benjamin chuckle along politely, before Mr Zelnick speaks again.

'How'd you like me to assign you to assist on the Chestnut divorce, Benjamin? It'd be a wonderful learning opportunity for you, I'm sure. When I was a young buck, I would have given my eye teeth to get in on something this juicy!'

Immediately, in every part of Fia's being, it is as though alarm bells begin to ring – deafeningly. She tips from extreme discomfort into a full-scale panic, practically tripping over her own tongue in protest.

'You know, I'm really not sure Benja—'

Horrifically, though, she finds herself cut off, Benjamin's voice rising over the top of hers.

'That sounds amazing, Mr Zelnick, thank you,' he says, all sincerity. And again, he looks right at Fia as he finishes: 'I can't wait.'

Mr Zelnick claps his hands together. 'That's settled, then!'

Fia says nothing, looking between the two men hopelessly. Her mind races, searching for some other escape, some new protest she might legitimately raise.

There's nothing, though. She knows when she's beaten.

And, undeniably, that is what has happened here. Benjamin Lowry has beaten her. More than that, from the expression on his face, he's all too aware of it. He has no genuine interest in learning about the legal mechanics of a divorce. She's also quite certain he has no genuine interest in working alongside her in any substantive way – *assisting* her. No. He has seized upon his opportunity for one reason and for one reason only, which is to cause her the maximum possible aggravation.

'All right,' she manages weakly, after a moment. 'Well. Maybe you could' – this was where, if she were speaking to any other lawyer in the office and perhaps the world, Fia would suggest the sending of an email, but Mr Zelnick does not do emails – 'drop a memo on my desk at some point? Just with this woman's contact info and whatever other details you have. I'll give her a call.'

'No need,' Mr Zelnick beams. 'She's in the lobby.'

Fia's eyebrows shoot up. 'She's in the lobby *now*?'

'I'll bring her up, shall I? Meeting room six?'

There's an expectant look on his face, and Fia lets out a helpless laugh. There is, at this point, nothing else to do.

As she gets to her feet, Benjamin does the same. They look at one another, and he gestures towards the door with an open palm, his voice silky smooth. 'After you.'

Of course, it doesn't take long for him to drop the gentleman act.

'You're a fucking divorce lawyer?' he asks, through practically gritted teeth, the second they're alone. Specifically, they've cleared the open-plan atrium and are marching down a long corridor now, at breakneck pace.

'Sometimes, yes,' Fia replies tightly, and she only wishes she could go faster. Not for the first time since Benjamin has joined her at ZOLA, she wishes she could take off her heels and *run*, as hard as she knows how, just for the sheer release of it.

'What does that mean?'

'Remember when I said rich people die?' she asks, and she watches as Benjamin nods irritably. 'Yeah, well, sometimes they also get divorced. You heard Mr Zelnick. We're a full-service law firm.'

'And you didn't think you should have mentioned this to me?'

Maybe, yes, comes some reflective, inexplicable response in her own mind. Of course, she cannot utter it.

'And when would I have done that in the last eight years, Benjamin?' she demands instead. 'At what point in your very regular, very mature communication with me?'

Benjamin cannot seem to restrain a choked grunt of frustration. 'Jesus, Fia, I get it! I didn't write you back or whatever. You were sad. But what do you want me to do – this is not *The Notebook*. And let's be honest, you've made the best of things in the interim, haven't you? Very much so, I'd say.'

Now it's her turn for an outright gasp. 'Of course I have – what other choice did you give me?'

'Well, for one thing—'

'Shh!' she commands, the sound much more staccato than soothing. They've turned a corner now, another long corridor stretching out before them, a woman advancing from the opposite direction. Fia has no clue who this person is, but her mere presence is enough to force a temporary halt in their conversation.

Fia and Benjamin do nothing to slow their pace or to soften

their expressions, but that's fine. There are plenty of reasons, inside this building, why two young professionals might validly seem extremely panicked and unhappy. It's just the specific nature of Fia and Benjamin's unhappiness that must be concealed.

The very moment they seem to be alone again, Benjamin turns back to Fia. 'Anyhow, you'll forgive me if this latest development doesn't exactly put my mind at rest about Susan Followill,' he says, his voice a little more hushed now, but still dripping in disdain.

'What does this have to do with Susan Followill?'

'I just think it's pretty suss. Nine to five you're apparently divorcing people left and right, taking no prisoners. You're a *shark*. But you're telling *me* "oh, let's definitely just go with this nice therapist lady." And I'm supposed to just take that in good faith?'

Every part of this feels offensive to Fia – illogical, inaccurate, grossly mischaracterized. She doesn't know why, in terms of her response, she starts where she does. 'Susan is *not* a therapist!'

She cuts herself off then, before she can finish the thought, physically stopping in her tracks while she's at it.

Benjamin halts right alongside her. It's discombobulating, like stepping off a moving walkway at the airport.

They look at each other, as though they're both a little dizzy. To their right is conference room six, and through the glass, Fia can see that their client has beaten them there.

'We'll have to discuss this later,' she tells Benjamin, forcing herself to take a deep breath in and out. Then, for the record: 'Do not talk when we get in here. I mean *not one word*.'

Of course, as soon as she says it, she realizes her error – and it's a rookie mistake at that. The most likely way of ensuring

Benjamin's silence would doubtless have been to ask that he contribute as much as humanly possible.

He follows her eyeline, peering into the conference room for a moment. Then, he returns to face her, affecting confusion.

'But, Fia, what if I have some insight to bring to bear? What if that woman in there says "my spouse is a total fucking lunatic, who's entirely abusing his power over me"? What then? You expect me to just say nothing?'

'Yes, I do!' she hisses, and in this precise moment, she *feels* like a lunatic. He has made her into a lunatic.

'I just don't think I can make that sort of a promise,' he tosses back airily and then gives her a particular sort of smile, the one she never finds at all comforting. 'But, hey, I'll do my best.'

Chapter Eleven

'So, you're Olivia,' Fia says, after briefly introducing both herself and Benjamin. She injects as much brightness into her voice as she can manage, looking across the conference room table at her new client.

The space is designed so that the visiting party has a view of Manhattan – sunshine glinting off skyscrapers again today – plus a vast bookcase full of hardbound law reports. Fia sincerely thinks these might be literal props, housing nothing but blank pages, but she has to admit they do look the part. Conversely, from the lawyer's vantage point, there is little to be seen in this room but pristine white walls, glass, and the client.

Olivia Chestnut has blonde and brown hair, trailing down her back in artful waves, and her outfit seems to involve a lot of component parts, all various shades of muted. Add in the designer handbag, and Fia's first impression is of a very particular kind of Manhattan 40-year-old: the sort of woman who could recommend, loudly, a good serum and, quietly, a good surgeon.

'Ah-liv-i-a,' comes the reply. 'With an "a". And a "y". A-L-Y-V-I-A.'

'. . . Alyvia,' Fia repeats, uncertainly. She can't imagine it's anything but obvious to everyone present that this sounds exactly the same as her prior attempt. Nonetheless, 'Alyvia' smiles her approval.

'Great!' Fia continues. She pours from the jug of iced water in the centre of the table, distributing three full glasses.

'Is this alkaline water?' Alyvia asks, her brow furrowing as she stares down at her glass.

Fia halts. Alkaline water sounds suspiciously like the sort of thing that rich people might try to pay for in America but that everyone gets accidentally in Ireland, at no extra charge – like grass-fed beef or a sense of community.

'Uh, I'm not sure,' she replies, and she watches Alyvia gingerly take a sip. When she swallows, her lips pucker slightly as though she's sucking on a lemon.

Fia elects to ignore it. 'So, I understand you're in the process of separating from your husband,' she says instead.

Incidentally, she always starts exactly here, when it comes to this conversation. Many people don't. An expression of sympathy, of regret, seems to trip off the tongue. Fia knows better, though. A divorce is often a sad, sorry thing, but not always.

'Teddy said you were Irish!' Alyvia exclaims then, in lieu of a proper answer. Her expression brightens. 'What a darling he is, eh? He's really helped me out so much already. Anyway, I love Irish people. Have you been at the firm for long?'

'Eight years,' Fia replies, and beside her, Benjamin mumbles something – some indistinct grievance or criticism – under his breath. She shoots a sidelong glance his way, her irritation just barely concealed, then does her best to get on with ignoring him.

'I suppose you're like me now then, eh?' Alyvia continues, obliviously. 'A proper New Yorker.'

The fact that Fia hasn't actually spent all of the past eight years in Manhattan feels pretty tangential to the exchange Alyvia evidently wants to have here.

'How long have *you* been in the US?' Fia duly enquires. It's the call-and-response of immigrants everywhere – or, as she suspects Alyvia might say, of expats. Given her slightly mangled twang – still mostly English, but with a little unmistakable American cadence in the mix – Fia would guess that the other woman has been on this side of the pond for a while. As it turns out, she's right on the money.

'Nearly fifteen years,' Alyvia says. 'Usual story. Came over from London for work, stayed for love. Much good it's done me.'

'Mmm,' Fia murmurs sympathetically. Then, she seizes the opportunity to get things back on track. 'On that note, Mr Zelnick . . . uh, *Teddy* . . . he mentioned that your husband has already served you with a divorce summons. Do you have that with you?'

Alyvia appears, in fact, to have come armed with a small forest's worth of paper. She plucks a document from the top of her pile, handing it over. Fia flips through the pages expertly. She knows enough, by now, to be able to get to the good bits fast. When Benjamin leans in for a look too, the sudden proximity makes her jump. She just about restrains a scowl, passing the document across for his perusal, turning her own attention back to Alyvia.

'So, this says your husband is alleging adultery on your part,' she says, not beating around the bush. 'Is that true? If it is, that's fine – we can deal with it. You just need to tell me.'

'Pfft,' Alyvia mutters, with a dismissive wave of her hand. 'He was always jealous. As if I can help it that people are, like, sometimes a bit obsessed with me!' She lets out a conspiratorial little laugh. 'Anyway. Jonathan has some nerve claiming *I* committed adultery when *he's* the one who's got a fancy woman on the go already.'

Fia raises an eyebrow, making a quick note on the yellow legal pad in front of her. 'Okay, so, we'll contest that. And I presume you want to contest his application for full custody of your son?'

'You're fucking right I do!' Alyvia fires back, before she seems to catch herself. 'Sorry. I'm sorry for swearing. But, yes, I do. My son will be staying with me.'

Fia's jotting that down, too, when Alyvia speaks again. Her voice has returned to its normal volume, but the slightly affected, sing-song inflection she arrived with seems suddenly to be gone. In the glint in her eye, the steadiness of her gaze, Fia can see the steel in this woman now.

'And I'll tell you something else,' she continues, 'when this hits the press, the story will *not* be that I cheated on Jonathan. If it's the last thing I do, the story will be *him* – how he's sabotaged me, how he's tried to ruin my business, kill my career . . .'

Fia frowns, struggling to follow. She's handled divorces for some of ZOLA's well-known corporate clients before. But such clients tend to be *Forbes*-magazine famous. Their business deals will get a mention in there, and – in due course – perhaps their deaths. Their divorces, though? Not so much. And that's normally exactly how they like it. By contrast, Alyvia seems almost enthused to arrive at the point of airing her dirty laundry in public – or, rather, Jonathan's.

'Sorry, let's just . . . rewind a bit here,' Fia says. 'What is it that you do exactly?'

'Well, gosh! I suppose I'm a jack of all trades, you might say. I'm a content creator – and *curator*, really. I'm a luxury brand ambassador, and I work a lot with companies on their consumer outreach and so on. But it's all very much passion driven. I've got quite a large following across various different platforms and verticals.'

It takes Fia a moment to process this, piece it all together. She squints across the table. 'Are you an . . . influencer?'

The descriptor seems to leave a slightly sour taste in Alyvia's mouth. 'I suppose you might say that.'

'What do you do, Instagram, or . . . ?'

'Mostly Instagram, yeah. BabyGAndMe is the account, if you've heard of it?'

Fia definitely *hasn't* heard of it, and she conveys this via a sheepish smile. 'Do you mind if I just . . .' She gestures at her iPhone, currently resting face down on the table. 'Just to get an idea, you know? Might be the quickest thing.'

This is true, but also, she finds she's just plain intrigued. Once she pulls up the account, the first thing she notices is that it has almost three million followers. She tries to keep her face impassive and professional as she takes in that number – perhaps, then, the notion of press interest is not so out of the question as she'd thought. Rapidly, this case feels like it is expanding, stretching into new and unfamiliar territory.

Below, on the Instagram grid, Fia scans dozens upon dozens of photographs of a little boy: him wearing burgundy braces and a bow tie, him atop a wooden rocking horse, him grinning over a cupcake mixing bowl. Every twentieth post or so is a photograph of Alyvia alone or perhaps a meal or a landscape.

But mostly, it seems to be the kid. He looks about 10 or 11 now, by Fia's estimation, but as she scrolls back through time, she can see his entire childhood, or some version of it, before her eyes.

'So, this is . . . BabyG?' she asks, sliding the phone towards Benjamin. It's less through any genuine desire to involve him in proceedings and more on account of the need to keep up an appearance of collegiality. Not to mention the need to keep him out of her personal space.

'That's my Gus, yeah,' Alyvia replies fondly. 'And' – she hands over all her other paperwork – '*this* is really why I'm here.'

Again, Fia thumbs through the pages. On them are screenshots of some of the photographs she's just seen, all re-posted by another user this time – Silverfish29. Below each re-post, Alyvia has highlighted the accompanying captions in yellow marker:

Guess what she has to do to make the kid keep taking these pics

Lol this isn't even ur real house

Ask Alyvia what happened litrally five minutes before this though

What you see isn't always the truth remember that

Hahahaha everyone can tell Gus fucking hates doing this

Fia gets the gist. Whoever is behind this account, she wouldn't give them any major points for spelling or eloquence, but for sheer dogged consistency, they cannot be faulted. Again, she passes the sheets Benjamin's way before turning back to Alyvia.

'That's my husband,' the other woman says, a slight waver in her voice that she swiftly moves to correct. 'Or my soon-to-be ex-husband, I should say. Silverfish29 and Jonathan Chestnut are one and the same.'

Huh. Fia couldn't say she'd seen that one coming.

'I can't have this,' Alyvia continues intently. 'I mean, it's just plain defamation of character, isn't it? And it's harming my brand. I've had emails about it from sponsors – some companies have already started using me less. For a while it was just comments under my posts – I could delete those. That's when the separate account popped up. And enough people seem know about it now that I still have to deal with the fallout on my feed, too. I've got people, like, *debating* in my comments whether I'm an unfit mother. *Thousands* of people. Every day. It's sort of ironic, really, because I've never had as much engagement and yet so little actual work coming in.'

Her outrage seems to be contagious, because – as Fia absorbs this new information – she begins to feel more than a little exercised herself. For all Alyvia's . . . quirks, it seems undeniable that she has good reason to be aggrieved here.

'Well, we can absolutely make sure the court factors that into any assessment of alimony and child support,' Fia says, scribbling frantically on her notepad. 'I mean, this is just . . . it's ridiculous! If Jonathan is deliberately reducing your capacity to earn a living and provide for your child, believe me, we'll be making sure he pays for that. Literally.'

Alyvia nods enthusiastically, and Fia senses herself well and truly on a roll now, a familiar sort of energy ramping up inside her. Divorce cases don't represent the bulk of her practice or anything close to it, but on the occasions they come up, she knows that Celia Hannity's assessment of her is probably an accurate one. She knows that she is tenacious, unyielding – propelled by some swirl of emotion that she absolutely never encounters when drafting a will or administering an estate. Perhaps that is just the nature of a divorce – inherently more adversarial than her other work. Might Fia also have a particular capacity for empathy in this domain? Might she have a personal well of resentment, all ready to tap into on behalf of her clients?

It's possible. She can acknowledge, if only to herself, that it's possible.

'And we'll cite "cruel and inhuman treatment" as our grounds for divorce,' she continues now. 'Not adultery. It's like you said. He doesn't get to control the narrative here.'

Alyvia murmurs her approval, and Fia again scrawls on her legal pad, this time with the pleasing sense of a plan coming together.

Then, into the silence, suddenly a third voice inserts itself into the mix. 'How do you know it's your ex?' Benjamin asks calmly. He's still scanning the pages of screenshots, but soon looks up. 'Behind these posts. How do you know it's him? Has he admitted it?'

Fia turns to stare daggers at him, any effort to maintain the appearance of united front suddenly forgotten. His input is about as unexpected and about as unwelcome as an objection at a wedding.

Alyvia, too, looks fairly taken aback. 'Well, *obviously* he doesn't use his name when he's *trolling me*,' she replies, with all the emphasis of the recently insulted. 'And no, he hasn't *told me* he's doing it. But I *know*.'

'Has he told you he doesn't want Gus featured on your page?' Benjamin continues.

'He had no bloody problem with it when we were still together, that's for sure!' Alyvia snaps. 'When he was seeing half the income. Who d'you think was taking most of those pictures? The fucking ringlights don't set themselves up, I can tell you that!' This time, she does not apologize for swearing. Instead, she lets out a sour laugh. 'These past six months, with Jonathan and me . . . it's been brutal – in more ways than you could possibly imagine. Who else would want to hurt me like this? Plus, who else would even know th—'

She cuts herself off, and somehow the silence that follows feels very loud indeed. Fia is attempting to formulate a response – something to smooth things over, right this ship – when again (*again*) Benjamin takes it upon himself to chip in.

'The thing is, Alyvia, for something to be defamatory – in the legal sense, I mean – it doesn't just have to be unflattering.' Benjamin gestures with the paperwork in his hand. 'Obviously we've, uh, cleared that hurdle with these statements. It has to be unflattering *and untrue*. Is this stuff untrue?'

It's not accusatory, the way he asks the question. His tone remains perfectly neutral, in fact. And, if it occurs to Fia that this is a bit of a turn-up for the books, for Benjamin to prove so measured in this scenario . . .

If there is some tiny portion of her that can't help but be impressed . . .

Well, she squashes that quickly. Their client, more importantly, is not one *bit* impressed. She looks completely aghast.

'Oh my gosh! Gussy loves our shoots! Are there times when he's a bit tired or a bit grumpy or whatever? Well, yes. I mean, he's 11 years old. Does he like some products better than

95

others? Of course he does. But I incorporate that into my honest reviews! All this bullshit from Jonathan is just bullying – and it's misogyny, frankly – and I don't see why I should have to stand for it.'

Benjamin cocks his head. 'Well, I—'

Fia scrambles to intercept. 'You *shouldn't* have to stand for it,' she says firmly, with another deadly glare in Benjamin's direction. 'And you *won't* have to. That's what we're here for.'

Somewhat mollified, Alyvia takes a large sip from her water, its pH levels evidently forgotten by this stage. When she sets the glass back down, it meets the table with an audible clink, and she looks between Fia and Benjamin for a moment.

'Are you guys married?' she asks then. Fia senses her entire body seize, before Alyvia lets out a titter of laughter. 'Not to each other, obviously!'

That's better, but not by much. Still, Fia just can't quite seem to formulate a response, and this time it's actually a bit of a relief to hear Benjamin piping up beside her. He answers in the negative for them both.

It's another potential black mark in their personnel files: misrepresenting themselves to clients. Another big reason – if one were needed – to ensure the truth of their relationship never leaks.

Across the desk, Alyvia just nods. 'Good,' she replies, a world of disenchantment in that one gesture, that one word. 'Don't ever fucking get married.'

Chapter Twelve

They go down to the lobby to see Alyvia off, and even as he's waving to her from the other side of the security turnstile, Benjamin shakes his head a little, his exhale coming in a whoosh.

'Wow. That woman is lying through her teeth,' he murmurs. 'I'm not sure how exactly, but she definitely is.'

Fia waits to be certain Alyvia is well on her way before she turns to Benjamin, all scorn. 'Oh yeah. She's got to be lying, right? Or crazy. Or both! I'm sure this guy she's accusing of abusing her is probably actually the victim.'

Benjamin lets out a huff of irritation. 'That's not what I said. But I mean, my God, she can't seem to answer a straight question.'

'Well, you certainly had plenty of questions lined up for her, didn't you?'

'You didn't seem to have any,' he fires back. 'Or none of the hard ones, at least.'

'I was getting to it! There's a way to handle these things. What part of *don't talk* was hard for you to understand?'

Benjamin blasts right past that one, with no apparent awareness of the irony involved in doing so. Evidently, neither self-awareness nor irony are among his strong suits. 'So, what?' he says instead. 'We're just supposed to take her word for it, when she tells us her husband is the one behind that account?'

'What else would you suggest? You want to put a tracker on his phone? Creep around Manhattan after him, invite his confidence in some cocktail bar? News flash, Benjamin, this is not *Suits*. This is not *The Good Wife*. Taking our client's word for it is kind of a core part of the gig.'

'We could subpoena Instagram,' he suggests. 'That happened all the time when I was at GameCab. It seemed like courts were constantly making us disclose people's IP addresses for one reason or another. Wouldn't that be helpful to our case – to know it's definitely Jonathan?'

Fia purses her lips, unable to issue an outright denial. 'Potentially,' she says.

'And even if Jonathan *is* behind the posts,' Benjamin continues, 'can we say for sure they're untrue? Didn't you think Alyvia was super weird about that?'

'The kid certainly *looks* happy enough, if the pictures are anything to go by,' Fia replies. She's no stranger herself to evading a question she'd rather not directly answer. 'I'd say he looks like he has everything a child could possibly want, actually.'

'I guess if we don't count the super annoying mother,' Benjamin mutters, almost as though to himself. He manages to take note of her glare though, his eyes widening in self-defence. 'I'm sorry, but she *is* pretty annoying.'

Once again, Fia finds herself unable to explicitly contradict him there. She hates that. 'Well, you know what, Benjamin?'

she says hotly. 'That's how it goes. You wanted to be on this case so badly? Congratulations – you're on it. Five years from now, ten years from now, when you're busy getting people off death row or whatever, I guarantee you that some of them will be the biggest arseholes you've ever met in your life. You don't get to pick the clients. You don't always get to like them. But Alyvia Chestnut *is* our client now. It's not our job to make this process more difficult for her. And you heard what she said – that guy Jonathan has made her life *miserable* for the last *six months*! Don't you think she's been through *enough*?'

Horrifyingly, Fia realizes she's almost breathless at the end of this little speech, having picked up speed and volume all the way along. And, by the end of it, she's not altogether sure she's talking only about Alyvia. Her voice cracks slightly on that final question. She feels, suddenly, as though it might not take very much for tears to spring to her eyes, right here in ZOLA's lobby – not from sadness but from sheer tension and tiredness. Perhaps that's why she says the next thing. She forces herself to take a deep breath first, with a quick glance around to ensure they haven't been overheard so far.

'Look. You want to do it that way? With us? Because the Alyvia and Jonathan model . . . that's what divorce can be, Benjamin. A huge, toxic, expensive, time-consuming, public mess.'

He just shrugs.

'No, no – answer me. You don't get to shrug your way out of this one. Do you want to do that? Because if you do, that's fine. We don't have to go down the mediation route with Susan. Feel free to find yourself another lawyer – someone who's available *immediately*, and someone who's never so much as heard of me or this firm. And then we can go ahead and start making this as terrible as it possibly can be. After all, you *know* I know what I'm doing. Ours will be your first divorce but it won't be mine.'

She delivers the whole thing with impressive flourish, if she does say so herself, and with it, she finally manages to cow him a little. His mouth twists in displeasure.

'Some things never change, do they?' he mutters, after a moment. 'It's your way or the highway, right? You always know best.' His eyes shift to the floor, darting about uncomfortably, and when he speaks again, he's barely looking at her. 'Whatever. We can use your woman. The attorney mediator. What do I care?'

Fia knows this is as wholehearted an agreement as she's ever going to get, as much of an active participant as she can ever expect him to be.

'Great. I'll confirm for next week then,' she says tightly. She's got what she wanted, but right now, it somehow doesn't feel like much of a triumph. She simply cannot *bear* the notion of going back upstairs to sit beside him all afternoon. She needs a breather, needs an opportunity to collect herself without him right there to witness it. She gestures past the turnstile, towards the same revolving doors that Alyvia has just exited.

'I haven't eaten yet. I'm going to go grab lunch,' she says.

Benjamin offers a grunt of acquiescence, and she's already on her way when he speaks again, a bit of a warning in his tone now.

'I'm going to draft that subpoena for Instagram, though. And I'm gonna do some more digging into this whole defamation thing generally. It's our job to represent the clients – I get that – but I don't think that means we just take down exactly what they tell us, fill in the form, and done. Sorry. That's not the kind of lawyer I want to be.'

Fia swallows thickly, sensing her heartbeat quicken. How can it be, that she suddenly feels like she's the one who might be floundering here?

It's this case, she thinks: the not-quite-standard nature of it, the way it's been thrust upon her today, the way it threatens to push her slightly outside her comfort zone.

And of course, yet again, the problem is Benjamin, too: his mere presence, yes, but also his questions that she cannot exactly answer; his snippets of knowledge that she hasn't provided; the fact that he appears to have selected Alyvia Chestnut's divorce as the one area in which he will refuse to be passive.

'Have at it,' she replies flatly. And then, she hardly knows why she says it: 'I have another box of photocopying that I'll need back for tomorrow, too.'

It's just the most familiar way, at this point, to reassert herself as officially the one in charge. Never mind that in doing so, she is surely only reconfirming all his worst prejudices against her.

For a moment, silence.

'Sure,' Benjamin replies, with a curt little nod. He just can't seem to leave it alone, though – it's as though maybe his own efforts to contain himself have finally failed altogether when he pipes up again. 'You know you're not my boss, right, Fia? I mean, just so we're completely clear about that.'

More dead air follows, tension pulsing between them.

'. . . I'm your *senior*,' she replies.

Benjamin doesn't miss a beat. 'That's for sure. How's 30 treating you?'

It's such a stupid dig – really so incredibly dumb and meaningless – but still it manages to grind Fia's gears. She absolutely hated turning 30, hates being 30, hates the thought of all the 30-somethings that are to come. What she doesn't hate – at all, actually – is her life at 30. She just would like to still be 27 and living it. She would even settle, as it happens, for Benjamin's 29.

'The point is: you're supposed to be providing me with *emotional support* this summer,' he continues, all mock-earnestness.

'I'm supposed to be providing you with an insight into the practice of law at a big corporate firm,' she snaps. 'There's literally zero emotional support involved in that, let me tell you.'

'Still, you know I get to evaluate you at the end of the summer, too, right?'

'Whatever,' she replies impatiently. 'I'll be back in twenty minutes.'

And as she flashes her security pass, strides through the turnstile and out towards Madison Avenue in search of food, Fia's mind races all the while. She can feel heat flooding through her whole body, and it has nothing to do with the rising Midtown temperatures.

She had, in fact, *not* known that.

Chapter Thirteen

By the time the workday finally ends, Fia is like a caged animal. The moment she can escape the office, she's out of there, stopping only briefly at her apartment to change clothes. Then, she's back outside again, and it's all about the stretch of her calves, the thud of her feet against the ground, the blood pumping in her veins. She's been running more in the past ten days – longer distances, faster speeds – than she thinks she ever has in her life. It feels, at this point, like the only thing keeping her even halfway sane.

That, and the thought of the Summer Summit. The thought of going *home* home. It's just three short weeks, now, before Fia will be leaving Benjamin behind in Manhattan with the secretaries and the paralegals and heading off to Dublin with the other lawyers.

Of course, once she arrives, there'll be the work aspect of things to endure. She'll have to look interested in boring things, and she'll have to enquire after so many people's children. But that will only be for three days. At the end of the conference, she's taken some precious annual leave, so that she'll get to be home for more than a week in total. No Benjamin, no Alyvia Chestnut, none of her own or other people's legal problems. Just the thought of letting her mam and dad look after her is completely, utterly heavenly. At this point, Fia hasn't actually been back in Ireland for more than eighteen months; her parents and siblings came to New York last Christmas. It's the longest she's ever been away, and – for that and probably other reasons – she feels like she's been pining for the respite of Dublin more keenly than ever before.

Right now, though, the evening air is a tonic; cooler and less humid than during the day, it makes her feel instantly enlivened. She puts her headphones in, setting a buoyant pace across 81st Street as she falls into step with the rhythm of her music. There is something about a soundtrack that just makes one's life feel a lot more cinematic. And, right now, honestly, Fia would have to say things are already fairly cinematic on the Upper East Side.

Weaving her way towards Central Park, she runs past brownstones bathed in peachy light, past people walking their silly bougie pets and that hotdog stand she likes on Lexington. The frozen yoghurt shop on 5th Avenue that seems to have had a constant line outside it for weeks is doing a roaring trade. Then, she's in the park, the beeps and screeches of traffic dampening a bit, and all around her she can see buskers, yogis, little kids on scooters, people in suits and people in shorts, tourists taking pictures – the hum of life in all its diversity.

It's at times like this – when she has music, movement, Manhattan – that Fia feels she is at the very centre of the universe. The city is so all-encompassing that she struggles even to really think of Dublin, or indeed anywhere else, in a concrete fashion. How impossible it is to look around and truly grasp that out there, right this second, whole *other* cities exist, too. Across the ocean, her parents will be methodically checking window latches, unplugging electrical items, pouring glasses of water before bed. Those things are definitely true. And yet, they feel so remote. The world seems instead to begin at the Hudson and end at the East River – that's what George always used to say.

Fia feels a slight pang, thinking about that. Another one. Sometimes, she can go weeks and weeks without thinking about George Ferarra at all. Other days, it seems downright cruel how many small, stubborn, reminders of her pop up at every turn.

The thing is, the two of them had a friendship that really could only be described as romantic. Fia knows that might sound odd, proclaimed aloud. She probably never *would* proclaim it aloud, for exactly that reason. But it's true. They had even had a meet-cute, right here in Central Park.

Fia was out running on the Sunday morning in question, the Autumn leaves in all their glory around her. Back then, running wasn't so much about the endorphin boost, or even the physical fitness – it was mostly just about giving herself something to *do*. Almost all her time was taken up with work – seventy hours a week, she wished desperately for a break. But then, it was the strangest thing. Once she did manage to escape the office, she found herself struggling to fill the time. How could that be so, in New York City, of all places? She didn't quite understand it herself – certainly she didn't know how to explain it to anyone she'd left behind in Ireland – but that was how she felt.

Anyway. She was jogging perfectly uneventfully through the park that Sunday morning when she realized she'd gone past the path she wanted – or at least, she thought maybe she had. It was hard to tell.

She turned on her heel, pulling her phone out to check the map, and that was when it happened: she slammed right into another runner, the pair of them colliding in a brutal mash of limbs, water somehow spilling all over the place from their respective bottles.

'What the fuck?!' this stranger exclaimed, more in shock than in anger. Still, though, Fia was instinctively a little intimidated.

'Sorry! I . . .'

She stopped, then, to really take in the person before her. Oddly, Fia realized she'd seen this girl before – here in the park, running. She had sleek jet-black hair and perfect, black arched eyebrows. Add in the olive skin and shapely figure, and the full effect was just about the polar opposite of Fia herself, looks-wise. In the past few weeks, Fia had spotted the girl over and over, and she'd been struck by the coincidence of it, in a city of this size, intrigued by the evident parallel in their schedules. She'd begun to think of this stranger as kind of her counterpart – even an alternate version of herself, somehow. She'd used her sometimes to help measure and better her own pace along the running paths. *She's two trees' distance ahead of me today*, Fia would think to herself. *I can get that down to one.*

Of course, she admitted none of that, post-collision.

'Sorry,' she repeated instead. 'I was looking for the 66th Street exit but I realized I'd gone past it.' She offered a chagrined sort of smile. 'I just moved here.'

At the time, this seemed like the single most significant, and most obvious, fact about her. At any given moment of any given day, she felt sure that a blind man could have seen that she, Fia Callaghan, had just moved to New York City.

The other girl smiled, everything about her seeming to brighten with interest. 'Hey, me too,' she replied, and she stuck out her hand. 'Just arrived from D.C. two months ago. I'm George Ferarra. Georgina, really, but everybody calls me George.'

Americans were excellent at that, Fia always thought – they introduced themselves right away, even when it seemed like an interaction was going to be a short-term one. In Dublin, you could easily speak to someone every day for a year without knowing their name, by which point it seemed humiliating to ask.

'I've seen you here before,' George added then. '. . . I mean, if that's not too weird a thing to say.'

Fia just smiled. Before she could even get a response out, her enthusiasm seemed to have emboldened the other girl.

'Can I tell you another secret?' she asked.

'Do it!' Fia tossed back, a proper grin beginning to pull at her lips. It was hard to explain, the way George just managed to make her feel exactly like herself right from the get-go.

'Sometimes, when you're running, I try to beat you.'

Fia could only laugh out loud, full-throated and giddy, her own reciprocal admission following easily.

And so, that was how it started. The two of them jogged together for a bit afterwards, chatting all the while, and eventually they stopped at a coffee kiosk near the playground. They sat on a bench, drinking takeaway lattes and watching little kids squeal with laughter on the monkey bars. It was one of the first times Fia could remember seeing anything in

New York that did not appear to have making or spending money at its heart. People, apparently, were living real lives here. They were taking their toddlers to the park. She, too, was living a real life here, it seemed. She was working in Midtown during the week, just like everybody else, and exercising in Central Park on the weekend. She was making a new friend.

After that day, things moved fast. Fia and George quickly became pretty much inseparable. They lived no more than five minutes' walk away from one another on the Upper East Side, and it felt as though there was something a little bit miraculous, something a little bit meant-to-be about that. Together, they explored the city, so many options opening up to each of them by virtue of having a wingwoman. Fia no longer had any difficulty whatsoever in occupying herself outside of work. She and George stayed out late and drank too much, safe in the knowledge that they'd be sharing a taxi home. They made pilgrimages to the Empire State Building and Magnolia Bakery, to the Statue of Liberty and the museum on Ellis Island – all activities Fia would have been mortified to suggest to any of the new people she'd met at ZOLA, much less to the three roommates she was living with at the time, all of whom seemed extremely, constantly busy.

Even after those first early weeks and months of friendship passed – once they could no longer be called a whirlwind romance – something richer and more lovely took its place. Fia and George began to clock up birthdays, Thanksgivings, Saint Patrick's Days together. A patchwork history developed, their lives increasingly interweaving until, more often than not, George's became the first text Fia typically got in the morning and the last one she got at night. Their workdays were peppered with memes and in-jokes, stream-of-consciousness nonsense.

Fia could honestly tell her mother back in Dublin that if she got run over and killed by a cab on a Friday night, at least one person in Manhattan would definitely notice this in advance of her not showing up to work on Monday morning.

Any time Fia passed Sarge's Deli and Diner, she'd call in and get George a slice of the cheesecake she loved, dropping it in unannounced on her way home. Before they went *out* out, a ritual developed where George – a dab hand at the smoky eye – would do her own makeup first, then Fia's, the two of them sipping cava together in George's tiny studio. Tragically (given the way things panned out), Fia is, to this day, pretty sure that she's never looked better than on the nights when George did her face. So many good times in dive bars and on rooftops, before they'd return unsteadily to one or other of their places, *I love you*s murmured drunkenly before sleep.

As Fia makes her way back to her apartment now, forcing herself to slow her pace a little, she plays and replays all those moments and many more besides. She's just not sure what she is meant to *do* with the memories. Is she supposed to have reached the stage of looking back fondly? Is she supposed to have forgotten them altogether? The attempt to box them up in her brain – the very same strategy she employed so success-fully when it came to, say, Benjamin Lowry – just doesn't seem to have worked so well with George.

It was never a sexual thing between them. Fia doesn't think she would necessarily have to clarify that point, were she telling the story to another woman, and she's absolutely sure she *would*, were she telling the story to a man. She would probably have to say it twice. *It was never a sexual thing between us.* Fia never wanted it to be so, nor did she ever get the slightest hint that George did. Imagining, though, some fantasy scenario in which George had initiated something . . . who knows? Looking back on it now, Fia can't say with 100 per cent certainty how she would have felt about that or what she would have done in response. Their usual gender preferences aside, the two of them certainly were not without the basic ingredients that tended to make for good sex. With George – more so than with any boyfriend she'd ever had – Fia felt understood, intimately; she felt like part of a pair; she felt interesting, valuable, beautiful in someone else's eyes.

When all was said and done, it really was very simple. For those first couple of years in New York, George Ferarra had been the absolute love of her life.

WEEK THREE

Chapter Fourteen

At noon on Monday, Benjamin and Fia meet at the lifts on the fifty-eighth floor, just as planned. Having spent all morning in a client consultation, it is the first time Fia has had to lay eyes on her summer associate today.

'Hello, Benjamin,' she says, all pleasantness, conscious – as ever – of peaking eyes, listening ears. She's going to be better this week, she's decided – a whole new woman. She's going to rise above it when he goads her; she's going to remember what's really at stake here: nothing less than her entire career.

'Fia,' he replies, giving her a cordial little nod in response.

And thus ends their display of collegiality, until the lift opens, and Celia Hannity steps out of it. She's in her trademark flats and a simple linen dress, probably the least adorned and most successful woman in this entire office. Fia cannot wait to reach that stage of her professional life, where no effort – no particular outward projection on her part – is required in order for other people to take her seriously. For the moment, though, she is still in the high heels and business suit every day, dressing up like a TV lawyer, just like everyone else.

'Good morning,' Celia says, and she checks her watch, as though to make sure that's still accurate. 'Or just about. Where are you two off to?'

'Oh!' Her boss's question is casual, not interrogatory at all, but still, Fia feels suddenly as though she's been caught with her hand in the till. 'We're just, uh . . .' Her mind races. 'We're going down to Bluestone Lane for one of our mentor-mentee catch-ups.'

These (Fia has ascertained via an email attachment hunted out over the weekend) are supposed to happen on a weekly basis. She is supposed to be offering Benjamin a safe space – ideally outside the office – in which to periodically confide in her. He was correct last week; emotional support does seem to be a big part of the mentorship gig. It's her job to instruct him, to teach him, to *involve him in her legal practice where appropriate within a supportive and empowering supervisory framework*. In that regard, having him on the Alyvia Chestnut case is actually ideal – it will at least give her an example to call upon when her application for promotion comes around.

'Wonderful! Glad to see Fia's not working you too hard, then, huh, Benjamin?' Celia says now.

Benjamin pauses for a moment – and just like with Mr Zelnick last week, Fia knows in her bones that he's doing this deliberately, dragging it out to unnerve her. At last, thankfully, a grin rises to his lips.

'Oh, I don't know about that. She *does* seem like kind of a tyrant.' he replies, as though entirely in fun. As his glance shifts over to Fia, though, she can see he absolutely means it. He's always been a pro at that, hasn't he? The joke with a jag.

Fia manages a smile in response. As part of the *new her*, she's undoubtedly going to have to dial down the general skivvying, find someone else to do her photocopying. She knows that. The fun of it had somewhat faded, anyway.

'I've been hearing good things about your work so far on the Goldsberry merger,' Celia continues, none the wiser.

'Oh,' Benjamin says, his expression shifting into what Fia – if she didn't know better – could easily mistake for sincerity. 'Thanks. That's really great to know.'

Beside them, the lift begins to close.

'Catch it before it goes!' Celia says, and Benjamin duly reaches out to stop it with his foot.

'You know, I'm actually meeting an old friend at Bluestone Lane in about an hour myself,' Celia adds then, in parting. 'So, I'll probably see you guys down there.'

Inside the lift now, Fia scrambles, both to locate the hold button on the console and to figure out some means of batting away this suggestion.

'Oh, uh, we'll probably be gone by then,' she manages. 'We're just grabbing a quick coffee. Lots to be getting back to and all.'

'Nonsense! You guys take your time! In fact' – Celia smiles indulgently – 'if you're not still having a nice, long lunch by the time I get down there, I'm going to take that as a direct breach of my instructions, ya hear?'

Fia murmurs some sound of assent, and as she releases the button on the lift, she can sense the same nervous smile on Benjamin's face as is plastered on her own. The two of them stand there, like gormless idiots, until at last the doors close fully.

'How far away's this lawyer's office?' Benjamin asks, the second they're alone.

'54th and 2nd,' she replies, and the rest – that they will now need to make sure they get over there and back within fifty minutes, for safety – goes unsaid.

He cocks his head to the side, considering it for a moment. 'We can make that work,' he says then.

Fia wants to believe him. She's dubious, though. 'D'you think?'

He looks down at her shoes pointedly, before coming back up to face her. 'Well. *I* can.'

It sounds like a challenge if ever Fia heard one. And she should have well and truly learned her lesson about those, especially when issued by the man before her. The new her should be immune to this sort of thing.

It turns out, though, that the new her is not. She really isn't at all.

By the time they arrive at Followill and Associates, they are both practically breathless. There was a time in her life when Fia might have imagined that dashing around Manhattan in a business suit would surely make her feel extremely glamorous and successful. As it is, her collar is sticking uncomfortably to the back of her neck, and she has a definite blister forming on one of her toes. But they're here.

It's a small little place, situated at street level; it has much more in common with some of the family-run outfits Fia remembers from back in Ireland than with ZOLA or its ilk in the US. But beggars, notoriously, cannot be choosers. Susan Followill, Fia reminds herself, has a lot of positive reviews on Yelp. And she is reasonably priced, and she was available at short notice. Tick, tick, tick.

When the woman herself emerges into the little reception area to greet them, both Fia and Benjamin leap to their feet immediately.

'Wow, I don't think I've ever seen two people in more of a hurry to get divorced,' Susan says with a chuckle, extending her hand to each of them in turn. 'And that's saying something! Why don't you guys come on in, have a seat?'

She is maybe fifty-ish, short and stocky, all of which combines to make Fia sure that she's bound to be a very capable and pragmatic sort of person. *Ideal.*

As Susan leads them into her personal office, though – there are no conference rooms here – Fia takes in the cascading piles of files, the photo of a black Lab on the desk, the mug declaring *Trust me, I'm a lawyer.* The vibe is, overall, a lot more folksy and chaotic than she might have expected. Susan picks up a sheet of paper to scan it, and in the hush that follows, Fia is struck – more than anything – by the strangeness of being on this side of the table. The image that floats into her head is of a child at the principal's office. Is this how her clients feel when they come in to see her? She's never much thought about it before.

It seems – in the way it always does when time is short – like an age before the other woman looks up.

'All right! So, like I said in my email, I think it's wonderful that the two of you have decided to approach this process in the spirit of collaboration, and non-adversarial resolution. As your attorney mediator, it's important you understand that I'm a neutral party in this process. I'm not *your* lawyer, Benjamin, nor *your* lawyer, Fia. I'm here to work with you *both*, holistically, to ensure that this process is as swift, as cost-effective, as fruitful, and – ultimately – as *peaceful* as it possibly can be.'

'That sounds great – the "swift" part especially. Unfortunately, we're, uh, we're actually on a bit of a time crunch right *now* as a matter of fact,' Benjamin says, with a sheepish smile.

Fia would have to acknowledge that it is probably the most charming possible way he could have encouraged Susan Followill to hurry the fuck up. Alas, the hint falls on deaf ears. Susan apparently has a speech, and she apparently is going to deliver it, by hook or by crook.

'Now, of course, nobody goes into a marriage hoping it will end in divorce,' she continues. 'That's why, here at Followill and Associates, we undertake a series of Exploratory Reconciliation and Reflection Discussions with our clients to really delve into all the possible options for your future. And that includes being absolutely sure that there is no path forward for you as a couple.'

Even the notion of enduring such an ordeal cements in Fia the sense that she may have picked badly here, may have unwittingly landed herself in some sort of wholly unsuitable law-firm-cum-Montessori-centre.

'Mmm, I don't think that'll be necessary,' she says.

Susan just smiles beatifically. 'You are not the first person to tell me that, Fia. But you'd be surprised how effective our Exploratory Reconciliation and Reflection Discussions can be. In any case, at least one session is mandatory, if you want to proceed with us. We just like to make sure that when couples are on a path to permanent separation, they really have thought through all the ramifications of that and considered any other options that might be on the table.'

'Look, Susan, this was a Vegas thing,' Benjamin says then, all bluntness. It is as though he thinks that nothing more need really be said on the matter. Fia, as it happens, would be inclined to agree with him.

'Oh!' Susan looks a little surprised by this turn of events. 'Okay. Not recently, though, right?' Again, she scans the page in front of her. 'You guys were married in . . . 2015?'

'That's right,' Fia says.

'And you're telling me this was an impulsive, maybe not-totally-sober situation, right?'

This time, Fia just nods, as Susan's face contorts in confusion.

'But then you guys stayed married for . . . eight more years?'

'Yep. *Somebody* was supposed to get in touch at a certain point, and then they just' – Fia shrugs exaggeratedly, not caring if her smile is the tiniest bit maniacal – 'didn't bother! Not only that, but they totally failed to respond to any communication! Isn't that the most hilarious thing you've ever heard?'

Beside her, Benjamin says nothing. But, for a guy so patently on the wrong side of this situation, he looks a lot less like it than she'd prefer. There's a tight, fixed sort of expression on his face. As though he is *tolerating* her.

And, now that she thinks about it, isn't it a little strange that he'd do that? Isn't a little strange that, back on that very first day he arrived at ZOLA, he would have even gone so far as to *apologize* to her? How was she not more suspicious of that from the get-go? Concocting some bullshit way in which the whole thing was actually *her* fault . . . surely that would have been much more on brand.

Even right now, in this moment, part of her seems to have been expecting the clap back from him. The *well, somebody . . . !* to follow her own outburst. That he seems, instead, to have just . . . opted out, backed down, ceded the moral high ground – that's weird. His silence strikes her as its own sort of oppressive.

She thinks, suddenly, of that box underneath her bed, the leaflet she can't look at and can't destroy.

'You know, Benjamin here even went to the bother of presenting me with a *contract*,' she continues breezily, 'within which he literally promised to divorce me on a certain date. But still – that date came and went. Not a word from him.'

'A contract?' Susan asks, ears seeming to prick up a bit.

'Yep,' Fia replies staunchly, much less concerned with accuracy now than with the attempt to stick the boot in, to flush out whatever it is that Benjamin's not saying. And it just might be working, because he jumps right in to correct her.

'Not a *real* contract.'

Fia scoffs. 'You've changed your tune.'

He hears her, ignores her. 'Would you call one sentence a contract, Susan?'

Susan hesitates for a second, as though this might be a trick question. '. . . A *clause* of a contract, maybe?'

'Ha!' Benjamin declares, deadpan. 'You've heard of a break clause. I guess Fia and I had the lesser-known break-*up* clause. Could really catch on, couldn't it?'

'Oh, excellent, Ben, let's have some comedy,' Fia snaps irritably, the conversation having careened wildly from where she wanted it, from the substance of things. 'That's great. Everybody loves a joker, don't they?'

'As opposed to a controlling, manipulative—'

'Manipulative?!'

'Yes! I don't know what else we would call it, using someone for a gr—'

'All righty!' Susan says brightly, like a practised parent of fractious children. 'Let's just . . . put a pin in all that, shall we? I guess it's not really relevant, anyhow. We are where we are.'

Fia nods. She's said that one before herself. *It is what it is, and we are where we are.* This is what lawyers say all the time when a situation is obviously terrible but they really don't want to get bogged down in the associated whys and wherefores.

In any event, Fia is more than happy to proceed straight to the point here.

'I was actually sort of thinking maybe an annulment might work?' she suggests. 'I mean, like Benjamin said, this wasn't even a real marriage to begin with, so . . .'

Susan looks confused. 'In what sense?' she asks. 'Was anybody underage or coerced?'

'Well . . . no,' Fia admits.

'Bigamy? Incest?'

'Christ, no!' she replies, and she barely gets her own words out before Benjamin's land on top of them.

'This whole thing is a clusterfuck, but it's not a *crime*,' he says.

'Okay.' Susan nods, and for a second, there's silence. 'So, then, I mean' – again, she pauses, waggling her index finger between the two of them – 'are you telling me that you guys have never had sex?'

For reasons that Fia truly cannot begin to fathom, everything about the other woman, from her tone of voice to the expression on her face, makes it clear that she finds this notion entirely ludicrous.

'Exactly,' Fia replies – and at the very same moment, Benjamin says, 'Well.'

They each halt then, their heads swivelling around to look at one another.

Benjamin quirks one eyebrow, just a little, and when he opens his mouth to speak again, the words come out quietly, maddeningly. '. . . I mean, it's probably not accurate to say *never*.'

Chapter Fifteen

The air between them seems to expand, intensify, and Fia suddenly cannot bear the sight of Benjamin's face – cannot bear the sense that within just a few more seconds, a smug smile might be twitching at his lips. She turns away from him, heat rising inside her.

Meanwhile, Susan's expression stays deadpan, unblinking.

'It's probably not accurate, or it's not accurate?' she asks dryly.

Fia takes a deep breath in and out, lets herself silently come to terms with what must be said next. It is possible that some of the very, *very* strong dislike she feels for Susan Followill in this moment may be transference.

'We never had sex after we were married,' she replies, doing her best to keep her voice neutral, calm, as though she's back at ZOLA, and this is a discussion of somebody else's life. 'Isn't that the relevant thing, here?'

'Non-consummation *after* marriage is one of the grounds on which an annulment can be sought, yes,' Susan agrees, 'but I don't know if that's the path I'd recommend.'

'Why not?' Fia asks. Having never actually had cause to handle an annulment herself, she doesn't know much about the ins and outs of them. She's glad, suddenly, that she hadn't bothered mentioning her own occupation, or Benjamin's, to Susan. Better, really, for her to treat them like any other clients, for her to assume no specialist knowledge on their parts.

Susan gives a little shrug. 'It's like . . . I don't know.' She casts around the room, her eyes landing on an object at the corner of her desk. 'This banana – let's imagine you bought this for lunch, okay? And now you say you don't want it anymore. Fine. What judge in the land is going to insist that you *do* want it? That's divorce.'

She pauses for breath, before beginning again. 'Whereas, if your whole thing is, like, "actually, I don't even accept that this *is* a banana, and maybe it never was . . ."' She lets her voice trail off, winces. 'That's tricky. It all gets very philosophical, y'know? Very subjective. And, I mean, at the very least, we're going to have to peel the friggin' thing, right?'

'So, our marriage is the banana here, is it?' Benjamin says, sounding amused.

'"Our marriage"!' Fia can't help but exclaim, though of course it's wholly beside the point and also a waste of valuable time. 'My God, Ben, we don't have a marriage!'

'Well, we *are* married, Irish.'

When she looks at him this time, there's mischief in his eyes – and provocation, and some other thing. The combination is suddenly, viscerally, familiar – exactly as it had been that first week in the office when he'd resurrected that moniker. It feels like her whole body remembers it.

'I know we are,' she replies, through practically gritted teeth. 'But that's not the same as having a marriage.'

'What would you call it, then?' he replies loftily. 'Give me a noun.'

For a second, Fia finds herself stumped, the language centre of her brain not working fast enough – how often does that happen? Almost never.

'You don't know,' he continues, all triumph, and then he turns to Susan, his voice dropping conspiratorially. 'She doesn't know.'

'A . . . a state of matrimony,' Fia manages at last.

Benjamin just rolls his eyes. 'So, the annulment,' he says pointedly, very much to Susan. 'How soon can we make that happen?'

'Well, that's precisely my point,' Susan replies. 'An annulment is going to take longer. And you know what that means . . .'

'It's going to cost more,' he says right away.

'Got it in one. Unless you have some deep-seated desire to avoid thinking of yourself as divorced, I would just . . . get divorced. Either of you guys Catholic?'

Fia suspects the question might be aimed more squarely at her – it's the accent.

'Culturally, I guess you could say. I'm fine with being divorced, though,' she replies.

'I would literally *love* to be divorced at this point,' Benjamin adds vehemently, glancing over at her, and Fia rolls her eyes.

'Wonderful!' Susan jumps in. 'I think let's park the annulment in that case and move forward on the basis of a negotiated divorce settlement, by way of attorney mediator.'

'Great,' Benjamin says. 'And how long do you think that whole thing will take?'

'If you both approach the matter productively?' Susan replies. 'And there's no property, no kids, no communal assets?'

She waits for their nods of confirmation before continuing. 'Typically, eight to twelve weeks.'

Just like that, all Fia's faith in Susan Followill is entirely restored. She doesn't even mind about the *Trust me I'm a lawyer* mug anymore. She feels relief flood through her. With a bit of luck, Benjamin will be exiting both her office on the fifty-eighth floor and her life generally right around the same time. August, from where she's sitting, suddenly looks set to be a banner month.

'That's amazing!' she exclaims. 'Seriously. That's just . . . *so* good. And if you need us to come and do one of your sessions, then fine. There's a process, and I suppose we'll just have to go through it. For now, though' – Fia looks at her watch – 'sorry to do this, but we actually have to go. We're on a bit of a tight schedule.'

Benjamin takes the cue. 'Our boss is kind of expecting us,' he adds, by way of explanation, as both he and Fia get to their feet hurriedly, gathering their belongings.

'Wait,' Susan says, and she's standing now, too. 'Hold up. You guys have the *same boss*? You . . . *work together*?' She looks, at this point, as though the pair of them are some sort of slow train crash, the sort that seems like it should hardly even be able to happen in the modern age.

'Temporarily,' Fia clarifies, already halfway out the door. 'It's sort of like . . . actually, you know what? Let's maybe save that one for the resolution-and-whatever discussion, shall we? Give ourselves something to talk about. Okay, bye!' she yelps – and then they're gone, poor Susan practically left open-mouthed in their wake.

'I'll email you guys with some dates!' she calls after them, the hint of forlornness almost comic. Behind her, Fia's pretty sure that Benjamin is, in fact, trying to mask a snort of laughter.

Once they're back out on the street, standing side by side now, they seem instinctively to pause, looking over at one another. Traffic whizzes past them in the usual cacophony of horns blaring, drivers yelling, but for a moment, Fia and Benjamin just stand there. Fia wonders what's going to come out of his mouth next. Based on everything that's just gone down, it could absolutely be an open expression of loathing. Or it could be . . . something else. Memory lane certainly took a few hard left turns in there.

'Should we try to get a cab?' he asks then.

Just like that, Fia's jolted back to the practicalities. It's the classic dilemma with which she finds herself faced time and time again in this city: via cab, a person can arrive somewhere less sweaty and dishevelled, but often no faster – and often, a lot more tightly wound, having sat powerlessly in gridlock for large portions of the journey.

As a matter of principle, Fia prefers to be moving, prefers the sense of progress being made, the sense of control of her own destiny. And by now, they have twenty minutes – maximum – in which to beat Celia to Bluestone Lane.

'What do you think? Probably quicker to walk?'

'Probably,' he agrees. It appears that about this one small thing, at least, they're on the same page.

'Come on, then,' she chivvies him along. 'Go, go, go!'

Chapter Sixteen

Inside the café, Benjamin and Fia each look around frantically: exposed brick, industrial lighting, a large poster reading GOOD VIBES ONLY – and no Celia Hannity. Their sighs of relief seem almost to be in unison.

'You grab a table, and I'll get some menus,' he says.

'Just get whatever they have pre-made,' she replies, peering at the counter. There's a glass case there that looks like it contains sandwiches and sweet treats. 'We need to be already eating when she gets here.'

Fia takes a seat by the window, sliding off her jacket and feeling her jitters start to subside. This is all, most likely, going to be fine now. Outside, the sun is shining – 'nature's filter', George used to call it – and just the sight seems to have its usual chemical effect on her mood.

Not everyone, she knows, is a fan of Manhattan at this time of year. It gets hot, and tourism kicks up a notch, and both of those things can make the subway incredibly unpleasant. On the pavements, groups of summer-school students trail around the city like long, infuriatingly slow snakes.

In short, there are valid reasons why many people, if they can, flee to the Hamptons or the Poconos or wherever. Fia gets it – but, still, much like the late Aaron Burr (sir), she personally thinks there is nothing like summer in the city. She loves the sense of energy as life moves outdoors, every green space and front stoop becoming akin to a communal backyard. She loves eating at rickety little tables on the kerb and going to Shakespeare in the Park and even having to put on a dab of sun cream before work.

What it all comes down to, she thinks, is that she grew up in a country where June, July and August were as much of a mixed bag, weather-wise, as the entire rest of the year. No matter the associated downsides, she simply cannot now bring herself to see several months of reliable sunshine – the ability to plan a picnic – as anything but glorious.

Benjamin arrives with two coffees and two baguettes, and they each wolf down about seven bites at speed without speaking a word. Fia is mid-mouthful when Celia walks in, and in her effort to swallow quickly, she almost chokes on a piece of chicken. She has just about finished coughing up a lung as the other woman glances around for them. She tosses a wave in their direction when she sees them, her meaningful little smile acting as a silent callback to their earlier conversation. Valiantly, Fia and Benjamin smile in return as Celia heads over to join her friend at a table in the corner – thankfully out of earshot, though still well within eyesight.

Smooth the whole thing is not. Fia's eyes are watery, and she can feel the burn lingering in her oesophagus.

Benjamin squints over at her. 'Are you alive?'

'Just about,' she replies, blinking furiously.

'Well. Mission accomplished, huh?' he says quietly.

And it seems to take each of them roughly the same amount of time to realize that, actually, the mission *isn't* quite accomplished. Not really. Because they can hardly pick up and leave right away, can they?

'I guess we should stay for a minute, look like we're enjoying each other's company,' he says, practically taking the words out of her mouth.

'I guess so,' she agrees, gulping down a large sip of her coffee.

Seconds later, she realizes that Benjamin is doing the exact same thing, both of their cups landing back on the table with a perfectly synchronized clink. It's . . . odd.

She clears her throat, tries to come up with something to say to him. Very obviously, it is not the time to recap any aspect of their meeting with Susan Followill. And one aspect of it in particular, Fia never ever wants to recap with Benjamin.

'So, um . . . week three, now. How've you been finding ZOLA so far?'

It does feel more than a little ridiculous to be talking to him this way, as though he's any other summer associate – the kind of summer associate she'd expected, a person with whom she might have actually *enjoyed* little jaunts out of the office under the guise of professional development. Something about Benjamin's expression tells her that he, too, recognizes the absurdity of the situation, and yet he, too, is willing to go with it right now.

'It's been good,' comes his response. 'Kind of a baptism of fire.'

'I bet,' Fia says, and what's strange is the way she can't sense any snideness or sarcasm in him. She thinks back to this

129

morning by the lifts, to the way he seemed genuinely pleased by Celia's praise. For the very first time, it occurs to her that, this summer, Benjamin might end up having exactly what ZOLA is doing its level best to provide him: namely, a net positive experience. Ruling out a big corporate law firm might just as easily turn to ruling it *in*. Of course, his initial detachment rubbed her up the wrong way, but it's suddenly clear to her that a late-blooming passion would be even more hideous. The only thing worse than Benjamin Lowry working at her law firm for the summer would be Benjamin Lowry working at her law firm for the *foreseeable*.

'Can I ask you something?' she says then. 'Why are you doing all this? Not just the summer. I mean, like, generally. What's the plan after law school? Back at Camp Birchwood' – she lowers her voice instinctively, as though she's referring to a former life of crime – 'I can't say I ever really saw you, um, heading down this path.'

She can think of no more polite way to put the fact that he always seemed, to her, so fundamentally . . . unserious.

'That's funny,' he murmurs, a smile playing on his lips.

'What is?'

'Just that you'd say that. Pretty much everybody else I knew, up until that point in my life, thought I'd eventually be a lawyer. I guess on account of my mom,' he continues, seeing Fia's look of astonishment. 'You remember she was—'

'Running for Attorney General, yeah,' Fia jumps in dryly. How could she forget that little detail? She googled the whole thing years ago, ascertained that Lisa Lowry had lost the race, would be continuing on as the District Attorney for Wake County. It was still, by any standards, a pretty big job.

'Right. And my dad, he was a lawyer, too. I used to hate it

when people would say I'd for sure be following in their foot-steps or I was bred for it or whatever. I hated the idea of just, like, drifting into it.' He pauses, takes a sip of his coffee, seeming to warm up to this subject now. 'Most of the time, that's what happens, right? It's, like, "Why are you in the seventh grade?" – "Because I was done with sixth grade." I don't know how much of our lives we ever actually choose. Anyhow, maybe that's why I tried something totally different with the software development and all. I guess I've ended up coming around to the same place now – I'm going to be an attorney, just like everyone always said I would be. But I feel a little differently about it than if I'd just come straight through after undergrad, y'know? More like it was my decision.'

It's a more thoughtful response than Fia would have predicted, a much harder one to mock or dismiss.

'So, what was it that made you decide?' she asks. 'The' – she resists, very admirably, in her own opinion, the urge to say 'video gaming' – 'the software development just wasn't doing it for you anymore?'

He shrugs a little, reaching for his sandwich. 'I guess you could say that.'

This doesn't exactly feel like an answer to Fia. Nonetheless, she's willing to move along. 'So, one more year of law school, and then you're done, right?'

'Assuming I pass the Bar exam next summer, yeah. I should be a real live lawyer by next September.'

'Well, I read Michelle Obama failed the Bar exam the first time. And Hillary Clinton did. So, y'know . . .'

He raises an eyebrow slyly. 'What? You think I'll fail it?'

She thinks back, suddenly, to what she heard about his class ranking. Evidently, Benjamin Lowry has a surprising capacity to pull it out of the bag when it comes to a standardized test. And/or, he is simply – could this really be it? – *a very academically gifted person*.

'No, no,' she replies loftily. 'I'm just saying, if you don't get it the first time . . . y'know, all isn't lost. You could still end up marrying a *very* successful man.'

He laughs at that, loud and hearty. And there's something so satisfying about the sound. It's totally unexpected, the way his laughter – his genuine laughter – seems to feel like a triumph, seems to fill her all the way up until she's laughing right along with him.

'I actually did the New York bar exam myself, about a year after I came over,' she finds herself telling him.

'Passed first time, I figure?'

'Passed first time,' she confirms, a smirk pulling at her lips to match his.

It's almost startling to Fia, this moment of . . . well, maybe not *connection*, exactly – connection would probably be too strong a word – but something other than outright hostility between them.

He coughs then, shifting in his seat a bit. It's awkward, somehow, and it forces Fia back to an awareness of the thing he seems to have just remembered: they are not friends. They never have been.

In a flash, the moment's gone.

Chapter Seventeen

Fia meets Annie and Kavita for a quick bite after work, the three of them having found their calendars empty for the evening. They're at The Butcher's Daughter in the West Village, a restaurant once disparagingly described to Fia as 'just white girls in yoga pants' by some random (and, incidentally, also white) man in a bar. This had not affected Fia's opinion of the place one bit. Over the past few years, The Butcher's Daughter has become one of her favourite dinner spots in the city. She loves this neighbourhood – the shorter buildings, with their colourful awnings and their fire escapes, the sense of familiarity that probably comes as much from episodes of *Friends* as from anything in her own real life. And in fact, as she looks around the restaurant now, there are all kinds of people here, dotted in between the hanging succulents. It's a crowd diverse, as seems so often to be the case in Manhattan, in all ways except economically.

By the time Fia, Annie and Kavita have each sipped their way through an Aperol Spritz, they've covered Kavita's ongoing feud with another accountant at her firm ('She double-emailed me today. Like, within an hour, to check if I'd received her previous one. This an *email*, Pamela. It's not a carrier pigeon! It's not a friggin' *Hogwarts owl*! Let's just go ahead and assume it's arrived safe and sound, shall we?'). And they've dissected Annie's ever-more-promising new relationship ('Last night, he talked to me about cycling for a solid fifteen minutes, and I didn't even really mind. I was *willing to overlook it*. That's the level we're talking about here, I think this might actually be something.').

Then, as Fia knew it would eventually, the conversation weaves its way in her direction.

'So. *Benjamin*,' is all Kavita says, as the waitress comes to top up their water. Fia cannot recall, in this country, having ever managed to get to the bottom of a glass of water.

'What about him?' she replies.

'What about him?' Kavita repeats, as though to underline the ridiculousness of such a question. 'How'd it go with the divorce lawyer today?!'

'Yeah, we want updates,' Annie chimes in. 'If you want to provide them, obviously.'

'Mmm.' Fia chews a bite from her Buddha bowl. There is quite a bit of chewing involved.

The basic upshot of today's meeting can be conveyed fairly briefly, and once she's done that, it doesn't take long for her roommates to swoop in, full of solidarity and enthusiasm.

'And what about that other divorce?' Annie asks eventually, turning towards the professional once the personal aspects of Fia's life have been well and truly parsed. 'For the Instagrammer. Is there really no getting Benjamin off of that one?'

'Don't think so. I'll probably have to broach that with him at some point this week, actually,' Fia says, letting out a heaving exhale at the reminder. 'Another special treat that'll be, I'm sure.'

Kavita waves away the concern, though. 'Whatever,' she says, 'the thing to remember is that's just short-term pain. Today is a good day.' She extends her glass in a toast. 'Here's to you, girl. Soon to be an official divorcée.'

'So *chic*,' Annie adds.

And even as Fia laughs along, she's conscious of a slight niggle of discomfort somewhere inside her. Of course, no part of her would ever have hoped for this to be a conversation she'd be having over dinner, aged 30. She would probably once have been all the more horrified to imagine that she would actually be clinking glasses with her friends, letting them amuse her, when the subject arose.

In fact, though, her unease isn't related to any of that.

'There *is* actually one other thing about Benjamin,' she tells the girls then, feeling antsy. This particular anecdote is not something she's ever offered up as gossip before – not to anyone at Camp Birchwood, not to her sister, Maeve, when she returned to Dublin that September, not even to George. She very deliberately omitted it, back when she first gave her roommates the rundown on her history with Benjamin.

This evening, though, Fia somehow feels a little dishonest about failing to mention it. Annie and Kavita seem to have been trying to be extra supportive of her lately. She suspects that this very dinner date, for example, might not truly be the result of coincidentally free schedules. It has been unexpectedly touching, feeling cared for in ways that can only be the result of some deliberate, joint planning on their parts.

Her roommates are not her family – she knows that. And there are times (oh God, are there times) when Fia very much would love to step into a bathroom and not find every inch of it soaked from someone else's shower. However, there is no question that Annie and Kavita have proven to be complete lifesavers since they found out about Benjamin. They've done their best to inject some fun into her life, to be there, to listen – careful, all the while, not to push too far beyond her boundaries. Having already confided in them part way, having had that vulnerability held with such a light touch, she's inclined to go the whole hog now.

And, beyond any of that, the simple fact is that for the entire afternoon, Fia has been able to hear it resounding in her ears. She's seen it in her mind's eye: Benjamin in Susan Followill's office:

Are you telling me that you guys have never had sex?
It's probably not accurate to say never.

The two of them had, in fact, had sex within ten days of their very first meeting.

During those ten days, they'd spent a bit of time sizing one another up and then had proceeded apace towards getting on each other's nerves. Already, they'd had a number of debates as stupid as they were lengthy and, in the process, had ruined more than one perfectly good game of dodgeball for the preteens caught in the crossfire.

All of that was true. But then, there was the other truth:

Benjamin Lowry, right from the very start, was one of the most attractive people Fia Callaghan had ever laid eyes on in real life. Even taking into consideration the people she'd seen on screens, he probably would have been in with a shot. Was it his dark eyes? Was it his sun-bronzed colouring? Was it the smile that seemed to come for free with so many US passports? It was, of course, the *combination*. And it was, too, the slight asymmetry in his features. It was the sense of his own inattention to maintaining his appearance in any specific way. Camp Birchwood very quickly provided Fia with ample opportunity to see Benjamin in all manner of states – sweaty, sunburned, sick from too many vodka shots. He was no preening Ken doll, that was for sure.

Nevertheless, Fia was absolutely certain that he must be aware of the baseline situation at hand – how could he not have been? It was actually part of what she disliked about him, right off the bat. The bravado, the lack of consideration – it all tied into the same thing: that prom-king, captain-of-the-football-team thing, the particular sort of confidence that could only, in her opinion, have come from knowing all too well that he was extremely hot. In the conventional way.

The lead-up to the whole . . . encounter – the one between him and her – was not memorable. He was late for some activity, and she went looking for him, rapping sharply on his bedroom door before striding on in. He was lolling on the bed – reading a *book*, of all things – and she stopped a few paces away from him. Some interaction of their usual flavour followed: no screaming fights, but snappy, snarky, smart-alecky. That was right in their wheelhouse.

She was on the verge of storming off when he grinned and said, 'You know what your problem is, Irish?'

It was the first time he'd ever called her that.

She leaned back a little and – there was no bun, back in those days – pushed her hair away from her face. This, she thought, should be good.

'I don't, Benjamin. Why don't you enlighten me. What's my problem?'

'Your problem is you're used to being followed. And yet you can't seem to stop chasing after me, can you?'

The profound arrogance of this statement – not to mention the inaccuracy of it, on both counts – boggled Fia's mind.

'Uh huh,' she muttered dryly, before letting her voice rise, as if in genuine curiosity. 'Do you know the difference between "chasing after" and "cleaning up after", Benjamin? It's actually quite an important distinction.'

He laughed out loud, glancing pointedly around his bedroom. It was small and functional – a double bed, a wardrobe, a few personal effects on the chest of drawers. 'Look where you *are* right now,' he replied, and he let the statement hang there for a moment. '. . . 'S'all I'm sayin'.'

Fia just rolled her eyes, in the special way she'd come to save just for him. She was turning on her heel to leave once and for all, when he leaped up and grabbed her hand. He stopped her in her tracks, forced her to spin back around to face him. And then, without even a second's pause, he kissed her.

It was a very risky manoeuvre, the sort of thing Fia would have wagered worked so much better on TV than in real life. In real life, when a woman appeared anywhere close to pissed off, she was rarely, in fact, just moments away from being very turned on. More men, in Fia's opinion, could do with realizing that.

But, in this particular case . . .

Well, in this particular case, who was to say what combination of factors was in the mix? Surprise. Youth. The one Fia knew was least flattering to her, but was perhaps the most significant, was that – again – Benjamin Lowry was undeniably extremely hot. In the conventional way. And there were moments in life when you discovered that you were not better than other people – not smarter, not more principled, not any less susceptible to an undesirable desire. This was one of those moments for Fia. Benjamin's breath on her neck, his hands on her skin . . . somehow those proved enough for her to set aside, at least temporarily, her distinct misgivings about his personality.

She found herself kissing him back – truly, it was like she was moving on nothing but pure instinct – and then clothes were coming off, and it turned out that despite the myriad ways she and Benjamin had already proven extremely incompatible, there were certain things they *could* do well.

Somehow, they found nothing over which to feud, here. Yes, she thoroughly enjoyed the way his eyes entirely glazed over, the moment she first so much as edged her fingertips under the waistband of his shorts. And yes, he did seem very pleased with himself when she cried out his name, begged him for *more*. There was no shortage, then, of teasing between the two of them, no shortage of a delicious form of torment, of one-upmanship, even – of showing off.

But it was not a battle. How could it be, really, when everything she wanted and everything he wanted . . . it all turned out to be one and the same. With each new movement – each smile, each strangled gasp – Benjamin's pleasure actually felt like it was Fia's. And hers seemed, too, like the ultimate source of his. What a revelation *that* was.

Afterwards, they lay together on his bed, each staring up at the ceiling, each breathing raggedly. Fia's mind raced. Obviously, she had always imagined that Americans would be better at sex. That Benjamin would prove to be so *very* good at it, though . . . it was almost irritating.

This thought, in combination with the melty, tingling sort of feeling in her limbs, suddenly struck her as very amusing.

'Ohhh, I must have lost my mind,' she said then, practically to herself, the words mumbled hazily, mid-laugh.

And, as she turned over on her side to look at Benjamin, she wasn't above admitting that it was the most positive she'd ever felt towards him – the most positive by a long shot.

He turned to look at her, too, his face flushed, holding her gaze for a second. Evidently, he was getting to grips with the new reality himself – with the unexpectedness of what had just happened, the undeniability of it.

Or maybe he very much wasn't doing any of that. Because then he told her, quiet and sure, 'This will never happen again.'

At once, Fia felt as if she'd had a bucket of cold water chucked over her. Meltiness? Gone. Tingling? She couldn't even imagine it. In a flash, though, the shock subsided, and then it wasn't so much the substance of what he'd said that bothered her: it was that he'd robbed her of the chance to say it first.

She pulled herself upwards in bed, staring down at him now, all wide eyes and sarcasm. 'Do you promise?'

And just like that, normal service between them resumed. It never did happen again.

'Oh my God!' Kavita says, when Fia's finished telling the story – or sketching out the skeleton of it, at least. 'That is just . . . I mean! Oh my God! This changes everything!'

Fia can't help but laugh at her roommate's exuberance. 'I mean, it doesn't really, though,' she replies.

'Well, for one thing, I feel like we need to get eyes on him now. Don't you, Annie? How could we make that happen?'

'Hmm. We could swing by the office for lunch some day?' Annie suggests. 'Or remember the time I crashed your Thursday night office drinks, Fia, 'cause it happened to be right by my chiropractor? That could work.'

The Break-Up Clause

'Ooh, yes, I like that!' Kavita jumps back in. 'We could just happen to be in the area – drop in, conduct a little light judgement on old Benji, talk you up. In fact, even better! You know what you should do?'

'What?' Fia replies indulgently, as their server arrives with another round of Aperol Spritzes. It's perfect timing. They seem to be descending further and further into the conversational rabbit hole here, but in a way that undeniably does feel a little bit fun – certainly more than she might have anticipated it would.

'You should bring a guy to one of those things!' Kavita says.

Fia snorts. 'Like who?'

'I don't know, whoever. What a bummer that Hot Irish Guy is in, like, Ireland, huh? He would have been perfect.'

At the mention of Ryan Sieman, Fia wonders idly what the situation will be with him once she gets to Dublin for this year's Summer Summit. From one of their encounters to the next, there is always the possibility that Ryan will have found a girl, settled down, etc.

He sent her a text last week, actually. She's somehow forgotten about it, until right this moment. Maybe that was a good sign, him having reached out. It was brief and out-of-the-blue, though – the sort of message that could have been flirty or could equally have been merely friendly. 'Breadcrumbing', she's heard this is called now. There is a term for everything these days. Fia didn't respond to the text, but not on account of any wider strategizing. She had simply – if she remembers rightly – been in the office at the time, distracted by some low-level dispute with Benjamin.

Her friends, meanwhile, aren't giving Ryan a second thought, focused instead on what more local gentleman might serve as suitable show pony for Benjamin's benefit.

'You could probably just find someone on the apps,' Annie continues, as Fia reaches for a sip of her fresh drink.

All three of them are, or have been from time to time, on the apps. Bumble, Hinge, Happn, Tinder, Coffee Meets Bagel, Thursday . . . it seems like a new one springs up every other month. Annie's current guy, in fact, was sourced via one of said apps. So, in among the very many men who are 'fluent in sarcasm', who are out there posting pictures of kids that aren't theirs, who are allegedly in open relationships, who like to photograph themselves oily and shirtless at the gym . . . somewhere in that mix, there apparently remain some hidden gems.

For her own part, Fia's enthusiasm waxes and wanes. Dating apps feel unavoidable – just another piece of the pie that makes up a modern existence. And, like HelloFresh meal kits and Amazon shopping and TaskRabbit handymen, sometimes they can be convenient. Does Fia still believe in them as a mechanism by which she, personally, is likely to find a lifelong romantic relationship? Probably no. Not really. She's not sure she sees that happening for her, full stop.

In any event, this is all by the by.

'I think you're both totally missing the point here,' she tells the others, though at this stage, she's not honestly sure what *is* the point. 'I'm not out to . . . I dunno, make Benjamin jealous or whatever.'

'Well, no. I mean, obviously that's not your *main goal*,' Kavita replies. 'And I do still think he's an asshole. But, girl, come on.' She cocks an eyebrow. 'If this is somebody who's a *snack* and who you once had excellent sex with . . . I don't know, call me crazy, but I think it wouldn't hurt for him to *also* be a little jealous.'

Together, they all laugh into their drinks – they downright *giggle*, in fact, in a fashion that their respective clients and co-workers could probably never imagine but that feels, in this moment, like it's who they really are.

'Wait,' Annie says then. 'Is *he* single? Benjamin.'

'I assume so. I mean, if he's in any sort of relationship, it can't be a serious one, can it?'

'Why not?'

''Cause otherwise he would have divorced me a long time ago,' Fia replies.

Annie tilts her head a little in acknowledgement. 'Good point.'

And now that Fia thinks about it, is it a little sad, that both she and Benjamin have evidently gone almost an entire decade without really falling in love? Maybe. But she pushes that thought away, reminds herself that something can be disappointing without being defining.

Being (mostly) single has not felt at all defining for her, in these past years.

Has it even, really, been all that disappointing? In fact, she's been inclined to think there are a lot of upsides.

And, more so than anything else, there is the principle of the thing:

It may be true that Fia was born pretty squarely in between the years 1981 and 1994. It may be true that she lives in one of the world's largest metropolises, and that she has plenty of bad days, in along with the good ones.

But these are merely discrete facts. She will not let them glom together, deepen and distend until they somehow flatten her. Whatever else Fia Callaghan is or might ever be, she simply *refuses* be a sad millennial girl in a city.

Chapter Eighteen

After dinner with Annie and Kavita on Monday, Tuesday evening is taken up by a company softball game in Central Park, attended (at least on Fia's part) purely for purposes of putting in some face time with the partners. When it comes to all the extra stuff connected to the summer associates' programme, she has not – for obvious reasons – found herself super keen to get involved this year. But then, she is all too aware that others of her age and stage at the firm are still showing up, showing willing. In that sense, at least some degree of participation is all but mandatory. She has her promotion to think of, after all. True, there is a sense in which just hanging on to her current job – just getting through the summer without being exposed as a big fat liar-by-omission – could be considered a win. But if there's a way to do more than that, to actually stay on track? Suffice to say, Fia doesn't want to watch her co-workers leapfrog her if she can help it, not when the whole reason she agreed to keep schtum in the first place – the whole reason she's now

enduring Benjamin's presence every single day – was to safe-
guard her own prospects.

Benjamin is already playing in the first round by the time
she arrives. She watches him bounding across the field with
that same easy athleticism he's always seemed to possess, the
kind she's always, in her own mind, slightly scorned as *acting
the sportsman*. And yet, on a summer's evening, with the
Manhattan skyline rising gloriously beyond lush greenery, it
turns out to be quite the picture, Benjamin acting the sportsman.
As shocking as she found it, just a few weeks ago, to see him
in a business suit, she is somehow equally shocked to suddenly
find him just as she remembers: shorts, T-shirt, tanned skin.
He still appears to have that ideal sort of definition in his
muscles – the sort that likely does not just occur naturally, without
any effort whatsoever on his part, but that seems like it *could*.

Maybe he finds the whole situation odd, too, because he
looks intently at her once he sees her during a break in play.
He jogs over to grab a bottle of water from the trestle tables
that someone from ZOLA has set up for the occasion, and . . .
yeah. Fia wouldn't know how else to say it. He *looks* at her
– takes in every single inch of her, in a very particular way, for
maybe three seconds, total. It's nothing anyone else would
notice. But, suddenly, she is conscious of her own outfit, of
the way it feels so much less like armour than her workwear.
Her arms are mostly bare, and her legs are, too, and she feels,
for just a fleeting snap of time, like she may as well be naked
right in the middle of Central Park.

She averts her eyes, letting them dart about a bit, and as she
does, the thought occurs to her that her face might be flushed.

'Blast from the past, right?' she finds herself saying, with a
slightly awkward little chuckle. It's just what comes out.

Benjamin's lips edge upwards the smallest bit, as though he, too, cannot help himself. 'Sure feels like it,' he replies.

His accent is a tad more Southern than usual, and as he takes a long glug from his water bottle, the faint sheen of sweat visible on his forehead, Fia finds herself struggling to formulate any further response.

The next thing she knows, there's a voice at her left-hand side. 'Blast from the past? What am I missing here?' asks Brett Sallinger, all curiosity. He's popped up from beside a cool-box on the ground and is loading drinks onto the trestle table now.

'Oh!' Fia exclaims. She actually jumps slightly. Her mind reels, trying to figure her way out of this one. And the worst part is, she can't even blame the situation on Benjamin. It was *her* blunder, really – her own carelessness, her own . . . nostalgia? Somehow, just for a second, all thoughts of discretion, of *safeguarding her own prospects*, had slipped away entirely. How could she have let that happen?

'Just an inside joke,' she manages, trying to keep her tone casual. '. . . About a case!'

And who knows if Brett buys it. Fia's not sure he looks altogether convinced. As she swiftly changes the subject, though, her heart in her mouth all the while, he lets the matter drop. Inaudibly, Fia releases a long, slow exhale of relief. She doesn't think she'll be so fortunate twice.

It is Wednesday afternoon before Fia has the mental space to even think about Alyvia Chestnut again. She and Benjamin are in the office, back in their usual attire, their usual positions. Thanks to the week's extra-curriculars, a familiar sort of stress is beginning creep up on her, the sort that seems to be unavoidable when she hasn't given herself the cushion of working late.

Printouts of all the Instagram posts from Silverfish29 are spread across her desk now. And, in her hand, she clutches Benjamin's attempt at a subpoena. It's in response to this order that Instagram will ideally disclose the user's identity – or, at the very least, they must explain why they're refusing to do so, and let a court decide whether the information should be released.

Eventually, Fia comes to the end of the document, having gone through it with the metaphorical fine-toothed comb. She looks over at Benjamin.

'This is good,' she says simply, waving her copy in his direction. Honesty compels her to admit it. And of course, she wouldn't want to overstate the matter. It is a simple subpoena, not a Supreme Court brief. However, she isn't going to have to make any amendments to it. That's more than could often be said for many of her *own* drafting attempts, back in her early days.

'I'm telling you, though, I think this is a waste of time,' she continues. 'Even if Instagram *is* eventually compelled to give us Silverfish's IP address, I doubt that's going to be quick. Alyvia and Jonathan will be divorced, remarried, and sending Gus off to college by the time we get it.'

Benjamin seems to think about that for a second. 'I don't know. Sometimes people – companies – just comply. Guess it depends if Instagram want to make a whole thing of this.'

Fia's surprised by the pragmatism of his response. It doesn't strike her as something he can have learned from a textbook.

'This is more intel from back in your tech days, is it?'

'Not really. There's this thing at Columbia called the Science, Health and Information Clinic,' he replies, and Fia recalls having heard about such 'clinics' in the past. They are, she's gathered, a common feature of American law schools, involving students actually representing clients, pro bono, under the supervision of qualified attorneys.

She nods along.

'I've been working there for the past two years,' Benjamin continues. 'Different kind of cases than this one, obviously. But, yeah. Similar processes I guess.'

Huh. This is somewhat interesting to Fia in and of itself – certainly it makes sense of the fact that he knows his way around a subpoena. Mostly, though, what's interesting is his delivery. No part of him is attempting to impress her – she can tell. Nor does she get the impression that he's trying to undercut her, one-up her in some way. He is purely conveying facts. So that's . . . different.

In return, she finds there's nothing with which to needle at him, no quip to be fired back. There seems to be nothing for it but to treat him like he is any other lawyer, with whom she's been having a slight disagreement on strategy.

'Okay, well, I suppose there's no harm in giving the subpoena a go,' she relents. 'Probably not a bad way to pressure Jonathan to just admitting he's Silverfish29, actually – if we can tell him we're going to find out one way or another, anyway.' She gestures with the document in her hand. 'I'll mark this for service today.'

Benjamin just nods his acknowledgement. He's pleased, though. She can tell. 'Cool. Have you seen today's offering on BabyGAndMe?' he asks then.

Fia has not. After all, she has a lot of clients. If she had to try to keep tabs on all their social media activity, she'd never do anything else. Nonetheless, she reaches for her phone now, pulling up the relevant post quickly. Unusually, it doesn't feature Gus in the photograph. Instead, it shows a bold graphic reading simply *Be Kind.*

As for the caption, Fia is surprised to find that, within it, Alyvia has addressed the trolling situation head-on. Maybe she *should* start keeping a closer eye on Instagram, she thinks to herself. Alyvia Chestnut might be a bit of a special case.

For no reason other than instinct, she finds herself reading the paragraph aloud:

'"Hi lovelies! Some of you will be aware that I've been the target of some really nasty bullying on here recently, and I don't mind admitting that it's had quite a detrimental impact on my mental health. I've always wanted this community to be a positive, loving place, and it's been so heartbreaking to see that not everyone can receive my little snapshots in the spirit they're offered. I understand that we're living in a new world now, with so much technology at our fingertips. But let's all remember that there's a real person at the other end of the screen, eh? In this case, there are actually two people: me and my darling Gus. In a world where you can be anything, be kind."'

Fia looks over at Benjamin when she's finished. He doesn't look anywhere close to convinced.

'Yeah, I mean it *sounds* nice . . .' he says.

'But . . . ?'

'Just this whole "be kind" thing. I don't know.'

'You *don't* think people should be kind to one another?' Fia asks drily.

'I just think, as slogans go, it's a pretty handy trick for deflecting any sort of legitimate criticism,' he says, and – almost as if he is reading her mind – he rushes to add a caveat. 'Not that I'm saying the way Jonathan's gone about it with those comments is legitimate – if he even turns out to be behind them. It definitely *isn't* legitimate. But, just in general, any time

I see the phrase "be kind" these days . . . I dunno – I always smell bullshit. Notice she hasn't actually *denied* anything in that statement.'

Fia did indeed notice that. But she's surprised that Benjamin did, too.

Or is she *really*, at this point?

The things that Benjamin Lowry cares about do not always align with the things that she cares about – and vice versa. That's for sure. But she's begun to see that when he *does* decide to take an interest in something, he doesn't miss much. He can be every bit as focused as she is herself. She'll need to watch out for that.

'Just you wait,' Benjamin continues. 'It'll be "we are the daughters of the witches you could not burn" from Alyvia Chestnut next. Never mind that her mother's probably alive and well, running a tea shop in fuckin' . . . Derbyshire.'

Fia raises an eyebrow, amusement flickering. 'Do you even know where that is?'

'I improvised,' he says, cracking a half-smile.

Fia shifts in her chair, smiling a little herself. Still, she clings to Team Alyvia. Perhaps that's in response to Benjamin in particular – perhaps it's about the habit the two of them have established for opposition. However, she suspects that most of it is just her usual instinct to play devil's advocate. She doesn't know if she's a lawyer because she's like this, or if she's like this because she's a lawyer.

'Well, I think you're being very harsh,' she says. 'This woman is a single mother! And an immigrant!'

'She's from London!'

'Yes, Benjamin, exactly – she *immigrated* here from London,' Fia replies, though even she can hardly deliver that one with a straight face.

For his part, Benjamin outright scoffs, because everyone knows, even in nice progressive Manhattan, there are immigrants and immigrants. The sort of foreign accent that Alyvia possesses has probably done her nothing but good in this country. The same is true of Fia's own.

'Look, I see what you're saying,' she continues, coming back around to the matter at hand. 'I do. Alyvia's probably not going to be everyone's cup of tea.'

'Is that how you guys put it in Ireland?' he asks wryly. 'Anyhow, it's like I said before: I'll bet you a month's salary that this whole case – the *custody of this kid* – won't come down to Alyvia's alleged adultery in the end. It won't even come down to whether Silverfish29 turns out to be Jonathan. Alyvia's biggest problem is gonna be if the comments are true. What if Gus *does* hate doing BabyGAndMe, and she's basically making him do it?'

'I mean, I'm not sure that's something anybody can ever objectively ascertain, one way or the other, though,' Fia counters. 'We haven't been there at every photoshoot, have we?'

'We could *ask* him,' Benjamin says, as though this is the most obvious thing in the world.

'What, just, like . . . bring him in here and ask him?'

'Yeah.'

Fia finds herself a little flummoxed. She has never seen a child anywhere in this building. The very idea of inviting one in, having them in the conference room, seems a bit like bringing one's mother along to a rave – or chucking one's hamster in a fish tank.

Or, maybe, in fact, it isn't at all like either of those things.

'I . . . suppose we *could*?' she offers. 'I mean, I don't think we would *outright ask* him,' she adds quickly, because based on what she's seen of Benjamin's lawyering style thus far, that seems precisely what he'd be liable to do. 'And obviously we couldn't *tell* Alyvia that was what was happening. But we could suggest she bring him along to our next meeting, try to get a general vibe.'

'Great,' he says simply, and then he seems to hesitate a bit. 'Do you, uh, want me to give her a call? Set it up?'

Fia frowns, taken aback. Then, she glances at her computer screen – at the sheer number of unread emails awaiting her response right now. Eighty-two and counting. Concurrently, a few feet away, someone is offering to take something off her plate. Not even a week ago, she's pretty sure Benjamin would have died before making such an offer, and she knows she would have died before accepting it. And yet.

'Uh, yeah. Sounds good. Thanks,' she finds herself replying, noting the way her own voice sounds a little disoriented somehow. This whole interaction – the very cooperativeness of it – is clearly foreign to them both. But, however awkwardly, however falteringly, they seem to have got there in the end.

Chapter Nineteen

For a while after that, there is relative quiet between them in the office. Fia gathers up all the papers from her desk, tidying them away carefully into different tabs of a file. Benjamin, surrounded by all his usual debris (or – is it her imagination? – could there be *slightly* less?) takes her in for a moment. He elects to say nothing, though, about her anal retentiveness or her control freak tendencies or whatever other choice phrase he surely has in mind. And Fia elects not to drag the criticism out of him. Another small sign of progress, perhaps.

'Oh!' he says, about a half an hour later, the exclamation seeming to come out of its own accord.

Fia glances over at him.

'Email from Susan Followill,' he explains. 'About our next . . . meeting.'

Fia can tell, by his deadpan delivery, exactly what he's referring to. Immediately, she pulls up said email on her computer, her existing client work cast aside altogether as she scans its contents:

Hi Fia and Benjamin,

It was great to meet you both earlier this week. I wanted to reach out in relation to the Exploratory Reconciliation and Reflection Discussion we talked about. As you know, participation in at least one session is a mandatory part of the process here at Followill and Associates. I am attaching a list of some time slots I have available next week.

I find that it is most fruitful to conduct an Exploratory Reconciliation and Reflection Discussion outside the confines of an office environment. Please can you propose a preferred location? Generally, I suggest that couples choose somewhere that has been special to them – a neutral space, associated with good memories for you both, tends to work well. You may also wish to consider the privacy component of any proposed location, given the sensitive nature of the matters to be discussed.

Yours,
Susan

'I kind of figured maybe this would be the kind of thing we could just put off and put off and then never actually have to do,' Benjamin says, right as Fia's coming to the end of the email.

She looks up from her screen, cocking an eyebrow. 'That's your speciality, eh?'

As soon as she says it, she wishes she hadn't. Things between them have been going so weirdly *well* all day. Why did she feel the need to antagonize him *now*, right when she most needs his cooperation? She braces herself for an argument.

In fact, though, Benjamin just rolls his eyes. It seems to be as much in annoyance with himself as with her. He did, after all, pretty much walk right into that one.

'Look, I could live without this, too,' Fia adds then. 'But if we have to do it, let's just get it done.'

Benjamin pauses, clicks his tongue against his teeth. 'Fine, I guess. Obviously, we don't have anywhere that's *special to us as a couple*, though. And the privacy thing . . . as long as we're not around work people, I don't really care. We could do this in a subway car as far as I'm concerned. We could do it in a diner.'

It's clear from his tone that Benjamin's examples are just that – hypothetical rather than real suggestions. A moment later, though, stream-of-consciousness in full flow, he's doubling back on himself. 'In fact, you know what? Maybe that's as good a place as any! How about Sarge's on 3rd Avenue? I'd say their lox bagel tends to put me in a very positive frame of mind.'

Fia's eyes widen in surprise. In *recognition*, really. Of course, though, Benjamin doesn't see that. Instead, he just sees uncertainty. Even distaste, perhaps.

'Okay, so maybe it's not going to be your natural habitat,' he continues, and he's on a roll now. He seems quite taken with the idea. He's taken, perhaps, with the mere prospect of winning a concession from her. 'I know you're probably not real big on, like, the possibility of a sticky surface. But look at it this way – there's next to zero chance of us running into anyone from ZOLA.'

That's true. And, in any case, Fia feels a certain realization dawning upon her for the first time: there is a direct benefit to her in maintaining good relations with Benjamin, in keeping him even somewhat on side. She can let him have this small win.

'Okay,' she agrees. 'Fine. I'll reply to Susan, figure out a time.'

Benjamin just nods, and there's a moment of quiet before he speaks again. 'Well, hey. I guess if this whole situation with the Chestnuts tells us anything, it's that we're not the only ones with . . . stuff to *untangle*, huh? No matter how well other people might hide the parts that don't photograph so well.'

Fia makes no reply. She's never quite thought of it in that way.

Meanwhile, Benjamin is still feeling chatty. 'It's kind of crazy, isn't it?' he adds. 'At one point, Alyvia and Jonathan loved each other more than anything – or, y'know, presumably they did. And now look where they are.'

'I know,' Fia murmurs. In fact, that's the one regard in which she can never relate to her divorce clients, the one aspect of their pain and frustration that she has no way into. But, seeing all that anguish up close . . . it often makes her downright grateful to be single. If she's being really honest with herself, it may even have some part to play in *why* she's single.

She's been told she has high standards, and perhaps that's true. What seems to her mere efficiency in eliminating no-hopers has sometimes been deemed unduly ruthless by her friends. Certainly, it's true that Fia has no time – quite literally no time – to play the numbers game, to treat dating like it's her second job.

But also, through her actual job, she has seen people at their ugliest, their most mercenary and vicious. Add that to the ways she's already been left high and dry in her own life? Starting, perhaps, with one Benjamin Lowry, with one very big promise left unfulfilled? It just doesn't make for an especially optimistic starting point, when faced with a stranger in a bar.

'Is it enough to put you off dating?' she asks Benjamin then, affecting a little chuckle.

And, okay, maybe it's not the *most* subtle way she could ever possibly have raised the issue. But she's curious – mildly curious.

She's been mildly curious since Annie's question in The Butcher's Daughter the other night. And, overall, she thinks she should probably get away with it, in the context at hand. She doesn't feel like she deserves the shit-eating grin that rises to Benjamin's lips, as though she has just been utterly, pathetically transparent.

He's opening his mouth to respond when one of the para-legals approaches the office, her presence in the doorway suspending all conversation.

Fia looks up expectantly, tries to switch her brain over to whatever Carole might want to discuss – the distribution of Mr Peterson's estate, no doubt. The man was hardly cold in the ground before his children began calling ZOLA about the matter constantly.

In fact, however, Carole tosses only the briefest glance in Fia's direction. 'Sorry to interrupt you guys,' she says. 'Hey, Benjamin, could you come look at the printer real quick? It's stuck again, and I don't know what magic you managed to work yesterday.'

Fia could hardly be more startled by this simple request. Apart from anything else, printer-wrangling does not fall even slightly within the realm of a summer associate's job descrip-tion. There is an entire IT department at the firm, albeit based all the way down on the forty-sixth floor. More than that, though, it's the mere fact that Benjamin appears to have made it on to Carole's radar – both at all, and in an apparently positive context. Carole Lindsay is one of the busiest and most frightening people in the entire office. She typically takes years even to offer fully fledged attorneys her grudging respect, and anyone else – particularly those whose presence at ZOLA is destined to be short-term – she treats with open impatience and/or hostility.

For his part, however, Benjamin doesn't seem to find any aspect of this present interaction even the slightest bit unusual.

'Sure, I'll give it a try,' he says, rising from his seat to follow Carole out of the office.

As she walks ahead, though, he lingers, turns in the doorframe. Evidently, he has one last word for Fia before he goes. A droll expression spreads across his face: smug and insufferable and the other thing, too, the thing Fia tries not to acknowledge.

'Oh, and in answer to your question, Irish,' he says, 'actually, I'm *not* seeing anyone right now – thanks for asking, though.'

Chapter Twenty

Once Fia notices it, she can't stop noticing it. Many more people than Carole appear to have already made a friend of Benjamin Lowry – or he's made a friend of them.

She watches him on Thursday, after a lunchtime seminar, chatting with a bunch of mid-level associates from the banking team: not holding court, not dominating, but certainly looking for all the world like he's one of the gang.

She clocks that on the way back downstairs after said seminar, an equity partner passes by, nodding to them *both*. 'Hi, Fia,' he says. 'Hi, Benjamin.'

And then, on Friday evening, Fia is down in the lobby. She's dressed for her run, having done a quick change in the bathroom, some part of her mind already bounding through Central Park. When she spots Benjamin, though, the sight of him jolts her back to the here and now. He's looking – in a way she can't put her finger on but would put money on – a little harried as he comes through the entry turnstiles, apparently heading back upstairs to the office. *That's* a turn-up for the books, she thinks, her mind flashing back to his first week, when he hightailed it out of ZOLA every evening at 5.30 p.m. as fast as his feet could carry him.

From the security desk, a guy in a white shirt and lanyard calls out to Benjamin.

'Hey, how 'bout them Yankees last night?' he says.

Fia does not know this man's name, despite having herself passed him most days for . . . she doesn't know how long. Months or years.

Benjamin hardly slows his pace, but still he grins. 'Reggie, when I tell you I almost cried with happiness . . .' he replies, and the pair of them chuckle together.

There really are no two ways about it, Fia thinks, as she sneaks out the exit turnstiles on Reggie's other side, before she can be seen: Benjamin Lowry is *popular*.

Of course, he always *was* popular. She remembers that from Camp Birchwood. Back then, his type of friendliness was often grating to her. It seemed overfamiliar – insincere in its reach and its force. Fia didn't know the word *performative* at the time, but if she had, it would absolutely have been the one she'd have used. Setting aside the snarkiness he'd saved just for her, Benjamin Lowry had, with other people, always been given to what struck Fia as excessive affability.

She would have to admit, though, that she doesn't get that impression from Benjamin now. In some perverse way, she actually wishes that she did. But, aside from anything else, the fact of the matter is that he appears to be pretty genial even towards people who can offer him no advantage whatsoever. He doesn't do what she's seen so many other summer associates do over the years: namely, dedicate themselves to the full-time brown-nosing of senior partners.

The whole thing just makes her think, as she heads out into Midtown, starts off at a brisk walk through the Park Avenue crowds: maybe Benjamin has settled into himself a little since Camp Birchwood, dialled the bonhomie down a notch.

Or maybe he has always been exactly like this. Maybe he simply is now and has always been an *American*.

It took Fia a while – probably at least a year – to really adjust to the particular frequency of American life: the *have a great day* of it all. Eventually, though, she came to realize that a lot of what she instinctively considered phony was, in fact, not phony at all. And even when it *was*, it undeniably contributed, nonetheless, to a general sense of buoyancy; it added a warmth and positivity to the most ordinary of interactions, in a way that eventually proved somewhat catching. For as long as she lives, Fia never plans to shop for jeans anywhere else but the United States, such is the perkiness – the sheer determination and fortitude – of the sales associates in this country. If she could somehow take what she knows now and rewind all the way back to 2015, she wonders what she'd make of Benjamin.

Needless to say, it's very disconcerting, this notion that the things she'd once felt sure of could now be up for debate. Absolutely everyone thinks they are a good judge of character, and Fia is no exception. But what, she wonders, if she's not? What if she's *terrible* at seeing people for who they really are? Or worse, what if she herself is the problem?

She thinks about all this as she circles Central Park with her headphones in, her heartbeat throbbing in her chest. Sometimes, she's not sure whether running is very good for her at all, psychologically-speaking. Sometimes, it seems to dredge up as many issues as it resolves. She might be much better off simply binging reality TV or drinking herself into oblivion.

By the time she gets home, Annie's in the kitchen, stirring a pot of some delicious-smelling thing on the hob.

'Hey, d'you remember my friend George?' Fia says, once they've done the general exchange about one another's respective days, their weekend plans. And she knows absolutely that the fact she is bringing this up now – out of nowhere, when she never has before – all goes back to Benjamin Lowry. Evidently, his ability to knock her off her equilibrium doesn't even directly require his presence any longer. It is extending, uninvited, into all sorts of other areas of her life.

'Of course,' Annie replies.

For the last year or so before George disappeared from Fia's life, Fia was living here, in this apartment, with Annie and another girl named Brie. At that time, Annie actually spent most of her time inside her own bedroom – as, in fact, did Fia. It took Kavita's arrival in Brie's place – Kavita's particular energy and disposition – to bring them together, make something of a trio out of three people.

However, that is all by the by. The point is that, at least sporadically, Annie's path *did* occasionally cross with George's in this very kitchen.

'Did you think I was . . . I don't know, controlling or intense or . . .' Fia stops, tries to think of other negative attributes. '. . . dismissive or unkind or just . . . anything weird with her?'

Having examined her own conscience (over and over throughout the past two years, and then once more this evening for good measure), Fia doesn't think she was any of those things. But she suddenly thinks it might be prudent to double-check.

'No,' Annie says, and her slightly perplexed chuckle is more comforting to Fia than any words could be.

'And what about her with me?' Fia continues, approaching it from the other angle – because this is the other thing that plagues her now: the thought that maybe, all along, there was some glaring red flag in George's character, and she was simply blind to it.

'No,' Annie repeats, with a little shrug. 'I liked her. She seemed nice.'

Fia just nods, tapping her fingernails a little against the granite countertop. In the circumstances, she isn't sure if that feels good to hear or not.

'Did something happen with you guys?' Annie asks then. 'I guess at a certain point I noticed I hadn't seen her around much, but I figured you just drifted apart after she moved out to Brooklyn.'

Fia gives herself a little shake, as though to return her focus to the here and now. 'Yeah,' she murmurs. 'I suppose we did.'

The two of them *hadn't* just drifted apart, though – of that she is certain. Having now reached the age of 30 and having moved around a bit, Fia has drifted apart from plenty of people in her life – case in point: every single person she knew at Camp Birchwood, save for the one she married. She hasn't heard a dicky bird from anyone else in that whole gang for years. These are people whom she now thinks of entirely without pain, without confusion, without any negative emotion whatsoever.

By contrast, with George, it was not a gentle, gradual sort of thing, a reality of life as natural as the changing of the seasons. It was like a severance – a break-up. Something, to use Annie's language, did indeed *happen*. Fia has just never been able to work out what.

WEEK FOUR

Chapter Twenty-One

Sarge's Deli and Diner has terracotta floor tiles and burgundy leather seats, strong filter coffee and generous portions. Its walls are lined with photographs of famous faces who may (or, equally likely, may not) have visited through the years. Overhead, glass lightshades – their mosaics of green and yellow pieces – cast the whole place in a slightly jaundiced hue. In short, it could not be further from mushroom toast and latte art, from millennial pink and teal velvet sofas. At times, Fia loves all those things. But she's always loved it here, too.

From across the booth, Susan Followill's expression is almost ludicrously pleasant. The basic greetings out of the way, and everyone having already ordered something to eat at the deli counter, this is a woman now ready, in earnest, to begin her tried-and-tested spiel.

Fia takes a deep breath. The contemplation of recent days has clung on, a bit. Maybe, she thinks, she actually *can* learn a thing or two from this process. In any event, she reminds herself that it is not in her interests to rock the boat too much this afternoon. She cannot have Benjamin storming off, refusing to even participate.

'So!' Susan declares. 'I'm always so interested when I talk to couples – what was it that first attracted you to each other?'

Right away, Fia can sense her insides seizing. It's not the best start. Denial is on the tip of her tongue – a repudiation of the basic assumption that underpins the question – when suddenly she can sense Benjamin's eyes on her.

She lets herself sneak a glance in his direction, and the expression on his face, to nine out of ten onlookers, would surely seem entirely neutral – blank, even. Fia can read him very clearly, though. It's in the very slight twitch of his lips, the minuscule arch of his eyebrow: that hint of challenge – and something else, too.

Just like that, Fia can sense her efforts to stay zen slipping away. She is thrown off her game – aware, suddenly, of the scent of him, even stronger now than it is inside the confines of their office. Why on earth, she wonders, did she chose to slide in alongside him, when another option – across the booth, next to Susan – was equally available to her? She tries to focus on Susan.

'Uh, what first attracted me to Benjamin?' she wonders aloud, buying time, letting her voice rise with sarcasm. 'That's a hard one. I would say it's got to be when I told him my name and where I was from, and he said, "Hey, I had no idea you guys spoke such good English".'

For a brief second, when Fia turns back to him, it looks like Benjamin might be recollecting that moment for the first time ever, even cringing a little. It's over fast, though. It may never have happened to begin with.

'And, for me, it would have to be Fia's sense of humour,' he tosses back, barely a missed beat. 'She's always been *so* good at taking a joke.'

'Well, what can I say? Benjamin's jokes just haven't always been to my taste,' Fia replies breezily. Again, her attention is ostensibly concentrated entirely on Susan now. 'Let me tell you about one time. We were working together, although not in the same job we're doing now – a different one.'

This – a fairly unremarkable fact, in Fia's mind – appears to take Susan rather by surprise. If she perhaps wonders why her warring clients seem to repeatedly find ways to work in the same place, she doesn't voice this aloud. But the look on her face tells Fia that at least slightly more context is needed.

'It was at a summer camp,' she supplies briefly. 'Anyway, I worked our entire evening shift by myself. Benjamin was nowhere to be seen, of course, but that was no big loss. Now, bear in mind that I had just managed to get ten 12-year-old boys settled down for the night. I could practically *taste* the cold beer that was waiting for me. When guess who comes bounding into the dorm room like Billy Big Bollocks, all "who wants to see a magic trick?"?' Fia pauses, allowing herself a brief sideways glance. 'Bingo! Benjamin here. And I won't bore you with every step of the process, but let's just say it ended with a bunch of preteen boys effectively holding me hostage, attempting to *saw me in half* with a baseball bat!'

Beside her, Benjamin lets out an unrestrained snort of laughter. Evidently, he's not a bit sorry about that one, even to this day. And, when it comes to anecdotes, he's not about to be outdone. 'Susan,' he says intently, 'would you believe that Fia and I were once out on a lake, and she sai—'

Susan, however, halts him with a gently raised hand. 'Okay. Maybe this isn't especially productive for anybody right now, huh?'

Across the table, neither Fia nor Benjamin say anything, both suddenly like reprimanded children. And is it weird that Fia feels slightly . . . disappointed? The two of them were just getting going; they were just ramping up that rhythm and pace. Furthermore, she has no idea what incident he was about to recall. The thought that she, too, might have said and done things in the past of which she now has no memory . . . that's a bit disorienting.

'So, I know you guys were married in . . . unconventional circumstances,' Susan continues calmly. 'And we're going to come on to talk about challenges in a moment. But what would you say was the biggest *success* of your marriage?'

Fia lets out a hearty, satirical sort of laugh. Magnanimity, moderation – prudent as those things would doubtless be, they've gone entirely out the window now. They just seem to be incredibly hard to achieve in Benjamin's presence. Apart from anything else, it strikes her that the alternatives are so much more *fun*.

'Pass,' she says drily, at the exact same moment as Benjamin says, 'I'll let Fia answer that one.'

She turns to him swiftly. 'What's that supposed to mean?'

He just rolls his eyes. 'Oh, come on.'

'No. What do you mean by that?'

He shrugs, in that maddening would-be casual way of his. 'You talk a good game, Fia. "All these years I've been helpless and trapped—"'

'I have been!' she interrupts, though it goes entirely ignored.

'—But I'd say that green card's been working out pretty good for you so far, huh? If anything, you should be thanking me!'

Fia doesn't give herself time to grasp the full implications of this. 'Thanking you?!' she finds herself all but shrieking in response.

And he is, now, every bit as emphatic as she is incredulous. 'Yes! Thanking me!'

'How d'you figure that one?'

'You've probably been in the US long enough by now, right? You'll probably qualify for some sort of residency-based permit, once we're divorced? If anyone's done their research, I'm sure it's you. But let's face it, Irish: you wouldn't even be here – much less would you be able to stay here – if it weren't for me. If it weren't for us getting married – and maybe more to the point, us having *stayed married*, all this time.'

When he's finished, even Benjamin himself seems a bit surprised by this little speech – the density of it, the frankness. For her part, Fia is nothing short of stunned. In under a minute, it's as though the conversation has somehow got away from her altogether, as if she's being dragged along behind it at speed.

'Hang on,' she manages eventually. 'Are you saying . . . Benjamin.' She pauses, hardly able to help the little grunt of disbelief that escapes her. 'Do you think I married you for a *green card*?'

Benjamin does not seem to register her tone. 'I don't think you married me for one,' he replies gruffly. 'But look at you now: feet under the desk at a big US firm? I think even *you'd* have to admit it's been a hell of a silver lining.'

Fia remains so completely astonished that it takes her another moment to formulate a response. 'I'm in the US on a work visa,' she says then, keeping each word slow and simple for Benjamin's benefit.

And she can practically hear the cogs begin to turn in his mind, in real time. She can practically *see* him wrestling with this new information – deciding whether or not to accept it, feeling his former sense of triumph slipping away.

His response, when it comes, is staccato and flustered. 'But . . . but! You *said*, that day we had the meeting with Alyvia Chestnut . . . you said you'd worked at ZOLA for *eight years*!'

Fia barely remembers that. Nonetheless, she's unperturbed. 'Yeah. Four years in the Dublin office, and then I came here. Fully legally, I might add, on an Intra-Company Transfer Visa.'

Benjamin looks utterly dumbfounded now – somehow indignant and embarrassed at once, and the combination is undeniably comedic. Or at least, Fia thinks it is. All of a sudden, she can't help the peal of laughter that bubbles up and escapes her, reverberating through her whole body.

Another one follows, and another, until it's an uncontrollable, self-perpetuating thing. She throws her head back with it, tears leaking from her eyes, the noise drawing glances from other diners. Fia herself knows this is probably a disproportionate reaction, but that very knowledge, in fact, seems only to make her cackle all the more. Plus, the expression on Benjamin's face – oh God, the expression on his face! – is just too much, too hilarious.

Even Susan's valiant efforts to interject, to redirect the conversation, make no difference.

'But . . . I don't understand!' Fia manages eventually, once her laughter has slowed to a wheeze. 'Why would I have hounded you about getting divorced – for months – if I secretly wanted to stay married? That's the stupidest thing I've ever heard, Ben! Can you even *get* a spouse visa without the two of you, like, literally showing up somewhere to be interrogated by an immigration officer?'

Unbelievably, Benjamin doesn't seem to have answers to these questions. It seems like they have never even occurred to him. He just shifts uncomfortably in his seat.

'Why didn't you say anything about this before?!' she continues.

'I *did*!' he splutters.

'You did *not*!'

Even as she speaks, though, certain moments come back to her in flashes. Benjamin absolutely *hadn't* declared this theory aloud before. Fia knows she would remember that. Had there been a few loaded accusations here and there, though – a few complaints grumbled under his breath?

She has to admit she's just never been much interested in pulling at those threads. Even now, she's momentarily distracted before she can really get into the specifics – it's the waiter, arriving with their food. Plain white plates clink down onto the wooden table, and Fia wastes no time before reaching for her sandwich. She's postponed lunch for this, and she's ravenous.

She's wolfed down a few glorious mouthfuls by the time she clocks that Susan is looking curiously across the table.

'Pretty good, huh?' Susan says, with a little smile.

In truth, Fia is just about restraining a moan. '*Oh my God*,' she replies, 'this is the best corned beef and pastrami in the city, bar none. Just never lets you down – I don't know what they do to it.'

She hears her own words aloud, as if they've come from someone else's mouth. And once again, she'd swear she can feel the very second Benjamin twists his neck to look over at her. She twists hers to look at him, their eyes meeting.

He is still mid-bite, a lick of cream cheese having escaped his bagel and made it to his upper lip. Evidently, he, too, has dived right in, approached this meal like he was in some sort of contest. Perhaps, she realizes, it was their very synchronicity that amused Susan.

For a few seconds, silence. He swallows, frowning a little now, as though he's slowly putting two and two together.

'You come here,' he says quietly, no question about it.

'Uh, yeah,' Fia replies, and though she didn't necessarily

intend to reveal that information, some part of her is glad he knows. She caught his little dig, last week, to the effect that she'd surely be far too high and mighty for a place like this.

'Oh,' is all he can seem to muster in response now.

And, yes, to be able to shock Benjamin Lowry twice, within a matter of minutes . . . undeniably that's pretty satisfying. It's a slightly uncomfortable feeling, too, though.

'And *you* come here,' she finds herself saying, a little disjointedly – because *that's* the source of discomfort, really. It's the having something in common. She just doesn't have much practice in that, with him.

Benjamin nods. 'Yeah,' he replies gruffly.

Fia supposes she has, at least, had a little longer than him to digest the coincidence. Still, though. How strange, that one of her favourite places in the city – this tiny place, on an unremarkable block – should apparently be one of his favourites, too. How *extra* strange to imagine that they could even have run into one another here, over the years. If she'd missed her subway one morning, arrived a little later than planned, if he'd decided to linger over an extra cup of coffee – that's all it would have taken.

Then, as if with the wave of a wand, the snap of someone's fingers, she's bounced right out of such thoughts, back into the present moment. She remembers Susan's existence, and the reason they're all here at Sarge's in the first place.

Another sudden peal of laughter escapes unbidden as she raises her coffee cup to her lips. 'Seriously, I just can't believe that all this time, you've been thinking I needed you for a visa!'

Chapter Twenty-Two

Fia practically giggles all the way back to ZOLA. Even when she has returned to her desk, with all sorts of other work matters to absorb her attention, she can't seem to help the sniggers that burst forth periodically. The sound pierces the silence of their little room, and Benjamin no longer needs to ask what's so funny.

'Sorry,' she tells him, not sounding hugely sorry. 'I just—' Another snort of laughter, another half-hearted attempt to smother it. 'I'm sorry.'

There is, by now, an almost permanent expression of chagrin on Benjamin's face. And, really, Fia knows she should try to be more sensitive. She supposes she cannot entirely blame him if – in the period since finding her here, at the firm – he hasn't exactly been at his most logical. She hasn't been at *her* most logical.

The remainder of their meeting with Susan was fairly uneventful. It didn't take long for the other woman to accept, once and for all, that she was on a hiding to nothing, as far as the emotional availability of her clients went. None of her questions or insights – none of the ways she must usually have been able to draw people out, bring them together – seemed to quite apply to the situation at hand. Any sort of romantic reconciliation was off the cards.

Onwards, then, to the practicalities of separation. The good news was that neither Fia nor Benjamin wanted to take anything from (or give anything to) the other. As such, there wasn't much to thrash out there. It was agreed that Susan would email both parties a form to complete and sign, and that they would all three meet just once more to approve Susan's draft marital settlement agreement. After that, Susan would file said agreement with the court. A judge would stamp it, issue a final degree of divorce, and they were done. Easy.

It's almost 6 p.m. when Fia receives the follow-up email from Susan, and she glances over at Benjamin, a moment of silent recognition passing between them. He's received one, too.

'I guess the seventh won't work since we're in Dublin,' he says then, no preamble. 'But could you do the following week? Or maybe we could even just sign off on the whole thing by email, depending on—'

'Hang on,' Fia interrupts, her mind beginning to reel ever so slightly. 'Go back to that last part. What did you just say?'

'Susan wants to meet with us again on July seventh to discuss the draft settlement agreement,' Benjamin says, enunciating deliberately this time, as though, in her, he is faced unavoidably with a moron. 'But that's when you and I are out of town for the Summer Summit, and so I thought . . . *oh*.' Benjamin trails to a stop, his mouth tugging upwards in sly amusement.

Whatever expression is on Fia's own face right now, she could not precisely say – abject horror, maybe, disbelief. In any case, as the seconds pass and the silence stretches out, it seems like Benjamin is getting the picture.

'. . . Did you not know?' he asks, a new impishness in his voice. 'The summer associates are going on that now.'

And, all of a sudden, it is as though Fia is propelled by some force outside herself. Leaving Benjamin there in her (their) office, perhaps literally mid-sentence, she takes off like a rocket.

Why does she do it? Why doesn't she simply address the matter with Benjamin directly? She doesn't know. But, for whatever reason, Fia speeds all the way to the far side of the fifty-eighth floor – no small distance away – until she's approaching Celia Hannity's corner office. Then, in those last few seconds, she reduces her pace a bit, smooths her hands over her suit, tries generally to create a slightly less frenzied impression before she appears in her boss's view.

For a moment, the two exchange pleasantries, Fia hovering in Celia's doorway. That can only last so long, though. Fia would simply never, in ordinary circumstances, come to an equity partner for random chit-chat. It is for this reason that she finds herself making up some bullshit question about a probate case, purely by way of explaining her own lingering presence. This really isn't ideal. She isn't afraid to ask Celia things, but she normally takes a lot of care to make sure these aren't things she could possibly find out via any other resource available to her. Celia is always fair, but she does not suffer fools.

When they're done with that whole charade, Fia, as casually as she can muster, says, 'By the way, Celia, the, uh . . . the summer associates aren't coming to the Summer Summit are they?'

'No, they are,' Celia corrects. 'Did you miss the email about it last week?'

Quite likely Fia *has* missed the email. She gets a million fucking emails every minute of the day. This – a thing she can never say out loud – sometimes feels like the central truth of her professional existence.

'But . . . the paralegals don't come,' she all but bleats. 'Or the PAs.'

At this, Celia looks more than slightly perturbed. 'Fia, the summer associates aren't paralegals or PAs. The summer associates are the *future of the profession* – the future of this *firm*. And it's important for them to have some insight into the cross-jurisdictional nature of our work here at ZOLA. That's why we decided to invite them this year. Really, we should have been doing it long before now. I've been saying so for years, but not all the equity partners were . . . like-minded.'

Celia's frustration with her fellow partners is thinly veiled, and likewise, Fia can sense that the older woman is somewhat disappointed in *her* now, too – in her failure to fully embrace the firm's ethos or whatnot. She sets about redeeming herself at short notice.

'Right. Of course. That makes total sense,' she says, doing her best to sound enthusiastic, or at least to sound normal.

Perhaps she doesn't quite get there, though, because Celia's eyes narrow.

'Is there something I need to know, with you and Benjamin?'

'What? No!'

'Because if you're having some sort of an issue – if you guys just aren't gelling, or if there's anything else . . . *challenging* happening . . . I can't help you unless you tell me about it.'

And, for the briefest of brief seconds, Fia actually does consider telling Celia all about it – the whole mess. There would be a relief in doing so, she's sure. But then, she gets a hold of herself. Along with the relief, there'd be a bunch of other stuff, too: the mortification, the very real fear for her future.

'No, no, everything's good,' she replies.

'You sure? I'd like to think we've made some kind of progress since I was your age, but I don't know. Some guys still can't seem to see a woman for anything other than T&A.'

This time, Fia catches her boss's meaning exactly. She's fairly horrified by the impression she might have inadvertently given Celia.

'Oh, no!' she replies, more fulsomely. 'There's nothing like that with Benjamin. He's great. Honestly. No problem at all.'

She smiles brightly, even as this new reality settles like lead in her stomach: Benjamin Lowry – not just here, but in Dublin, too, encroaching on her much-anticipated safe haven.

At least, however, he is not a sex pest. She can say that much for him.

Chapter Twenty-Three

'You'll probably barely even see him,' Annie says, when she hears the news. 'Didn't you say, like, a billion people go to this thing – like, from all the different branches of your firm?'

Kavita jumps in, right on cue. 'Plus, you're staying with your parents, right – as opposed to at the hotel with everyone else? I agree – you can totally avoid him. And, I mean, work stuff is work stuff. Benjamin in your office in New York, Benjamin in some conference room in Ireland . . . what's the difference, really?'

In some intangible, indescribable sort of way, it feels like quite a big difference to Fia. Nonetheless, by midweek, and for lack of much else to do, she has come around somewhat, chosen to believe her roommates unless and until they are actively proven incorrect.

If nothing else, she's grateful not to have had to explicitly discuss the matter with Benjamin, having blamed Monday's hasty exit on some unrelated – and entirely fictional – matter. Of course, Benjamin didn't really buy that. Fia could see it written all over his stupid grinning face, the second she arrived back into the office after seeing Celia. He *knew* she'd been caught unawares. Thankfully, though, he didn't quiz her any further, didn't especially rub it in. Frankly, he made things a lot easier on her than she made things on him, when it came to *his* misunderstanding about the visa situation.

Now, it's late on Wednesday evening – much later than Fia generally likes to be in the office, really, but it cannot be helped. She's certainly not the only one still around. While the sky outside is pitch black, there are lights in the windows of all the neighbouring buildings. And, on the fifty-eighth floor of her own building, the lights are very much still on, too. With her office door flung open, every so often Fia hears a burst of chatter from the break room, spots co-workers criss-crossing the atrium, ties loosened by now, high heels slipped off.

In other words, the lateness of the hour does not, at least, translate to creepiness. Fia has tried to explain this to her very worried mother once or twice: that on the occasions where it is not accompanied by huge time pressure, being at ZOLA after hours like this can actually be sort of nice. There's something about the calm of the place, the camaraderie, the commiseration. At some point after 8 p.m. this evening, everyone still around had gone in on a mammoth Grubhub order from the Vietnamese place nearby, and it felt almost festive, padding into the break room to poke through cardboard containers, see what surprises were on offer.

All that said, by 9.30 p.m., there are still so many things on her to-do list. Even as she finishes drafting ten codicils for wills, a stack of trust documents wait on her desk, all to be checked for accuracy. It isn't a particularly complex job, just time-consuming, and she can't restrain a weary exhale when she looks at them. As it happens, this is *not* overly what she wants to be doing with her one wild and precious life.

In the corner, she senses eyes flicking towards her at the sound of her sigh, but by the time she looks up, Benjamin's gaze has shifted away again. Because, yes, Benjamin is here, too.

As though he can perhaps feel *her* regarding *him* now, he glances back upwards, meeting her eyes this time.

'Your hair . . .' he mumbles.

And, for a second, Fia has no idea what he's talking about. She frowns, reaching a hand up towards her hair instinctively. She's pulled it down from the bun, she realizes, so that it's tumbling down past her shoulders, doubtless as voluminous as ever. She ruffles at her scalp a little, sweeping unruly strands back from her face. 'What about it?' she asks.

There's a funny sort of expression on his face, one she can't quite pinpoint. 'Nothing, it's just . . . it's how I remember it, that's all,' he says quietly, before they each return – somewhat hurriedly, it might be said – to their respective tasks.

It doesn't take long for peace to settle between them again. And, as he types away, as she reaches for the next document in her pile, Fia finds herself suddenly very aware of just that: the sense of peace. That peace might ever reign in this little office would once have seemed unthinkable – an entirely, absolutely unachievable thing. So, what has changed? On his end, perhaps Benjamin has found himself less inclined to deliberately press her buttons since learning that she *hasn't* in fact used him for immigration purposes.

On hers, she's not quite sure. She's reminded, though, of something that her mother has always said: *There is no such thing as quality time. There is only time.*

Inside the confines of these four walls, over the course of the summer so far, Fia and Benjamin probably haven't said or done anything very significant in the grand scheme of things. There certainly have been no tears or apologies or the like. She still wouldn't have to think too hard to come up with the top five most annoying and/or perhaps fundamentally immoral things he's ever done. Nonetheless, it would seem that the simple fact of having been in one another's presence, unavoidably, for hours and hours, has perhaps begun to have some sort of impact. It may have started to rub the very sharpest points from their corners, made them just a little softer on each other, even when they collide.

It helps to know their divorce is well and truly underway. It helps to see that he is trying, at work; no matter what he'd implied at the beginning, he's evidently a lot more conscientious than Fia initially thought. It helps that he is nice to security guards and paralegals and partners alike. It helps that he is, occasionally, quite amusing.

Out of the corner of her eye, she can see him moving now, pushing back in his chair a little, stretching his neck from side to side.

'Do you want to see something cool?' he asks her, and she looks over at him, her eyes narrowing suspiciously.

'What kind of thing?'

'God!' he replies, the word exhaled on a half-laugh. For a moment, he just studies her. 'How 'bout this, Fia? How 'bout you have to just . . . trust me.'

Trust him.

That seems like quite a big ask, given his background when it comes to repaying trust. It's on the tip of her tongue to tell him exactly that, and yet, for some reason, she doesn't.

The thing is that, so often in her life, she's been able identify moments like this only in retrospect, if at all. But th^re is just something about the expression on his face now, the tone of his voice: this is a rare occasion on which Fia can tell – right this second, *live* – that she has arrived at something of an inflection point. She could pass, politely, keep him at a distance. She could consider the fact that she and Benjamin Lowry are now able to mostly sit in professional – maybe even companionable – silence to be a major win, and leave it at that. Or she could show herself receptive, let them inch towards something . . .

Well, something else.

Some sort of a work-friendship, she tells herself. A temporary one, for the remainder of the summer and until their divorce is done once and for all.

That would probably be to her benefit, on a purely practical level. It could help reduce her stress levels back to somewhere near normal. Plus, she's grown so very irritatingly *curious* about him – that's the truth of the matter. Where once she saw absolutely no depth, no reason for intrigue, in Benjamin Lowry, now she finds herself less and less sure that's right. She wants to find out what other people see in him. She doesn't want to be left with him, the way she has been with George: left wondering.

And so, she glances at the stack of paperwork on her desk, sighing again heavily. It does present a fairly unappealing prospect. However, that's not the only reason she looks back at him, holding his gaze for a second or two, clicking her tongue against her teeth.

'Okay, fine. I'll trust you,' she says quietly. 'Just this once.'

Chapter Twenty-Four

Fia hasn't been up here since that breakfast buffet on the morning all the summer associates arrived. It's a lot quieter now, on the roof terrace of the sixtieth floor. Fia and Benjamin are the only ones around; even the traffic noise is dampened at this height. All the way down at street level, cars and pedestrians look like little Lego pieces.

Fia walks a few paces, her eyes darting around as though some sort of surprise new addition to the space is going to jump out at her – but none appears. The rooftop looks precisely the same as it always does.

'Please tell me this isn't where you chuck me off,' she says.

Benjamin doesn't miss a beat. 'And ruin my career before it's even really started?' he replies. 'I'd never get away with it.'

She just looks over him, her question asked in the silence.

He smirks. 'Always the husband, right?'

Fia has to admit, she somewhat set herself up for that one, and she rolls her eyes, unable to help the smile that comes with it.

'So, then, what are we doing up here?' she asks, following him as he turns the corner towards the other side of the building.

A few seconds later, he stops dead, nodding out to the horizon. 'That's what we're doing.'

Before them, the moon is larger than Fia has ever seen it: a perfect circle, nestled low in the sky as though held there by the tallest towers of 49th and 50th Street. It looks slightly pink in colour – almost cartoonish in its dimension and definition.

'Pretty cool, huh?' Benjamin says.

Fia just nods, taking it in for a moment. 'Pretty cool,' she agrees softly. 'Is it a supermoon?'

'Yeah. That's literally about the extent of my knowledge, though. I just read in the paper – by which I obviously mean the internet – that it was happening tonight.'

He moves to pull up a slatted wooden chair – one of many dotted around – before her warning comes.

'Oh, I think that's the banjaxed one,' she tells him. 'I don't know why it hasn't been removed.'

About six weeks ago, at a client reception, Fia watched a man – quite an important man – literally fall through that chair. By way of a deep and sincere apology, someone from ZOLA was now going to be taking him to the New York City Ballet more or less in perpetuity.

Fia hoists herself up onto the concrete surround of an enormous planter, trying not to disturb the actual plants in the process. 'View's better up here anyway,' she says, and he hops up to join her.

They each look out, in comfortable quiet, and for some reason Fia is struck by the thing – or one of the things – she's just said to him: *banjaxed*.

These days, she's more and more American in the way she speaks (even if not always in the way she thinks). It's not just vocabulary – *elevator, eggplant, eraser*. She can also hear the way her own cadence, her own turn of phrase, has changed: she's all about 'taking' a shower now, 'grabbing' a coffee, 'calling' a client. She has adapted in order to assimilate. With Benjamin, though, it is the oddest thing: she has caught herself, more than once, talking to him in her old language – the same way she did just now. And if, on any occasion, he hasn't understood her . . . well, he's done a good job of hiding it.

She really has no explanation for that. Maybe, she realizes, it is just a history thing. For obvious reasons, she's never been inclined to think of her history with Benjamin Lowry as having any sort of positive connotation. But, sitting beside him now, it occurs to her that of the eight million people in this city, he is in fact the one who has known her the longest – or at least, who knew her first. That's a strange one to think about.

Fia gives herself a shake, as if to snap herself out of such ruminations.

It's just the view, she thinks. It's very hard to look out at that cityscape – that incredible moon – without having some thought approaching the philosophical, some musing beyond the minutiae of one's own little to-do list.

'So, you're here late tonight,' she says, because that feels like a safe topic: work.

'Yeah. You know, they told us all this stuff at Columbia about work-life balance and how you gotta set boundaries and whatever,' he replies. 'And I thought, great. I'll do that. Right off the bat, you know? Get into good habits. But it turns out – and I'm 100 per cent sure you don't need me to tell you this – you actually *cannot do* this job between the hours of nine and five. Like . . . that very literally just isn't enough time to do the whole job.'

Fia smiles drolly. 'I don't know. Have you tried a meditation app?'

They both snigger, and for a moment, there's quiet before she continues.

'Seriously, though, I get it. I mean, I definitely don't think it's just this firm or just the law. I think it might just be modern working. Both my roommates are the same, and my brother and sister. It's like we don't even get to just be crazy-busy and stressed about it anymore. Now we have to be stressed about our stress, too – as if it's completely our own problem that we've dropped the ball on self-care.'

Benjamin squints over at her. 'Can I ask you something? About the job?'

'Go for it.'

'I guess, it just doesn't always seem like you . . . exactly love it,' he says then, his tone delicate, as though he is doing his best to be sensitive, to tiptoe into a very difficult topic

Meanwhile, Fia barely bats an eyelid. 'Oh, I don't love it,' she agrees readily. She's long past any angst about this subject. 'I like being good at it, and I like the clients – most of them. And, obviously, showing up here every day is what pays for, like . . . my entire life. But am I giddy over trusts and estates? Wills? The occasional *divorce*?' She cocks an eyebrow, like the very notion is ridiculous. 'No, I'm not.'

Benjamin looks sincerely a little thrown by this turn of events. Fia would wager she might be the first person since he stepped through the doors at ZOLA – and maybe the first among all those he's met through law school, too – not to have waxed lyrical at him about an alleged passion for the profession.

'But, so, you're up for promotion, right?' he says, and maybe she's the one who looks surprised now, because then he shrugs, all innocence. '. . . I hear things.'

He probably, Fia realizes right then, hears *all sorts of things*. He's been at the firm so much less time than her, and yet there are doubtless already ways in which he could well and truly school her. Dashing from one team to another as he does, in and out of partner's offices, chatting away with the secretaries . . . he must now have a whole array of information, both reliable and less reliable, in his back pocket.

'So, if you're not necessarily super into any of this, why do you stay at all? Never mind actually seeking out . . . more of it?' he continues. 'I mean, that'd be the basic consequence, right? More work, more responsibility.'

'More money,' she points out. 'That's definitely part of it. New York is expensive.'

Manhattan, specifically, is sickeningly – perhaps unsustainably – expensive, even for someone like her who already gets paid comparatively well. A hike in salary would go some way towards offsetting what has started to feel like an incurable financial deficit – namely the absence of a partner who also gets paid well. And, at least as much as the practical aspect, there is also the principle of the thing. Fia has come to understand that cold hard cash is really the number one way in which an employer demonstrates the extent to which they value an employee. It isn't unladylike to say so. Praise and promises can be nice to hear from time to time, but they are ultimately *not it*.

Of course, in Fia's particular case, there is an added wrinkle: if she wants to stay in New York, she really has no option to walk away from ZOLA, get a better-paid role in some comparable firm that would end up being the same but would briefly pretend to be different. She can't ever tell Celia and the other partners that if they liked it, they should have put a ring on it. Her right to be in the United States at all is tied to the firm.

That Benjamin doesn't readily grasp all this is not something she holds against him. It isn't his fault. There are just certain things you can never know about a job before you are some way down the path of actually doing said job. For that matter, there are certain things about the practice of law as a woman and – yes – as an immigrant that Benjamin might never really understand. That doesn't make him a bad guy. It just . . . is what it is. They are where they are.

And then, there is another, simpler truth to all of this, too.

'You know what?' she says, looking over at him. 'Mostly, I want to get promoted because I just fucking deserve to get promoted.'

He laughs out loud at that, the frankness of it, and it makes her grin as well.

'That seems like an excellent reason,' he says. 'I think you should tell Celia Hannity exactly that when it comes up.'

Fia just chuckles, twisting around a little to take in the panorama. That huge moon – this particular vantage point from which to experience it – might be one of the coolest things she's ever seen in this city. It somehow makes the familiar view seem magical again, as if she's seeing it with brand-new eyes.

'What neighbourhood do you live in?' she finds herself asking Benjamin then – the stuff of a very first meeting.

'East Village. Like, Little Ukraine, Alphabet City kind of area?' he replies, and he waits for her nod of recognition before he continues. 'I have this new roommate, he just moved in two months ago. He's a dancer, like, Cirque du Soleil kind of stuff, you know? Anyhow, he's broken up with his boyfriend, and he's been crying – and I mean *wailing* – for weeks. He's in the flex bedroom, so that's been . . . interesting.'

Fia laughs along with Benjamin, but even as she does, other thoughts are coming to her, running like ticker tape in her brain. Is it surprising to her, that he is living in that neck of the woods? With a roommate? With a roommate whose bedroom in fact comprises a partitioned section of the living room? Yes, as it happens, all of that is *very* surprising to Fia. It doesn't quite tally with what she envisaged of his life here: the apartment in a doorman-building, somewhere Uptown, decorated to his parents' taste.

In fact, of the two of them, *she's* the one closer to that scenario. She's struck by an unsettling, itchy sort of sensation – as though her insides are shifting, and she can't stop them. Feeling the sudden need for some variation, some movement, she hops down from her spot on the planter, heading to the perimeter of the roof terrace.

She walks all the way over to the very edge, until she can – if she tilts forward a little – see the street below. It's all very well-secured, of course, not exactly a *Spiderman* situation, but nonetheless, her brother and sister would be nearly vomiting already. Neither Eoin nor Maeve have ever, even in all their visits here, quite acclimatized to high-rise living.

Fia, by contrast, has a head for heights. She looks down for a moment, before switching instead to look up. And, all the while, she can sense Benjamin's eyes on *her*. She can sense it, too, when he sidles up to stand alongside her, lets his gaze follow hers. You can never see the stars in Manhattan, the way you can in Ireland. This is something Fia appreciates about her home country when she's back there, more so than something she necessarily misses all that much when she's away. There's a lot of stuff like that.

'Y'know,' she says then. 'The thing about New York is that it's dirty and crowded and probably vulnerable to terror attacks . . .'

'Not to mention your run of the mill mass shootings,' he interjects dryly, and she smirks a little, because she was born into, raised on, just that sort of black humour.

'Right. And some people are not that nice, and it can definitely be lonely, and everything's crazy expensive. The work culture is – as discussed – completely terrible. But I love it.'

Benjamin smiles over at her. His smile, in its full force, is . . . something. Fia tells herself that it is fine to have noticed this, that any person would have done, that there really was no way not to have noticed it.

'Yeah. Me too,' he replies, and for another moment, there's quiet between them.

'I could live here the rest of my life, I think,' Fia declares.

'Yeah?'

In fact, in the few months before turning 30 and the few months that have followed it, this very subject has been occupying more and more of Fia's thoughts. And, depending on the day – sometimes the hour – she comes down on different sides of the whole thing. But at least right now, what she's told him feels solid, true.

'Yeah. It's weird, isn't it? Have you ever seen those Hallmark films where the girl's, like, I don't know, a big city lawyer, let's say.'

'Let's say,' he agrees, a smile pulling at his lips.

'And she has to go to the sticks for whatever reason, and

she's super bitchy about it at first. Maybe it's Christmas. Maybe there's, like, a local festival of some sort that needs saving.'

'She meets a hot single dad,' he chimes in.

Fia laughs. 'Exactly. What's the message there? Small towns are great, and big cities are terrible, right? Knowing all your neighbours by name is meaningful, and working in a skyscraper is vapid. But I don't know.' She sighs, lets her gaze span the horizon once more. 'I still look out at that view and feel . . .'

'Alive,' he says softly.

She turns to look at him, and her own voice seems to come out sounding just the same. 'Yeah. Alive.'

Chapter Twenty-Five

Thursday night, and at least thirty of ZOLA's mid-level, junior and summer associates are all crammed into a sports bar near Bryant Park. Jackets have been cast aside by this stage, though. A few of the women have gone to the toilets and attempted some subtle day-to-night modifications, red or fuchsia painted on their lips. Twenty-four hours from now, the Fourth of July long weekend will have begun in earnest, and already there appears to have been a collective agreement that tomorrow's workday barely counts. It's a mere formality. Just the thought of four solid days, and *soon*, on which the office will actually be closed – nobody will be able to get in there even if they want to – seems to have made everyone a little loopy.

Waiting at the bar for her gin and tonic, Fia couldn't be less interested in whatever baseball game is being shown on a dozen HD screens. Instead, she surveys the scene. While it does involve a lot of the same people, this is not at all like the events scheduled as part of ZOLA's official summer programme. The firm's higher echelons are not circulating tonight. There is not even the pretence of any edifying element. This a piss-up, plain and simple.

And Fia's all for that, to a point. She's not immune to the sensation of having been somehow *unleashed*. She hasn't, throughout her twenties, entirely denied herself the pleasure of occasionally drinking far more than is medically advisable. But she picks her moments. And her moments are absolutely never in large groups of people, none of whom owe her any very close allegiance. Once bitten, eight years shy, and all that. In the time it's taken for her to arrive at her third drink of the evening, others around her have easily had four, plus two shots. Already, she can see some people beginning to get a very specific sort of messy. Tongues are loosening, hands are wandering, professional distance is falling away little by little.

As far as workplace relationships go, ZOLA can only outright forbid them where there is a power differential. Even among employees of equal standing in the hierarchy, though, fraternization is certainly not encouraged. Lawyers wanting to date one another are obliged to declare such an intention in advance to Human Resources, and to sign what Fia thinks is technically called a Consensual Relationship Agreement – more commonly known, and mocked, as a 'love contract': the opposite, perhaps, to the scrap of paper she and Benjamin once signed in a Vegas hotel lobby.

As for more casual liaisons – non-sanctioned ones – of course, they happen. They happen all the time, and often thanks to nights just like this one. There is a certain honour code, though, within the resulting whisper network and rumour mill. Like highschoolers who agree, on pain of death, *not to tell our parents*, so, too, do ZOLA's young and young-ish lawyers conspire to keep certain exploits beyond the eyes and ears of the firm's partners. Not that Fia has ever needed the benefit of such solidarity. She herself has never dipped her pen in the company ink – setting aside Ryan Sieman, of course, who is so far away it barely counts, and with whom she has never actually shared an office building.

She's on her way back from the bar when she spots Benjamin, lingering by a large barrel functioning as a table. Beside him is another of the summer associates – a girl named Riley – and she stops Fia on her way past.

'Oh my gosh, Fia! Will you *tell* this guy,' she says, giving Benjamin a playful nudge, 'that the Hamptons is not *all* bougie. I swear, parts of it are actually very low-key and unspoiled.' Her words are the slightest bit slurred as she gazes up at him. 'Maybe you just haven't had the best tour guide.'

This is all it takes – ten seconds maximum – for Fia to get the measure of the situation before her: this girl is a walking, talking heart-eyes emoji.

Meanwhile, Benjamin himself does not seem remotely aware of it – or if he is, he certainly isn't encouraging it. He just shrugs, taking a sip from his beer. 'You could be right,' he says easily.

And from the tone of his voice, the expression on his face, Fia can tell: he isn't flirting. He isn't feigning nonchalance. Neither is he being rude or dismissive. This is simply a conversation in which he has an extremely average amount of interest. He's also about as sober as she is herself – in other words, maybe not altogether, but mostly. That's the other thing that Fia can see right away. Maybe, she thinks, he learned some lessons from their little trip to Las Vegas, too.

Returning to the discussion at hand, Fia has absolutely nothing to contribute on the subject of the Hamptons, other than that she always thought they were – or rather, apparently, *it was* – plural. Instead, she just smiles and moves things along.

'So, uh, how's everything been going?' she asks Riley, purely for something to say to her. 'You still enjoying it okay at ZOLA?'

Despite the effusiveness with which the other girl greeted her, their previous interaction has in fact amounted to one single conversation, at a 'lunchtime symposium' on securities lending. On that occasion, a fortnight ago, Riley happily referred to both herself and all the other summer associates as 'baby lawyers', which was up there with 'pretty please' and 'mama bear' in terms of phrases Fia could not stand. However, she tried not to fixate on it.

'Absolutely.' Riley beams, and even in her present state of inebriation, she still turns out to be a talker. Americans are often like that, in Fia's experience. Presumably it is to do with the way they have been socialized – or educated, maybe. They seem to assume that the thing they have to say is valuable, and that you are bound to be very interested in hearing it.

Of course, Fia actually isn't at all interested in whatever Riley has learned about the finer workings of one company taking over another company. What's more, she strongly suspects that, beside her, Benjamin knows it. Last night, just briefly, she took off the mask she typically wears at work, and now she has the sense that he can see right through her, can read her true thoughts even as she nods along with Riley, making the appropriate sounds at appropriate intervals. It's an odd sensation – as if two conversations are somehow happening at once, one of them entirely silent.

'I'm learning a *ton*, though,' Riley eventually concludes, draining her wine glass. 'And it's awesome to be able to try a little bit of everything. Before I started at ZOLA, my friend from back home – he's a first-year associate at Dentons in Boston now – was telling me that the whole experience is, like, basically summer camp for lawyers. So far, he's been kinda right!'

At this, Benjamin suddenly looks a bit more alive. 'Summer camp, huh?' he says slyly. 'You know anything about those, Fia?' His eyes narrow as they land on her, amusement flickering.

She looks right back at him, and she feels something – some little spark of energy, of interest – ignite in her brain, too. 'I don't,' she says smoothly, feigning innocence, curiosity. 'Do you, Benjamin?'

'Not really. I hear the supervision can be very . . .'

'Lax?' she suggests.

'I was going to say "rigid",' he replies.

She can't help but snort out a laugh, even as she rolls her eyes.

Riley opens her mouth to add something, but she's quickly cut off.

'Boo!' comes a voice from behind them, and Fia jumps, feeling an arm loop around her shoulders. When she turns, Kavita is standing there, Annie beside her.

'Oh my God!' she exclaims, caught wholly unawares. 'What are you two doing here?'

'Oh, you know. We just thought we'd drop by,' Kavita says with a grin, and in the circumstances, Fia feels that her only response can be via some very intense *wtf* eye contact aimed at each of her roommates in turn.

A flurry of introductions follow, shortly after which Riley absents herself to replenish her drink. Then, there's a slightly awkward lull, the strangeness of this little group rising unavoidably to the forefront of Fia's mind.

Kavita leaps into the conversational gap, undaunted. 'So, you guys are all off to the old Emerald Isle next week, huh?' she begins, and every time Fia is reminded of that, some part of her seems to be shocked anew. Just the thought of *Benjamin in Dublin* still feels like such an oxymoron.

'Right,' he replies.

'You excited to meet the in-laws?' Kavita continues, new bite in her tone this time. 'You know, Benjamin, this really is none of my business, but I have to say, you've got *some nerve*, dude. Have you ever thought about ghosting in the Olympics? Let's be honest, it's a pretty competitive sport these days, but you were such an early adopter that I'm sure—'

'All right,' Fia interrupts, with a little laugh intended somehow to be conciliatory, 'let's all get back in our corners, shall we?'

Her eyes dart around as if to ensure there are no listening ears. Undoubtedly, that's a huge part of her concern right now. She can't afford another slip-up, like the one with Brett back at the company softball game. However, she's prepared to admit – at least to herself – that there might be other reasons why she jumped in, too. For a second there, she could see that hard, closed expression begin to cloud Benjamin's features – the same one she's seen before when this topic arises. She doesn't like it. Naked hostility, bullshit assertions – those things she can take from him and toss right back at him if need be. But she doesn't like that expression.

And, by now, perhaps she simply is somewhat tired of re-treading this particular ground. While, in principle, there should be a major appeal to watching Kavita expertly rip Benjamin Lowry a new one, in practice she finds she's just . . . not in the mood for it. Not tonight.

'So, Benjamin, Fia tells us you guys are working together on this influencer thing,' Annie starts then, in the interests of smoothing things over. 'BabyGAndMe? How's all that going?'

Fia, too, does her bit to get the conversation back on track. 'How come you're never this interested in my trusts and estates?' she jokes.

Annie just smiles sweetly. ''Cause they're so much less interesting.'

'Ha *ha*,' Fia says sarcastically, but she's smiling herself.

'Well, I think Fia and I maybe have slightly different instincts about Alyvia Chestnut,' Benjamin chimes in, and then he turns to look at Fia. 'Actually, I finally got a hold of her earlier about coming back into the office – with Gus. Turns out she's been on some sort of sponsored trip to Montana. You ever wondered how Gus would look in a cowboy hat? Maybe a little lasso? 'Cause you can be damned sure you're about to find out in the next week.'

Fia chuckles into her drink, even though it's probably thoroughly unprofessional. She can't help it.

'Anyhow, at this point I figure we'll have to wait 'til after the Summer Summit, right?' Benjamin continues.

'I suppose so. And remember I'm in Ireland an extra week afterwards.'

Benjamin arches both eyebrows, his voice rising teasingly, too. 'Oh, what, so you don't trust me to handle the meeting without you, is that it?'

'That's *absolutely* it,' Fia tosses back, zero hesitation.

She has to say, Benjamin doesn't look too put out, though. Instead, he cracks a smile. 'Fine, I'll schedule it for as soon as you're back.'

'Back from Dublin,' Kavita prompts from beside them. Momentarily, Fia had somewhat forgotten that anyone else was present at all.

'Right,' Benjamin says.

'It really is so fun that your firm sets up these trips every year,' Kavita replies, and she seizes upon the chance to say the thing she's maybe wanted to say all along. 'Do you think Ryan Sieman will be there this time, Fi?'

'Uh . . . as far as I know, yeah,' Fia replies, and for Benjamin's benefit, she adds, 'Ryan's a lawyer – a solicitor – in the Dublin office.'

'*Very* cute,' Kavita says, which – though something Kavita herself has observed only from photographs – is true. And, as she lowers her voice conspiratorially, she, too, is clearly talking directly to Benjamin now. 'He's kind of obsessed with her.'

That part isn't true at all, but Fia finds she doesn't especially mind. In some way that's bound to be very juvenile and illogical, she can't deny that it's nice for Benjamin to know she hasn't been living an entirely sexless existence all these years.

'Is that right?' Benjamin replies, before looking over at Fia, his eyebrow quirking slightly. 'Obsessed, huh, Irish?'

And, for a second, she finds herself unable to do anything but look back at him. 'You need to stop with that,' she tells him, but when she hears her own voice aloud, it doesn't seem to have much force to it. Could it be this third drink, hitting her now? She does seem to feel unusually . . . floaty – as though she is being carried along by something, some force that, for good or for bad, is a little outside her control.

'Stop with what?' he asks.

'You know what.'

He smiles a half-smile in return, and in the silence that follows between them, Fia's peripherally aware of Annie and Kavita having some sort of wordless communication of their own.

'Hey, Benjamin, can you excuse us for just one second?' Kavita pipes up, and she wastes no time waiting for a response. 'Thanks so much, we'll be right back!'

She tugs Fia by the hand, Annie in tow, too, until the three of them have found a quiet corner on the far side of the bar.

'What are we doing?' Fia yelps. 'You've made me spill half my drink!'

Kavita hops up onto a bar stool, letting Fia settle herself before she continues. 'Girl, I have some *bad news* for you,' she says, and just like that, Fia's on high alert.

'What?'

Kavita waits a beat. 'You're enjoying this.'

'Enjoying what?' Fia frowns.

Her roommate nods over at Benjamin. 'Him,' she says, and she doesn't seem one bit dissuaded by the surprise that shows up on Fia's face. 'Yeah. Maybe you weren't at first, but you are now.'

'What?!' Fia exclaims, as soon as she can get the word out. 'Of course I'm not. I'm counting down the days until he's gone. This whole thing has been an *untold nightmare*.'

Kavita looks amused, incredulous. 'Oh, girl. That's *definitely* not true. You've told us about it *so* much.'

'So much,' Annie murmurs, almost soothingly, and something about it makes all three of them laugh. They laugh their heads off, at themselves, at the ridiculousness of this whole situation.

'He's very good-looking,' Annie manages eventually, giddiness subsiding. 'Can I just say that? He's *very* good-looking.'

Fia chooses not to respond to that one. 'I can't believe you two! Talk about an ambush!' she says instead.

'We couldn't resist. We actually haven't even eaten,' Annie replies. 'We really *did* just swing by to scope Benjamin out on our way to dinner. You wanna come with?'

It's a turn of phrase that no matter how much she loves the speaker, always grates on Fia a tiny bit.

'Oh, we ordered some food when we arrived,' she says. 'Sliders and wings and whatever. I don't think I could eat another thing.'

'Cool. So, you're gonna . . . stay here, then,' Kavita concludes, as though there is something extremely meaningful about this decision.

Fia ignores the smile twitching on her roommate's lips, strives to keep her tone extra casual in response. 'Um, yeah. Y'know. I'll probably just . . . stay for one more and then head home.'

And she doesn't look at Benjamin when she says it. Of course she doesn't. The not looking at him, though – the very deliberately, definitely, wouldn't even dream of looking at him . . . part of Fia can't help but suspect that might be an even worse sign.

Chapter Twenty-Six

One drink turns, as it so often does, into a couple more than one. Still, though, Fia manages to make an exit before midnight. It's muggy on the street outside, and of course there is the usual amount of revelry and traffic. Compared with the heat and the concentrated din of the bar, though, it feels like a relief.

She's at the corner of Bryant Park, on the lookout for a cab, when she senses him approaching. And, truthfully, that's what it has felt like all night, in the hours since Annie and Kavita left. She and Benjamin haven't had deep and meaningful conversations – in fact, surrounded as they have been by lots of other people, they've barely had anything that could be called a conversation at all. However, all the while, there has been something – just a certain awareness. Fia had actually forgotten about that – about the fact that for a brief time in her life, across the summer of 2015, the first thing she could have said about any room was whether or not Benjamin Lowry was in it. Such was the degree to which he . . . *aggravated* her.

'You headed home?' he asks, once he gets near enough to be heard. And without the presence of other, much more inebriated people to skew the data range, he does sound a little buzzed now. Fia realizes that, undeniably, she is probably in the same state herself.

'Yep,' she replies. 'You?'

'Yep.'

If this strikes Fia as coincidental (which it certainly does), she elects not to mention it. For a moment or two, they stand alongside each other on the corner – she attempting to flag a cab heading Uptown on 6th Avenue, his attention on the cars going across town on 42nd Street.

It doesn't necessarily feel as though either of them is doing their best work on that front, though. A taxi with its light on actually whizzes right past Benjamin, because his arm is raised so half-heartedly.

'So, you looking forward to getting back to Ireland?' he asks, conversationally.

'Yeah.'

'To see your *special friend*,' he prompts, and although she can see now that his opening gambit wasn't just conversational at all – it was a trap – something about his goofiness makes it hard for Fia to stay serious.

She gives it a solid attempt, though. 'Ryan and I are *co-workers*,' she replies.

'Well, that's a relief. I mean' – he holds his hands up, as though by way of a disclaimer – 'I'm just thinking of you, here. Ryan *Sieman?*'

It takes her a second to catch his meaning. 'Oh, hilarious, yes,' she says then, deadpan. 'It sounds like semen.'

'Literally exactly like it,' he replies, nothing short of gleefully.

She rolls her eyes – although, again, she just can't quite seem to fully commit to disdain. 'I might have known that would appeal to your sophisticated sensibilities.'

'Come on! It's not a good name,' he protests laughingly, as Fia does her best to remain po-faced.

'. . . You're telling me you'd want to be Mrs Sieman?' he presses.

'Like I said, Ryan and I are co-workers, so that's not really a relevant question,' she replies. And then, because she can't help it, because he really seems almost to have purposefully set her up for it: 'But I have to say, at this point, if it's a choice between that and being Mrs Lowry . . .'

Even as he grins, Benjamin clutches at his chest like he's been shot. 'Oh, Fia! You wound me!' he exclaims, and Fia lets herself laugh out loud, at last. She just can't seem to help it.

'So, your roommates . . . at this point, I should just take it that they know everything about me, huh?' he asks, after a moment.

She studies him for a second, to work out if he's genuinely annoyed. He doesn't seem to be, though. So, her response comes casually. 'Whatever *I* know about you, *they* know about you, yeah,' she replies. She's beginning to suspect that, for all his many friends and acquaintances, there might actually be very few people who know Benjamin Lowry all the way. The tidbits of information he offered last night, on the rooftop, don't seem to have satisfied her at all. If anything, they have only *increased* her curiosity about him.

It is at this point that one of the most undeniably impressive things she's ever seen in her life occurs. With a brief glance out into the traffic, Benjamin spots his mark, and suddenly he lets out a shrill whistle. No fingers to his lips, no apparent effort whatsoever, and yet – like magic – the yellow cab coming across 42nd Street pulls over, slows to a stop a few feet away.

Benjamin doesn't immediately go towards it, though. Instead, with a brief gesture to the driver that he's on his way, he veers in her direction. She's about to comment on the whole display – how could she not? – but he gets in there first.

'You know what, Fia?' he says, and he has ended up pretty close to her now. A few more inches, she realizes, and she'd probably be able to feel his breath. 'The thing is, we can do all this,' he says quietly, with a vague gesture between the two of them. 'It's fun, or it's fucking irritating, or it's both. Whatever.'

She watches his Adam's apple bob, feels him move just fractionally closer into her space, notices how his voice drops even further until it's little more than a murmur.

'But let's not pretend I couldn't have you begging inside about a minute.'

Fia's breath hitches in her chest, and she finds herself frozen – powerless to deny or confirm or even to look away from him. And probably the noise of the city does *not* dampen, as though she's been suddenly plunged underwater; probably all the surrounding activity does *not* smudge into a blur, and time does *not* suspend – but, standing there, with Benjamin, it feels an awful lot like that.

She doesn't know if it's a relief or a let-down when he turns away from her at last. She seems to hear her own exhale inside her head, slow and tremulous as he strides off towards his cab.

When he opens the door, though, he stands back from it, holding it out. He has, apparently, hailed this cab for her. It occurs to Fia that perhaps his purpose out here in the first place – or, at least, one of them – has been to make sure she gets home safely.

She is gobsmacked, on just about every level a person can be gobsmacked, and she makes her way over to the taxi as if she's operated by a remote control. As she slides into the backseat, he lingers, his hand resting on the doorframe.

In the circumstances, part of Fia wouldn't be at all surprised if Benjamin intended on following her into this car, and again, she cannot honestly say how she feels about such a prospect, how she might respond to it. However, he makes no move to join her. He just looks down at her. She realizes that she must, in turn, be looking up at him.

'I mean, I'm not saying the reverse isn't true,' he continues, in that same quiet, almost pragmatic, tone of voice. 'The reverse is definitely true. We both know that, too.'

And then he closes the door, gives the roof a quick tap by way of signal to the driver. Fia watches him through the window for a second until it strikes her that her face could very well be flushing, betraying her somehow.

She turns instead to stare resolutely forwards, every part of her abuzz as the car speeds off into the night.

Chapter Twenty-Seven

In an ideal world, Fia might have taken the following day off work – lengthened an already long weekend. However, her period of annual leave in Dublin is fast approaching. She is conscious of the backlog that cannot be cleared, but must at least be reduced, before she goes. Furthermore, there's an element of laying the groundwork to be done; people could feel very let down – practically slapped in the face, digitally speaking – by an unforeseen *out of office* response. Hence, she's at her desk as promptly as ever on Friday morning, nose to the grindstone.

She is at least spared the hangover that some of her co-workers appear to be contending with – in the break room during the mid-morning coffee rush, the residual alcohol and anguish seems to seep from their very pores.

It's the hottest day of the year so far, and in response, building management have gone with their usual strategy, which is to crank the a/c all the way up. The height of summer often makes for a very tricky wardrobe situation at ZOLA, with staff thus forced to choose between dressing for their commute (hotter than a furnace) or their workplace (chilled to morgue levels).

By noon, Fia's reaching absently for her pashmina, wrapping it tightly around herself, when a red alert pops up on her computer screen.

Serve Alyvia Chestnut response and counterclaim, it says, and she switches over to her calendar, a little startled. How can it be time to do that already? She thought she had ages yet.

She tenses a little, steels herself to break the news to her office-mate.

'Hey, Benjamin?' she begins, and in the corner, he glances up at her.

Suddenly, Fia's a slightly different sort of tense. After last night, things between the two of them are different, in a way that is undeniable and that neither of them have mentioned so far today. Fia isn't sure how she would put it into words, even if she wanted to.

She could tell him, perhaps, that what he said to her was extremely unprofessional – she is his mentor, and they have to work together, and he has put her in a difficult position.

She could tell him that he's created a lot of unnecessary complication in the midst of a situation – namely their secret marriage and equally secret and ongoing divorce – that they agreed to keep as simple as possible.

Can she tell him, though, that he was wrong – that the things he said were untrue?

At least in her own mind, Fia has to admit that she probably cannot. And there's just something about him having said the quiet part out loud. It can't be taken back.

She's maybe been looking at him for a couple of seconds too long now, and he's looking right back at her, a hint of a smile on his face as though he can read her mind. She swallows, tries to refocus on the matter at hand.

'Uh . . . so, the thing is, I actually need to serve our response to Jonathan Chestnut today,' she tells him. 'Or next week, latest. If we wait 'til I'm back from Ireland, we're going to be time-barred, and he'll get a default judgment.'

Admitting it aloud, Fia winces slightly. For her to be caught on the hop like this, saved only by the gods of technology . . . that's actually not especially unusual. Despite her best efforts, so often she seems to fall short – to avoid a fuck-up by no more than a hair's breadth. Of course, that's not always a question of her own failings. Part of it's just about the volume of cases, the pace of things. Sometimes, in her job, it's impossible to be anything but reactive.

On this occasion, though, she isn't the only one affected. Whether she likes it or not, there seem to be two of them involved now, and Fia can't help but curse herself all the more for that. Even last night, when she and Benjamin talked about the Chestnut case, no part of her thought they were running out of time.

Across the room, Benjamin seems to be putting the pieces together. 'So, we can't wait 'til Alyvia comes in again – with Gus – after all?' he asks.

Fia winces again. ''Fraid not.'

Benjamin says nothing. And, as the seconds tick by, the rant she'd imagined would surely follow doesn't come. She can tell by looking at him, though, that he's far from thrilled.

'I'll tell you what,' she says, and how it has reached this point – the point at which she is willing to appease him, treat him like an equal – she has no idea. 'I'll deny the adultery on Alyvia's part. And on the other stuff – our counterclaims about the online harassment – I'll try to be vague. I just need to serve *something* before the deadline. We can always amend it down the line if necessary.'

Benjamin looks sceptical. 'Mmm. I'm not sure how you can accuse this guy of being an online troll and sabotaging his family while also, like . . . *not* accusing him of it.'

'Are you joking? Ben, we're lawyers – that's literally what we do.'

He sniggers, his resistance seeming to melt a little before her eyes. 'Okay, cool,' he replies then. 'Yeah. Try to curb your sharklike tendencies.'

'I'll see what I can do,' she says, and as she looks back at her computer screen, she can feel the little smile on his lips – it's the same one that's pulling at hers.

At this point, she knows she probably won't start the actual drafting until next week. She may even do it over the weekend, such are the extent of her Fourth of July plans. In the meantime, it occurs to her that, with Benjamin so focused on Alyvia, she might be wise to do a little digging on Jonathan Chestnut herself. While she's not as talented an online sleuth as many others of her generation – she's sure her sister, Maeve, could rival MI5 for the speed, depth and discretion of her investigations – she's not totally incapable.

A ton of people come up when she googles Jonathan's name, but it's the image search that ultimately leads right to her source. In seconds, she spots a picture of him, Alyvia and Gus as a toddler, all of them grinning at Coney Island. It's not quite the aesthetic of BabyGAndMe – even the *perfectly imperfect, Instagram versus reality* posts from Alyvia have a cultivated quality to them. This one is just a family, unfiltered, at the funfair. It makes Fia a little sad to look at it.

Jonathan himself apparently uploaded this photo to his Facebook account, and Fia pulls up the full profile, hoping for the best. There really is no predicting the permissions that other people might have set or failed to set on their social media accounts. Sadly, what new information she can glean about Jonathan Chestnut turns out to be fairly limited. He went to Rutgers University, he works for Bank of America and, six years ago, he contributed to someone's JustGiving campaign in aid of the Alzheimer's Association.

Added to that, one more photo – a much more recent one – is visible. It's been taken at the beach and shows a man's legs – Jonathan's, presumably – with a woman's, intertwined. **My love**, he's captioned it.

The woman isn't identifiable, but her skin tone, her body shape and the date all combine to let Fia know that it's not Alyvia. *Interesting*, Fia thinks. So, Alyvia was right about that one – for a guy who is accusing his wife of cheating, he certainly hasn't hung around.

Fia's own Facebook profile has been dormant for some time, used now exclusively by aunts sending birthday wishes. Absently, she scrolls through her newsfeed, coming upon names she hasn't seen or thought of in years – people she knew at school, people who once briefly dated some of her friends.

She looks up George for some reason, even though she never knew George to be active on Facebook. And, sure enough, there is nothing recent to see there, no hint at whatever life George might be living now – where or with whom. So, that's that.

In any event, it's unclear exactly how Fia ends up in the precise corner of this website that she eventually does. She's been looking over an old chat with her sister, chucking internally at the text abbreviations they used back then, when somehow or other she finds herself faced with a list of private messages she's never seen before. Most of them are of the *singles in your area* or the *one weird trick to reduce belly fat* variety. But then, in the midst of them, a name catches her eye. It takes a second for her to properly register it, in this context. There's just a certain degree of incongruity, like seeing one's teacher turn up in a H&M. She squints, making sure she hasn't misread.

Benjamin Lowry, it says.

Instinctively, Fia looks over at the man himself, opening her mouth to get his attention. Equally instinctively, though, she soon thinks better of it. Her breath suspends in mid-air as he types away on his keyboard, oblivious, and she shuts her mouth again like a goldfish. She leans forwards a little in her chair, feeling her heart speed up when she sees the litany of messages.

There's no profile picture on the account, just a generic, greyscale silhouette – and, when she clicks on his name, she can see he has no Facebook posts, no friends. As far as she can see, the communication with her constitutes Benjamin's only activity on the site. She scrolls all the way back to the first attempt at contact. It is, she notes immediately, dated just nine months after the two of them got hitched.

15/05/2016, 18:24

Hi Fia – hope you're good. You might have noticed some missed calls from me this past week. I know we talked about waiting a year before we settled things after what happened in LV. But, actually, I'm thinking maybe we should just go ahead and deal with it now? Not sure if you already have a lawyer on your side of the pond, but if not, maybe you would have a think about who you'll want to use, and let me know. Like I said, I know we talked about waiting, but on reflection, I think that might have just been a really dumb idea (I know, I know, MY really dumb idea). I can handle things on this end with my mom. Benjamin

As Fia reaches the end of the message, it's now almost impossible for her to stay quiet. Some exclamation of disbelief or the demand for an explanation is on the very tip of her tongue. Again, though, the greater part of her seems somehow to know that she should hold off. She has, after all, plenty more reading to be getting on with.

22/05/2016, 21:05

Hey Fia – just checking to see if you've had a chance to think about this? I know you weren't totally sold on the whole 'waiting' thing anyhow, so I'm assuming you'll be fine with getting the show on the road. Why postpone the inevitable, right? Have you managed to track down a lawyer yet? I'll probably use a guy named Fred Malcolm – he's at the firm of Malcolm, Jones and Frankfurt here in Durham, NC. I've made him aware of our situation, and he's happy to have a quick chat with whoever you're using, just to go over the process. Apparently, it could be a little slower with you being outside of the US, but obviously we can't do anything about that. Ben

25/05/2016, 17:11

Fia – I'm not gonna lie, I'm starting to get a little worried that I haven't heard from you. Is everything okay? I called your cell a couple more times today, but no reply.

That's the whole reason I set up this Facebook account, even though I really genuinely believe Mark Zuckerberg is the devil in a pair of loafers. Anyhow, if it's a financial issue on your end, I can figure it out and cover the costs. My main thing right now is just to get this handled as soon as possible. I've actually been seeing someone for the past couple of months and, as you can imagine, being married to somebody else – even if just on paper – really isn't ideal.

27/05/2016, 03:44

You know I can see your status updates, right? I know you're on here. You can post thirty pictures of your friends at some stupid bar, and yet you can't reply to me? Nice.

20/06/2016, 16:45

Okay, Fia. We've run the gamut here – I've been polite, I've been confused, I've been friendly, I've been angry. I'm gonna try laying it all out on the table. Seven months ago, I met a girl. Her name is Jessy. She's a history major here at Duke University, and she's the worst cook you've ever met in your life, and I'm crazy about her. I've never felt this way about anybody. But every time I look at her, I feel like I'm lying to her a little bit. The thought of telling her I already have a divorce under my belt before even graduating college kind of kills me inside, but the thought of telling her I'm still married is so, so much worse. I just don't want anything to jeopardize what we have, and I don't want there to be anything that stops our relationship moving forward. I guess it's like they say – when you know, you know. And Jessy and I are both all in with this thing.

The situation between you and me is my baggage to deal with, not Jessy's. I need you to help me deal with it, though. I've tried to give you some space – obviously I don't know what shit you might have going on in your own life right now – but I'm feeling the weight of this whole mess more and more every day. I don't care about my mom or her campaign or the money or any of it. I just want us to be divorced. Please get in touch. I'll try calling you again this week if I don't hear from you here.

02/07/2016, 11:38

Have you changed your number? I guess that's probably clutching at straws given, you know, ALL THE ABOVE. Blanking me on this is just so low, Fia. One thing I know for sure is that you don't want to be married to me. But the fact that I don't want to be married to you . . . that's what's going to make you cling on, isn't it? I get it, that's kind of how things were with us. But this really isn't a game anymore. It's just not an opportunity for you to get the upper hand. I want to move on with my life and propose to my girlfriend. Literally not sure how much clearer I can make that. Can you imagine if the situation were reversed, if you were the one left contacting me over and over, wondering where to go next? 'Cause I can. You would be having a fit.

02/07/2016, 11:45

I feel like I need to tell Jessy, one way or another. Keeping this a secret is killing me, and she's starting to see that something's up. I have no idea how she's going to take it. You are seriously just blowing my fucking mind with this, Fia. I thought you were a lot of things, but I didn't think you were cruel.

02/07/2016, 11:46

Please.

At last, Fia finishes, her heart going a mile a minute now. She tries to drag the cursor downwards, as though more will magically appear. It doesn't, though. That single word – dating back seven years, almost to the day, is all she's left with.

She knows that the time for restraint, for information gathering, is over now. It's time to talk to Benjamin. And, handily or horrendously, he's sitting only four feet away.

But, still, when she opens her mouth, she just can't seem to find the words.

Chapter Twenty-Eight

For hours and hours, Fia says nothing. This is not because she is figuring out how best to broach the subject or preparing any sort of grand speech in her mind – not at all. Lunchtime comes and goes, the afternoon hours beginning to slip away, too, and all the while, even so much as an opening gambit seems to be entirely beyond her.

'My God, it's like a tundra in here!' Benjamin mumbles at some stage, with a sudden shiver, and she can manage only a weak smile in response.

If she weren't so distracted, Fia's sure she would be beside herself by now, wondering how it was possible for Benjamin Lowry to say what he said to her just last night, and then to make small talk with her today. Was he waiting for *her* to mention it? Maybe, if things were different, she *would* have mentioned it by now.

As it is, she's stumbled upon a few other places to put her attention.

'Hey, Ben?' she begins, seized with a sudden burst of bravery.

As he looks over at her expectantly, though, she senses herself freeze again. She considers a swift retreat. She could wait for a better time to do this, she thinks; she could wait for a more natural way into the whole subject . . .

But then, she suspects she would be waiting a very long time.

'I got your messages,' she blurts out, dearly hoping this one sentence might be all that's required. Alas, however, she watches as confusion spreads across his face. '. . . The ones on Facebook?' she continues uncertainly. 'From, like . . . a while back?'

'Oh.' He shifts a little in his seat, as realization dawns. 'That . . . you can just ignore those,' he says gruffly.

'No, but I . . . what I mean to say is that I *just* got them. They were in some kind of secondary inbox thing, I think because they didn't come from a friend, or . . . anyway, that's not important. The point is I . . . well, obviously I would have replied if I'd seen them at the time.'

For a long moment, there is silence. Fia braces herself for disbelief, for confusion, for anger.

But then, at last, he speaks. 'It's cool,' is all he says, and he averts his eyes, suddenly fascinated by his computer screen.

Whatever else this situation is, Fia can sense it is not – not even remotely – *cool*. By now, she's spent the better part of the last four hours reading and rereading Benjamin's messages, as though she might find some new clarity in any specific word choice – in the time stamps, maybe, or the punctuation.

Needless to say, there is nothing. And, on one level, that is probably just as well. It's destabilizing enough, to find herself on the receiving end of what can only be described as the modern iteration of long-lost letters. For there to be some sort of hidden meaning, a secret code contained within them . . . that might push her over the edge altogether.

Instead, she's reached for logic, lined up a list of the things she knows are true:

Shortly after their lives intersected at Camp Birchwood – and more notably in Las Vegas – Benjamin Lowry fell in love.

He tried and failed to contact her via Facebook and appeared convinced that she was deliberately ignoring his messages.

He called her on the phone, too – via a number that, yes, she remembered now, she *had* changed shortly after she got back to Dublin that September. Her shiny new job gave her a shiny new Blackberry, all texts and calls included, and Fia didn't see the need to keep paying for her own separate contract, much less lug two devices around with her.

Armed with this information, Fia has some new insight into Benjamin's weirdness this summer, when it came to any mention of *his* noncommunication. But then, *why* was he like that? Why did he not simply confront her right away? Why didn't he say 'before you even thought about contacting me, I was doing my damnedest to contact *you*'? It made absolutely no sense. If there's one thing she's absolutely never known Benjamin to do, it is let her off easy.

And, if he was every bit as keen as her to get divorced – seemingly more so – why didn't he respond when she began to reach out to him? The very first day he arrived here at ZOLA, he outright admitted to having deliberately ignored her attempts at contact. Yet, between his very last message to her and her very first to him, she'd guess there might have been no more than six weeks.

Then, of course, there is the Jessy of it all. Benjamin is not with her now – that much is obvious. But why? Did she find out about Las Vegas – about the wife Benjamin not only acquired but seemed powerless to get shot of – and bail?

That's absolutely what Fia would have advised, were she one of Jessy's friends back then.

In any case, what Fia knows for sure is that Benjamin loved this person. And he lost her. The thought of that – the guilt of it – makes Fia feel sincerely queasy now.

'No, but I just . . . I really want you to know that this wasn't, like, a "mark as unread" situation, you know?' she continues disjointedly, looking over at him in the office. 'This was an *actually* unr—'

'Fia,' he interrupts, the sharpness in his tone unmistakable, 'I said it's cool, okay? Whatever. I'm over it.' He looks pointedly around the office and out to the atrium. 'I don't think we need to get into that shit here, do you?'

'Okay. Do you want to . . . I don't know – go for lunch? Or we probably are due a mentor-mentee catch-up anyway, we could go and grab a coffee right n—'

He interrupts her this time with a hollow laugh. 'Mentor-mentee catch-up! My God, Fia! You really just can't take no for an answer, can you? I *don't want to talk about this with you*,' he says, enunciating each word deliberately. 'I'm not in the market for your *mentorship* here. Is that so impossible to understand?'

Fia feels the question land like an assault. In the time they've spent together in this office – and for that matter, out of it – she's seen Benjamin Lowry sarcastic and frustrated and tired and bored and all kinds of other things . . . but never quite *this* – whatever exactly this is.

And the thing is that everyone, when they begin to feel attacked, has some response they reach for right away: counter-aggression, maybe, or silence or humour. Fia's tendency – she knows this about herself – is towards haughtiness. She can hear that high-and-mighty tone in her own voice when she replies.

'Well! I think it's perfectly reasonable for me to ask why you didn't just *tell* m—'

'Oh my God, *you*!' he explodes, having apparently tipped just past the point of restraint. 'You, you, you! Sorry – you don't actually get to be in control on this one, Fia! I can imagine it's a shock to the system.'

'What?!' she fires back, and it seems like this might be the first thought he actually lets her finish. 'Okay, at what point since you walked into my office unannounced has it seemed like I've been in control of *anything*, Ben? Do you think I wanted *any* of this?'

Both his eyebrows shoot upwards, and he leans back a little in his chair, as though he's settling in to queue up Netflix, as if he knows this is the thing that irritates her most of all – when he affects nonchalance.

'Oh, you want to have that same fight again?' he asks. 'Cool, that's always a fun one.'

For the moment that follows, though, neither of them say anything, tension pulsing between them like a heartbeat. Fia doesn't know how things have ended up this way – how the conversation seems to have spiralled so swiftly, so completely, out of her control.

'You know, you're exactly how you've always been?' he continues then, and it's almost conversational, the way he says it. Were it not for that slight edge in his voice, she might think he were discussing the weather, the traffic, the price of a flat white these days.

'And how's that?' she asks. A glutton for punishment. 'How have I always been?'

He seems to cast around a bit, as though desperately searching for the words, as though he is fit to burst, this office suddenly far too small to contain him. '. . . Aggravating!' he lands on at last. 'You are the most *aggravating* person I've ever met, Fia. You want to hear me say it? Fine. I never should have come to work at ZOLA. That first morning, I should have fucking hightailed it out of this building the second I saw you and never looked back.'

'You think?' she tosses out caustically, but he doesn't even pause to acknowledge it.

'So, there we have it,' he concludes instead. 'You were right, again. You're the victim, again. Wow, we got back there fast, didn't we? Crazy how nothing's ever really your fault, huh? Nothing's ever your choice.'

Fia feels the burn of that. Of course she does. She's a person. But she pushes it down, argues this one like a lawyer. 'What? I'm confused. Ten seconds ago, I was a controlling psychopath – now I never take responsibility for anything? I don't know how I can be both?'

'I don't know either, Fia, but somehow you fucking manage it!'

'Well, hey. I thought we'd wait 'til the end of the summer, but if we're doing feedback now, then *you*, Benjamin . . . I don't even know where I would start with you! You are entitled, you're flighty, yo—'

'Yeah, yeah, I get it. You've always made it perfectly clear what you think of me – don't worry,' he mutters.

Another beat of silence follows, during which Fia's eyes dart out into the atrium, all too rapidly recalling they might have an audience here. With the door closed, she's pretty sure they can't be heard. Through all that glass, though, they can certainly

224

still be observed. Fortunately, nobody appears to be paying them much notice.

'I'm going to call Susan Followill today,' Benjamin says then, newly decisive, 'tell her we're not doing any more stupid meetings. She can't make us. Have you sent back your paperwork?'

'Of course I have.'

'Of course you have,' he repeats, with a joyless little laugh. 'Me too. So, what more is there to say? Susan can send us the marital settlement agreement by email, we'll approve it by email too, and then she needs to just go ahead and submit everything to the judge. That's what we're paying her for.'

Fia lets her eyes widen, as if in naivety, in genuine surprise. 'But, Benjamin, I didn't think you were a fan of lawyers who just filled out the forms? I thought you were all about digging down into the mess, exploring it from all angles, you know – dragging it out to serve your own ego?'

He doesn't take the bait. Oddly, more so than anything else, that's how she knows: things are really bad here.

'We're a special case,' is all he says, sourly. 'If I have to go up there and courier those papers to the courthouse myself before we leave for Dublin, I will. I don't know what in the hell I've been thinking with you, this pas—' He pauses, cuts himself off, takes a breath in and out. 'Bottom line? A few more weeks, and you and I will never have to see each other again.'

Fia's eyes narrow. 'Do you promise?'

If he remembers that old exchange – such a long time ago now, in his little bedroom at Camp Birchwood – no part of him shows it. Instead, he turns away from her. Very clearly, he has decided that they've reached the end of this particular conversational road.

Fia snaps her head in the other direction, too, staring briefly at nothing but a blank wall.

By the time she glances back over at Benjamin, a few seconds later, he is clutching his mouse in a death grip, and she has the sense that she could be on *fire* over here, and still, he wouldn't so much as look in her direction.

She turns back to her computer, pulling up Alyvia Chestnut's file.

Perhaps, she thinks, she *won't* put this one off until after the weekend. Perhaps – her fingers are already flying across the keyboard, as if of their own accord – she will draft her reply to Jonathan Chestnut right now.

And, suddenly, she is in no mood to pull any punches. If she cannot scream from the rooftops everything she'd currently like to say about her own husband – if, *in the spirit of collaboration and non-adversarial resolution, blah blah blah*, she cannot even commit those grievances to writing . . . well. Somebody else's husband will have to do.

WEEK FIVE

Chapter Twenty-Nine

It's always interesting to Fia, the variety of ways in which people dress for the airport.

In her direct line of vision in the departure lounge of JFK, there are travellers who, upon arrival at their destination, could head straight to a boardroom. Right alongside them are people who are head-to-toe beach-ready, and a few others who wouldn't look hugely out of place in a nightclub.

Generally speaking, Fia has a very definite airport aesthetic, which – if she were called upon to describe – she might characterize as 'on the way to the hospital to undergo major surgery.' Maybe even 'on the way home from the hospital after major surgery'.

The point is, she likes to be comfortable. Style typically doesn't come into it whatsoever. Sadly, on this occasion, given the presence of everyone she works with, she's had to step it up a little – quite a big ask, given she left her apartment at 4.30 a.m. In the darkness of her bedroom, she plumped for a stretchy cotton maxi dress and flat trainers, and now, yawning into her coffee at the airport, she idly assesses the outfits of whatever female co-workers are around.

As for the sartorial choices of her male co-workers, she really has no interest in those. Obviously, she spotted Benjamin earlier, as they all stood in line at check-in – she briefly took in his jeans and T-shirt. Nothing special. Still, though. How maddening that despite everything that went down between them last week, she hadn't been able to help seeking out that little mental note, filing it away. By this stage of the summer, in the course of various activities and events, she has had time to notice how Benjamin's clothes always seem to hang just right on him, no matter what he wears.

After their bust-up on Friday came the reprieve of the four-day weekend. Kavita and Annie having both left to celebrate American independence with their families, Fia had the apartment to herself the whole time. On an ordinary weekend, she wouldn't have minded that one bit. In fact, for the rest of the year, it almost never happens, and sometimes she veritably longs for it. The Fourth of July can be a bit of a tricky one, though.

Is it that Fia has a strong desire to put on some stars-and-stripes clothing, have a barbecue? Not really. Having never celebrated the holiday growing up, she has no particular affection for it, no nostalgia for its traditions.

Nonetheless, there turns out to be a slight sense of loss, of inadequacy, when everyone else has a plan and you do not. Everyone Fia knows well is either American or – in a few instances – in a committed relationship with an American, such that they have some natural place at their partner's family celebrations. Not so for her. And, George aside, she has never much wanted to be a friend's plus one, imagining she'd feel unavoidably like a hanger-on.

Of course, had she made more effort to specifically befriend other immigrants in the city, it would probably have been different. She could have spent this past weekend in Central Park, cosplaying Americanness with a bunch of fellow Irish people. As it is, she spent most of the weekend by herself, just doing her ordinary things. That was the best way. The year she went to watch the fireworks over the Brooklyn Bridge, stood in the crowds with everyone else, it somehow only made the sense of loneliness even more acute.

After that – after a whole four days of stewing by herself, of trying and failing to distract herself from certain recent developments – she and Benjamin had only one day to endure together in the office yesterday. He made it his business to be elsewhere as much as possible – as, for that matter, did she. To the extent they overlapped, communication was sparse – terse. It was every bit as bad as their very first week together in the office, if not even worse.

And now, this morning, he hasn't said a single word to her for the entire time they've been at JFK.

Of course, plenty of other people haven't said a word to Fia either – there must be fifty of ZOLA's lawyers milling around the departure lounge, killing time before boarding. But, just as Benjamin's was the appearance she'd noticed, his is the silence she's noticed. She tries hard not to think about what the significance of that – if any – might be.

The flight, when at last they get to it, is more or less uneventful. Fia is seated beside a guy from the banking team whom she barely knows, and he makes his intentions clear from the outset via a monstrous pair of noise-cancelling headphones. It could seem quite hostile – the implication that *she* is the noise he wishes to cancel – but, in fact, it comes as a complete relief to Fia. Freed from the need to make small talk, she watches a mediocre film and picks at her in-flight meal. Below her armrest, the socked foot of a stranger appears from the seat behind, rotating unappealingly at intervals. A second mediocre film and one fitful nap later, and all of a sudden, the captain has switched the seatbelt sign back on. Their tray tables need to be stowed; the toilets are no longer in use.

It's 8 p.m. local time when they land at Dublin Airport, but still broad daylight outside. And, though the air is chilly as they all troop down the aeroplane steps, it's light and fresh – gloriously free of Manhattan's humidity. Fia feels, in that same fundamental, cellular way she always does, happy to be home.

Inside the arrivals lounge, her eyes dart about, relieved to find no sign of her mam and dad. She had strong, repeated words with them to the effect that she did not need them to pick her up from the airport this time, and thankfully, they seem to have heeded her. That collision of worlds would just have been too discombobulating – probably at any time, but especially after such an early start, such a long flight. And, needless to say, there is one co-worker in particular whom she's very keen for her parents never to so much as lay eyes on.

The Summer Summit is taking place at a big hotel outside Dublin proper, near the coast, and as everyone else from ZOLA boards coaches bound for Garrett Castle, Fia says her goodbyes, then jumps in a taxi. It's an expensive option, but she barely registers it. At this point, she is used to things costing so much more than it seems they have any right to. Only days ago, at the Whole Foods on 86th Street, she spent $10 on a punnet of raspberries. So, she just taps her card on the machine as the driver at last slows to a stop on a familiar street, outside a familiar red-bricked semi. Already, she can see a face at the living room window, and Fia feels another unexpected well of emotion, just at the thought that her mother has been looking out for her, waiting for her.

Of course, she's made this journey back to Dublin a fair few times by now. She's not sure why she seems to feel like such a wreck this time around. It might be the tumult of the past five weeks – that seems reasonable – or it might be the tumult of the past few *days*. That feels a lot less reasonable – the notion that a falling-out with Benjamin Lowry, of all people, would leave her feeling fragile and off-kilter. Hasn't she more or less been in one long falling-out with Benjamin Lowry for the guts of the past decade? Why would this latest conflict be any different?

In any case, she's home now, at long last. The front door is opening before Fia's even out of the car, and her father is rushing out to help the driver with her suitcase. He gives her a smile and a little pat on the shoulder.

'Flight all right?' he asks.

'Yep, it was perfect,' she replies, leaning forwards to kiss him on the cheek.

This is his way of saying that he could not be more delighted to have her home, and her way of saying that she could not be more delighted to be here.

With her mother, meanwhile, these sentiments are exchanged much more literally, and Fia lets herself be wrapped in a big hug, ushered inside.

In the living room, she finds Maeve, and they each let out an involuntary little squeal of delight, rushing towards each other.

'Oh my God, you're here!' Fia exclaims.

Maeve still lives at home, but she spends plenty of nights at her boyfriend's place, too, so, Fia didn't necessarily expect to see her immediately.

''Course I'm here – I wanted to be part of the welcoming committee, didn't I?'

They hug each other tight, and as they pull apart, Fia looks at her sister appraisingly.

'You look nice,' she says. 'I'm liking these jeans.'

A tell-tale pause follows.

'Do not tell me,' Fia warns then. 'Do *not*.'

'TK Maxx. Twenty euro, down from eighty-five!'

Fia shakes her head as if in disbelief, though she's smiling all the while. 'I swear to God – just tell me the stuff is from Anthropologie and have done with it, would you? It would make me happier. I've seriously never met anybody who's as lucky as you in that place.'

'It's not a question of luck, Fia,' Maeve corrects, and she's grinning, too. 'It's a question of *commitment*.'

They flop down on the sofa together – the same floral one that's been there since their childhood – their mother lingering in the door frame.

'Will you have a bit of dinner, Fia? Or a wee sandwich even?' she asks, her northern lilt as strong as ever, despite forty years down south. 'Did you get something to eat on the plane?'

'Mmm, not really,' Fia replies. She doesn't know that she could face a full meal right now, though. She has that unsettled feeling in her stomach that comes with having eaten odd things at odd times. 'A sandwich would be amazing.'

Her mam nods. 'I'll make you a wee cup of tea with it, will I?'

'Oh yeah, no odds about me, Mother,' Maeve chimes in, though her voice is all teasing, no malice.

'Sure, I'm never done making you cups of tea that you never drink!' their mother tosses back.

'I do! I drink at least half the cup all the time!' Maeve exclaims, laughing, and Fia's not entirely sure she gets the joke on this one. There's some inconsequential little snippet of history she might have missed.

In any event, their mother just tuts affectionately at Maeve. 'Come into the kitchen, the pair of you, and give us a bit of your craic from the big smoke, Fia,' she says. She makes her way through the hall, both girls following obediently as though they are children again. '. . . And Maeve might have a bit of news of her own, mightn't you, Maeve?'

'What is it?' Fia pounces, as Maeve just grins.

In the kitchen, their father already has the kettle on, and by the expression on his face, Fia suddenly has the unmistakable impression that everyone here knows something she doesn't.

When she turns back to Maeve, her sister is holding up her left hand, a diamond sparking on her ring finger. 'Conor proposed!'

'Oh my God!' Fia says, and she can only hope, in this moment, that her face looks right. She hopes it displays the sort of utter, unqualified joy that she could perhaps only really feel if she, herself, were already extremely happily married. As it is, she's sort of . . . the opposite. Right now, she feels like she'd be only too delighted never to hear the words *wedding, marriage, matrimony* or any variants for the rest of her natural life. That's probably a futile hope, though. Even setting aside the demands of her professional life, she's a woman with more or less her entire thirties ahead of her.

'It just happened last week, and I wanted to wait and tell you in person! Can you believe it?' Maeve exclaims.

There is no right answer to that one. *Yes, I've been expecting this every time you went on a mini-break for the past three years* and *No, this has come like a total bolt from the blue* would both seem inappropriate. Oddly, Fia feels like they are both sort of true.

'It's *so* great!' is what she settles for instead. And then – because this is what you say to people, even your own sister – 'Congratulations!'

'You'll be my chief bridesmaid, obviously.' Maeve beams, and Fia can only smile in return. Of course, she would want nobody else to fulfil that role for her only sister. But, equally, the thought of fulfilling it herself does make her feel a little . . . off balance, somehow.

'I have to say, Conor timed it well, all right,' their mam says, reaching for the bread in the cupboard. 'We're going to have a wee engagement party next Friday, just here at the house – take advantage of you being home to celebrate, Fia. Eoin's going to come up from Cork as well.'

'Oh, fab. I know how you like to have all your offspring under the one roof,' Fia says, slightly teasingly.

Her mother merely smiles in response. 'Ah well, you can laugh. But I'm telling you, it's the most contentment I ever feel in the world, when I know yous are all home and all safe.'

And, as it turns out, Fia can't find it in herself to come up with a silly reply to that. She can only offer a little smile of her own, a little nudge of a shoulder against her mother's. Every minute of the journey here – every minute of the boredom she'll have to endure at the Summer Summit, the potential weirdness with Benjamin fucking Lowry – feels suddenly well worth it.

Chapter Thirty

Garrett Castle is the sort of hotel that Fia thinks Ireland does particularly well: luxurious, but unpretentious. By now, thanks to her job, Fia has seen inside more fancy, five-star establishments than she once would have ever expected to. And she enjoys them – what's not to like? – but deep down, she's not sure she's a five-star person. She doesn't expect, or especially want, some minimum-wage employee to delicately place a napkin in her lap.

The Garrett Castle brand of things is more her style – which is to say, attentiveness that is warm, rather than subservient, in nature. It strikes her as what true hospitality should feel like. With turf fires in winter, unspoiled views and, of course, that grand facade with its turrets and battlements, it is the sort of place where one can rely on a good Sunday carvery, a little bit of whiskey in the porridge at breakfast, and nice hand creams in the bathrooms. What it must have cost for ZOLA to block book the hotel slap bang in the middle of wedding season, Fia dreads to think.

Although there's a bus from Dublin, her father insisted on giving her a lift down here this morning, and it felt so nice – having someone *insist* on making her life that little bit easier – that Fia didn't put up much of a protest.

By the time she makes her way into the hotel's function room, the day's programme is just about to begin. They're starting with the financials, apparently, then moving on to a series of addresses from the managing partners of each of the firm's four branches. Then . . . Fia's not sure. She didn't get that far in the email.

She lets her gaze scan the space, all set up for the occasion with chairs in concentric circles, a podium and a projector screen. The place is also swarming with people – several hundred of them, some looking more tired than others. Thankfully, Fia's never suffered much with jetlag herself. Quickly, she finds herself swallowed up into the melee, moving from one half-conversation to the next, exchanging greetings and promises to catch up properly later. While there are plenty of people here, especially from the San Francisco and London offices, whom she's never seen before in her life, there are lots of familiar faces, too.

It's always a little strange, at the Summer Summit, seeing those she used to work with at the Dublin office. Simultaneously, Fia is one of them and not one of them. Especially with the lawyers around her own age, she feels obliged to demonstrate that she hasn't, since flitting off to America, lost her accent or her interest in local happenings or otherwise become *up her own arse*. In conversation, she finds herself keen to make sure that they know that *she* knows that the whole New York business was just a matter of luck, really. There can be a fair bit of eye rolling on her part about the city and the work that she's not sure she entirely means.

Then, there are those who used to be her superiors at the Dublin office. Seeing them is weird, too, but in a different way. For a long time, Fia remained keen to impress them – on the assumption that, at some point, she'd be returned to their purview. Today, her former supervisor spots her almost as soon as she walks in the door. And, even as they catch up, exchanging tidbits of professional news, Fia is struck by how little she actually cares about what this man thinks of her now. Does that mean she's decided she's really never coming back to Dublin, she wonders? She's never made that mental leap consciously – but subconsciously?

In any event, the irony is that Damien McNulty – a man who once had her continually protest his entirely deserved parking fine for over a year, on the pretence that this constituted vital legal training – seems to be showing more interest in her than he ever has before. There's a certain comradery in his approach, maybe even something – dare she imagine it – slightly *deferential* in his tone as he congratulates her on a recent contentious case, one involving the sort of large estate that is commonplace in Manhattan and entirely unheard of anywhere on the island of Ireland.

It's all very peculiar, and Fia excuses herself, heading for the coffee station before the day kicks off properly. A long, white banqueting table has been set up in front of huge, floor-to-ceiling windows, and the woman ahead of Fia in line is staring out at the landscape.

'Some view, huh?' she says, in a broad American accent, and Fia looks outwards, too, as though seeing the place with new eyes: lush green hills in every direction and, in the distance, a blue strip of the sea. It *is* beautiful. She feels, in this moment, proud of it, as though somehow it reflects on her personally.

She's inordinately grateful that the weather looks set to hold up at least reasonably well.

'Well, look what the cat dragged in,' comes a voice from behind her then, and when she turns, Ryan Sieman is standing there, his arms already opening.

'Look what the dog threw up,' she tosses back, stepping into his hug. Driving down here this morning, Fia wondered when she might see him – *if* she'd see him.

'That's . . . gross,' he says as they pull apart, though judging by his grin, he's not too repulsed.

He's as attractive as he ever was, Fia notes: nice suit, nice face, nice aftershave. More than any of that, there's just something about Ryan that is, after several years of acquaintance by now, comforting – or maybe comforting is the wrong word. Familiar. She knows where she's at with this guy.

'And your thing wasn't?' she counters.

'My thing was a *common saying*,' he replies, and anything more she might offer is supplanted instead by a voice on a microphone, telling everyone to please take their seats for the first session.

'Suppose we better do what we're told,' Ryan says, once the announcement concludes.

Fia nods towards the banqueting table. There are only two people ahead of her, now. 'I'm going to hang on here for a sec, see if they'll take pity on me. But . . . I'm sure our paths will cross at some stage.'

'I'm sure they will. It's good to see you, Fia,' he says, meaningfully – flirtatiously.

'It's good to see you, too, Ryan,' she replies, a lot less meaningfully, and with a roll of her eyes to boot. But the whole effect, she would admit, is likely just as flirtatious.

And why should it not be? She's had a rough ride this past while, she tells herself. And her little sister has just got engaged, and it's hard to meet an attractive man – most men are just so incredibly easy *not* to have sex with – and there really is no reason why this Summer Summit cannot proceed exactly as all the others have done before it.

No reason whatsoever.

It is well after lunch by the time Fia realizes that Benjamin is not here. There are so many people, and there is so much movement among them all, that reaching this conclusion actually requires an inordinate amount of effort on her part. She dedicates the entire morning and a good part of the afternoon session to the investigation. Scanning the room subtly while a panel of speakers chat away about client-centric lawyering, she's finally able to move in her mind from *he must be around here somewhere* to *no, he definitely is not*.

She doesn't know quite how to feel about that.

Of course, rewinding just a few weeks, she hadn't wanted Benjamin anywhere near the Summer Summit. And, given how things have panned out between the two of them more recently, she's certain that were he here, he'd only be glowering at her from across the room or resolutely disregarding her.

Still, it's . . . unsettling, not knowing where he is.

By 7 p.m., however, Ryan is doing a remarkable job of distracting her. Once the buffet dinner arrived (and the bar opened), everyone began filtering out of the conference room, spreading out around the ground floor, finding surfaces on which to perch. Dotted among all the other little groups, Fia and Ryan have hit the jackpot with two plush wingback chairs in a bay window, paper plates of food in their laps.

As they chat away about work and life, she's struck again by the sense of ease with him. He tells her about some irritating client (an absolute *dose*) and another (a pure *chancer*), and Fia delights in the phrases, in the feeling that Ryan pours into them. In the US, she's often conscious of certain words, certain constructions, rubbing her up the wrong way. There's nothing wrong with them as such; she can use them and understand them, but they just don't quite feel like *hers*. In Ireland, by contrast, language always strikes her as delicious. She luxuriates in it, savours the way it all feels like it fits just right.

Eventually, their conversation meanders to the subject of upcoming summer holidays. Fia: none. Ryan: two weeks in Thailand.

'I just thought *feck it*, you know? What's the point of working if you can't enjoy yourself?' he says. 'Things have been so mental this past six months with the new financial regulations coming in and all the clients going up the wall and blah blah. It's been hard to fit in . . . anything else.'

'So, you're still single then,' Fia says, taking her cue from him – she wants explicit confirmation of the situation there, and they've always had the type of relationship whereupon there was no need to beat about the bush. Such short pockets of time together, at these Summer Summits, are simply not compatible with maintaining any air of mystery. By necessity, it is a cards-on-the-table approach. *I'll show you mine if you show me yours*, so to speak.

'Very single,' he confirms. 'Just can't seem to find the right girl, you know?' He says this last bit in the slightly ironic way that only a confident, attractive man can. 'The mother's nearly beside herself at this stage – doesn't know where she went wrong.

Will she ever have grandchildren? The whole shebang,' he continues, and Fia smiles.

'My sister's just got engaged actually,' she finds herself replying – and how funny to hear that aloud, like a perfectly ordinary fact.

'Oh, great stuff,' Ryan replies. 'That's brilliant news. What about you then? Don't tell me you've been swept off your feet by some big Yank at long last, have you?'

Fia's opening her mouth to respond when, in her pocket, her phone vibrates. *Unknown number*, the screen says when she looks at it. Nonetheless, at Ryan's urging, Fia accepts the call, lifting the phone to her ear.

'Is that Mrs Lowry?' comes an unfamiliar Irish accent on the other end of the line.

'No,' Fia replies, and the words *wrong number* are almost out of her mouth, too, before she realizes. Her voice lowers instinctively into the handset, even as she flashes Ryan a re-assuring smile. 'I mean, um, yes? Who's speaking?'

'This is Janette,' the caller replies. 'I'm one of the nurses at the Mater Hospital. I'm just giving you a ring about your husband.'

Chapter Thirty-One

Fia's jittery the whole way there, her mind zigzagging in all sorts of different directions even as the Friday evening traffic crawls. What's happened? And when and how and with what precise result?

It seems to take an absolute *age* to get back into Dublin and across the city, and when at last she makes it through the doors of Accident and Emergency, the whole place is rammed. All human life appears to be here – plus, in the far corner, a border collie, to boot. Several red-cheeked toddlers are screaming their heads off; the phone rings shrilly in reception, medical and domestic staff tripping over one another all the while. That there might be any actual *healing* going on in the middle of this seems so unlikely. But then, Fia supposes, that's hospitals.

It takes at least another fifteen minutes just to make herself known, to establish Benjamin's whereabouts.

'Round the corner, cubicle seven,' an orderly tells her eventually, and as Fia makes her way there, she can feel the unease in her chest ramp up another little bit.

Then, as she slips in past the cubicle's curtain, Benjamin appears in front of her at last. She lets herself take him in from head to toe.

'Oh my God, look at you!' she exclaims. She isn't sure what she was expecting – she just didn't know *what* to expect, really – and she isn't sure how to categorize the sensation that seems to flood through her entire body at the sight of him. He's sitting up on the bed, on top of the covers, still fully clothed. 'You look healthy as a fucking trout!' she all but yelps.

'Wow. Your concern is so touching,' Benjamin replies, deadpan. 'Honestly, dial it back a notch, will you? I can only cope with so much wifely affection from my sick bed.'

She huffs impatiently. 'I'm here, aren't I? I took a bus and then a DART and then I walked for fifteen minutes. If that's not wifely affection, I don't know what is!'

He says nothing, and Fia feels a little jolt of confusion, hearing her own words aloud. What she'd intended as a barb somehow seems to have got a bit mangled in the delivery.

'What happened anyway?' she continues, barking out the question, lest he seize upon any perceived weakness on her part. 'The woman on the phone just said you'd had an accident.'

For another second, silence. In truth, the nurse barely had the chance to say much more – Fia was in such a hurry just to *get here*, she didn't hang around on the phone for details. She sinks down into a hard seat at Benjamin's bedside, taking the opportunity to reinspect him, more carefully this time. There's a gash on his forehead, already cleaned and treated, from what she can tell – but no other injury or malady is visible to the naked eye.

'I don't want to talk about it,' Benjamin replies.

'You don't want to talk about it?' Fia's voice rises sarcastically, before dropping to a bitter chuckle. 'Figures. There's not much you want to talk about these days, is there?'

Benjamin ignores that altogether. 'I can't believe they called you,' he mutters, almost as though to himself.

Fia feels defensiveness surge in her anew. 'Oh, right. Charming! Magicked my number out of thin air, did they?'

'Well, you *are* my next of kin,' he grumps. 'I guess technically you're my next of kin anywhere, but this side of the Atlantic? Who else was I supposed to write on the form?' He pauses for breath. It would seem that he, too, feels somewhat on the defensive. 'They said they don't like to send people home alone with head injuries, and I said I was fine. I definitely didn't ask them to *summon* you. I've been here for like two hours and the first I heard of the whole thing was ten minutes ago when Janette said you were on your way.'

'Well, I'm here now,' Fia replies, the sentence superfluous even to her own ears. *Of course*, she thinks, Benjamin has managed to reach first name terms with the hospital staff in double-quick time. Of course, his appearance and his accent and his manner would combine to ensure that someone decided, entirely unbidden, to take him under her wing.

She says none of that aloud. In fact, neither she nor Benjamin say anything at all for a long moment. The silence stretches out between them as they each look here and there, anywhere to avoid one another's eyes.

He does not ask her to leave, though. And she doesn't make any move to. If Fia were asked to explain that, she'd be stumped on both fronts. Perhaps it is just that, as she said, she's here now.

'You weren't at the conference today,' she offers eventually, letting her gaze settle on him at last.

246

'Oh.' He sounds a little taken aback, as though it's odd she would even raise such a subject, as though his response is the most obvious, prosaic thing in the world – as though he surely could never have been expected to be there in the first place. 'No, I skipped it.'

'You *skipped it?*' she repeats dumbly.

'Well, it was pretty obvious when we arrived at the hotel last night to find literally *hordes* of lawyers – I don't actually think anyone is staying there who doesn't work at ZOLA – that I wasn't exactly going to be missed.'

On this point, he is entirely correct. Still, though, Fia's brain seems to be struggling to compute the concept.

'So, what? You just took off?'

'Pretty much. I mean, it's different for you – you're from here – but I'm probably never going to be in Ireland again in my life. Am I going to spend my day watching a bunch of presentations – most of which could have been emails – about a law firm I don't even permanently work for? Or am I going to get out and explore?'

And there was a time, long ago – and maybe even not so long ago – when Fia might have tutted at this, less because she actually disapproved than because it served to put Benjamin Lowry ever more squarely into the box that she'd assigned him: the pleasure-seeker who proved himself more irresponsible by the day.

And, in the present scenario, it is true that, one way or another, he does seem to have landed himself in A&E. But, nonetheless, listening to the rationale for his truancy, she cannot help but think that he probably has the exact right idea. Last year, at the Summer Summit in San Francisco, she could perhaps have simply taken herself off to Alcatraz one afternoon.

247

How has that not occurred to her before now? She wishes she *had* gone to Alcatraz. Certainly, the time she spent staring at profit projections in some conference room instead has left no impression, been of absolutely no benefit.

Her attention is caught, then, by some movement behind her. Fia twists in her seat to see a doctor emerge through the curtains, at least six different clipboards clutched in the crook of his arm. He looks barely more than 25, and – judging by the paleness of his face, the rings under his eyes – he's thoroughly exhausted. This whole environment frankly strikes Fia as one in which he could hardly be anything *but* thoroughly exhausted – harried. By comparison, the fifty-eighth floor of Zelnick, O'Leary and Abbott's Manhattan office actually feels like an incredibly soothing workplace.

'You must be Ben's wife,' the doctor says, extending a handshake.

And, as her hand closes around his, Fia decides – for both their sakes – to go with the path of least resistance here. Just this once. 'Uh . . . that's right, yeah,' she says, resolutely not looking anywhere near Benjamin. 'Hi.'

Already, the doctor has stepped forwards to peer at the wound on Benjamin's head. 'That's looking pretty good, if I do say so myself. You were lucky not to need stitches – it was a deep enough little wound. But the surgical glue seems to be holding grand there. How does it feel?'

'Fine,' Benjamin replies. 'A little sore but fine.'

'I'd hate to see what the other fella looked like, eh?' the doctor jokes. 'Or should I say the—'

'Tell me about it,' Benjamin interjects, with a laugh of his own.

And, from her seat beside him, Fia just about restrains the urge to shake him. It would be poor form, in front of the doctor and all – but if there is one thing (among many and various other things) that Fia does not enjoy, it's being out of the loop.

'So, I had a chat to the registrar there, and I think we *will* give you a tetanus jab, just to be sure,' the doctor continues. 'One of the nurses will be along asap to administer it. Obviously, things are a bit busy this evening, so if you could . . .'

'Got it,' Benjamin fills in. 'No hurry. I'll just sit tight.'

The doctor nods gratefully. 'There are vending machines down the corridor if you fancy something,' he says, and he's on his way back out of the cubicle when he tosses another glance in Fia's direction.

'Don't worry. A good night's sleep, a few painkillers for the headache, and your husband will be back to his old self in no time.'

Fia raises an eyebrow. 'Well, that's a relief,' she offers drily, looking not at the doctor now but at Benjamin himself. The moment they're alone, the white curtain dragged closed again, her voice drops to a dramatic hiss.

'Oh my God! Did you get in a *fight* with someone?'

'Come on, Fia. I'm a lover not a fighter. You know that.' His lips twitch with what might be irritation, but she thinks it's something else: amusement.

'. . . *Debatable*,' she hears herself reply, a certain lightness in her own voice now, too.

And, within those ten seconds and the ten that follow, something in the atmosphere seems to shift between them – just fractionally. In the strangeness of the scenario in which they now find themselves, they appear both to have given up the fight to be the one who ignores the other hardest, longest.

'Look, I'm sorry about . . . God, I don't even know what day it was, I'm losing track,' Benjamin begins, and there is suddenly something insistent about his voice, like he just wants to get this said. 'But . . . the thing in the office – about the messages. I'm sorry.'

Fia scrambles to adjust to the sudden change in subject, to adjust to what seems like sincere repentance and regret coming from the mouth of Benjamin Lowry.

'No, *I'm* sorry,' she replies. 'That's how the whole thing started – with me trying to say I was sorry about not picking up the messages before now. And, somehow, we just . . . got off-track.'

'That sort of seems to happen with us, doesn't it?' he replies, with a sheepish sort of smile.

Agreement is on the tip of Fia's tongue. But then she thinks about it – for real – and offers a little shrug. 'Sometimes,' she says instead. Because the strange thing is that, at other times, she's found that the two of them seem to be quite remarkably in sync. Like the night up on the roof at ZOLA – and the thing that he said to her, when they were hailing cabs at Bryant Park, the thing they've still not talked about and, knowing them, perhaps never will.

Given everything that's happened between them, before this summer and in the course of it, there are undoubtedly ways in which Benjamin Lowry knows her – the *real* her – better than any of the co-workers she's just spent the day with. And, in truth, there may even be ways in which he can understand her – can understand her life as it is now – better than the family members she's on her way home to later this evening.

'We don't have to talk about it,' she says then. 'I shouldn't have pushed you on it.'

He shakes his head. 'It was my fault. I *did* think you were just ignoring me, back when I first sent you all those messages.

And I was *pissed*. So, then, when you started to reach out to me, I was . . . let's say *disinclined* to get back to you.'

Fia stays silent, squashing the instinctive urge to jump in.

'I guess at this point, it's not a spoiler to say that we're not still together – me and Jessy, I mean. Kind of an unceremonious ending, to be honest. By the time I started to hear from you, it was over. You caught me right at the intersection of angry and heartbroken.'

She sucks a breath in through her teeth. 'Not fun.'

'No. I know that's no excuse though. I shouldn't have just ignored you.'

And, of course, he *shouldn't* have just ignored her. At another time, she wouldn't hold back in telling him so. But, faced with his own acknowledgement of that fact . . . there doesn't seem much need for her to underline it again.

Added to that is the reality that has revealed itself to her, unavoidably, over the past five weeks. Before then, she told herself that she'd done her darnedest. What else could she have done, she asked herself incredulously, in the face of his radio silence, his unreasonableness and cruelty? Hired a PI to find him?

But, in truth, of course she *could* have hired a PI. She's arranged it for clients in the past. And she probably wouldn't even have needed to go to such lengths. She could have easily found Benjamin's mother's name and work phone number, made contact with him that way. In short, this could all have been handled a long time ago, had she been absolutely minded to handle it – had it been someone else's divorce.

And yet, that was not how it went. A part of her, she has to concede now, has perhaps actually enjoyed feeling like the wronged party. Loath as she is to admit it, Benjamin might have had a point about that, last week. In a certain kind of way, action and avoidance may have suited her. They have allowed her, for almost a decade, to avoid confronting the biggest, most embarrassing, most expensive mistake she's ever made.

It's for all these reasons that Fia, staring across at Benjamin in A&E now, doesn't overly feel the need to stick the boot in. She *is* curious about other things, though.

'Okay. But, so, I still don't understand why you didn't just tell me about Jessy – about your messages – at the start of the summer. Why not just say you'd tried to contact me – get angry with me, even?'

'Oh *yeah*,' he replies, as though the notion is so ludicrous as to be almost comedic. 'So, I show up at ZOLA, that first day. I'm *shocked* to see you – every bit as shocked as you were. I'm basically your *intern*, which, I don't mind telling you, was not exactly my dream situation. And you made it pretty clear, pretty fast, that all my attempts at communication had somehow passed you by. At that point, what was I going to say? "Hey, *also*, take a look at some ridiculous, lovestruck nonsense I sent you about a girl who subsequently dumped me"? Not if I could help it, no.'

Fia just nods, taking that in. She still isn't sure that everything Benjamin has done or failed to do, across the past eight years and across the summer, makes total sense to her. She'd wager that not all of his logic would stand up to cross-examination. But then, the same is true of herself. And life is not a court of law.

All around them, there remains a steady cacophony of noise: footsteps and conversations, fractious children and drunken adults, trolleys being wheeled across linoleum floors. But between Fia and Benjamin, there's quiet for a moment.

'So, I don't want to pry,' she says, carefully. 'But can I just ask – with Jessy, was that 'cause of me? Like, 'cause you had to tell her you were married to me, or 'cause it seemed like I was never going to divorce you or whatever?'

'No,' Benjamin replies simply, and Fia seems to feel every muscle in her body loosen, just a little bit. She's told herself over and over, this past week, that even if she once managed to destroy the love of Benjamin's life, she didn't do so on purpose. She could hardly be blamed. Nonetheless, it's a profound relief to realize now that, in fact, he *doesn't* blame her.

'So, what happened?' she asks, and she knows she's skating on ever-thinner ice here. 'You don't have to tell me if you don't want to.'

Benjamin sighs. 'You know what? There's a long answer to that, obviously, but the short one is probably just as true. I think she just . . . didn't love me as much as I loved her – which is really a shitty thing to wrap your head around, let me tell you.'

Fia lets herself absorb that, properly, for a moment. The very simplicity of the statement suddenly strikes her as kind of revelatory, kind of profound. 'Wow. Yeah. It really *is*, isn't it?'

'Are you . . . speaking from experience?' he asks then.

Fia's slightly lost in her own world, so it's almost a little surprising to hear his voice again. 'What? Oh, no. Well, kind of. Maybe this is stupid.'

After all, in the years since Vegas, she has never been on the verge of issuing or receiving a marriage proposal. Far from it.

Meanwhile, Benjamin just raises an eyebrow. 'You know what, Fia? One benefit of getting married drunkenly – and also, like, just kind of *stubbornly* – in Las Vegas? We've each had a front-row seat to the stupidest thing either of us *ever* did. And I'm gonna go ahead and say we haven't exactly outdone ourselves since then, either. I think it can be pretty much radical honesty from here on out, don't you?'

She tilts her head a little, as if in consideration. When he puts it that way . . . 'All right, well. It's not the same. I know it's not the same. But when you said that, about Jessy – about her maybe just not caring as much as you did . . . do you know what I thought about?'

'What?'

Fia hesitates, figuring out in her own mind whether to proceed or reverse, here. What she thought about, of course, was George.

Chapter Thirty-Two

The beginning of the end was when George moved to Bushwick. Deep Brooklyn. It was an hour on the train from the Upper East Side, but Fia imagined that George would still be in Manhattan a lot, for both work and play. For her own part, she was more than happy to make the journey across the bridge, too. She pictured lots of weekends in George's lovely, airy one-bedroom loft, the square footage making up for all those extra subway stops.

Somehow, though, it never really worked out that way.

For a while, things stayed the same. There *were* a few such weekends in the loft. 'This is the happiest I've ever been in my life,' Fia could remember George joking once, as they holed up with pizza and ice cream and *Gilmore Girls*.

Of course, overall, the two of them did see each other less regularly and certainly on a much less spontaneous basis – they couldn't really run together after work anymore or grab a quick bite the way they used to. But via text, their involvement in the everyday minutiae of one another's lives – the intimacy between them – endured.

Until, at some point – and, in the two years since, Fia has dearly wished she could pinpoint exactly when – George seemed to become harder and harder to get hold of. Communication began to feel more one-sided, George's responses briefer, more delayed. Fia often thought that friendship – true friendship – could basically boil down to a simple yes/no question. *Does this person unreservedly want the best for me?* And, little by little, with George, she became less sure of the answer.

Omg, I got a pay rise today! Fia could remember texting, once. **Minuscule, obviously, but Celia said they wanted to recognize the hours I put in on the Patterson thing. I'm at Sarge's celebrating the best way I know how – with coleslaw AND pickles.**

Cool! George replied, roughly fifteen hours later.

Fia couldn't help feeling a bit defeated when she read that. Her little piece of good news really wasn't a huge deal – she knew it wasn't – but, once upon a time, George would have acted like it was.

She told herself that this was just the way of things sometimes, with texts. One person's idle moment could easily meet someone else at a time of high-stress, chaos, preoccupation. There was nothing sinister to be inferred from that.

On the occasions that she and George met in person, though, things gradually became different there, too. A slight, unspoken stiffness developed between them – or at least, Fia thought so. As time went on, she sincerely found it hard to know whether it was all in her imagination. And, if it *was* real, did it come from George? Or did it come, in some subconscious way, from *her* – from her own vague sense of grievance, of groundlessness? It was all, essentially, a bit of a mindfuck.

Then, one unremarkable Saturday, they had a downright

horrible brunch in Williamsburg. It took forever to arrange, and Fia still came more than halfway, but that was fine. It was all fine, she told herself, and they were going to get back on track. A long afternoon of mimosas and chatter was all that was needed to make things right, to make things easy and fun again.

George seemed a little irritable from the outset, though, distracted – and not in the way that Fia had seen her so many times before, where she'd spill out her latest drama or disgruntlement, make it something for them to share. She appeared, instead, to be dissatisfied in a distant sort of way – one that neither volunteered details nor invited questions. Put frankly, it seemed very much like she could do without this brunch altogether.

'Oh wow,' Fia said at some point, looking out the window onto the street. Somehow, unfathomably, that was what it had come to between them: commenting on their physical surroundings. 'That's quite the, uh, *interpretation* happening over there.'

On the corner, four people were performing what appeared to be a sort of slow-motion dance-slash-puppet show. They all looked extremely doleful, and behind them, a large placard featured a range of images so disparate as to reveal little about the theme of the whole thing. It could have been anything from veganism to the futility of war. COME SEE US TONIGHT AT THE BRICK THEATRE, 10 P.M. 'TIL LATE! was the oddly jaunty exclamation at the top of the placard.

For a moment or two, Fia and George simply watched this all play out.

'Classic Brooklyn, eh? Shall we go along this evening, see what the craic is?' Fia proposed then, in jest.

'I guess it could be interesting,' George replied placidly, and

Fia tried (once more with feeling) to steer the conversation towards some sort of life, some sort of their old repartee.

'What?!' she asked with a grin. 'And here I thought we were friends, Georgina Ferarra. Have you forgotten the great spoken-word poetry disaster of 2019? I've barely recovered. How could you even consider subjecting us to two hours of whatever this thing is?'

However, George showed no recognition of the memory, no hint of amusement. Instead, she just offered an implacable shrug. 'I don't know. I guess maybe I'm just a little more open-minded than you are.'

And, right away, Fia knew that she'd never be able to explain how or why that sentence – *we are not the same* – hit her like such a slap in the face. She could imagine recounting it to her mother or sister, having them suggest that it didn't sound so very terrible. And maybe they'd be right. Maybe she *was* being oversensitive. Again: mindfuck.

But, one way or another, rightly or wrongly, Fia suddenly felt as though she was eating with a stranger – worse than that, even, since she could only presume that a stranger would regard her with neutrality, maybe a little curiosity. From George, she now sensed – at best – disinterest, potentially even a species of mild contempt. The realization, right then and there over huevos rancheros, broke Fia's heart a bit.

Of course, there was probably an opportunity – in that moment, and maybe in certain others, too – for her to have taken the bull by the horns; confronted the situation head on, demanded an explanation from George, issued an apology if it emerged that one were needed. In the eyes of any third party, all of this would have been, if not necessarily easy, then at least doable. Fia and George had, after all, spent the past two years laughing and crying together, sharing all sorts of private and pointless things. They'd spoken, sometimes, in unison. Or in overlapping sentences, spurring one another on. Their conversations had often had sudden, wild digressions, promises to *come back to that in a second*. There was always *too much* to say between the two of them. Throughout the course of their friendship, they'd covered such an extraordinary amount of ground.

In the end, though, somehow Fia simply wasn't able to find the words. Perhaps the questions she really wanted to ask just felt too juvenile, too vulnerable. *Why don't you like me anymore? Why are you being so mean to me?*

In her heart, she knew, sitting in that Williamsburg café, that this would very likely be the last time she and George Ferarra would ever set eyes on one another.

And, in the years since, there has been no joy in being proven entirely right.

Why Fia tells Benjamin Lowry any of this – much less tells him *all* of it, and more – is not clear to her. However, one way or another, that's what she does, over the course of two vending machine coffees in a hospital cubicle and, astonishingly, more than an hour.

She even adds some flavour along the way, specifically for his benefit.

'I mean, I know you probably can't even *imagine* it,' she says facetiously, at one point. 'Someone accusing *me* of being close-minded and no fun?'

Maybe she doesn't quite nail the delivery, though, maybe it comes out a bit less cavalier than she hoped – because, now that she thinks about it, is that a little concerning? That, in fact, Benjamin is not the only person ever to have levelled such accusations at her?

He just smiles, though, a little secretively. 'Mmm, I don't know. You might be a little more fun than I gave you credit for, Irish.'

A smile tugs on her own lips in response. 'Yeah, well. You're a lot less "fun",' she replies, a bit brusquely, and then she cannot help softening herself. '. . . But you're funnier.'

It's odd, that moment.

Odder still are all Benjamin's little nods and questions along the way as she tells him about George, all the overlap she discovers in his experience. His break-up with Jessy, too, had apparently been a bolt from the blue, a mystery to this day.

'The thing is: you don't even get to look back fondly,' he says. 'I don't care if it's a friend, a family member, or a significant other. I mean, I guess that's the point, right? A "significant other" can be anybody. When something ends like that, it's all the same – every good memory is just kind of soured by the ending.'

'Exactly!' Fia replies, feeling almost giddy with the affirmation of it – the validation.

And, in her mind, she returns again to what started her on this whole story in the first place: that thing he'd said about Jessy, the clarity it suddenly offered her about George. She's spent two years trying to detangle the situation, unable to perceive it as anything other than incredibly complex, as a riddle it was her job to solve. She's tortured herself over it, periodically. But sometimes the simplest explanations are the most accurate: the relationship just was not one that, in the end, George cared enough to maintain. Perhaps that really is all there is to it.

'You know what's weird,' she says eventually, draining

the last sip of her horrible coffee, 'despite everything, if George showed up next week and just wanted to go back to the way things were . . . that would be so tempting. I like to think I'd be all "you burned your bridges, I'm done," and I'm sure that would be the smart thing to say. But, as pathetic as it sounds, I still don't know if I could say it.'

'I get that,' Benjamin replies quietly.

And, though she would never in a million years have predicted it, Fia thinks he really does.

Chapter Thirty-Three

'So what *did* you get up to today?' she asks him, some unknown amount of time later. They're sitting cross-legged on the bed opposite one another now, still no tetanus shot in sight, but an array of unhealthy snacks spread out between them. It seems so peculiar that a hospital would sell such things.

'Oh my God,' he says, and there is something – she might as well admit it – downright *adorable* about the way his face brightens with enthusiasm. 'I did all the things – all the touristy things, I mean, but, like, fuck it, I *am* a tourist. So, I got the bus from Garrett Castle, which turned out to be, uh . . . let's say a scenic route.'

'Stops at every hole in the hedge, yeah,' Fia agrees, making him smile.

'It actually *was* incredibly scenic though, so I guess I can't complain. Anyhow, I went to Trinity College first,' he continues, ''cause I wanted to see the Book of Kells, and I read the lines can be crazy. After that, I went out to Kilmainham Gaol and did the Guinness Storehouse, and then I made my way back into the city centre, wandered around a little, came across this really great bookstore . . . Hodges Figgis – do you know it?'

Fia nods, a smile rising to her lips unbidden. Her mother used to take her there often as a child. It feels so strange to think that Benjamin – *Benjamin Lowry* – has been in there, that there is now one more small thing on their list of common experiences.

'Oldest bookshop in Ireland,' she says, but then suddenly she doubts herself. 'Or one of them at least, I think.'

Benjamin squints over at her. 'Did you know that Garrett Castle was built in 2002?' he asks, a hint of accusation in his tone.

Fia doesn't know whether to wince or laugh, and she ends up in some amalgam of the two. 'I did know that, yeah,' she replies. 'I thought they tried to kind of keep it on the downlow from visitors, though. How'd you find out?'

'I asked.'

She just nods, like this is a hard truth and one that must come to everybody eventually. 'I think there *was* some sort of ruin there to begin with,' she adds, in case this is any comfort. 'But, I dunno – it didn't exactly scream *luxury spa weekends* in its natural state, I suppose. It's like the Vikings and the Normans weren't even *thinking* about a Mother's Day brunch when they landed here. So, yeah. Most of the facade was just built new. It's a pretty good job though, don't you think? A blind man on a galloping horse wouldn't know the difference.'

This is one of her mother's favoured expressions, and from the look on his face, Benjamin quite enjoys it, too.

Still, he puts on scepticism. 'It's made me very mistrustful of the shit you guys are claiming is old, that's all I'm saying.

Anyhow, after Hodges Figgis, I wanted to have an Irish stew for dinner, but I couldn't find any. So – I guess you can take the boy out of New York, right? – I just grabbed a slice of pizza. And, after that . . . well, after *that*, I guess I ended up bleeding profusely from the head, so . . .' He shrugs. 'As per the recommendation of some very concerned locals, I came here.'

Fia just nods. As to the precise source of his injury, she knows better than to try to press him again. If he doesn't want to tell her, she cannot make him. That's every single bit as true as the reverse would be.

'I suppose, when you think about it, no trip to Dublin would be complete *without* seeing inside the Mater Hospital, though,' she offers instead. 'Kind of a hidden gem, you might say. Was it not in your guidebook?'

He smiles, grabbing a few crisps from the bag that's split open between them. She waits as he chews, swallows.

'You sound different here,' he offers then, *à propos* of nothing whatsoever.

Fia blinks, taken aback slightly by the comment, by the admission underlying it: he has been paying attention. Here, and in New York, he has been noticing things about her, filing them away. As ammunition? Maybe, yes. But maybe not only for that purpose. Maybe also because he simply cannot seem to help it.

Once again, this notion occurs to Fia for one main reason: because she knows the reverse is also true.

'Different how?' she asks.

'I dunno. Your accent's just stronger, I guess. Same thing happens to me when I get back to North Carolina.'

'There's just an ease, isn't there?' she says, and her mind flashes back, of its own accord, to her conversation with Ryan earlier – to the shorthand that existed so naturally between them. Then, another example springs to mind. 'Or, like, even here, tonight. They made me sign in at reception when I arrived, and I got to write my actual name, which was nice.'

'Yeah, I've been noticing that, on all the paperwork for Susan,' Benjamin replies conversationally, and Fia is startled anew to find that this is another thing he's registered.

Fiadh. It just looks, at least to her eyes, so much more beautiful that way – so much less like a car model or a macOS update.

'How come you don't spell it that way at ZOLA?' he continues.

She shrugs. 'Just wasn't worth the hassle I suppose.'

Truthfully, there are often times these days when she wishes she'd pushed through the hassle – or more to the point, made other people push through it. She'd only had so much fortitude, though. There were only so many times she could smile along with the whole *omg that's so crazy and unnecessary, lols lols lols* thing.

It's an understandable reaction, she supposes, among those who happen not to speak Irish. It doesn't make Fia like people less, exactly. It's just that . . . well, maybe it makes her like them a *tiny* bit less. Part of her half expects something similar from Benjamin right now. Not for the first time, though, he surprises her.

'Well, I'm into it,' he proclaims. 'With the *d* and the *h*, I mean. I can't say I *understand* it, exactly, but I like it.'

For a second, Fia says nothing. It's difficult to explain how very far this response puts him ahead of the curve. And, as it turns out, she has no time to try.

At long last, a nurse arrives to administer Benjamin's injection, swooping through the curtain with a rickety trolley.

She makes conversation, snaps on a fresh pair of gloves, and the job is done and dusted in little more than a minute.

Afterwards, Benjamin barely has the sleeve of his T-shirt tugged back down before it's made clear that he and Fia must vacate the cubicle sharpish. There will be no hanging around to finish off their last few crisps, no more bickering over the various confections she chose earlier. Someone else needs the bed. Though they've spent all night waiting for this – to be cleared to go – it feels like quite an unceremonious eviction.

'Sorry again about the delay,' the nurse says, as Fia and Benjamin hop down from the bed, gathering their belongings.

'That's okay,' Benjamin replies easily. 'What else would we have been doing, right?'

The nurse offers a grateful little half-laugh, before disappearing off to her next task.

'I'll have you know I left a very . . . promising evening for this,' Fia says, once they're alone again. Just for the record.

Benjamin stops in his tracks, looking over at her. It's clear he catches her meaning perfectly. 'Did you now?'

She just smiles cryptically, heading out of the cubicle with a swoosh of the curtain, leaving him to trail behind her.

'It was good of you to come,' he says, a few minutes later. They've cleared the chaos of the reception area by now and fallen into step on their way to the exit. 'The four buses and the six-hour walk and whatever. Thank you.'

It's unexpectedly nice, the simplicity of those last two words – the sincerity of them.

'You're welcome,' she replies softly.

And it occurs to her once more that they are the *same*, she and him. They have always met and matched each other. When it comes to debates and wisecracks, criticisms and harsh truths, what one offers, the other will always reciprocate. But what if they were – even just every now and then – gentle with one another? What, Fia wonders, might *that* be like? If this evening is anything to go by, it might be quite nice.

All of a sudden, though, another thought altogether crosses her mind. Just like that, the spell is broken.

'Oh my God,' she exclaims, glancing down at her watch. 'Ben! *Your* bus! You'll have missed the last one now!'

He's entirely unconcerned. 'I won't. It's, what, like ten thirty, eleven o'clock?'

However, as he takes out his phone – presumably to check the app – his face soon falls. He looks back up at her. 'In Ne—'

'Do not say "in New York", Benjamin! Do not! This is not New York! This is Ireland. You can't just *assume there will be buses.*'

'Well, could I have assumed that the *Irish woman I was with* might have *warned* me about the no buses?'

'If she was your *mother*, maybe yes.'

Despite themselves, they each give in to a quick burst of laughter, because they're both so ridiculously dramatic – almost a parody of themselves at this point – and it's funny.

'I guess that whole process in there couldn't exactly have been sped up, anyhow,' he admits then. 'Could I get a cab?'

Fia thinks about it. 'It would be pricey,' she says then. 'Like, a hotel might even work out cheaper. And – Friday night . . . I'm not sure how many Dublin drivers are wanting to head out to the middle of Wicklow, to be honest.'

For a moment, there's silence, as they each process the predicament. They're hovering just shy of the hospital's exit now, and as they look across at one another, an obvious solution seems to come creeping towards them. Fia imagines she can feel a moment of impact, the prospect hitting her once and for all, spurring her into a reaction.

'You're not staying at my house,' she tells him resolutely, though of course he hasn't asked yet, and perhaps he never would have. 'I'm sorry. No. I know we've had this whole night and it's been . . . y'know. It's been unexpected. But I think a sleepover with you, me, and my mam and dad would just be pushing it.'

Benjamin all but pouts. 'You would send me out, into an unknown city, *injured*, seeking whatever Travelodge might take me?'

And Fia can tell, from the look on his face, the tone of his voice, that he's just joking. He's not really trying to put the guilts on her. But, when said aloud, it *does* sound a bit mean, the prospect of just leaving him here. It's true that he has just been discharged from a hospital; it's true that he has nowhere obvious to go. Not to mention that, quite aside from those things, he is a very good-looking American man. He has, sometimes, the hint of a southern drawl. Once word gets around among the women of Dublin, there's a possibility he could be in real danger.

What she says next seems to come out of her mouth entirely of its own accord. 'I will consider it – *if* you tell me what happened to you today.'

Benjamin lets out an exhale that's half surprise, half amusement. 'Always with the transactions, aren't you, Fia? Always the quid pro quo. I think you should worry about that, maybe. Are you in therapy?'

Fia is unmoved. She just stares at him, until he rolls his eyes in capitulation.

'All right, fine,' he says, and she's sure the slight pause he takes is purely to build her anticipation.

'So, I was at that famous bridge in the city centre – the little white one. Ha'penny Bridge?'

Fia nods a confirmation.

'Right. Just walking along the Liffey, eating my pizza slice, minding my own business.'

'You never mind your own business,' she interjects, but even she can hear the affection that seems to come out along with it.

'*Minding my own business*,' Benjamin repeats, his voice rising over the top of hers. 'And – I guess there's really no other way to say this – I was full on attacked, unprovoked, by one of your Irish seagulls. Attacked in my *face*.'

It's his delivery, more than anything. It's his wide eyes, his affronted expression.

Fia can barely restrain a guffaw, her whole face animating in response. 'Oh my God! That's . . .' She bites back another giggle, the effort creating a strangled sort of sound at the back of her throat. 'I'm sorry – that sounds terrible.'

When she thinks about it properly, it *does* sound quite terrible.

'Did it want your food?' she asks.

'I think so, yeah. Which it did manage to get, in the end. But I put up a bit of a fight, which in retrospect was . . . unwise.'

'Mmm,' she murmurs. She is, in her own good opinion, doing a remarkable job of being sympathetic here, of resisting the urge to tease. *Remarkable*.

'What are seagulls even *doing* in a city centre, anyhow?' he continues, all indignance. 'It just makes no sense. There's nothing *there* for them.'

'I mean, there's the odd slice of pizza knocking about,' she can hardly help but point out, and then – at the look

269

on his face – she recants. 'No, I know! I know. You're right. They *have* got incredibly bold in the past few years, it seems like.'

'The whole escapade actually drew quite a crowd,' Benjamin says. 'People were a lot more sympathetic than they would have been in Manhattan, that's for sure.'

Fia can well imagine. By this point, she's seen countless fender-benders on New York City streets, spied her fair share of people crying on the subway. Passersby, including herself, tend overwhelmingly towards not poking their noses in. By contrast, in Ireland, there is the opposite inclination. People very much want to find out what the craic is, get involved, offer some bit of assistance or advice. There is, like every other thing on earth, good and bad in both scenarios.

'So!' Benjamin says, new jollity in his voice now. 'Which way to your place? Is it close enough to walk? I gotta say, I'm pretty excited to meet the in-laws. You think they'll ask me to call them Mom and Dad?'

Fia feels herself jolted back to the present moment, to the basis on which she extracted Benjamin's confidence in the first place. She opens her mouth in protest, but before she can even get the words out, he beats her to it.

'A deal's a deal,' he trills.

What she said, in fact, was simply that she would consider the idea. So, consider it she does, letting out a long-suffering sigh for his benefit. For another moment, she says nothing, just looks at him, the notion making itself real in her mind for the first time.

Perhaps, at this point, it is just the simplest, swiftest option.

'You'd have to be on your best behaviour . . .' she warns then.

He smiles beatifically. 'I always am.'

'I'm serious. It's not the time for your funny, funny jokes, okay?'

'You think my jokes are funny?' he returns, and she just rolls her eyes. He does, too, snorting out a laugh. 'Okay,' he adds. 'I get it. I'll be the perfect, non-husband houseguest, I promise.'

Perhaps she still looks sceptical, because he's soon reassuring her once more. 'For real. I'm actually great with parents.'

Fia clicks her tongue against her teeth. She doesn't know if that's true or not – but, unfathomably, it seems she is about to find out.

Chapter Thirty-Four

It's unspeakably bizarre, sitting in the little front room of her childhood home, having tea and toast with her parents and Benjamin Lowry. Unspeakably bizarre.

And, at the same time, it's also . . . fine.

Her parents accepted the situation at face value (what else could they do?) and welcomed Benjamin in, all politeness and concern for his health. That Maeve – who would surely have had some slightly different questions or comments – is at Conor's for the night feels like nothing short of a gift from God.

Meanwhile, as Fia has seen so many times before with Benjamin, the guy really *can* make conversation with a brick wall. Or, as might apparently be more accurate, he can *draw out* conversation from a brick wall. Because, in a turn of events Fia could never have predicted, it's actually her dad who does lots of the talking. He offers up all sorts of tidbits of local knowledge about Dublin, encouraged by Benjamin's rapt attention, by the questions extended here and there. To boot, Fia's father – an avid watcher of television documentaries –

seems to have quite a surprising amount of information about North Carolina at his fingertips – enough on which to base a conversation, at least. In turn, Benjamin talks a little about where he's from. No personal anecdotes – Fia notices that. No tales from his childhood or early adulthood. But he does an engaging job of sketching out the politics and the geography of the place, nonetheless.

Aside from being interesting, it's also sort of . . . sweet, the effort on both men's parts. Fia can't help but think, just briefly, that if things were different – if Benjamin wasn't her summer associate, and if he wasn't her soon-to-be (secret) ex-husband . . . if she'd brought him home to meet the parents, say. Well, in that circumstance – there's no denying it – her heart would be about fit to burst right about now.

'So, you're surfing tomorrow, is that it?' Fia's mother asks eventually, once the teapot is empty, and they must all try to bring this interaction to a close somehow.

It occurs to Fia, then, that she hasn't even asked Benjamin what activity he was allocated. Because of the volume of people involved in the Summer Summit, they've been separated into different groups – and different beaches – for tomorrow's team-building offerings. Surfing, kayaking, or stand-up paddle boarding – those are the options. One thing about Ireland is that there is easy access to quite a lot of water. It is not, generally speaking, warm water, but there is plenty of it around.

On Sunday, more small-group activities will follow (this time, more land-based, more law-based); after that, there's a formal dinner for the whole firm to round out the weekend.

'I did get surfing, yeah,' Benjamin says, which works out handily, for transportation purposes. 'Although' – he turns back to Fia's mam – 'in my case, it's more like I'll be in the water, and a surfboard will also be there, you know what I mean? I'm not really a surfer.'

'I don't believe that,' Fia finds herself blurting out, before she can edit herself.

'Why not?'

She thinks about it for a moment, and once she's figured out the answer in her own mind, she decides just to go with the truth. 'Because I've never seen you be bad at anything like that, ever.'

There's a compliment in there, but Benjamin skates right past it. Instead, he just cocks his head sceptically, his voice deadpan. 'Well, get ready.'

'How much sport do they have you playing over there?' Fia's father pipes up then, his brow furrowing.

'What?' Fia replies instinctively, and a slightly awkward sort of pause follows, during which she realizes that, yes, her previous comment was a fairly questionable thing for one lawyer to say about another lawyer

'Oh!' she continues, flustered suddenly. 'Just . . . you know what the firm's like, Dad, especially in the summer. We're all out playing rounders every whip about. If we give any legal advice at all, that's a good day!'

She thinks she gets away with it. After all, what she's said is semi-accurate. Mostly, though, Fia knows what saves her: it is that her parents do not think she would lie to them, not even by omission. The thought makes her insides tighten with sudden guilt. How gutted they would be, if they found out the full truth of her history with Benjamin.

'Do you think you'll be all right to be in the water, with your injury, Benjamin?' her mother asks worriedly now, peering again at the gash on his forehead. 'You might be better not to get that wet.'

'I asked. Sadly, the glue's waterproof,' Benjamin replies.

Fia's mother looks thoroughly unconvinced.

'Mam's got one of those medical degrees you don't need to go to college for,' Fia tells Benjamin, teasing lightly. It's funny, the urge to slightly perform your family dynamic in front of other people. 'She doesn't even need Google. It's pure instinct.'

'Get away with that, you,' her mother says, taking her own cue seamlessly. 'Benjamin, I hope Fia's a bit nicer to you over there in New York. Or have you had her sass to put up with as well?'

Benjamin turns to look at Fia, mischief in his eyes. 'Literally none at all,' he says.

The next morning, Fia wakes up several times before she *really* wakes up. The events of last night come flooding back to her, of course, but they're quickly overtaken by thoughts of the events that are ahead today. Cursing herself (as usual) for being so slap-happy with the snooze button, she leaps up and hops into the shower, taking her toothbrush in there, too, for speed.

She has finished in the bathroom and is dashing around her bedroom when she hears a rap on the doorframe.

'I know, I know, I'm coming!' she says, her head still halfway inside the wardrobe. She riffles urgently through items, on the hunt not for anything specific, but merely for some suitable thing she's going to know when she sees. As ever, she seems to have packed extremely badly for this entire trip, leaving herself doomed to cobble together outfits from whichever of her clothes happen to have stuck around in the house.

'Your mom said that your dad is revving the engine,' comes a voice then, and Fia leans all the way back, her attention

275

suddenly very much piqued. Just a few feet away, hovering by her bedside table, it's Benjamin.

'Oh my God!' she all but yelps. She clutches the hoodie against her chest instinctively, as though he is catching her naked, which he isn't, exactly. She has her jeans and a bra on. But he *could have caught her naked*, which feels much more like the point. 'What are you doing in here?!'

'Uh . . . ' Benjamin looks momentarily a little paralysed. 'Your mom said I should just "give you a quick knock to make sure you were definitely out of your pit"', he says then, his eyes flicking downwards briefly, then resolutely upwards again to face her. 'That's a direct quote. I really like her, by the way – she's great.'

Suddenly, Fia feels slightly faint. The reality of Benjamin's presence – the same reality she's barely had a chance to think about this morning, in her haste – is now *all* she can think about. How on earth could she possibly have invited him here? What had seemed like a sort-of-unusual-but-okay decision last night seems borderline psychotic in the cold light of day.

Needless to say, Benjamin has not slept in her bedroom. Fia is fairly certain she could have claimed that herself and Benjamin were madly in love and shacked up together in Manhattan, and still her mother would have directed Benjamin towards Eoin's single bed, handed him that pair of Eoin's old pyjamas.

But here he is now.

'Oh Jesus,' she says weakly. 'How long have you been awake?'

'A while, I guess,' he replies, right as Fia's gaze makes its way to the half-eaten thing he's holding.

'What's that?' she asks, though of course she can see exactly.

Benjamin glances at it, too. 'Oh. This is something called a "sausage sandwich", Fia. And I don't mind telling you, based on the name, I had my doubts. But, my God – your mom could set up a food truck selling just these in Brooklyn, and I swear she'd be making six figures easy.'

He takes a large bite, as if by way of illustration, somehow managing to grin even as he chomps through it.

Fia just stares at him, stunned and aggravated and . . . she doesn't know what. Not even a minute previously, she'd been hurried, harried, but now her mind seems to be a complete blank. What had she even been intending to look for next? Her little mini hairbrush? A tampon, just in case? What is on the list of things she might need for a compulsory outing to the Wicklow coast with all her Yank co-workers? She suddenly has no idea. She's hyper-conscious of whatever slivers of her skin might still be visible.

Meanwhile, Benjamin's eyes scan the room, without even the slightest attempt at subtlety.

Fia is powerless to stop it, and immediately, she knows in her bones that this – *this* – is why she didn't want him to come to the Summer Summit. It wasn't only about the thought that she would have to see more of him. It was the thought that *he* would be seeing more of *her* – perhaps, in some intangible, unavoidable sort of way, seeing parts of her that she'd rather he didn't.

And of course, that was when she merely envisaged him in Ireland generally – never mind sitting in A&E, improbably getting her to spill her guts about George; never mind, for example, in the kitchen of her parents' house enjoying a minor fry-up, unsupervised; never mind here, while she is *semi-clothed* in her *childhood bedroom*.

As for that last bit in particular, he's not seeing the place at anywhere close to its best.

Among Fia's special skills has always been the ability to decimate a hotel room in less than half an hour. This house, as was brought to her attention repeatedly in adolescence, is not a hotel. But, nonetheless, she's taken a very similar approach upon her return to it within the past few days. Clothes are strewn on various surfaces, her semi-unpacked suitcase still splayed open on the floor. On the bedside table, a collection of crockery and water glasses has accumulated.

'You're *messy*,' Benjamin declares, as he takes in the scene. It's not a question, not a hypothesis; it's just an observation. The facts speak for themselves.

'Uh, yeah,' Fia mumbles. What she sometimes likes to tell other people, when the subject comes up, is that she is untidy, rather than messy. People like that. It is a relatable flaw to admit to. Not gross. But the truth is that, left to her own devices, she has the capacity to be untidy, messy, dirty – all of them. Of course, she makes an effort, given her usual communal living situation. And she makes even *more* of an effort in work – a colossal, constant, necessity-driven effort. But, in the privacy of her own space, it's very different. She has been known to let things congeal.

'And you're *late*,' Benjamin continues. He looks, at this point, about as happy as a human being can be. Fia imagines she could tell him he's won the lottery, and still his grin could hardly get wider.

'I'm not late,' she says, and then, with a quick glance down at her watch, honesty forces her to amend. 'Yet.'

This, in fact, is the usual way of it. She is very rarely late for things – she's trained herself out of that – but she is almost always cutting it fine.

Benjamin says nothing – it is as though, in this moment,

he might be recalibrating everything he ever thought to be true of her – and suddenly, Fia snaps back into action.

'Turn around,' she commands, and to his credit, he does so right away, with a bit of a chuckle. Swiftly, she wrestles on a T-shirt and the same hoodie she's been grasping like armour. She reaches for an elastic band on her dressing table, sweeping her hair up into a ponytail. From the window, she can see the car on the driveway. Her father – somehow at once the most patient and most impatient man in the world – is indeed already sitting there, raring to go.

Haphazardly, she throws a few other items into her handbag, and then she's pushing – physically pushing – Benjamin back out onto the landing and down the stairs.

He lets out a noise of protest that quickly becomes mostly laughter. His voice works its way into mock earnestness.

'I gotta say, this doesn't feel very welcoming, Fia. What happened to that famous Irish hospitality, huh?' He polishes off the last of his sausage sandwich. 'So far, you're my least favourite member of this family by a mile.'

Chapter Thirty-Five

Several hours later, Fia is looking around at a metaphorical sea of lawyers in the literal sea.

Upon arrival this morning, everyone got into wetsuits (an ordeal only ever exceeded in indignity by the inevitable process of wrestling out of said wetsuits). Then they split into smaller groups, had a talk about water safety, and practised on their surfboards on the sand, like beached whales. All of that seemed to go on interminably.

Conditions were also, it had to be said, less than ideal. Certainly, it was far from the coldest Fia had ever known an Irish beach to be – and, despite some fairly ominous-looking grey clouds, at least the rain held off. Still, though, it became clear very quickly that this was not going to be surfing like they did it in Summer Bay.

Between the weather, the basic fact of participating in an organized activity, and the forced jollity with lots of people whom she barely knew and would probably never really get to know, the whole thing was more or less a royal flush in terms of stuff Fia could very much live without. It reminded her of precisely why she had hoped never to attend another hen weekend in her life – although of course, it occurred to her then, she'd probably have to attend, and indeed organize, Maeve's. Why did that make her feel so weird, thinking again about Maeve's wedding? She wished it didn't. She wished she could just be wholeheartedly excited about it, as any good sister surely would be.

In any case, having at last reached the main event, now, Fia can't help but suspect that all the on-land preparation was an utter waste of time. Around her, in the water, the whole scene is chaos. Despite their instructors' best efforts, most people either have given up altogether, or are being brutally battered about by a combination of the wind, the sea, and their own surfboard.

Only a tiny handful among their group have reached the stage at which this sport seems like it could actually feel unbelievably freeing and fun. One such person catches Fia's attention after a while: it's Ryan Sieman, out in the distance, riding the crest of a wave like he was born to do it. His sandy hair, slick with water now, looks five shades darker, his general bearing so easy and undaunted.

Fia doesn't know how long she stands there watching him, the water up to her hips, her surfboard floating prostrate beside her, before she becomes aware of someone else watching Ryan, too. Or is that it? Watching *her* watching Ryan – that might be more accurate.

Stationed maybe twenty feet down the shore, half a dozen other bodies in between them, is Benjamin. He looks away in double-quick time once her eyes meet his, and steadfastly tries instead to mount his own surfboard once more. He does his best to catch the next wave that comes, and he really, very nearly, almost does . . . until he doesn't. Seconds later, he's tumbling off balance, emerging from under the water breathless and spluttering.

Fia watches as he spits out a mouthful of sea foam, unable to help the little giggle that comes. There's no malice in it, though. In fact, some part of her is pretty concerned about that cut on his head. She's inclined to agree with her mother that the water is no place for him right now, what with the potential for a second injury.

If it were Ryan? That might be fine. There doesn't seem to be much risk of *him*, say, hitting debris, knocking himself out with his own board or body parts.

But, as it's turned out, Benjamin didn't lie to her. He can make friends, and he can fix tech issues, and he can play baseball. He can swim, and do half a dozen other sports well, and he can whip a cab like nobody she's ever seen. He is, on top of everything else, probably going to make a pretty good lawyer. He is not a surfer, though.

She watches him try again, and be thwarted again.

Really not a surfer.

Thirty minutes later, everyone is mercifully allowed out of the water at last. ZOLA has arranged for burgers, pizza, beers, and hot drinks, all of which are being served out of food trucks on the sand.

Fia does some jumping jacks in her wetsuit to warm herself up and makes conversation about the weather and the food and the Celtic heritages of some of her American and British colleagues. It's the best part of the day by far, and she wonders why they couldn't all have done this – just this – in the first place.

She's jogged a little away from the pack to put her rubbish in the bin when Ryan sidles up to her, ostensibly doing the same thing.

'How were you so good out there?' she asks him with a grin, once they've dealt with the preliminaries.

He chuckles. 'I don't think I'm headed for the World Championships or anything. But I'm down here most weekends. Just good to get the head cleared, you know?'

Fia nods, thinking of her runs in Manhattan. 'I know what you mean.'

'So, you disappeared yesterday,' he begins, after a moment – not a question, just a statement.

'I'm not actually staying at Garrett Castle,' she replies. 'I don't get loads of time with the parentals these days, so I just thought I'd stay with them, commute for the few days.'

It's Ryan's turn, now, to nod in understanding. 'Yeah, of course. Sure it's a handy enough drive down the road. Saying that, I'm pretty sure everybody from the Dublin office is taking full advantage of the free bed and board for the weekend. Hard to beat that breakfast.'

Fia just smiles in response, and there's a second's pause before Ryan continues.

'If you wanted a place to kip after the dinner thing tomorrow night . . .' he offers then, and of course Fia hears what he is actually proposing loud and clear.

As has been very well established, she would normally be happy to take him up on his invitation. It's just that, this year, she has had her family to occupy some of her time and energy during the Summer Summit. Her family and . . . other people. It occurs to her that perhaps what she needs in her life, at this juncture, is not to add yet one more element, one more complication.

But then, hasn't that always been the best thing about Ryan Sieman? He has always been so wonderfully uncomplicated. He might, in fact, be *precisely* what she needs in her life right now.

If there is a part of Fia that is hesitant – that is maybe just slightly less enthused than she would ideally like to be, that instinctively makes a certain comparison in her mind – she pushes all those thoughts away. *Stupid.* Because it's not, she reminds herself, like she actually has two choices here. She's not a Regency lady, confronted with a pair of competing suitors. What she has is one reliable friend-with-benefits who wants to temporarily renew the benefits, plus, one . . . well, one *Benjamin.*

Benjamin, who only very recently stopped actively hating her guts; Benjamin, who might still be pining for his college girlfriend; Benjamin, who really should have no influence whatsoever on the way she lives her life.

So, Fia looks up at Ryan, letting her eyes widen a little, letting a half-smile play about her lips.

It has been a while since she has been in a nightclub, and she has begun to think she mightn't mind never being in one again. In years gone by, however, she has frequently seen other girls on dance floors, essentially gyrating in essentially underwear, and she has only ever hoped that they personally found this activity to be lots of fun. Because, in Fia's experience, there is absolutely no need to go to such efforts merely to attract the attention of the average heterosexual man. The basics work like a charm.

'That sounds good,' she says, a little coyly, and Ryan smiles back now, getting the message.

'Well, I'll look forward to it,' he replies, and then he gestures up past the sand dune, towards the car park. 'I'm just going to run and grab my phone from the car here, but I'll see you in a minute?'

He's looking at her hopefully, and she feels a little flash of fondness for him as she nods her agreement.

She makes her way back to the rest of their group, and as she gets closer, she sees Benjamin striding across to meet her. Even the visual contrast between him and Ryan is suddenly so striking to her, Ryan's fair complexion the antithesis of Benjamin's dark eyes and dark hair.

Again, Fia catches herself, berates herself slightly. It is pointless, making this an exercise in comparison.

Once Benjamin arrives within talking distance, the two of them just look at each other for a moment, greetings exchanged wordlessly.

With a jerk of his head (Fia is silently relieved to see no blood gushing from his wound), Benjamin gestures to Ryan's retreating back, already well in the distance.

'So . . . that's your guy, is it?' Benjamin asks, almost idly, as if it's not much to him one way or another.

'Wouldn't you like to know,' she replies, and she lets her own gaze travel out towards the shore. 'You were keeping a good eye on him out there, anyway.'

Benjamin grimaces in such a way as to pooh-pooh the very idea. He can't seem to quite bring himself to deny it out loud, though. Maybe, Fia decides then and there, she can let herself do a *little* bit of comparison – have a little fun with this.

'He was very good, wasn't he?' she continues wickedly. Needling Benjamin just seems, as it has always seemed, to come so very naturally. 'Sort of majestic, you might say.'

Benjamin doesn't fire back a riposte, as she imagined he would, though. Instead, irritation or some adjacent emotion is written all over his face. It makes Fia feel briefly . . . unsettled.

But, no. Her mind flashes back to this morning, when he was the one making her squirm, all too delighted with himself as he took in every detail of her bedroom. This is just what they do to one another, she reminds herself. It's the game they play.

'Oh, look, Benjamin,' she continues, letting her gaze drift, gesturing with her hand. 'It's one of your friends. A whole load of them, in fact.'

Fifty feet away, a cluster of seagulls have arrived and are squawking around some sort of prize on the sand. A forgotten slice of pizza, potentially.

This time, Benjamin bites back a laugh.

'Wow. Two out of ten for sensitivity, Fia,' he says, and she can tell he's doing his best to keep his tone serious. 'Imagine you had suffered a trauma, and you were far from home, and then you were forced to re-confront that trauma . . .'

'Well, it's interesting you should put it that way. How do you think I feel every day you're bunked into the corner of my office?'

He actually does laugh then, pulling a stupid face at her, and Fia does nothing to hide her own smirk.

See? she thinks to herself. This is just the game.

Chapter Thirty-Six

The following day consists of ZOLA's staff again being divided into groups, this time at the hotel, alternately participating in team-building activities (Fia has her two truths and a lie already locked and loaded) and thinking quite serious thoughts about the law.

Later that evening, Fia walks back into Garrett Castle with just minutes to spare – she's been like a yo-yo today, having had to return home again in the afternoon to get changed. Not for the first time, it occurs to her that it would probably have been much simpler to just stay down here for the whole Summit. That's how she's explained to her parents that she'll be staying tonight: a matter of pure convenience.

In the ballroom, other people are already beginning to take their seats, and Fia rushes to consult the chart. She sees, with some surprise, that she's been graced with a seat at Celia Hannity's table. It's Celia, a few other partners – including her old boss Damien from the Dublin office – plus miscellaneous senior associates from different branches. She is going to be the most junior person at the table. Of course, she notices that. To be a lawyer at a large firm is to be unrelentingly aware of the hierarchy, your own place within it, and any micro-interactions that might indicate an imminent climb or fall.

In fact, though, as Fia takes her seat, as the goat's cheese tartlet turns to the salmon-or-beef, and one glass of champagne turns to two or three, she somehow finds that sense of the pecking order melting away. Maybe, she thinks, this is exactly the point of the Summer Summit. Maybe somebody, some-where, had the wisdom to know that a few days away from one's usual routines, usual friendships, usual clothes would be just the ticket for breaking down some barriers.

Undeniably, it *is* sort of fun to take in the grandeur of the space, the slight sense of excess to it all, with everyone dressed in their finery. Most of Fia's normal life seems to be spent in either a suit or in running gear. In the slice of time that remains, she's a fairly simple dresser. She's not a sequins-just-because type of girl. Tonight, though, she's borrowed a frock from Maeve – an over-the-head, no-zips-or-buttons number that falls to the ground in a sheath of shimmery gold. Maeve was also drafted in to create some sort of chignon at the back of Fia's head – not a million miles from her usual workplace bun, but a little softer, wisps of hair left loose to frame her face.

The whole combination of factors seems to conspire to make her feel like a slightly different person tonight. Certainly not the version of herself who, just hours ago, sat in an old dressing gown while her little sister did her hair, dripping the juice from a peach down her chin and cackling with laughter – but then, not quite her typical ZOLA self, either. A more glamorous version of that, perhaps: a lawyer like the ones on television, whose days seemed to involve a lot of sex and not much photocopying.

Celia encourages her to tell their tablemates about a recent case, and as Fia does just that, some hybrid of excitement and contentment buzzes in the back of her mind. This train, she thinks, is well and truly on the tracks. How incredible, after all the anxiety of recent weeks, to know that for sure. Despite a few close shaves along the way, she's somehow managed not to fuck up at least this one thing, embarrassingly, keen for any new morsel of information.

It was true, what she told Benjamin that night on the roof: she has no great love for the inherent substance of her work – none whatsoever. She was not born caring about powers of attorney, and she will not die caring about them. But the feeling of accomplishment, the feeling that she is at last beginning to be properly noticed, valued . . . if there is a person alive who doesn't enjoy those things, Fia would like to meet them.

Benjamin, incidentally, is way across the room right now at another (less illustrious) table. The two of them having been placed in separate groups for today's activities, she hasn't seen him since the beach yesterday. However, she's let herself observe him over the first two courses of this evening's meal – just for a few seconds here or there, watching as he nodded along in conversation.

'Seemed a very civil fella, that Benjamin,' her mother said when Fia arrived home yesterday. 'And very easy to feed.'

Fia just chuckled. Overall, she finds stereotypes about Irish mammies to be incredibly wearying. She has never heard her own mother so much as mention immersion heaters or wooden spoons, for instance. Undeniably, though, perhaps it is the fate of every Irish person to veer occasionally towards the caricature version of themselves. And one of Rosemary Callaghan's absolute favourite qualities in another human being is willingness to eat what is put in front of them. Woe betide the vegan, the coeliac, or the fusspot who enters her kitchen.

'What did the two of you talk about at breakfast?' she asked her mam, then. Had he said anything about what he planned to do after the summer, she wondered to herself silently. Or even about Fia herself? As regards the latter, especially, she found herself almost unbearably, embarrassingly, keen for any new morsel of information.

Her mother, however, was of no help whatsoever.

'Oh, just this and that,' she replied breezily. 'Isn't it great how he's having the career change? I couldn't believe it when he told me he'd never had a sausage sandwich in his life. And them such fans of the hot dog in America. You wouldn't just run that parcel in next door there, would you, Fia? I've told the postman a dozen times that we're number 24 and *they're* number 26, but sure what's the use? Any more of a dope and, I'm telling you, that fella would need watering twice a day.'

By the time the dessert plates and coffee cups are cleared, there is the usual sense of release that comes with the end of speeches and a sit-down meal. Everyone is ready to get up and mingle, and Garrett Castle is perfectly appointed for just that. Outside the ballroom, the whole ground floor appears to be one reception space after another: a reading room here, another little nook there, and in the entire north-east corner of the hotel, a large extended lounge area.

Plush floral sofas are arranged in clusters, and Fia sinks down into one, among a bunch of people she knows. Someone from the London office with whom she's had many a chat at Summer Summits past presses a white wine into her hands, and Fia takes it with a grateful smile. No matter the apparent success of dinner, there's a certain relief in finding herself back with those of her own age and stage.

Ryan shows up not too long after – handsome as ever in his suit, smiling as he settles himself beside her on the sofa, his hip nestled against hers. Of course, their history has taught them nothing if not discretion. Surrounded as they are by others, there are no wandering hands, no flirtatious comments – the occasional secret smirk or raised eyebrow from Ryan is about as risqué as things get.

Sadly, however, Fia can hardly even enjoy it. She can't enjoy it because she's distracted – and, specifically, she's distracted by Benjamin Lowry.

Benjamin, in the far corner of the room near the bar, looking at her.

Over and over, she feels his eyes on her. She can just sense it. Each time she turns her neck in his direction, though, he's already looking away, all innocence. Has the reverse been happening a little bit, too? Fia could neither confirm nor deny.

This time, however, it's different. When Fia casually lets her glance wander over towards Benjamin, he is nowhere to be seen. She scans the room, feeling her heartbeat quicken in her chest, and . . . it's true. He appears to be gone altogether.

She turns her attention back to her group, doing her best to concentrate on the story someone is telling – but the feeling in her stomach as she looks at Ryan suddenly makes at least one thing undeniably clear to her.

'I'll be back in a sec, okay? I'm just going to run to the bathroom,' she murmurs to him, barely awaiting his nod before she slips away.

She doesn't go to the bathroom, though. She goes, instead,

out to the hotel lobby, a little away from the cacophony of people. Then, one quick phone call later (and a few minutes to try to settle herself), she's headed back to the lounge. She's just approaching its open doorway, in fact, when suddenly, there he is.

Right in front of her, for the first time all day, it's her summer associate.

Chapter Thirty-Seven

Benjamin is headed for the same place she is, apparently, but he stops short as soon as he notices her. How startling it seems to be, finally seeing him like this, when it feels like they have been orbiting one another all night.

'Uh, hi,' she says.

'Hi,' he replies. 'You look nice.'

And the thing is that so many other people have said that – or something like it – to her already this evening. But it hasn't felt at all the way it does when he says it.

'Thanks,' she says, hearing how her own voice comes out sounding a little thin, a little fluttery. 'Are you having a good night?'

'It's been all right,' Benjamin says, and Fia tracks his gaze as he nods through the doorway towards Ryan, still chatting happily with the others in the group she left. 'So, you and him. Real talk. Is it a romantic thing?'

Fia thinks about it for a second. 'No,' she replies, and then, for the sake of full disclosure, she clarifies, her voice low.

'I mean, I've had sex with him. But not in a romantic way.' She watches that information land before she speaks again. 'Also, this really is none of your business.'

A smile twitches at his lips. 'Hey, I can't know who my wife is bumping uglies with?'

Fia's expression contorts into sudden alarm. Of all the people coming and going or clustered in groups around the lounge, there's probably nobody quite within earshot. However, that seems much more like a matter of good fortune than any calculation on Benjamin's part. And by now, they're five weeks into the summer. Having made it to the halfway point, she'd much prefer not to let their particular cat out of its bag at this stage. Instinctively, she edges into an open door just adjacent to where they're standing.

'That's a horrendous expression,' she says, aware of him following her as she moves. 'And less of the wife talk,' she adds, though she'd acknowledge the hushed tones are probably unnecessary now. There's no longer much of a threat of being overheard.

Benjamin looks around, taking in their new surroundings. It's all wood panelling and heavy curtains, an empty grate in the fireplace and, in the centre of the room, a large mahogany billiard table. Or is it pool? Snooker? Fia has no idea what the difference is. She's a pretty decent shot, though, having been schooled by her brother in her younger years.

'Why are we in here?' Benjamin asks.

Actually, Fia isn't altogether sure. She didn't deliberately decide to come into this room, much less did she deliberately decide to bring him with her.

'We're in here because you can't be trusted to keep your big mouth shut,' she hisses, which feels like it must be the truth.

It does, at least, feed into a very familiar dynamic between the two of them. It avoids anything more . . . nebulous.

In any event, he ignores it altogether.

'You wanna play pool?' he asks.

She's taken aback. 'Not really.'

He just cocks his head, as if in sympathy with her. 'Are you afraid you'll lose?'

Fia fights the sudden urge to laugh out loud. 'Oh, Benjamin,' she replies instead, all condescension, with a little sigh to boot. 'Is it 2015 again already? You forget – I'm *not* actually a 13-year-old boy. Stuff like "are you afraid you'll lose" or "are you too chicken" . . . ?' She gives an exaggerated shrug. 'What can I tell you? It just doesn't have much effect on me.'

'Mmm, I think it has a *little bit* of an effect on you,' he replies softly, and suddenly he seems to be very close to her. When did that happen? When did he inch forwards into her space, near enough that she imagines she can feel the heat from his body? Or, at least, one way or another, she's newly aware of being very warm.

She can't quite seem to formulate a response – it feels like she's floundering, grasping for words just out of reach – when he stretches to grab one of the cues from the table. He places its tip on the ground between them with a gentle thud.

'You can start,' he says.

Then he reaches for the other cue, lifting the triangle rack from the balls and making his way to the other side of the table. He pushes the room's door closed while he's at it. Fia notices that.

She takes a shot, misses, and Benjamin grins, until his own foul just seconds later wipes the smile off his face.

Next, it's Fia's turn again, and this time, she hits it right into the pocket. She looks over at him, a half-smile pulling at her lips.

'Jealousy is so unbecoming, Benjamin.'

He scoffs as he leans down, lining up his next move. His eyes flick from her to the ball and back again. 'It's early days, Irish. One half-decent shot? Who said I was jealous of that?'

She quirks one eyebrow, just a millimetre. 'Who said I was talking about the game?'

Benjamin makes no reply, but she watches the muscles in his lower jaw clench, in what might be aggravation or might be concealed amusement – or might be the other thing: *want*. It is starting to feel as though perhaps they are all one and the same, anyway.

When he finally takes his shot, it's perfect – a purple number four hurtling neatly into the top right-hand corner – and he straightens to meet her eyes again, thoroughly satisfied with himself now.

Fia just breaths out a little laugh. She reassumes her own shooting stance, ready to reassert her lead, eyeing up her next move. She is jittery, though, second guessing herself. From beyond that heavy wooden door, she can still hear muffled sounds of the party going on. But in here, it's quiet. And there is no energy that crackles like potential.

Once or twice, she adjusts her positioning, just the slightest shifts in her hands, in the angle of her body. She doesn't know if it would even be apparent to the average onlooker, but at this point, she expects nothing less than for Benjamin Lowry to notice, and to make a thing of it.

In fact, though, she doesn't get any of his usual choice commentary. Instead, she hears his pool cue drop, and the next thing she knows, he's striding purposefully over to her end of the table.

She rolls her eyes. 'I swear to God, Ben, if you plan to instruct me on how to use this cue, I will shove it—'

That's *not* what he plans, though, if indeed he's planned this whatsoever. Actually, it doesn't seem like he has. He's a little like a man possessed as reaches her side – and then, with both hands, he pulls her into him, pressing his mouth to hers.

Fia's stunned, both of her eyebrows shooting up, and together, they stumble backwards a little bit from the sheer force of their collision. As they steady themselves, though, she appears to be clutching at him just as desperately as he is her. How about that? It takes her brain a second to catch up to what her body seems to already know. Because, yes, she's kissing him back with everything she has now, her hands moving to whatever parts of him she can reach, her blood coursing through her like liquid heat.

For his part, Benjamin's equally frantic, but not sloppy with it – he kisses her as though he's thought about this, wanted it, knew exactly what she'd like. When he lets his teeth catch just slightly on her lower lip, lets his tongue ghost across the skin he's nipped, Fia doesn't understand how every bit of tension in her body seems to drain away and ratchet up simultaneously. She'll have to figure it out later, though. Because in this moment, she can't think. She can only feel.

'Oh my God!' she exclaims, when eventually they pull apart. 'What the fuck?!'

Benjamin says nothing, only looks at her, and there is something new in his expression – something that seems suddenly, deliciously, untamed. It makes Fia's stomach clench anew, just the sight of it

As for the next thing, what she might tell Annie and Kavita later – if she decides to tell them at all – is that everything just happens so fast. This would be a complete lie.

All those years ago, in Benjamin's little room at Camp Birchwood, *that* happened fast. And the kiss they've just pulled away from, that happened pretty damn quickly, too.

But this time around, the truth Fia might acknowledge only to herself is that she knows exactly what she is doing.

As Benjamin moves in towards her once more, it is extremely clear to her what is about to happen. She can feel his breath hot on her skin. She has so much time to stop this, so much time to exercise her better judgement. And yet, she doesn't. When his lips finally meet hers again and they sink into one another, it's five seconds before they're right back to kissing hungrily, madly. The scent of him up close – that same scent she's had lingering in her office for weeks now – makes Fia feel truly a bit lightheaded. She isn't sure how long they stand there, hands grasping, tension building, but eventually, they break apart once more. It might be the need for air, or it might be the call of sanity beckoning.

They stare at one other, and as Fia's heartbeat starts to slow to a normal rate, her eyes widen. The full significance of what has just happened hits her hard.

'What the fuck,' she says once again, but it's less of an exclamation this time, less of a question. Instead, the words tumble out on a dazed sort of exhale.

'You kissed me back,' he murmurs, as though some part of him is actually telling *himself* that fact, as though he can't altogether believe it's true.

'No, I know,' she agrees immediately, and then she repeats it like a chant. 'I know, I know. It's just, like . . . this can't be a good idea, can it? I mean, apart from anything else, I'm basically your boss.'

He rolls his eyes, suddenly entertained. 'I don't know how many times I need to break it to you that you're *not* my boss, Irish.'

Fia barely hears him. 'I just can't believe this has happened!' she exclaims. 'Again!'

Benjamin looks at her for a moment, and when he speaks, there's no ego in it. It's simple, guileless. 'Yeah, you can.'

For once, she finds herself disinclined to argue with him. 'Yeah,' she admits quietly. In a way it's a relief, after all this time, to say it out loud. 'I suppose I can.'

Still, though.

Boss or not, she knows for sure that the partners at the firm would not take kindly to this pairing. And even within the gossip and lore that exists below partner level, she absolutely does not want to be known as the woman who's always up for a fling with one of the summer associates. That's how it works, in the fishbowl that is ZOLA: you only have to do something once for it to stay with you forever.

Added to that, of course, there is the small matter of her ongoing divorce from Benjamin – all the cash and emotional energy she's already spent with the direct aim of never speaking to him ever again.

Fia's mind whirls as she thinks about all that – and then she thinks about Ryan, in the next room, assuming he's on a promise tonight.

It's a lot to assimilate at once.

'I have to go,' she blurts out.

Benjamin opens his mouth to say something – to protest, she imagines, although maybe she's flattering herself. In any event, she jumps in again before he can get the words out.

'No, honestly, I really do. My mam's picking me up.'

It sounds incredibly childish, said out loud like that. Her New York self would never – could never – say such a thing. She's projects nothing but independence there. It's funny how all sorts of practical things – things you didn't even particularly choose – can eventually come to make up your personality. Anyway, right now, what she's just told Benjamin is the simple truth of the matter. When she called the house earlier, Fia barely had time to issue the request before her mother was rushing to hang up the phone, grab her car keys.

Even if she wanted to, it would be tricky at this point to have her mam arrive at Garrett Castle and then turn right back round again, without her.

Would she want such a thing, if it were possible? Instinctively, Fia thinks that she would. Her instincts have been known to lead her badly astray in the past, though. And the feeling she had just a moment ago, with Benjamin's hands on her hips – that sense of *abandon* . . . some very long-buried part of herself remembers that. She knows it can only end in disaster.

'Okay,' Benjamin replies, his eyes still fixed right on her. There's a moment's pause before he shakes his head a little. '*God*, your mother loves me,' he adds then.

And it's immediately obvious to Fia that he is in some sense letting her off the hook here – or letting both of them of the hook, maybe, allowing them to revert once more to something more playful, more arch, more like it was before they remembered how incredibly good they seem to be at kissing one another.

'All right, steady on,' Fia replies drily – because she can play her part, too.

'I'm like the son she never had,' Benjamin continues blithely, undeterred.

'Well, I'll make sure to mention that to the son she *does* have.'

He smiles, and there are another few seconds of quiet between them: an acknowledgement, Fia imagines, of the fact that this will probably never happen again, but that neither will regret it having happened tonight.

Or it could be none of that. She really does not know.

'So, I'll just . . . see you back at the office?' he asks then, squinting over at her. Along with all their co-workers, he's flying out first thing tomorrow. Fia will have a whole seven days here, without him.

'Yeah,' she replies softly. 'I'll see you back at the office.'

WEEK SIX

Chapter Thirty-Eight

The following week goes by quickly – too quickly, as it always does when Fia's off work. She makes a valiant effort to stay off her emails, too, and is mostly – although not entirely – successful.

'Just don't answer it,' her mother suggests, when something particularly urgent pops up on Fia's phone. It is so hard to explain that such an option is actually not an option at all. Fia does, at least, have Maeve there for backup. Her sister works in events management, which appears to offer a similar work-life balance to the law.

Their mother worked all her life, too, as a dental nurse at a local surgery. Although now retired, she'd definitely had her share of work-related issues over the years. Tiredness, irritation with co-workers, pressure from superiors – she knew all about those things. But it was different. There came a point, every single evening, when their mother left work, knowing for sure that she was off the clock, and knowing that absolutely nobody would expect anything different. By contrast, neither Fia nor

Maeve have ever experienced working life without constant
– literally constant – accessibility. The threat of a sudden
demand from a boss or a client, even when that demand doesn't
ultimately materialise, is simply something to be managed.

In this particular week, it strikes Fia that she actually feels
lucky – as though she is getting off lightly, as if she could
hardly expect anything better – while her mother is veritably
appalled by the degree of contact. How has this happened,
within one generation? She wonders if perhaps everyone her
age might have some kind of Stockholm syndrome. She thinks
back to that first Blackberry she'd been gifted from ZOLA,
aged twenty-two. How delighted she'd been. She hadn't realized
then that it was a tracking device, a leash.

Work aside, she spends lots of her week outside, tramping
around the beaches and hills that did not, throughout her
childhood and adolescence, seem like even remotely exciting
excursions (no matter the ease of access from Dublin). At 30
years old, though, Fia discovers she's pretty content in her jeans
and raincoat, taking in the fresh air. Expansive views seem to
stretch in every direction – Ireland encouraging her to look
out, not up – and she's struck, not for the first time on this
trip, by how lovely it all is.

Plenty of time, also, is spent at home. That's another thing
that's different for Fia. In New York, she is lucky to have a
relatively spacious apartment – but still, there's the urge to get
out of it. Manhattan is just no place for an indoor cat. People
do their work and their socializing and often even their relaxing
outside their homes. Fia can't remember the last time she spent
a full day inside her own four walls. In Dublin, by contrast,
she passes hours just chilling on the sofa and pottering around
and – as an act of pure altruism – helping her dad create a

better system for all the cascading paperwork in his office. How it all got so out of control, she has no idea.

She feels younger, in the way a person cannot help but feel when they return to their parents' house, sit down to a meal they haven't made, have someone suggest they take a coat. Equally, though, on this trip, she somehow feels older, too – and not older as in wiser: older as in *ageing*.

On Thursday, she goes for brunch with Lauren, an old school friend who's followed the Irish playbook to the letter. That is to say, she has taken the allocated window for adventure – university in Glasgow, a year or two in Australia – before returning home to recommence her real life. Her 5-month-old son turns out not to exist only in photographs but in fact to be a real, living infant, sleeping contentedly in the pram beside them.

'It's so crazy that you have a *child*!' Fia says, her eyes widening in what she thinks is an obviously comedic fashion.

'I know,' Lauren replies. 'Sometimes, I look at him, and I just think "oh my goodness, I can't believe he's really mine", you know?'

And the utterly lovestruck tone of her voice makes it clear that they have somewhat missed the mark with each other here. Fia meant something more along the lines of *how alarming*, not *how marvellous*.

Somehow, she has just been unable to shake off a certain reaction, every time she learns that someone she knew in adolescence is now pregnant. There remains the slight whiff of scandal to it in her mind. She still wonders, instinctively, what the parents will think – when, of course, the parents are probably absolutely beside themselves with joy.

On Friday afternoon, Fia overhears her mother in the kitchen with Auntie Anne. They are talking about Maeve and Conor, the upcoming wedding and all. Twenty-seven is 'a lovely age to get engaged,' her mother says, and Fia knows that her mam would never dream of making such a comment around her. In a certain way, she is grateful for that – not everyone is lucky enough to have such a mother; this she knows for sure. Equally, though, it does make her a little sad, the idea that there are certain things her mam would not say in front of her: the idea that there are ways in which her whole family is probably trying to be sensitive.

People, it has to be said, get a lot *less* sensitive by the time Friday evening comes around and a few drinks have been imbibed. The engagement party brings a crowd of friends and relatives to her parents' house, the furniture rearranged slightly to make space for everyone, the kitchen well-stocked with beverages. Even Fia's brother, Eoin, arrives from Cork – greeted by their mother, as ever, as though he is the Lord Jesus Christ, risen again and popping in from Jerusalem.

'Any men on the go, over there?' one of Maeve's friends asks Fia conspiratorially, barely three sentences into the conversation.

Fia's mind flashes instinctively to Benjamin. She can't help it. Over the course of the past week, her mind has flashed in his direction quite a bit. Incidentally, he was right when he claimed that there'd be no need to physically meet with Susan Followill again. Perhaps one in-person session had proved quite enough for Susan, too. She emailed just yesterday with their draft settlement agreement, and Fia approved it in ten seconds. Across the Atlantic, she can only assume Benjamin has done the same. The document must be winging its way to a judge this very moment. For now, she pushes all such thoughts aside, focuses on the question she's been asked.

'No,' she replies, feeling slightly pathetic. She shouldn't feel that way – she hates that she does – but she knows it's not her fault. It's because of *society*.

'Ah well, I'm sure you'll meet somebody soon. Probably when you least expect it!' the other girl replies.

'Fia's about to be made a senior associate at her firm,' Maeve chimes in proudly. 'She's basically running a little legal empire at this point. In *Manhattan*. Can you believe it?'

'Ooh, you go girl!' says the friend, then, sounding more Americanized than plenty of Americans Fia knows, even though she is – according to her own recently offered bio – from Bray. 'That's what I like to hear. Hashtag boss bitch!'

Fia smiles along, clinks her glass when prompted, because what else is there to do? As it happens, she has zero time for the whole boss-bitch, boss-lady, girl-boss thing. Each to their own, and all – if some people found it inspirational to consider what Beyoncé might do in a given scenario, then more power to them. It just happens to leave Fia entirely cold. If she *is* ever put in charge of anything or anyone (beyond Benjamin Lowry), she's certain she'll see that as much more a matter of practicality than of personality. Even now, she doesn't think she has any major attachment to herself as a *high-powered lawyer*, a *career woman*.

Sadly, Maeve's friend does not know any of that. She simply cannot be stopped from launching into an impassioned speech about modern women – confident, *fierce* modern women – and the ways in which modern men (for shame!) are threatened by all the confidence and the fierceness.

'I mean, look at you, Fia, you're such a babe!' she finishes ardently. 'You should be fighting them off with a stick!'

Again, Fia can only smile weakly. This type of thing – almost invariably offered in some sort of feminine solidarity – has always struck her as the worst kind of compliment. Some variant of *you seem too nice to be single*, or *too cool, too pretty* – as though there is any sort of correlation.

Perhaps she might feel differently, if she found herself bowled over by every person she knows whose 'best friend in the world' had one day asked them to 'do forever', etc. And/or if she were routinely underwhelmed by those who were uncoupled, if they seemed clearly deficient in one way or another.

However, the truth is that when Fia thinks about her single friends – her single *female* friends, that is – the very opposite is true. They are sociable, hard-working, attractive. They are keeping pets and plants alive. They are travelling and volunteering, and they've read *The Secret History*. The idea that they are, in some sense, the exception – the confusing, unfortunate minority who somehow haven't found love despite really deserving it – just doesn't ring true for Fia. What a person deserves doesn't much come into the equation, as far as she can see. There is no star system at play here. If domestic partnership illustrates anything about a person, she reckons it is merely their capacity for faith in others, their capacity for compromise with others. More than anything, it illustrates the sheer unplannable, unpredictable happenstance of life.

Of course, she can say none of that. But, as the conversation moves along, as the party continues, there is a lot Fia *can* contribute. There are toasts and hugs, and she feels so naturally a part of things – so intrinsically connected to these people, this place. It's not a question of whether she wants to be; she just is. She meets neighbours she hasn't seen for years, and she roars along to Christy Moore songs with everybody else, and when her brother Eoin throws her a precious last bag of Tayto crisps across the room – 'Here, catch, Elle Woods!' – she throws back her head and laughs.

Undeniably, there are a fair amount more questions about her life – how it's going, *where* it's going – from people who mean well. That Eoin (35 years old but, crucially, male) does not seem to be subject to the same questioning is not even particularly surprising to Fia any longer. It does mean, however, that she finds it necessary to consume quite a lot of wine.

Meanwhile, Maeve (for reasons presumably much more fully rooted in celebration) consumes quite a lot *more* wine. By the early hours of the morning, the two of them are squished together on the couch, feet on the coffee table, their mother thankfully not around to witness it. The party has thinned out considerably now, just a few remaining friends and relatives clustered around the house or back garden, the groom-to-be presumably somewhere in the middle of them.

'Fia, I love you so, so much,' Maeve slurs.

Fia laughs. 'I love you, too, Maevey.'

'No, but I mean, like, I *really* love you. I miss you so much when you're in New York. I worry about you over there, you know.'

Fia did not know this, not even a little bit. 'Worry about me?' she replies, perplexed. 'Why?'

Maeve shrugs, cuddling into her. It's almost impossible for Fia to believe that this girl, her baby sister, is going to be someone's wife soon. Maeve will have the church and the three-course dinner, the disco and the residents' bar until the wee hours . . . the very specific Irish version of a wedding. None of that, of course, is the version for which Fia had been destined. In her more lucid moments, she doesn't even overly want it. So why, right now, does it feel like a bit of a loss?

'I dunno. Just America, you know?' Maeve continues. 'The guns and the healthcare. And, like, your Instagram . . . ?'

Of all the places Fia might have expected the conversation to go, this was not it. She barely even posts on Instagram. Maybe once every couple of months, at most.

'What about my Instagram?' she asks with a laugh.

Maeve wriggles a bit, pulls her phone from her pocket. It seems to take her an inordinate length of time to find what she wants on there, but eventually, she does. She brandishes the screen at Fia, as though the content speaks for itself.

'There, see?'

Fia recognizes the photo as her most recent post. It is a photograph of the exterior of her apartment building, taken back in the spring. With the cherry blossoms in full bloom, the sun shining, and a filter discreetly applied, it looks beautiful. Below, in the caption, she's written:

> Spring has sprung! But also, today I saw a rat inside an empty Ritz crackers box right here on the pavement. Everyone – EVERYONE – thinking about moving to NY should be forced to see such a sight before they sign a lease agreement.

'And then this one . . .' Maeve continues, flicking to the previous post. It shows an obscenely large slice of chocolate cake.

Fia squints, to read what she wrote there.

> Hi, this is my boyfriend now. #dinnerforone

That amuses her slightly, even now, and she's chuckling when Maeve swipes to yet another post.

By now, they're all the way back in 2022, and Fia barely even remembers taking the photo. It's of a 'delayed' sign on the metro – which, to be fair, could be practically any day of the week.

Carrie Bradshaw never had to put up with this shite, her caption reads on that one.

And, suddenly, she feels like maybe she sees where her sister is coming from.

She has never wanted to post anything online that screamed *look at my fabulous life*. But perhaps, she realizes now, she might have over-egged it slightly. If a brunch was enjoyed with the gals, but it didn't make the grid, had it even really happened? She might be the only person in the world who actually makes her life look worse on the internet than it really is. She's got the opposite problem to the likes of Alyvia Chestnut. And why, with that thought, does Benjamin pop into her head? Why is he the one to whom she wants to convey her dumb little late-night realization?

Next, a totally separate line of thinking springs to mind. Maybe, in some weird way, these photos are telling her a truth she hasn't wanted to see. Maybe Maeve is exactly right to be concerned. Maybe, on balance, Fia *doesn't* actually have a very good quality of life in New York. Maybe the levels of stress and work and expense and effort that she has come to accept as normal and necessary are in fact neither.

Could that be true? It's very taxing to think about, in her current state of inebriation.

'What do you want me to put?' she challenges Maeve then. '"Wow, today's view definitely beats the one from the top of O'Connell Street"? "Fantastic shag with 'this one' last night"?'

Maeve doesn't laugh along, though. She's actually almost out cold, Fia realizes.

Her sister's reply is drowsy and affectionate. 'I just want you to come home, Fia,' she murmurs. 'Me and Mam and Dad and Eoin. We all just want you to come home.'

Chapter Thirty-Nine

So it is that, by Sunday, Fia's about to leave Dublin, and some significant part of her is thinking about staying – or rather, about returning. Permanently.

Precisely why that's happened now – as opposed to two years ago, or three years ago – is hard to say. Fia lies in her childhood bedroom on the last morning of her trip, turning the whole thing over in her mind. It is, she decides, probably a combination of factors.

Part of it must simply be that, having spent last Christmas in New York, she'd been away for so long, this time. And, on this trip home, more than on any other, she's had the sense of things changing here. People just haven't had the decency to stay where she put them.

Of course, Maeve's engagement is the biggest example. Babies will surely follow the marriage, and some day all too soon, the conversation that Fia had with her friend Lauren this past week is the one she'll be having with Maeve. They will not love each other less, but they will inevitably have less in common, their window for gadding about as equals all but over.

In truth, though, is not *only* Maeve's engagement. Fia also can see, in the smallest of ways, that her parents are getting older. Any time she feels homesick in New York, she often reminds herself that home will always be there. People have said that to her, over the years, and the phrase has stuck with her, comforted her. However, this past week, it has struck Fia (profoundly, irrefutably, and for the first time ever) that in truth her home will *not* always be here. Not the way it is now.

In the time she's lived in New York, she's lucky that her family have had the money and the energy for frequent visits. They have gone up the Empire State Building and the Freedom Tower and Top of the Rock – together, they have climbed more or less any structure that can be climbed in Manhattan. So many great pictures, great memories. But for how long will those trips continue, once there are infants in the mix, once advancing age begins to do what it does?

And, although it is perhaps less exciting than jetting off to the Big Apple, there is something equally lovely about the way that Maeve will always – even when she officially moves out – be able to call into their parents' house unannounced. Or the way that Eoin can drive up from Cork and be home within a few hours if necessary. Fia can see that she is missing things, here – all sorts of little threads of connectivity – and she's reminded again of her mother's saying: *There is no such thing as quality time. There is only time.*

Added to all that, of course, is the small matter of her own age. Thirty (and counting). Fia can't rule out the idea that she's unnecessarily hung up on the milestone, but still – she feels how she feels. Don't people always say that New York is a city for one's twenties – that you should get out, before it makes you hard?

Professionally speaking, the last four years in Manhattan have been one long phase of Working Like A Demon. That's what she'd call the album, if she were a musician. As for romantically, she might define the era, broadly, as Kissing Random People. And maybe those are exactly the things she should have been doing in this time period. She's learned some lessons, had some fun, made some money.

She feels like she can see the new decade stretching out in front of her, though. This is the time. The decisions she makes in these next couple of years will probably decide – in practical, rather than necessarily philosophical, ways – who she is for the rest of her life. Where she puts her time matters now, in a way it didn't before.

What if she gets to sixty, and realizes that she's done all the wrong things? What if it doesn't take anywhere near that long? That night on the rooftop with Benjamin, telling him that she loved New York – as if it were just that simple – suddenly seems a long time ago.

She lies in her childhood bedroom on Sunday morning and thinks again about those $10 raspberries she bought from Whole Foods, about her upstairs neighbour whom she has to hear having sex and listening to terrible music. She thinks even about Annie and Kavita – about how their version of domesticity, as nice as it can often feel, is surely not destined to last. Maybe the end has already begun, in fact, with the arrival of Annie's promising new man.

Where would that leave Fia? If George Ferarra has taught her anything, it is that even the best of friends can ultimately disappear without a trace. Will her life in New York eventually come to feel like one long Fourth of July weekend? She's considered it something of an achievement, the way she can fit into the city almost seamlessly these days. But *belonging*. There is something deeper, more elemental, to that. She has a sense of belonging in Dublin that hasn't gone away. That is undeniable.

By Sunday afternoon, she's at the airport, killing time at the departure gate, when her phone buzzes in her hand. She looks down at the text. It's from Ryan Sieman and, even at first glance, it's a bit of a change from all their previous one-liners and emojis.

> Hey Fia. Sorry we didn't end up getting to spend much time together over the Summer Summit this year. I hope I didn't do anything to upset you? Obviously, our thing has been going on for a while now, and I can only think that maybe you have been wanting something more from me – like, some sort of commitment? Sorry if I've just been really blind to this! I totally get that you don't want to do the casual thing forever, and it was probably on me to step up this year!

Fia's first urge, when she finishes reading, is to laugh out loud. She actually *does* laugh out loud. Men are sometimes too hilarious. They profess to want women who want no-strings relationships with them, but they also fundamentally do not believe such women can exist. Even as Fia chuckles, though, another text pops up.

> Anyway, I just wanted to let you know that I think you're great. I'm truly sorry if you didn't know that. And, message received loud and clear. Actually, I think you're probably right – maybe it's time for us to make a real go of things (assuming you want to, that is)? Obviously, you're still in

New York at the moment and everything, but I have it on pretty good authority that the partners in the Dublin office would have you back here in a heartbeat. Damien McNulty is such a fan, he's ready to have T-shirts printed with your face on them. And I wouldn't mind seeing a bit more of you either ;)

Fia lets out another little exhale of disbelief. Her instinct is to forward both messages to her sister or to her roommates – to find the fun in them. But she stops herself, tries to take all of this at face value, to take it seriously.

Could this be some sort of sign?

Before her, at least figuratively, is a 30-something single man from Dublin. He works hard, and at the weekend, he likes to go surfing on the coast. He takes two-week holidays to Thailand – *she* would like to go to Thailand – and he's attractive and enjoyable to be around. This year more than ever, actually, she found herself genuinely appreciating his company at the Summer Summit. He never makes her feel jittery or confused. Even his vast mischaracterization of her feelings, as plain to see from these texts, somehow seems to strike her as more comical than aggravating. She doesn't actually think Ryan would have the capacity to really piss her off.

In short, she could probably do a lot, lot worse.

And as for the job portion of it all . . . well, maybe that's something to think about, too. Another thing.

WEEK SEVEN

Chapter Forty

Fia half-expects that New York will have changed somehow when she returns to it – or, at least, that the way she feels about it might have changed. In fact, things are much the same on both counts.

Traffic on the way into the city from JFK feels as soul-destroying as it ever has, but all the life on the pavements once they cross the bridge into Manhattan feels as heartening as it ever has, too. Fia still loves the sunshine, still hates the humidity. Kavita's home when she gets into the apartment, and they order a pizza from Numero 28, eating quietly together as they each work at their laptop screens. By the time Fia goes to bed that night – surrounded no longer by remnants of adolescence but by all the ephemera of her current self – it feels like her life here has just been waiting for her to slot right back into it.

Monday morning brings more bright blue skies, and she's on her way to work – high heels back on as she marches across the lobby – when she spots him.

That Benjamin would be here, walking into this skyscraper where thousands of people are employed, at the exact same second as she is? Honestly, that doesn't even strike Fia as especially unusual at this point. She feels as though Benjamin Lowry could show up at her gynaecologist's office, as her gynaecologist's part-time fucking apprentice, and she'd be about ready to accept that as simply another manifestation of God's sense of humour.

'Hi,' she says, as they each come to a stop, standing just a few feet away from one another.

'Hi,' he replies.

'Your forehead looks a lot better,' she says, which is true. The gash is just a neat little line now.

They take each other in for another moment, before Benjamin turns pointedly to look at the turnstiles that will lead them to the lifts. She follows his gaze; then they each turn back to one another, time seeming to stretch out, even amid the masses of other people.

Of course, it's extremely clear that they should go on upstairs. They should settle into their office, do some work, get through the reminder of the time they must spend together this summer. They should stick to the plan.

Benjamin tilts his head, nodding backwards at the street. 'You wanna just . . .'

And it must be some sort of sorcery, Fia thinks, or perhaps a more delightful kind of magic. Whether it's ultimately for good or for evil, what else could explain the way everything but the man in front of her seems to melt away?

'Yeah,' Fia hears herself agree, with barely a second's pause, no hint of hesitation in her tone.

He turns on his heel then – and, wordlessly, she follows

him. She follows him all the way outside, into the sunshine and a swarm of commuters.

They march across 52nd Street together, not another word spoken, and Fia wonders if Benjamin knows where they're going, because she has no idea. From the way his eyes are darting around, she'd guess he's winging it here, too.

They come to a parking garage belonging to a hotel and – though they're a tolerable distance from the office by now – still Benjamin takes a cursory glance around before he grabs her hand, tugging her into the space.

It's dark and cavernous, and Fia senses her heartbeat quickening as he leads them to a corner hidden from view.

Though she'd never say so out loud, what she imagines might happen next is that he might grab her – take her in his arms and kiss her so thoroughly she can only respond in kind.

He doesn't, though. Instead, he edges backwards so that he is resting against a wall, with her facing him.

This time, he's going to make her do it. Choose it.

And, in the end, she doesn't waste any time wondering whether it's a good idea or what it will mean. She's spent the last week in Dublin, one way or another, thinking and thinking and *thinking*. It feels incredibly good, now – it feels like such a profound relief – to just let herself have this: one thing that, at least in this moment, she suddenly knows for sure that she wants.

She presses her lips to his, her hands on his face, and immediately, they're in it together, utterly. He wraps his arms around her waist, pulling her close to him, and she remembers this feeling from Garrett Castle: the way he angles into her, seems to kiss her with his entire body. All-encompassing, intoxicating.

At some point, she leans back from him just a little. She lets her thumb drag over his lower lip and down his chin, and it's unbelievable, the thing that she can see in his eyes when she does. She's spent so much time trying to make sense of the particular power he seems to have over her that she really hasn't given much thought to the other side of the equation: the power she has over him. It's written as plainly as day on his face now, though. It's in his blown pupils, the slight hitch in his breath. In this moment, he would probably do absolutely anything that she wanted him to. That's quite a thing to realize.

He dives forwards again, his mouth recapturing hers hungrily, and Fia is only too happy to allow it, her hands clutching at whatever parts of him she can reach.

Whatever is happening between them, it won't be until death does them part. She knows that. But could it be until their *divorce* does them part? Strange as it may sound, she's starting to think that might be an excellent way to spend the remainder of what could even be her last summer in New York. She'll need to keep her wits about her, make sure it doesn't get out at work. But doesn't she have quite a lot of practice in that regard by now?

The key will be in picking the right moment to end things. And *she* will be the one to end things with Benjamin – she promises herself that, even as he's kissing her, as her own good sense threatens to desert her altogether. In any relationship, it is much better to be the one who leaves than the one who is left. Fia knows that all too well by now. This time around, she will be better at protecting herself.

In the meantime, though, it seems there could be all sorts of new things to be discovered. When eventually they pull away from one another properly, Benjamin is smiling an almost shy little smile – one just for her.

'Welcome back,' he says.

'Thanks,' she replies, sounding no less dizzy than he does.

She watches his gaze shift to the surroundings then, taking in the cars, the general grubbiness, the big dumpsters in the corner.

'I take you to all the best places, don't I?' he asks, and she laughs.

'Turns out this would actually be ideal content for my Instagram account.'

'What?' he asks, his brow furrowing in confusion.

'I'll tell you later,' she replies. Because right now – at least for ten minutes, before they are both officially late for work – she wants to do nothing but *this*.

What follows over the next few days is complicated sometimes, in its practical aspects. There is so much fucking *glass* at ZOLA. And, annoyingly, they each have so much *legal advice* to be getting on with providing.

It's undeniably a little bit exciting, though – the sneaking around.

Midmorning on Thursday, and Alyvia Chestnut is waiting for them downstairs, this time with her son in tow. Fia and Benjamin are on their way to greet her, marching along a corridor, when suddenly Fia finds herself tugged through a doorway on the left-hand side. It's a stationery cupboard, apparently, though she barely has time to take that in.

'What are you doing?' she squeaks, but he doesn't answer. Instead, he just reaches for her right away, pressing hungry open-mouthed kisses to her cheeks, her jawline and – at last – her lips.

She sucks in a breath through her nose. By now, that clench low in her stomach is familiar to her in a way, but still deliciously new.

'So, I don't even know what the point of this meeting is,' she manages, as he makes his way down her neck. She snakes her hand in underneath his suit jacket, his skin tantalizingly close through the thin fabric of his shirt. 'Just, by the way. Like, I've served our response to Jonathan's lawyer already . . .'

She loses her train of thought slightly then, as Benjamin's lower half angles into hers just so. Still, she makes a valiant attempt to continue. Whoever said two people couldn't make out among the paperclips and notepads of their workplace, while also keeping it extremely professional?

'All we can do at this point is wait for the reply. Also, I was kind of . . .'

She trails off again, and something about it makes Benjamin pull backwards a little to look at her this time.

'Arsey,' she confesses. 'In my letter. I, uh . . . I didn't really go for the "keeping it vague" in the end. It was more of a "let me burn you and everything you own to the ground" sort of approach, to be honest. I may have . . . had some personal feelings to work out on the page.'

That had been the day of her fight with Benjamin, after she discovered his Facebook messages, after all the ugliness that followed.

Making the admission to him now, she finds her body tensing a little, bracing for the possible fallout. As it is, though, Benjamin still has that look in his eyes as he scans every bit of her. Fia wouldn't know how to characterize it, exactly, but it makes her mouth go dry. Suffice to say his interest in arguing with her over matters of legal strategy seems to be at an all-time low.

'. . . *Arsey?*' he repeats, and the tone of his voice, the expression on his face, draws a peal of laughter from her.

'That's a Latin term,' she says, as condescendingly as she can manage in the circumstances. 'You wouldn't understand.'

He laughs then, too, so loudly it makes her worry about being overheard from the corridor outside. There's no time to raise the issue, though, because he's kissing her fiercely again. It's all she can do to stop her knees from buckling under her as he moves from her mouth to her clavicle, smoothing his tongue across her skin, dipping lower to the part of her chest left exposed by her top. As he does, he lets out a strangled, indistinct sort of sound from the back of his throat, his fingers pressing a little more firmly into her hip. And, in response, Fia feels something surge inside her, like a quickening of her pulse that she feels everywhere.

It is the way of things in films – and, perhaps consequently, in life – that women are often the ones who make all the noise, all the faces. They are the ones socialized not just to enjoy an experience, but perhaps also to slightly *perform* their enjoyment of it. With Benjamin, these past few days, it hasn't been that way at all, though. There has been no one-sidedness in that regard.

When they are together like this, he moans into her mouth, the sound always instinctive, as though he's swallowed a delicious morsel, been massaged at just the right pressure point. He smiles against her lips and breathes out her name, and none of it ever feels even remotely like a performance. It simply could not be clearer to her, when he is kissing her, that it is entirely his pleasure to do so.

For her own part, Fia isn't sure what's wrong with her, but she's starting to feel as though she has never before known what it was like to want anyone or anything. The need for the next fix, the next stolen moment, seems to heighten, not lessen as the days (the hours) go on.

She grabs for a handful of his hair now, tugging him upwards to look at her for a moment. '. . . How does this feel so good?' she asks him, when their eyes meet. The question tumbles out of her mouth before she has a chance to edit it, and when it does, he seems somehow to understand that it is not rhetorical; she's actually asking him.

For a moment, he appears to think about it right along with her. Then, he just shakes his head a little. 'I have no idea.'

Chapter Forty-One

Across the conference room table from Alyvia, Fia cannot believe it has only been five weeks since they all were last here together. So much seems to have changed in the interim – at least, on her and Benjamin's side of the desk. His sheer proximity still creates a supercharged awareness on her part, but in a very different way from before.

Meanwhile, on Alyvia's side – with her son still waiting in reception – things appear to be much as they were. Again, she comes armed with reams of screenshots of the recent Instagram activity from Silverfish29. He continues to repost all of Alyvia's content, each time with his own caption added, and, truthfully, this is not news to Fia. She's been keeping tabs. Nevertheless, she goes through the motions of reviewing some of the first few highlighted captions:

When will u learn that nobody cares about these stupid pictures

> Lol lol not your real house though, not your kid's real clothes . . .

> This is litrally child abuse.

Silverfish29's spelling, evidently, hasn't much improved. The allegations, too, remain much as they ever have been – just variations on the same themes, with no particular escalation. Oddly, the more ferocious feedback appears now to be coming from perfect strangers. Under both the troll account's posts, and Alyvia's original ones, the comments come thick and fast:

> ALL of Alyvia Chestnut's sponsors need to IMMEDIATELY STOP bankrolling this MONEY-GRABBING WHORE

> I'm not going to lie, I used to really like you, Alyvia, but this is becoming pathetic. Give it up, girl. Silverfish29 slipped that mask right off you, and there ain't no putting it back on.

> Guys, I am actually seriously worried about Gus at this point, does anyone have a connection to the family? Where in New York are they living? I think it's time child services got involved. PM me if you know their address.

Fia winces, passing the pages over to Benjamin. He, too, gives them a brief glance, before looking back up at Alyvia.

'Well, we'd love to go ahead and bring Gus in,' he tells her, swift as ever in getting to the point. 'Like I said on the phone, if this case does progress, there's a possibility he might ultimately have to give evidence. So, it's important we get a sense of how robust a witness he's likely to make.'

This, Fia has to admit, is good. So much better than *I wanted to get a gander at him, make sure none of the things in these allegations are actually true*.

'And it's probably good for Gus to start getting comfortable with us, too,' Benjamin continues. 'Or, well, I guess I'll actually be finishing up at ZOLA in a few weeks, but getting comfortable with Fia.'

He glances over at Fia, and she wonders when she started to kind of love the sound of her own name coming out of Benjamin's mouth.

A slight wave of heat comes over her, just thinking about the position they were in together not twenty minutes ago. She has *got* to find some way to get Kavita and Annie out of her apartment – *soon* – for the purpose of getting Benjamin into it. Failing that, she'd tolerate some sort of encounter with *his* roommate. She'd prefer to be overheard by a stranger than her own two friends. Hell, she'd almost pay to rent a hotel room at this point. But somehow, some way, she needs to be alone with Benjamin Lowry. That just feels like what's required here, before she can even begin to think about her exit strategy.

She reaches for a glass of water, feeling his eyes on her now, as if he knows exactly what's running through her mind.

Across the table, meanwhile, Alyvia just looks worried. 'Okay. I haven't told Gus anything about the trolling so far, though. And, needless to say, I haven't told him it's his fucking father. So, if you could just . . .'

'Absolutely,' Fia replies smoothly, before the obvious question occurs to her. 'Why does he think he's here, though?'

'Oh, he thinks it's just a business meeting. Gussy tags along with me on those all the time – welcome to single parenthood, am I right?'

Not being a parent, single or otherwise, Fia has nothing much to say to this, so she simply smiles. And one quick phone call later, someone is escorting Gus into the conference room. The boy sits down beside his mother.

The first thing Fia notices is that he's not in the blazer and bow tie of so many of his photographs. There's no corduroy anywhere in sight. Instead, he's dressed in jeans and a hoodie. With these, he's wearing Converse and a T-shirt showing a seventies rock band that Fia imagines he's lately begun to like more in notion than in sound. In short, he looks much more like the average American preteen than he seems on Instagram.

In other ways, though, Gus doesn't seem at all like a preteen. Conversationally, he's 11 going on 25. Only child syndrome, Fia guesses, noticing how he seems to know exactly when and how to speak up, where to listen politely. Even as Alyvia drones on about algorithms and optimization and engagement, he manages to appear reasonably attentive.

Overall, it takes less than fifteen minutes for Fia's mind to be put entirely at rest. She's no expert, of course, but she's pretty sure she would know an abused child, or even a troubled child, if one happened to turn up in ZOLA's conference room in front of her.

Very evidently, Gus falls into neither category. And Alyvia, for all her possible and probable faults, clearly adores this kid: it's in the affection of her body language, her tone of voice with and about him.

'So, is it fun doing the posts?' Benjamin asks Gus eventually, having – quite masterfully, actually – engineered the conversation so that this seems a natural question.

Gus shrugs. 'Sure.'

'How 'bout your friends at school,' Benjamin continues. 'Do they think it's pretty cool, too?'

At this, Gus hesitates slightly. 'Mmm, some of 'em can be kind of annoying sometimes. But I guess that's okay. You can't please everyone all the time, right?'

Beside him, Alyvia beams. 'That's right,' she says sagely. 'That's exactly what I always tell him.'

Benjamin seems to take this in. There's a slight suspension in the conversation for a minute, before he turns to smile at Gus, too. 'Well, that's a very mature attitude, dude. Took me at least 'til I was in my mid-20s to figure that one out. And you're, what, 11 years old?'

'Almost 12,' Gus replies.

'Oh, cool. When's your birthday?'

Fia barely registers the child's response though. She's long since seen, and heard, all she needs to here.

Once Alyvia and Gus are on their way, Fia and Benjamin take the lift back up to the fifty-eighth floor.

'Well?' she asks him, once the doors are closed. 'You satisfied?'

Benjamin's staring into space a little. 'Hmm? Oh. Yeah. I guess so.'

He's quiet for the whole remainder of the morning, though.

It's only after lunch, when they're both in their little office – Benjamin readying himself for some big conference upstairs with the M&A team – that Fia gets any hint as to why.

'So, I think I know who's posting all the shit on Instagram about Alyvia,' he offers as he stands, sliding his arms into his jacket.

Fia snaps to attention. By now, she's dealt with so many other matters that it takes her a second to refocus her mind accordingly.

'Oh my God! Did Instagram respond to the subpoena already?' she asks. 'Do we have an IP address for Silverfish?'

'No.'

'So, what, then?'

Benjamin tips his head back, rotating his neck in a circular motion, in the same way that he's done a zillion times since he arrived at the firm and that has now become inexplicably extra-attractive to Fia. There seem to be a lot of things like that. For the moment, she does her best to ignore it.

'I think it's Gus,' he says.

Fia practically does a comedy double-take. 'Gus, as in the kid?'

'Yeah.'

'How'd you figure that?'

'I don't know. Just . . . look around,' Benjamin says, and then he does exactly that, letting his gaze drift out into the atrium before landing back on Fia. 'This place isn't exactly a kid's idea of a perfect morning, okay? And with 90 per cent of kids, you're gonna very much know that. They're gonna act out, ask for the iPad – or be on their phones, I guess. At the very least they're gonna look bored. But Gus was just so . . . pleasing.'

Fia lets out a little laugh. 'And you think that's a problem?'

'I kinda do, yeah.'

'So, he's polite,' she counters. 'He's comfortable around adults. I don't think we can hold that against him.'

Benjamin shakes his head, unconvinced. 'Nah. He was, like, *too* polite. Didn't you think so?'

For no particular reason other than that he's planted the seed, Fia begins to doubt herself. 'I don't know. Maybe?'

Benjamin flicks through his armful of documents, checking to make sure he has everything for his meeting. 'Just, ask Alyvia, will you?'

'Ask her if she's in cahoots with her kid to basically frame her estranged-husband?'

'What? No. I don't think Alyvia *knows* this,' he clarifies. 'Just ask her if there's . . . any possibility it could be Gus.'

Fia exhales an incredulous little laugh. 'How 'bout *you* ask her?'

'Well, I couldn't possibly do that,' he replies, not missing a beat. 'I'm just the summer associate.'

There's a smile tugging at his lips, and it makes her want to kiss it off him.

'I'm not saying call her up and accuse Gus,' he continues. 'Just say . . . I don't know – say that you think it's important he knows what's going on and it wouldn't be a bad idea to broach the subject with him, ask him if he has any idea as to who it might be, yadda yadda . . .'

'We're talking about the *same child*, right?' Fia asks again, though it's mostly rhetorical at this point. And, when Benjamin offers no response, his expression still unmoved, she sighs aloud. 'Fine,' she agrees. 'But I'm only doing this for you.'

He makes a huge show of being touched, veritably bowled over by her declaration. She rolls her eyes.

'Because I *respect you as a professional*,' she clarifies, with a little bit of a smirk.

He smirks, too. 'Wow. That's big talk, Irish. This meeting is probably going to go long, and then I have a ton of other shit to do for Brett upstairs. I might be done by about seven thirty. Will you still be around by then?'

'I could be,' she replies.

'See you on the roof?' he asks quietly.

She gives him a little nod. 'Cool,' she says, and the thing is that nobody can hear them in here – there's no need for their discretion. It feels sort of nice, though, all the same: just, the intimacy of it.

Chapter Forty-Two

He's already there by the time she arrives – he's sitting atop the planter, just like the last time they were here, and Fia hoists herself up to join him. Once more, she has to fight the urge to reach out and touch him – to lean over and kiss him, maybe. Somehow, she can tell that similar calculations are running through his mind, but in the end, they keep their hands to themselves. It's just too risky. Anyone could arrive up here, any time.

This morning, in the stationery cupboard, was risky as well – insanely so. What on earth is wrong with Fia's brain? Nothing like that can happen again, she knows. She needs to be better at controlling herself.

It's sort of ironic, really. After weeks and weeks of worrying that someone at ZOLA would notice something off between her and Benjamin – would wonder why they didn't seem to like each other very much – there is now a new kind of danger. Fia's biggest fear has become the thought of someone clocking that she and Benjamin Lowry seem to like each other a little bit *too* much.

'How was your thing this afternoon?' she asks him.

He shrugs. 'Fine. I mean, shitty, but fine.'

Fia gets that. Sometimes, you need a person to listen to every detail of your work problems, to behave as though they are interested in the nitty-gritty of it all. Other times, you just don't want to get into it.

'So, I phoned Alyvia,' she tells him next.

At this, his ears seem to prick up, metaphorically if not literally. 'And? What'd she say?'

'Nothing, really. Said she'd talk to Gus. I have to say, though, I'm still really not sure I'm with you on this whole theory. A weird feeling across a twenty-minute meeting does not a little mini online troll make.'

'But it's not just that!' Benjamin protests. 'You heard what he said. His birthday is October *twenty-ninth*.'

Fia doesn't even try to hold back her laughter. 'Oh my God! That's what you're basing this on?!'

'Well, and "silverfish"!' he adds. 'Turns out "silverfish" is some kind of Minecraft thing. I googled it this afternoon. We probably should have googled that before now.'

Fia takes this in for a moment. 'Probably,' she agrees, and she lets a few more seconds pass, for effect. 'Or, y'know, if only we'd spent like seven years working in video games, we might have just . . . *already known it*.'

It's the type of thing that could have easily soured their whole morning, six weeks ago. As it is, her jibe isn't serious, and the snarky face he makes back at her isn't either.

Fia clicks her tongue against her teeth, forcing herself to genuinely consider the possibility for the first time. She casts her mind back to whatever specific Instagram comments she can remember. Upon reflection, *was* there something slightly juvenile to them? Some slight whiff of impotence or innocence? It would certainly explain the spelling deficiencies.

She supposes perhaps the idea isn't entirely ridiculous. She doesn't feel, as she did even a minute ago, that there's zero chance. But she's far from convinced.

'Still, Gus wouldn't be putting out those comments unless he just basically hates his mother, and it didn't seem like he did – far from it. They seemed really close, to me.'

'Yeah, well. I'm close to *my* mom. But did I love being paraded around like a show pony every time she needed to seem relatable? No, I really didn't.'

Fia wasn't expecting that one – the fervour of it. Nevertheless, she just nods, trying not to show her surprise. She feels, in some instinctive way, like she should try not to spook Benjamin right now.

'Did that happen a lot?' she asks evenly.

'Pretty often. She was always trying to get elected for something, you know? Or re-elected. Ran for District Attorney twice and won twice. Ran for Attorney General of North Carolina twice and lost twice. That's a lot of fundraising luncheons.'

'I'm never totally sure what the difference is between a lunch and a luncheon.'

Benjamin chuckles, slightly ruefully. 'About two grand. Anyhow, none of it was my mom's fault – she basically needed to bring me and Dad along to all those things, 'cause that's what everybody does, right? I get it. Even back then, as a kid, I got it. It was part of her job. But it wasn't always a whole lot of fun for me. And . . . Alyvia's putting food on the table with these posts. But I'll bet it's not a whole lot of fun for Gus, either.'

For a moment, they both just sit with that, in silence. 'Well, I suppose we'll see what Alyvia comes back with,' Fia replies. Right now, she finds she doesn't actually care all that much about Alyvia or Gus or any of it. She just wants Benjamin to keep talking.

'So, you're an only child, too?' she prods. 'Same as Gus, I mean.'

'Yeah.'

'And that thing of, like . . . wanting adults to like you – that was kind of ingrained in you as a kid, was it?'

'Not just adults,' he replies, and some expression that's half wince, half smile rises to his lips. 'I don't know if you've noticed, but I have some latent people-pleasing tendencies.'

'I don't know if *I've* always had the benefit of them,' she teases.

He smiles, more fully this time. 'No. I don't know what it was with you, but . . . you pretty much always got the unfiltered version. Back in Camp Birchwood days, I think you were the first person I ever met who could kinda . . . see through me, I guess, would be the best way to put it. Everybody else? Yeah. I knew how to just . . . make them like me. But then, that's weird, right? It shouldn't be that way. You can only have everyone like you if you're changing like the fucking wind.'

'I think you're hard on yourself,' Fia replies, and she's ready to admit it out loud: 'I think *I* was hard on you. Being able to talk to people . . . adapting to your situation, trying to take an interest . . . Those are good things.'

'I guess so. I've been trying to kind of re-programme myself, these last couple of years,' he says. 'But, yeah, it's definitely a balance. Trying to figure out how to be a little more myself, while also not being . . .'

'A total dick,' she fills in, at the same time as he says, 'Dislikeable.'

'Dislikeable, yeah,' she repeats, and they both laugh out loud.

For a moment, there's an easy silence between them before she speaks again. 'So, go on then. Tell me some dislikeable things about you,' she says, and though there's a buoyancy to it, she thinks it's clear to both of them what she's actually saying here: tell me the things you don't tell other people – the stupid things, as well as the serious things.

'Well, obviously there's the stuff you already know,' he replies, his voice rising jocularly. 'Marries drunk women and then never calls them, etc. Or do you mean aside from that?'

'Yes, aside from that,' she replies, and who could have predicted that she'd ever have such an exchange with Benjamin Lowry and feel warmth spreading through her, feel a laugh bubbling over.

Another beat of silence follows as he thinks, or at least pretends to.

'I'm not, like, a real big dog person?' he offers then, and she gasps dramatically, on cue.

'I know, right?' he continues. 'It's like the last unsayable thing. I mean, I don't hate all dogs. I wouldn't *harm* a dog. But do I want some random dog licking all over me on the subway? Do I love a dog-friendly café? Not really.'

'Well, you are a rarity in the world of New York dating apps, my friend,' she replies. 'Every guy on there, it's him in the park with a Golden Retriever, him up a mountain with a Great Dane. I always wonder where they're *keeping* these pets. Like, a lot of these dogs are not apartment-sized dogs.'

It's a little strange, suddenly, just the suggestion of that aspect of her life. Even as Benjamin smiles along valiantly, Fia wishes, for some reason, that she hadn't brought it up.

'Anyway. Okay. What else?' she says, in the attempt to blast past it.

He tilts his head, thinking again. 'Not that into sports. I mean, I do like watching baseball. A lot. But all the others . . . I'm honestly kinda faking it.'

She sniggers. 'I won't tell,' she says, and he holds her gaze for a second. When he replies, it's almost as though he's speaking to himself.

'You know, Fia, I don't think you will.'

She feels something bloom in her, at the tone of his voice, the look on his face. She can't process it any other way than as a physical want. And it takes absolutely everything in her not to kiss him, not to reach a hand out to his thigh, not to pull him into her, on top of her, all over her.

'What are you doing this weekend?' he asks her.

She's distracted. 'Mmm, life admin. Laundry. I think Annie and Kavita and I might go down to the South Street Seaport for lunch on Sunday.'

'Oh,' Benjamin replies, a little awkwardly. 'Cool.'

Immediately, Fia realizes her mistake and rushes to amend it, feeling a little awkward herself. 'Well, but I could . . . I mean, I could *not* do any of that. If you, um . . . have a better offer.'

And, as it turns out, he does.

Chapter Forty-Three

So it is that Fia discovers Benjamin's family has a cabin in Greenport, Long Island.

So it is that he ends up outside her apartment in a rental car at 8 a.m. on Saturday morning, sunglasses on, windows rolled all the way down.

It's a Toyota Camry, and they are headed for the Queensboro Bridge, but as she gets into that car, Fia feels as though she may as well be hopping into a convertible to be whisked off to Monaco.

They put the radio on, chatting idly, and as Manhattan begins to recede behind them, there's the sense of an exhale. Both metaphorically and literally, they are getting further from ZOLA by the minute – further from the people they each have to be there. The relief, the sense of escape, is so real that at some point, Fia laughs out loud, just from the sheer joy of it.

'What?' Benjamin asks, squinting over at her.

'. . . Nothing,' she replies, with a little shrug. But they're both smiling now.

She watches as the buildings gradually start to get lower, further apart, and by the time they've hit two hours of driving, it's all wide lawns and Saturday morning soccer games, banks and grocery stores with lots of parking outside. Fia has no idea how much property costs on Long Island – it's probably crazy expensive – and she's heard there are a lot of racists out here – but it sure feels nice to have some extra breathing space.

Of course, not for the first time, it occurs to her that she could have nothing *but* breathing space, if she went back to Ireland. Not for the first time, she pushes that thought to the back of her mind. She still hasn't replied to Ryan Sieman's text. Neither has she replied to the feeler email that – sure enough – Damien McNulty in the Dublin office sent her earlier in the week. There will be time, she tells herself, to think about all that once the summer's over.

She sneaks another glance over at Benjamin now, taking in the way his elbow is propped on the open window frame. His hand lightly grasps the steering wheel, his head bobbing along with the music a little, and she feels something vibrate inside her.

It's hard to explain how appealing she finds it, that he can rent a car in Manhattan and pick her up at her door and drive into the unknown, weaving in and out of traffic with ease. The same sequence of events would feel essentially impossible for Fia. And that's even if she were driving in Dublin, on the correct side of the road, never mind here, where she'd be driving on the wrong one. Unfortunate as it is for the cause of women drivers everywhere, the fact of the matter is that she – a woman – is not a good driver, nor an enthusiastic one. Something she's always appreciated about New York, in fact, is that there is really no expectation a person will drive. The assumption, in fact, is that they will not. Not driving does not immobilize a person or infantilize them in the way it sometimes seems to in Ireland.

That *Benjamin* can drive, though. That's sexy to her. When he stops to refuel and then reverses back out of the forecourt, one hand on her headrest as he looks out the rear windscreen, she honestly nearly loses her mind.

'Hey, Fia?' he says, once they begin to see signs for Greenport.

'Yeah?'

'Just so we're clear, you know how I said the place was rustic?'

'Yeah . . .' she replies.

'That's, like, *actually* rustic, okay? Not, like, Instagram rustic.'

'So, what? You're telling me there aren't going be any macramé wall hangings?'

'. . . I don't even know what that is, so no,' he says.

She thinks for a moment. 'Is there running water?'

'Mmm, you sometimes have to take what you get in terms of temperature, but yes.'

'Are there any dead animal carcasses knocking about? Mounted on walls or what have you?'

'What? No.'

She chuckles. 'Then we'll be fine.'

Based on this conversation, she still doesn't have any clear sense of what to expect, but soon, they come to a little town – or village might be more accurate. It has a marina and a main street full of trinket shops and eateries, and Fia can hardly believe that they are still in New York – New York State, at least. This place feels more like how she's always imagined Rhode Island or Maine. People are strolling around with takeaway coffees, enjoying the midmorning sun, and Fia begins to suspect that she could be sleeping in a tent tonight and, still, she would love it here.

That said, it's nice that she is *not* sleeping in a tent. Away from the main drag, and down one windy side road, then another, Benjamin eventually pulls up alongside a tiny little house. It's made of timber, with a wraparound porch, and as they make their way inside, it's immediately clear that Benjamin wasn't lying. The interior is not quite Scandi-chic – or, at least, not yet. It's more of a work-in-progress, and a very petite one at that. Still, though. There are gnarled wooden beams and a comfy-looking couch and huge stack of books piling from the ground up in the corner. Much as with the town itself, Fia can sense herself being won over almost instantly.

Walking around, her overwhelming feeling, in fact, is that she'd quite like to get her hands on this place: re-tile the kitchen maybe, source some hanging baskets for the porch . . . It wouldn't take much.

The tour is a fairly swift affair, given the size of the place, and when they arrive at what appears to be the sole bedroom, Fia stops in the doorframe.

'Oh, Benjamin,' she says, all mock concern, giving it everything she can muster. 'There's only one bed. What ever will we do?'

A look of much more genuine worry crosses his features. 'Yeah. I was thinking that, if you want, I can sl—'

It's sweet, and Fia so charmed by him, by this entire experience, that she hears herself let out a little giggle. Sincerely. A *giggle*. Wrapping her arms around his neck, she interrupts whatever proposal he might have, pressing her lips to his.

As ever, it takes no time at all for Benjamin to respond in kind, for the energy between them to shift into something feverish, something frantic. He grasps for the hem of her dress, clutching a fistful of the material against her thigh as they kiss, his other hand in her hair, and Fia senses heat rising inside her. Just the certainty that they are totally alone here – that nobody they work with is going to pop up or pop in – is so incredibly freeing.

They pull apart for air, and her glance flicks over towards the bed again.

'I'm sure we can make this work,' she breathes out.

'I feel so much better,' she mumbles against his skin, once the two of them are lying boneless and sticky-sweaty, sheets tangled around their limbs.

And it's true. Fia's whole body feels heavy and wrung out, but her mind is clearer than it's been in a long time. She feels, finally, like she could properly concentrate on something. She doesn't really *want* to have to concentrate on anything too strenuous, as it happens. But this past week – maybe longer than a week – it has been as though she actually, physically, *couldn't* – not fully. Her brain has just been so foggy.

She's partially blamed the heat – and truly, this past week in Manhattan, it has been hotter than hell, not a breath of fresh air to be found anywhere in the city. But, also, she's known that it wasn't the heat, not really. She's known what she needed. The phrase *getting it out of her system* has crossed her mind.

And she really thought that once might do it – enough to scratch the itch, allow her to return to her usual self, call it quits with Benjamin before he calls it quits with her. Now, though . . . that just seems slightly premature. It seems, more than anything, like such a *waste*. They're here for the whole weekend, after all.

The thing about good sex, Fia thinks, is that communication is key. Asking questions is definitely to be encouraged. But sometimes, at the same time, a person wants to be surprised. Sometimes, a person wants their partner to take charge, to seem a little unbridled – or, in the alternative, to let themselves be led, to yield their own power willingly. One way or another, to *just know*. It is, in Fia's experience, almost impossible to create that balance of dialogue and intuition if it doesn't exist to begin with.

And, with Benjamin, it exists more perfectly than she's ever known it.

'Maybe we should have just done that the very first day you arrived at ZOLA,' she continues, shifting to prop herself up on her elbow, looking down at him.

That the frustration between them may always have been – at least in part – of a very particular sort . . . it does feel like they've passed the point of deniability there.

Benjamin grins. 'So, you *don't* want me to sleep on the couch, tonight. Am I picking that up right?'

She lets out a little hum, as though she's considering it. 'Well, why don't we see how the day goes?'

She can't keep a straight face though, and when he pulls her down on top of him again, half-kissing, half-tickling her bare skin, neither of them can do anything but laugh.

'Where *do* you sleep, though?' she asks him then, once their laughter has faded, once her capacity for rational thought seems to have somewhat returned to her. 'Like, when you come here with your parents?'

Benjamin hesitates. 'Uh . . . yeah. About that. When I said this was my family's place . . . it's actually *my* place. I, uh, ended up with some spare cash a couple years back – before I started law school – and I bought it.'

Fia just looks at him, one eyebrow raised. 'Hmm. Okay. You ended up with some spare cash. *That* doesn't sound dodgy at all. You know lawyers can't also be *criminals*, right, Ben? Or they can, but it's sort of frowned upon.'

He just chuckles. 'It's all pretty much gone now. I mean, I'm not choosing to live with Vasyl as some sort of personal penance. After I paid for my tuition at Columbia, there wasn't much I could afford to buy in the city, except maybe a parking space . . . but then, I saw this place.'

Fia lets out a little exhale of disbelief. She thinks back to the day he first arrived in her office – to her assumption that he was living off his parents, that his summer associateship was all by their arrangement. There does not seem to be a limit to the number of ways she can be proven wrong about this guy. Of course, he has managed to neatly circumvent the matter of where exactly the money – and by Fia's calculation, it has to have been quite a lot of money – came from. She does notice that. How much money did video game people make? Had Benjamin *invented* some sort of video game? Fia doesn't know. But, at least for right now, if he doesn't want to discuss it, then she doesn't want to, either. What she's learning about Benjamin is that he gets to things when he's good and ready.

'So, hang on,' she replies slowly, as though she's piecing a jigsaw together in her mind. 'You made a shit ton of money, and you decided to spend it on . . . law school and property investment?'

'Yeah.'

'Oh my God. Are you a grown-up, Benjamin? Is that what you're telling me here?' she asks, and she lets her eyes widen dramatically. 'Do you have *house insurance?*'

He laughs. 'I do, but mostly I just hope that covers my own fuck-ups. My adventures in DIY have been . . . something.'

At this, she lets her gaze travel through the bedroom doorway and out towards the little hall. 'Yeah, what's happening there?'

In her direct line of vision, Fia can see five thick stripes of green painted on the wall, each one similar but different.

'Oh, I was just trying to pick a colour. In, like, February. Sometimes I get a little . . . sidetracked.'

Fia points at a pale sage. 'I like that one in the middle. D'you want to do it today?'

Benjamin lets out another laugh, this time of undisguised surprise. 'You want to help me paint?'

As it happens, Fia has never painted anything in her life before. She knows nothing about primers or masking tape or exactly what process and equipment is most likely to yield good results. Yet somehow, today, it strikes her that people can just have a go at things things – grown-up things, for which they've been given no advance permission slip. They can get in cars and just drive; they can buy ramshackle cabins in the middle of nowhere. Trial and error and enthusiasm – these have never seemed, to Fia, like the hallmarks of adulthood. But she's starting to think that, actually, they might be the secrets at the heart of the whole gig.

And so, painting a small hallway in Long Island sage green, this afternoon.

She gives a shrug. 'Why not?'

Chapter Forty-Four

If it were a film, the day would go by in a montage – and, somehow, the whole thing does kind of feel like a film to Fia. They go to the little hardware store in town to choose the paint, taking a wander through some of the other shops while they're there. It seems only sensible to pick up a few basics in the grocery store, to treat themselves to an ice cream cone each. Benjamin grabs her hand at some point and never lets it go, and part of Fia actually hates how good it feels. She hates that she feels somehow validated, in other people's eyes, just by presenting as part of a pair.

They come back to the house and get to work, making rapid progress in the small space. Again, there's something a bit aggravating, in principle, about that – about the fact that a task really does turn out to be so much easier when shared between two.

'What do you think?' she asks, once the first coat is done, and they stand together regarding their handiwork.

Benjamin has a cold drink in one hand, and his other comes to rest lightly at the juncture of her neck and shoulder.

'I think . . . I hope we don't die of fume inhalation tonight,' he replies, and in this moment, his fingers pressing against her skin, Fia forgets all analysis of couple-privilege in modern society. She just doesn't know how to feel anything but happy.

Post-dinner, they're settled on the porch, a bottle of wine between them. Fia pads into the kitchen, taking care where she steps in her bare feet. Properly re-sanding the deck, Benjamin tells her, is another job on his to-do list. She re-emerges with two bowls of ice cream, having picked up a pint earlier, and she hands one to Benjamin wordlessly.

His eyes brighten at the sight, and it feels nice, being able to offer him this small surprise, being able to take care of him in this small way.

'Twice in one day, I know,' she says. 'But it's basically medicinal.'

Temperatures here are probably not one bit lower than they were in Manhattan. If anything, it might even be hotter. Hopping in the shower earlier, Fia was actually grateful, in the circumstances, for the periodic bursts of cold water.

'Works for me,' Benjamin says, and when he tugs at her forearm, somehow she knows instinctively what he wants. She leans down for a kiss that's, respectively, *thank you* and *you're welcome*.

The last of daylight has faded by now, but the heat hasn't. Benjamin's old plug-in fan is still whirring, its lead trailing out onto the deck from the living room. Fia can hear cicadas buzzing in the distance, too. For whatever reason, as she sits back down, she wonders briefly what it might be like here in winter.

Different, for sure. But she can imagine loving that, too. A fire in the grate in the living room and red wine instead of white, jazz in the background instead of nineties R&B. In the privacy of one's own fantasies, it is perfectly possible to become a jazz lover.

'So, here's a question for you,' she says, mouth half-full of Häagen-Dazs. 'That summer at Camp Birchwood. Did you . . . I mean,' she falters, feeling suddenly unsure about what she'd envisaged as merely a piss-take. Nonetheless, having started, she must find a way to finish. 'You didn't, like . . . have *feelings* for me back then or anything, did you?'

What, she wonders frantically, if he actually says *yes*? What if he has been pining for her, for almost a decade, everything he's ever done a manifestation of a love she's been too blind to see? But—

'No,' Benjamin replies frankly, with not so much as a blink of hesitation, and the relief of it is such that Fia laughs out loud.

'I mean, obviously I thought you were unbelievably, like, borderline *unfairly* gorgeous,' he continues, and for a brief second, Fia would swear she can see a bit of colour rising to his cheeks. Or might that be her own cheeks? In any event, he's not done.

'Irritating, though,' he adds wickedly. 'Very, very irritating.'

'Well, back at you,' she replies, and then she just can't resist. 'What about now?'

'Same,' he says, and she makes a face at him, spooning another generous helping of ice cream into her mouth.

'It's a good job we've got Susan Followill on the case then really, isn't it?' she says blithely.

'Thank *God* for her,' he agrees, extending his glass towards Fia.

She clinks hers against it in turn. Should it feel so easy to joke about this? She doesn't know or, at the present moment, care.

'Although . . .' Fia lets her eyes span the modest surroundings, with a little gesture of flourish. 'To think: of all this, I might have been mistress.'

'That's a *Pride and Prejudice* reference,' she tells him, when he just smiles vaguely in response.

He brushes it off, all bluster. 'I know.'

She lets out a peal of laughter, prodding whatever part of his leg she can reach with her foot. 'Bullshit – you didn't know!'

'Okay, I didn't know,' he relents straight away, not trying to hide it in earnest. 'Honestly, I still don't really know. I'll google it.'

'*Do* that, Benjamin,' she says indulgently. 'You have to be willing to put in the work, you know? Educate yourself.'

For a minute, there's quiet between them, the playlist in the background tailing off as they each eat their ice cream, sip from their wine – it's a pretty unusual combination. But neither of them is complaining.

'I bought this place 'cause of my dad, really,' Benjamin says then, into the silence. 'In a manner of speaking. He died four years ago.'

The suddenness of this information, the simplicity in Benjamin's delivery of it, somewhat takes Fia's breath away. She has just about managed to open her mouth in reply when the expression on his face, the slight flinch in his upper body, stops her.

In that second, she can see that he doesn't want sympathy – or, at least, not the outward expression of it, not platitudes he'll only have to find a polite response to. He's probably heard plenty of those already.

'He had a brain tumour, and it was slow, and just . . . yeah, hard to watch. We did get to go on some good trips, have some good conversations. We sure read a lot of books together, towards the end.'

Fia manages a bit of a smile, her mind conjuring the stack in the living room just inside.

'People say all that should be a comfort. And I guess it is, sort of. But, still, I don't think I'm ever going to get over it,' he says quietly. 'Not totally. My parents spent every dime they had looking for a cure – clinical trials, experimental treatments, the whole thing.'

The next logical statement – that none of it worked in the end – goes unsaid. Fia feels the weight, the finality, of it, nonetheless.

'I did end up getting a big life insurance payout, though, when Dad finally passed. Hence law school. Hence this house. And it's so hard to process, knowing that certain things – like, good things – probably wouldn't have happened if he hadn't died.'

Fia wishes she had something helpful to say in response to any of this, some sort of wisdom to offer. She doesn't, though, so she just nods, reaching out to lace her fingers through his.

'He was a lawyer, too,' Benjamin continues, and if Fia didn't already know, instinctively, that it is difficult for him to really open up about his life, then the somewhat stilted tone of his voice would tell her. 'My dad. He was a public defender.'

'Wow, how'd that go down with your mam?' Fia asks, chuckling lightly. It almost sounds like the beginning of a joke. *A public prosecutor and public defender walk into a bar . . .*

'Well, it was a huge practical nightmare, obviously – they were both constantly having to turn down cases the other one was already involved in. But, in terms of how they handled it, like, between the two of them . . . I don't know. I think, ultimately, they felt like they cared about the same thing, and they were just coming at it in different directions.'

'Must've made for some lively dinner table chat,' Fia says.

He smiles. 'Oh yeah. Neither of 'em were exactly the type to back down from a debate, that's for sure.'

'Now I know where you get it from.'

'Mmm, but what's *your* excuse?' Benjamin tosses out, and they share a brief smile before he gets back on topic. 'You know, one thing I'd say about with my mom is that any time she was campaigning . . . I don't think even *she* would disagree that the whole circus made her a little crazy. It would probably make anybody a little crazy. But she never asked my dad to quit, even when it would have been a lot better for her if he had.'

'That *is* pretty cool,' Fia murmurs in reply. She'd like to meet this woman, she thinks. She'd like to have met Benjamin's dad, too. Her own parents' relationship has always – at least as far as she's witnessed it – been harmonious, even-keeled. The idea that there could be conflict between a couple, a bit more fieriness but no less love . . . that's intriguing to her.

'The amount of people who sent letters after he died – clients he'd helped over the years, their family members . . . I still have them all. They're here actually, in the closet upstairs. Anyhow, that's why I'm in law school, I guess,' Benjamin says. 'I want to do medical law, if I can.'

Fia's expression shifts in surprise. 'What does that involve?'

'Depends if I start off at a firm or go straight to some kind of public body. I'd lean towards the latter, but working for more equitable access to medicines and healthcare . . . that's basically the goal. Those are the kind of cases we take at the clinic at

Columbia. I know, it's all very like "Daddy issues", "psychiatry 101" or whatever, but . . . yeah.'

And, of course, there was a time when Fia would have been all too ready to pounce on any hint of worthiness in him, any hint of naivety. In the circumstances, though, she finds she's not one bit inclined to make fun.

'I think you'll be great at that,' she says, and what's more, she means it. 'I'm sure the partners at ZOLA will be very sad not to have wooed you to the dark side, though.'

He chuckles. 'ZOLA's not the dark side. I don't know why I was such an asshole about that, at the beginning. I guess I was just insecure and—'

'I get it,' Fia interjects. She doesn't want to rehash all that now. It feels like they are so, so far past it. 'Didn't you say it was your mam who really wanted you to try corporate law?'

He nods. 'I think she actually *is* worried about Daddy issues. And I think she just sees it as an easier option somehow – better earning potential, obviously, but also just, like, less emotionally taxing than a lot of other practice areas. Everything's hard in its own way, though, isn't it? People at ZOLA are working at an insane pace, on crazy-complicated stuff. And most people there are pretty nice.'

Fia would probably agree with him. American corporate culture is terrible, but the majority of people involved in servicing the culture know this all too well. In other words, they themselves are fine.

'You don't think it was a total waste of time then? This summer?' she asks.

Where their hands are joined, he scratches a fingernail down the length of her palm playfully. The sensation makes her squirm, even as she grins along with him.

'Not a total waste of time, no,' he says.

'I meant in terms of the actual job!'

'No. If nothing else, I'll need the reference. Quickest way to get hired is always for it to seem like somebody else wants to hire you. And if the "somebody else" is a firm like ZOLA, then . . . all the better.'

After that, Benjamin talks and talks. And how long has it been, since Fia's heard a man talk and talk and only wanted more of it? In fact, this might have never happened before. As she gobbles up every detail he offers her about his family, his future plans, some part of her brain thinks back to that night in A&E, when she was the one feeling chatty. Perhaps she needed to be there, in Dublin, in order to tell him everything that she did that night – the things that make her feel most vulnerable. Perhaps he needs to be here. That thought – the fact that he brought her to this place at all – makes her feel kind of . . . honoured? Would that be too cringeworthy a word? It does feel fairly cringeworthy. She will have to figure out some other way to put it, when she tells Annie and Kavita.

But then, really, she knows she'll never tell Annie and Kavita any of this. This conversation – maybe this whole weekend – feels sacred. Just for them. Fia's roommates, right this moment, think she is visiting a friend in New Jersey.

By the time she and Benjamin retire to that one bedroom, that one bed, it's been an incredibly long day. Nonetheless, they both know what's about to happen. Fia feels, in fact, that she cannot wait a single second longer for it to happen, and it occurs to her that this is how a person in such a situation should *always* feel. As she and Benjamin gravitate towards each other in the semi-darkness, mouths finding one another, it is the most perfectly obvious thing.

They kiss more languidly – more deeply, deliberately – than they ever have before, taking their time, making this last. When he runs his hand along her sundress, from the curve of her breast down to her hip, she shivers despite the heat.

'Does this thing have a zip?' he murmurs. 'Or buttons or . . .?'

'No, you just pull it off,' she says, and she watches him swallow.

'Oh.'

She looks up at him, and even a week ago, she couldn't possibly have imagined it would be this way between them. She could have imagined frenzy, passion, fun, but she couldn't have imagined there'd be tenderness, too.

A smile tugs at her lips. 'So, pull it off.'

Chapter Forty-Five

The next day brings a long lie-in and, after breakfast, the second coat of paint on the upstairs hallway.

The edging is a bit messy in places, and a few spatters of green have made their way onto the white skirting board here and there. It's not the best job that could have ever been done. That's for certain. But it's the job they did.

Down in the living room, all sorts of miscellany has ended up strewn about, most of it Fia's, and she can sense Benjamin's eyes on her as she begins to gather up her belongings. It reminds her of that morning in Dublin when he walked into her bomb-site of a bedroom. Though he hasn't asked the question aloud, she feels the need to answer it anyway.

'Being organized in work and being on time or whatever . . . it's not like that comes naturally to me,' she says, a bit embarrassed in a way she can't precisely specify. 'As in . . . *not at all*. I don't get any personal joy out of a Post-it note. All that stuff . . . it's literally just about not getting struck off, for me. Even back at Camp Birchwood . . . I was sure that unless I made, like, pretty major efforts at self-improvement, I'd be fired within a week.'

Benjamin just nods, and Fia thinks that maybe he understands it, now – maybe she understands it, fully, for the first time herself. So much of her frustration with him, back then, was seeing herself in him: the self she tried to hide.

In all honesty, she could probably have afforded to work a lot less hard at hiding it back then. They were camp counsellors.

And conversely, as seems to have become clear to Benjamin over recent weeks, he will probably need to step up his efforts from here on out. They're lawyers.

Later, they make their way into town, veering towards the little marina. With a late lunch of bagels and iced coffee spread out between them, they sit on the wooden dock, letting their feet and shins dip into the water.

Leaning back on her forearms, her palms flat on the ground behind her, Fia lets out a little sigh. She's exhausted, but not in the way she usually is, after a long day at the office. This is a satisfying sort of tiredness, one born of physical activity, her limbs feeling almost pleasantly achy. In response to it, for once, she lets herself be idle, lets herself just take in the picture-perfect scene around her. A mere matter of days ago, she hadn't known this town existed. It doesn't have the excitement and opportunity of Manhattan, nor the comfort and familiarity of Dublin. After today, she knows that the odds are she'll probably never come back to Greenport again in her life. She knows that, for a whole host of reasons (not least the risk it poses to her future career and maybe his, too), this thing with Benjamin needs to end. Probably sharpish. Not for the first time, she reminds herself that she absolutely cannot let him get in there first – or rather, *get out of this* first. All that said, she's felt undeniably more peaceful this weekend than she has in a long time.

'So, I guess we'll pack up, hit the road about five?' Benjamin suggests.

Fia nods. 'I kind of wish we could stay,' she says, a minute later.

'I know. Me too. But we love New York City, right?' Benjamin adds dryly.

'Yep,' she says, and she recites it like an incantation. 'We love New York City, we love New York City.'

The funny thing is that actually, now that she's settled back in the US, that sort of feels true again. That mini existential crisis she had in Dublin seems to be receding ever-more in her mind. But then, she thinks to herself, any doubts that sprung up were never really about the day-to-day of her existence in Manhattan, were they? They're not really about the present. They are about sustainability – the future.

'Sometimes I think people at home – in Dublin, I mean – feel a bit sorry for me being here,' she finds herself telling Benjamin. 'And then, sometimes, I think they feel a bit jealous of me.'

It feels like an admission, like a big thing – a slightly raw thing – to talk about.

But Benjamin just takes another bite of his bagel, wholly unperturbed. 'So? Don't you feel a little sorry for them? Don't you use that feeling to validate your own choices, to counteract the part of you that's a little jealous of them? That's pretty much just life, I think.'

Fia takes that in for a moment.

'Ughhh.' She lies right back on the wooden dock, careful not to hit her head, reaching out blindly to swipe at him as she does. 'Stop making so much sense, would you?'

He just laughs, letting her lie there for a minute or two, in comfortable silence.

Then, Fia's phone rings in her bag, and she hauls herself back upwards, reaching for it. Unknown number.

'Fia! It's Susan Followill,' comes the voice on the other end of the line, and Fia jolts to attention. A low-level panic, inexplicable but instinctive, suddenly threatens to rise in her.

'Susan, hi!' she replies, and beside her, Benjamin's all ears now, too.

'I intended to call you on Friday with a quick update, but you know how it is. Did I get you at an okay time? Don't worry, I'm hoping I'll catch Ben this afternoon, too.'

'Oh! Um, he's actually here,' Fia says, and it only occurs to her afterwards that she didn't need to do that. She wouldn't even have needed to lie. Saying nothing would have been a perfectly legitimate option. In any case, it's too late now. On the other end of the line, there's silence.

'He's there right now?' Susan asks. 'With you? On a Sunday?'

'. . . Yeah,' Fia admits, feeling immediately like a toddler who's been caught with her hand in the cookie jar. *We've been playing house*, she adds, in her own mind. All at once, it occurs to her that maybe this weekend, while very enjoyable, has also been entirely ridiculous.

Susan, meanwhile, seems to be some mixture of bewildered and weary. 'I'm just . . . I'm not even gonna ask,' she says. 'I guess you may as well put me on speaker, then.'

Fia duly does so, setting her phone on the dock between herself and Benjamin.

'All right, so, as you know, I've submitted your settlement agreement to the court,' Susan continues, her voice coming out a bit crackly.

'What was that?' Benjamin asks. 'Sorry, the reception here kind of sucks. We're on Long Island.'

Another pause.

'You're on Long Island,' Susan repeats, deadpan. By now, it is as though she is being asked to accept that her divorcing clients are, right this second, wrapped up in bed together. Had she called just a few hours earlier, they might have been.

'You guys *are* still getting divorced, right?' she asks then. 'You don't want me to withdraw the petition? You sounded pretty definitive the last time we spoke, Benjamin, if I remember correctly.'

A hint of what looks like embarrassment crosses Benjamin's features, as though he's recollecting that conversation, too. As though, that day – before they left for Dublin very much at odds with one another – he might have been very definitive indeed.

'Uh, yeah,' he mumbles.

Susan takes this as a sort of generalized green light to proceed with the conversation she originally had in mind.

'All right, well, I called the court clerk on Friday. I just wanted to flag with her that this really is a remarkably clean-cut case, see if she couldn't maybe shuffle it up the judge's list a little for sign-off, you know?'

'Oh? And what did she say?' Fia asks.

'She hasn't made me any promises, but Sheila Katz and I have known each other twenty years. I'm gonna guess we're talking maybe two to four more weeks, tops, and then this is all done. You'll each get a copy of your final decree in the mail, so just keep an eye out. I gotta tell you, this'll be my fastest divorce ever. No mess, no fuss, huh?'

Susan chuckles lightly, and just about leaves space for Fia and Benjamin to do the same, before she's rushing to move the conversation along. This is a woman mopping up her work overspill on the weekend. Fia gets it.

'Anyhow, I just wanted to give you the good news! I know speed was of the essence for you guys. Like I said, I intended to call on Friday, but things were just hectic and tomorrow will be *hectic-er*!'

Again, there seems nothing to do but make the appropriate sounds as Susan wraps up the conversation, says her goodbyes. And, once she's gone, Fia and Benjamin say nothing. They just look at one another.

It's a matter of waiting on a signature, then. Substantively, their divorce is done – unless, of course, they were to take any steps to actively *un*do it.

Benjamin swings his legs a bit, the water sloshing around them noisily. Whatever he's thinking right now, Fia doesn't know, but for her, that whole conversation felt like being pulled back to reality. Another sudden, stark reminder of the situation that awaits them when they get back to Manhattan. Greenport is nice, but it is not real life.

She takes a slurp from her iced coffee, swirling her feet a little to match Benjamin's, as though she's tracing patterns in the water.

'Pretty weird, isn't it?' she says. 'I mean, just . . . given the way things have panned out with us.'

'Pretty weird,' he agrees. For a moment, there's quiet between them once more, before he speaks again. This time, he's faltering, stilted, as though some new prospect has just

365

struck him for the first time. 'Wait. Are you saying that you *don't* want to get—'

'What?!' Fia rushes to jump in. 'No, of course I do! Do *you* w—'

'Yes!' he yelps in turn and, somehow, despite how extremely emphatic they both are being, Fia's not totally clear on what they're actually saying to one another any longer. It seems like perhaps Benjamin isn't either.

She frowns, forces herself to take a minute.

'It would be insane for us to stay married,' she says then, for the sake of absolute clarity.

'Right,' he agrees readily. 'Insane.'

And, just for good measure, she agrees with him, too. 'Right.'

'Right.'

A beat of awkward silence follows, then another, and Fia's not sure where to go from here. He opens his mouth to speak just at the very moment she does, which makes them both clam up. Are they colliding with each other – or missing each other? The practical effect is the same.

'I'd still like you see you, though,' he offers eventually, his voice about as tentative as she's ever heard it. 'That's . . . if you want to.'

'You'll see me all the time,' Fia replies, wilfully misunderstanding him. She just needs a second, to process the fluttering sort of feeling in her chest. 'Practically everywhere you turn, about fourteen hours a day for the next three weeks, there I'll be.'

'You know what I mean.'

She does know what he means. There are so many reasons why it's a terrible idea. And yet.

'Yeah,' she finds herself saying. 'I'd like that, too.'

A little longer, she thinks to herself. If he's not ready to call time quite yet, then maybe she can hold off, too. They will just need to be extra, *extra* careful at work. And, of course, Fia knows she'll need to stay alert in other ways, too. But, provided she watches for the signs, provided she's prepared to cut and run before he does . . . why not, in the meantime, allow herself to enjoy this?

For just a little bit longer.

WEEK EIGHT

Chapter Forty-Six

In the main, it is women, Fia notices, who tend to be accused of *over*thinking things – of having, quite literally, more thoughts than can truly be good for them.

Consequently, she wouldn't describe herself as an over-thinker, purely as a matter of principle. But she does certainly find herself with plenty to think about on a daily basis.

Not always wills, or trusts and estates, or office politics, though those things are generally in the mix. Sometimes, instead, she's thinking about the cost of giving birth, in America, to a baby she's not expecting and perhaps never will be. She's thinking about why her best friend abandoned her two years ago, or about the simple fact of her sister's upcoming wedding, or about what would be the safest route to walk home. She's thinking relentlessly, every fucking night, of what to eat for dinner.

Benjamin Lowry, when he touches her, manages somehow to silence all of that.

He actually always has, now that she thinks about it. Even when she was 22 years old in that bedroom, Fia was able to come up with no explanation beyond *I must have lost my mind*.

It seemed like foolishness to her, back then – an aberration on her part. And maybe, in the circumstances, it was.

Maybe it still is – but Fia can't help it. All she wants to do is quiet her mind, lose her mind, as often as she possibly can. After their little road trip, even more so than before it, everything and everyone else in her life seems to have become a blur, just a slog of waiting to be alone with him.

In the office, the tension ratchets up to almost unbearable levels. Fia begins to worry that anyone who so much as lays eyes on her and Benjamin, in any context – including entirely innocent ones – will surely guess what is going on. If anything, it seems incredible that no one has guessed already. Fia feels like both she and Benjamin practically have it written across their faces every minute.

Thankfully, some moments of privacy do come, Benjamin's roommate having chosen this week for a post-break-up self-care trip to Mexico. Then, it's a different sort of blur, decadent and delicious. Yes, some creativity is required, with Annie and Kavita – alternately, Fia makes excuses for her absence or is vague about her whereabouts. However, she's inclined to think that's a very small price to pay.

On Friday morning, for reasons that have to do with poor planning and lack of self-control, they're in her bed rather than his for the very first time. They've agreed to be *just* on time for work – not a minute earlier. Fia curls into Benjamin's back when the alarm goes, her hands snaking around his middle, a kiss pressed between his shoulder blades.

Twenty minutes later, she's standing at her apartment's kitchen sink, gulping down half a cup of coffee. Around her,

Annie and Kavita are the usual whirl of activity, when out strolls Benjamin, happy as a clam.

And it isn't that he was supposed to hide in her bedroom, per se – she hadn't told him to *hide* – but neither did she necessarily think he'd choose to emerge before her roommates left for work – much less in just his boxers and a T-shirt. He looks unbelievably, heart-stoppingly good.

It's probably that schoolgirl thought, as well as the schoolgirl sense of being somehow caught red-handed, that makes Fia feel a little flustered.

At the sight of him, both Annie and Kavita stop in their tracks entirely, the gathering of jackets and KeepCups all but forgotten.

'You remember Ben,' Fia offers weakly, as if to the apartment at large.

'I do remember Ben,' Kavita says, not doing one thing to hide her delight. 'How 'bout you, Annie – do you remember Ben?'

'I do,' Annie confirms, equally thrilled, and she turns to address him directly. 'It's just *wonderful* to see you again. Although I have to say, it does seem a little early for you to, uh . . . drop by. Didn't your mom ever tell you it's kinda weird to make house calls before 8 a.m.?'

'And so casually dressed,' Kavita adds.

'*So* casually dressed.'

The two girls are looking him all the way up and down now, entirely unabashedly, and Benjamin flashes them a chagrined little grin, before glancing over at Fia.

It's her job, evidently, to say something at this point. Before she can, though, Kavita beats her to it.

'You're just in time for *Pocket Pema Chödrön*,' she tells Benjamin, thrusting the book at him. 'Do you want to do the honours?'

'You just pick one,' Annie clarifies, through a mouthful of a cereal bar. 'At random.'

Doing as he's told, Benjamin flicks through to land on a page, then clears his throat. '"If we learn to open our hearts, anyone, including the people who drive us crazy, can be our teacher."'

He pauses, raises an eyebrow. 'I mean, I'm not gonna lie, that feels pretty basic. Y'all call this great philosophy?'

'Well!' Kavita explodes, all would-be indignation. 'You have *some nerve*, Benjamin – coming in here, enjoying our hospitality, dissing our book . . .'

She trails off then, though, because Benjamin's not paying the slightest bit of attention to her teasing. Instead, his eyes are on Fia's, and Fia's are on him, and the two of them are laughing like fools.

He's safely in the shower when Fia's roommates seize the opportunity for some gossip, conducted at a frantic hiss.

'I knew it!' Kavita exclaims. 'Didn't I say so, Annie? I did! I said that the two of you wouldn't be in Dublin twenty-four hours before it was all hot-hate-sex on the friggin' Blarney Stone or whatever that thing is. And don't think we haven't noticed you've been gone *every night* this week.'

Fia must look a little surprised at that – a little insulted, even, by the slight against her own efforts at subterfuge – because both the other girls roll their eyes extravagantly.

'Oh, please,' Annie scoffs. 'I'm telling you, when it comes to vigilance, the parents of teenagers have nothing on the roommates of a single woman in New York City. Our eyes see everything. And for the record, we know you don't have any friends in New Jersey.'

374

Fia can't help sniggering in amusement.

The sentiment is oddly sweet, too, though. It makes her think, suddenly, about all the time she's spent, over the last couple of years, missing George, ruminating on the tiny ways in which Annie and Kavita are just not quite George.

And of course, they are *not* George. They can never be. But is that really such bad news? Because, for a long time, the main thing George Ferarra has been is *gone*. Meanwhile, the two girls presently staring across at Fia – all attention and affection, despite the million other priorities that doubtless lie ahead of each of them this morning – have been kind and funny and fun. They've been *here*.

As Fia opens her mouth to respond, she hesitates slightly. If they're going to talk about all this right now – and it pretty much seems like they are – then honesty compels her to rewind, course-correct just a little bit of the conversation.

'The thing is, with Benjamin, it hasn't really been, like, a hot-hate-sex situation,' she admits. 'It's been more like a sort of . . . romance.'

It feels ever so slightly mortifying to say that aloud. Why should it be, Fia wonders? There are so many other things she could say. She could say, 'this guy told me he never wants anything serious, but he never wants me to see any other men, not even as friends.' That would seem very normal. One time, Kavita came home from a date and informed both Fia and Annie that the dude had wanted to spit on her during sex. In the discussion that followed, the three girls were appalled but not necessarily shocked – it was as though the confrontation of such an issue was unfortunately just part and parcel of being a modern woman.

Romance, though. That doesn't seem a very modern word to use, a very modern thing to encounter.

But then, nothing about this situation with Benjamin seems to be going according to Fia's usual experience of sex and dating. She has always had the sense, in those areas of her life as much as in any other, of being in control. Now, though, with every day that passes, the risk to her gets only greater, things feel increasingly *beyond* her control.

'Okay, so.' Fia glances towards the bathroom now, and although she can still hear the shower running, she lowers her voice anyway. 'What do I do if I like a boy, and I'm already married to him? But we're getting divorced? And he works in my office? But he's leaving in two weeks? And' – she hesitates – 'also, I don't know if I should even stay in this country?'

That last bit, she realizes, might be the biggest revelation of all, from her roommates' perspective – or, at least, it's the one most likely to affect them personally. By now, though, Fia's ready to admit that she doesn't have the first clue about any of it.

And, as it turns out – at least in the hurried, hushed five minutes she gives them – Annie and Kavita really don't either.

Chapter Forty-Seven

Later that morning, they're in the office when the phone on Fia's desk rings.

'Oh my God, it's her!' Fia blurts out, as soon as she sees the caller ID. Benjamin glances up from his work.

'Who?' he asks.

'Alyvia Chestnut,' she replies. It's been over a week now with zero contact. Truthfully, though, Fia can't say she's given the whole situation much thought. She hasn't wondered why Alyvia hasn't been in touch or what that might mean. She hasn't even been checking up on BabyGAndMe. She's had other things on her mind.

'Well, answer it!' Benjamin urges her.

Fia does, and for the ten minutes that follow, she barely gets a word in edgeways. Alyvia talks and talks – and, try as Fia might to convey the situation to Benjamin with her eyes, she cannot. Then, at a certain point, she needs to give the other woman her full attention. It's actually more and more sobering, the longer she listens. At points, she is fairly certain that Alyvia is either crying or trying not to cry.

Fia makes all sorts of noises – sympathy, surprise, back to sympathy again – until eventually her client falls silent on the other end of the line. And, given the chance to properly contribute at last, Fia finds she isn't sure what to say.

'Alyvia, I'm, uh, I'm just going to put you on hold here for a sec, okay?' she manages eventually, barely waiting for agreement before she starts pressing buttons on her handset. 'I'll be right back! I promise, just . . . yeah! Two seconds!'

She looks over at Benjamin then, realizing that in fact she'll need many more than one, two or even three seconds to explain all of this. Where to start? By now, Benjamin is reabsorbed in his own task, having long since given up the attempt to follow along.

'Well,' she says, throwing her hands up in the air a little bit, as though in surrender, 'you were right.'

Benjamin looks over at her, and the wickedness in his expression is now intimately familiar to her. 'Oh, Fia. Could you say that again, but slower? Maybe come sit on my lap, whisper it in my ear?'

Even in the midst of a second-hand crisis, she can't help but snigger. 'Stop it! This is serious!' she says. She reaches for a balled-up page on her desk, chucking it in his direction, then hopes nobody out in the atrium has witnessed it. That could probably be termed workplace bullying – or workplace flirting.

'So, what?' he asks then, paying attention now, leaning back in his chair a little. '. . . The kid's not our troll after all, is he?'

Given he was the first one to come up with the notion, Fia doesn't know why he's now acting surprised about it. 'Benjamin! Yes! That was your whole theory, remember?'

'I mean, it was just a theory!' comes the reply. 'But, so . . . he's admitted it? For real?'

'Yep.'

Benjamin exhales, his breath coming out long and slow as he assimilates the new development. 'What'd Alyvia say, then?' he asks. 'Turns out Gus doesn't want to be 15 years old and posing with a fucking artisanal train set for likes and clicks?'

Despite herself, Fia laughs grimly. 'Pretty much, yeah. I think he just wanted to stop and didn't know how to broach it.'

'A hundred per cent fair, if you ask me. Give it another ten years, and all these influencers' kids are gonna be filing lawsuits against their parents on the daily.'

'Well, maybe. But, obviously, the way Gus went about *this* was . . . y'know. Terrible. And, my God, it sounds like they've had a hellish week. Gus is upset, and Alyvia's upset that *he's* upset. Also, she's sort of raging at him, though, so . . . it's just a whole big mess.'

'Does she want him to keep doing the posts?'

'I don't think so, but the reality is she's pretty screwed, income-wise, if he doesn't. The sponsors don't really give a shit about her selfies and brunch porn, apparently.'

Benjamin chuckles, and Fia feels compelled to clarify, for purposes of accuracy: 'I mean, that's not how she put it, but that's the gist. That's not even the biggest problem, though. Jonathan – Mister Let Me Flaunt My New Love on Facebook – *he* knows now, too. And, of course, he says he's just devastated to learn that his son's been so desperately unhappy all this time, blah blah. This is all his Christmases come at once, though, isn't it? In terms of the custody arrangements.'

Benjamin raises both eyebrows, a sharp intake of breath giving way to another heavy exhale. For a moment, he says nothing, but Fia can tell his mind is working. He's weighing it all up.

'Well, look, when all's said and done, I guess none of that is our fault,' he says then.

Fia's unconvinced, though. 'Mmm. I don't know. Maybe if my arsey letter hadn't been quite so arsey . . .' She trails off, her brow furrowing in worry. 'Alyvia could lose her kid here. And she *does* love Gus. He loves *her*. Okay, she's a bit of a melter, and she's made some mistakes. Does that make her a completely unfit parent?'

'No,' Benjamin says, 'it doesn't.'

And the endorsement means something to Fia. She knows that, on this subject and probably most others besides, he definitely wouldn't agree with her just to agree with her.

She glances over at the telephone, aware they've kept their client hanging for some time now. 'Bottom line is, Alyvia's going to get killed in court. We won't be able to stop it.'

Benjamin presses his tongue against the inside of his cheek, and for a moment, he looks every bit as glum as Fia feels. 'Well, no,' he offers then. 'But maybe we know someone who can.'

'What?' Fia replies, all confusion.

He nods towards the phone. 'Put Alyvia on speaker.'

'What?' she repeats.

'Just put her on speaker.'

And it might be her faith in him or it might be lack of other options that makes Fia do precisely as she's told.

'Alyvia!' Benjamin says smoothly, once they've reconnected the line. 'Hi. It's Benjamin. Fia read me in. We're so sorry to hear about how everything's gone this week. Have you, uh . . .'

He winces, his eyes travelling over to Fia's, as though he's half amused by, half apprehensive about the thing he must say next.

'. . . Have you ever heard of an Exploratory Reconciliation and Reflection Discussion?'

WEEK NINE

Chapter Forty-Eight

'I still can't believe Susan agreed to the whole thing!' Fia exclaims. It's Tuesday evening, and they're up on the roof terrace once again, sitting at one of the little tables, this time. They've spread out something of a picnic: nothing romantic – convenience food, the likes of which any two co-workers working late of an evening might decide to share.

It's perhaps not the *dream*, but needs must. Benjamin's roommate having now returned from Mexico, his apartment no longer feels like much of a retreat. Neither does Fia's own place offer a huge amount in the way of privacy, and heading out for dinner à deux in public feels like a no go. Even in a city the size of New York, Fia's sure they'd somehow be spotted. On all the occasions you least want it to, Manhattan can feel like a village.

'I didn't even really have to do much convincing,' Benjamin replies, picking at his sweet potato fries. 'Susan was more than *thrilled* to get involved in some reconciling.'

Fia cracks a smile. 'I can't believe Jonathan went for it either, to be honest. Susan gets that he and Alyvia are definitely not thinking about getting back together, though, right? She knows it's pretty much just about figuring out the custody at this point, untangling this whole business with Gus?'

Benjamin nods. 'Yep. We're all set up for a week from Friday at 9 a.m. You, me, Susan Followill, Alyvia, Jonathan, Jonathan's original lawyer, and Jonathan's new girlfriend – he insisted she's part of the package now. Doesn't that sound like a fun morning?'

'The best,' Fia says, taking a sip from her Diet Coke. In fact, it *is* a pretty remarkable achievement, Benjamin having managed – in double-quick time – to get all those different parties to agree on a plan of action, a date, a venue.

As for her part in bringing the whole arrangement together, that came down to two words: Celia Hannity.

Yesterday afternoon, Fia ventured to her boss's office, and explained the situation as clearly as she could. When she was finished, though, Celia still looked altogether confused.

'Wait, let's back up a second here,' she said, one eyebrow raised. 'You've sent our client to some other lawyer?'

Fia flinched internally. She supposed she could have killed Benjamin's suggestion the moment he offered it last week, on that call with Alyvia. She could have doubled down, made it her business to dig up some dirt on Jonathan, fought tooth and nail for the best possible result in court – she'd done all that before. Or, she could have simply accepted the inevitability of a poor result in court, collected the cheque just the same. She'd done that before too.

Either of those options would have been better for the firm. Better, in turn, for Fia herself.

On this occasion, though, even as her boss stared her down, Fia just couldn't feel too badly about having taken another route.

'I just. . .thought it would be the best thing for Alyvia. For her kid. We don't offer mediation at ZOLA.'

Celia seemed to note that, seemed to decide, in front of Fia's very eyes, that there was no point in crying over spilled milk. Did she, in the end, offer an enthusiastic, full-throated approval of the new plan? Fia wouldn't say so, no. But she signed off on it.

'And we're really doing it at the Met?' Fia continues now, looking across at Benjamin on the roof terrace.

'Yeah. Apparently, Jonathan and Alyvia had Gus's humanist naming ceremony there, in one of the private event spaces.'

'Of course they did.'

'There are smaller rooms you can rent out, too, so we've booked one of those for the whole morning. Costs a pretty penny but, hey, if they're willing to pay it.'

'I suppose I'll just walk from my apartment then, instead of coming into the office first,' Fia says, reaching for a few of Benjamin's fries. Their chairs are positioned almost beside one another's, for purposes of taking in the cityscape (among other reasons). She sighs a little as she looks out ahead. While they might be up here mostly for reasons of practicality, discretion, the view is undeniably as great as it's ever been – and actually, this has started to feel a bit like *their* place.

'What a way to end your summer associateship,' she says, trying to keep her voice light. Friday of next week will be Benjamin's last day on the job. With nothing of note having yet made its way to them in the post, Fia's beginning to suspect he'll be leaving ZOLA the same way he arrived, as far as marital status goes. That thought doesn't seem to panic her the way it once would have, though. She doesn't exactly know how to feel about it.

'It's been quite the ride, that's for sure,' he replies, and he leans forwards to kiss her.

She mumbles a half-hearted protest into his mouth. 'We can't – someone could come up.'

'Nobody's going to come up,' he replies, and when he moves in towards her again, it feels so natural to twist her body around to meet his, to let her lips part, to let him pull her hair free from its bun.

'I fucking love your hair,' he mumbles, leaning back to look at her for a second. 'Can I just tell you that? Any time you leave it down, I swear that's all I can think.'

And in a flash, every morning she's ever wrestled with it, wished it to be different, is forgotten. It is impossible, in this moment, to imagine that Benjamin might someday decide not to care a jot about her hair, or about any other part of her; that he might disappear (again) without a trace. Purely as a matter of fact, Fia supposes that's as true as it has ever been. But somehow, in her bones, she just doesn't *believe* it anymore. How can she, when he's looking at her like he is?

He pulls her mouth back to his, then, and the moan at the back of Fia's throat prompts an identical reaction in him, each of them sinking fully into this kiss. Fia can't hold back another strangled sound – she's not *inclined* to hold it back – when, all of a sudden, Benjamin is pushing her away from him. Not pulling apart for air, not seeking to reposition them or refocus his attention in some spectacular way . . . actually pushing her away from him.

'What's the matter?' she asks, all confusion, but she falls silent once she sees the panic in his eyes, once she follows where they're focused.

After that, the thing she's most conscious of feeling – honestly – is anger. As both she and Benjamin instinctively leap to their feet, there is an overwhelming sense, spreading swiftly throughout Fia's whole body, of *I told you so*.

Because behind them, someone has just stepped out onto the roof terrace. It is the one person, in the whole firm, who Fia would least like it to be.

It's Celia Hannity.

Celia, who for four years has consistently made it her business to acknowledge Fia; who has supported her, in bigger and smaller ways, including as recently as just yesterday; who has pushed her forward for things, been kind to her, said, 'We Irish girls have to stick together'.

Celia, who is presently looking at Fia and Benjamin with some combination of abject horror and profound disappointment.

Based on the cigarette packet she's clutching, she was on her way up here for a sneaky one. Everyone, it turns out, has their vices. But it is very clear whose are going to be up for discussion right now.

'What in the *hell* . . . ?' Celia says, apparently too shocked to even manage a full sentence. Instead, she lets out a joyless little huff of laughter – of disbelief, really – looking skywards for a moment before coming back to face her subordinates. She shakes her head, something about her seeming pent up, barely contained. 'For Christ's sake, Fia,' she hisses. 'What are you *thinking*? He's a summer associate! You're basically his boss!'

Fia shoots Benjamin a sidelong glance. In this precise moment, though, she doesn't feel even remotely smug.

This could all have been avoided, she thinks to herself, had Benjamin just *listened* to her. But no. He's always been about bending the rules, hasn't he? Always pushing the boundaries, always with the *it'll be fine*.

And look where they have ended up – so close to the finish line, but very far from fine.

'This . . . this isn't what it looks like!' she hears herself yelp, before she's even conscious of deciding to speak. 'I mean . . .' She feels her heart beat ever faster, her mouth go dry, her mind go blank. 'Uh, what I mean is . . . Benjamin and I, we're actually married!'

Of course, this revelation isn't planned either, it's just all she can think of in the moment. It's a desperate, spontaneous attempt to make things better – to somehow negate the impression of a certain kind of impropriety.

It doesn't make things better, though. One look at Celia's face tells Fia that, clearly and unequivocally. It doesn't make things better at all.

'Married?' Celia exclaims, utterly aghast. '*How*? When? You've only known each other a matter of weeks!'

'. . . We were actually married before this summer,' Benjamin admits then, shifting his weight awkwardly.

And with that, he tells Celia the whole story. Or certain key details, at least – the circumstances of their marriage, their mutual surprise that first day he'd arrived at the firm, the fact of their imminent divorce. Actually, when Fia thinks about it, that's nowhere near the whole story.

It's more than enough for Celia to digest in one go, though. Standing across from them, she looks nothing short of shellshocked now. She starts to pace back and forth across the terrace, every second of it feeling like an hour.

'I just . . . I don't even know where to *start* with this,' she says eventually. 'Is it that we offered a position – a very highly *competitive* position, might I add – to the husband of one of our associates? And then we went ahead and just put him in her office, under her supervision? Because that's bad.'

It seems like a rhetorical question, and so Fia stays silent. She just stands there, heat burning through her entire body, as Celia continues.

'Or is it that he's somehow not *really* her husband, he's just the guy we assigned her to mentor, and she decided to take advantage of that power dynamic? Because that's bad, too.'

Again, Fia can offer nothing in response. Because the thing is, she *knows* this. She has known absolutely all this for the entire summer, and yet she has chosen to ignore it.

'Obviously, I'm going to have to report this to Human Resources,' Celia continues. It seems almost as though she is taking to herself at this point. At last, she stops with the pacing.

Fia feels her heart sink, and when she looks over at Benjamin, she's sure the dread is written all over her face. They both know what that could mean. For him, there'd be no job offer from ZOLA once he finishes law school, which she knows he doesn't care about. There'd also be no reference. She knows he *does* care about that.

Nevertheless, she's inclined to think such a consequence pales in comparison to the ones she could face: dismissal – deportation.

And, once more, it is so, *so* hard not to blame him, at least substantially. Yes, she has free will, but for so much of the last fortnight especially, it hasn't felt much like it. *He* is the one who has got under her skin, who has made her reckless, made her risk all the years of care and control she's put in here at ZOLA.

She looks away from him swiftly. Somehow, even to meet his eyes, with Celia there to witness it, feels forbidden now.

'Please,' Benjamin says then. 'Can't we just . . . pretend tonight didn't happen?'

Celia laughs grimly, and Fia almost does, too. The request seems so ludicrous.

But then, perhaps if you don't ask, you don't get. Because the next thing Fia knows, Celia's eyes are narrowing, her lips pursing. Could it be that she is actually considering the idea?

'What is this, between the two of you?' she asks.

In response, from both Fia and Benjamin, there is only shock. Silence.

'I need to know,' Celia continues, 'if I'm going to even *consider* turning a blind eye to this. So, tell me: what is it? Not when you guys were in college or whatever, not when Benjamin got here back in June. Now.'

Fia sucks in a breath. That's a complicated, frightening question, even setting aside that her boss is the one asking it. Nonetheless, she's prepared to try to answer honestly. She barely has her mouth open to begin, though, when Benjamin beats her to it.

'Nothing,' he says simply.

'What?' Celia asks.

Fia, too, feels the jolt.

'It's nothing,' Benjamin repeats. 'Just . . . long hours, close quarters. Add a little bit of history into that mix?' He shrugs, looking suddenly every bit like the 21-year-old Fia once detested. 'I'm sure I don't need to join the dots for you. Fia and I were just . . . blowing off some steam.'

He doesn't look at her as he says it. Fia suddenly finds she can't take her eyes off him, though, Celia's presence be damned. She can't stop the cocktail of emotion that floods through her all at once, most of the constituent parts all too familiar to her: confusion, fury, foolishness.

'All right,' Celia replies. 'What I just saw tonight was a one-time thing, then, was it? It's done now?'

'Done,' Benjamin confirms, not a jot of uncertainty about it, not one bit of regret.

If Celia notices that he ignores her first enquiry altogether – and surely, she must notice – she chooses not to press the matter. Instead, she turns to Fia. 'What about for you? I need to know what your priority is here. It is your work? Or is it something else?'

And Fia still feels half-paralysed. She is not in a position to properly think. But the answer to this one trips off her tongue, so obvious as not even to require consideration.

'Work,' she says immediately. 'Of course. This was just a . . . a lapse in judgement.'

And, looking at Benjamin now – looking at how very *unaffected* he seems, by every bit of this – she finds she really means it.

Chapter Forty-Nine

'Benjamin, you should go,' Celia says, her usual decisiveness suddenly returned in full force. 'And I mean *go*. I don't want you waiting in the stairwell or in Fia's office or down in the lobby. You need to leave this building right now. And when you come in tomorrow morning, you come right to my office. Are we clear?'

He just nods. And then, with a last glance in Fia's direction – she feels it, ignores it – he's gone.

Celia and Fia say nothing until the lift doors close. Even after that, the silence between them lingers, the horns and screeches of city traffic audible but dampened at this height.

'I'm gonna have one of these,' Celia says after a moment, brandishing the cigarette packet that's still in her hand.

'Sure,' Fia replies, though it doesn't seem like her approval is truly being requested. Already, the other woman is lighting up, sinking into a wrought iron seat.

'. . . You want one?'

The offer is somewhat barked out. Nonetheless, Fia can sense an olive branch when it's offered to her.

'I'm good, thanks,' she replies, wishing heartily she were a smoker.

Even so, she feels bold enough to take the seat beside Celia. Unlike Benjamin, she does not seem to be dismissed just yet.

For another long moment, there's quiet. Celia inhales a drag, releasing it. 'I gotta say, Fia,' she murmurs, 'you would have been the last person . . .' She trails off, begins again. 'And before you say it, I *know* you're not the first. Not by a long shot. I know that. But, what? You think 'cause the men have always done this type of shit, that gives us licence to do it, too? That's not how this works.'

Fia feels the shame burn through her anew, still unable to offer anything in her own defence.

'Like I said, by rights, there should be an investigation here – a whole disciplinary process,' Celia continues, blowing out another long plume of smoke. 'If I don't report this, don't think I'm not aware of all the ways it could come back to bite *me* in the ass.' She lets out a heavy sigh, clicking her tongue against her teeth. 'I can't decide tonight. I need to think about it.'

Fia just nods. She once imagined that at the top of the tree, from where Celia sits, there would never be any fear for your own future, that you would always know exactly what to do.

'Might I get away with a warning?' she asks then, timidly. Maybe other people might not need to ask – maybe other people could be more dignified in the face of their own demise. But Fia suspects all of them would be independently wealthy. 'If HR gets involved, I mean. Or would it be . . . more than a warning?'

'I can't answer that,' Celia replies quietly. 'Of course, Benjamin is only here for another, what? Ten days or so? He'd be long gone in any case. Always the way.'

And there's a softness, almost a sympathy, to her delivery now. In a certain way, Fia thinks that might be even worse than anything that came before it.

'You'd do well to remember who gets left carrying the can in these situations, Fia,' her boss continues. 'Here's a tip: somehow, no matter what, it never seems to be the guy.'

Under the intensity of Celia's expression, the dead-seriousness of her tone of voice, Fia feels as though those words seep down into every cell of her. Consumed by utter, excruciating embarrassment, she lets her own gaze drift out towards the city skyscrapers, the sight not remotely magical any longer.

In her five years here, Manhattan has never seemed so huge, so hostile, as it does right now.

The following morning, Fia walks into her office to find Benjamin's desk gone.

The place feels veritably spacious without it, and it's certainly a lot quieter now that she has the place to herself again: no more of his clutter or his *clack clack clacking* away on the keyboard. Anyone would think he'd never been here at all.

The only thing that has lingered, just slightly, is that distinctive scent of his.

Fia has no idea how to describe it – she's sure a more creative person than her could come up with a better attempt. Rainwater and juniper and masculinity, or whatever. In fact, she knows it's just cologne. Some other sort of product, maybe. Whatever it is, Benjamin Lowry has always smelled incredibly, unbelievably good to her.

And yet, the thing is, she's never even been able to properly enjoy it.

There was, first of all, the period when she hated him – hated the fact that she liked anything about him.

Then, there was the period when she didn't hate him, not at all, and that smell was the most powerful temptation to be resisted inside this little space.

And now . . .

Well, now, there's a degree to which it actually slightly sickens her, this remnant she's been left with, the ghost of him.

She hasn't heard a dicky bird from Benjamin since he walked away from her last night. He hasn't contacted her to, for instance, apologize profusely, to take back everything he said, to provide some sort of account of himself.

Deep down, though, Fia doesn't really expect any of that. After all, wasn't Benjamin himself the one to teach her that sometimes the simplest explanations are the best?

What he said last night was what he meant. Perhaps he hadn't planned to say it right then or in precisely that way, but the substance, she's sure, was true. She and him, these past weeks, have merely been scratching an itch, having a bit of fun, *blowing off some steam*.

How naive to have even briefly imagined anything else. How mortifying, to have bleated on to her roommates about *romance*.

More than any of that, how utterly, unforgivably *stupid* Fia feels, having allowed Benjamin to be the one to decide that they were done. It was, all along, the very thing she least wanted.

All the speeches she composes in her head now, all the things she'd say if she could, the ways in which she might foreseeably claw back some agency . . . they are no use.

Because, as the hours tick by in her big empty office, as the hours become a day, and one day becomes two, the reality makes itself clear to Fia. It settles like concrete in her stomach.

Benjamin will not be texting or calling or dropping by to chat further about where they go from here. He won't be sending her any messages on Facebook.

He is just gone. Again.

And, of course, there are ways in which it's different from the last time he seemed to disappear off the face of the earth. For one thing, this time around, she knows exactly where he is. She hears on the grapevine that he's been moved up to the fifty-ninth floor, ostensibly to assist Brett more closely on the Goldsberry merger.

She simply *cannot* bring herself to go up there explicitly in search of him, though, no matter how much she wants a do-over on their coda. She will not chase after him. She does have some pride left.

Chapter Fifty

Without Benjamin, the remainder of Fia's week is made up of work, roommates, exercise. She even goes for a few too many late-night drinks on Thursday with an old friend – the one sane person from a book club she quit years ago. In other words, all the elements that made up her existence before Benjamin are present and correct. She makes damn sure that they are. She is, objectively speaking, living a fun and fast-paced life in the city that never sleeps.

She's not sure, then, why things seem to feel so empty.

On Friday afternoon, Maeve phones to talk bridesmaids' dresses, venues, save-the-dates, and it takes everything Fia has to dampen down the irritation that rises within her. They're on the tip of her tongue – a dozen caustic comments that she could brush off as witticisms but that would puncture, somehow. They would steal little pieces of Maeve's joy, in ways she'd be unable to quite express but would surely feel.

Why, Fia keeps asking herself, is she tempted by this, the worst kind of bitchiness?

It's not that she's envious of the idea of a wedding, per se, or even of the idea of a marriage. She's certainly not envious of Maeve having met and matched with Conor Quigley specifically. She's never found him to be exactly spectacular. But then, that is likely as it should be. If she found her little sister's boyfriend – now fiancé – to be spectacular, that would probably be a different, much worse, sort of problem. Conor is definitely nice, and he and Maeve definitely seem to do a lot of nice things together, albeit mostly at Maeve's instigation.

Maybe that's what it comes down to, in the end.

The simplicity of Maeve's happiness. It's as clear as a bell, even from three thousand miles away, down a phone line. She has a steady job, a fixed sense of home. And to boot, she is, for whatever reason, in love with this guy who loves her back. She is heading into her future, sure and contented about the shape of it.

That's the thing that Maeve has and that Fia feels further away from than ever.

Of course, her little sister can't remotely be blamed for the emergence of such a gap between them. Fia desperately, desperately doesn't want to blame her. So, she stays on the phone, trying to enjoy the privacy that's been restored to her little office at ZOLA, debating the merits of cake pops over the traditional fruit option. Lottery tickets, Fia agrees, *are* a fun idea for favours. And all the while, she reminds herself: *Love is always patient and kind. It is never jealous. It is never rude or selfish.*

Who said that stuff was just for spouses?

She thinks again about going back to Ireland – not just for Maeve's wedding, but generally. As things have panned out, that might end up more an imperative than a choice. She still hasn't heard from Celia about what she plans to do next.

If Fia gets the boot from ZOLA's New York office, would the Dublin branch take her back? Maybe not. Damien McNulty's enthusiasm could fade fast, once he knows he has a man-eater on his hands. However, at least she has the free-standing right to work on her own side of the pond. She could find a job in another law firm – or, potentially, in some other place altogether? That notion doesn't seem to excite her, though; all the fantasy-career options she's ever thrown out over drinks feel quite different in the cold light of day.

As it turns out, maybe she *is* a little bit attached to the idea of herself as a *high-powered lawyer*. Maybe there *is* a little bit of her identity, her sense of self, bound up in this job. Maybe she does like the way others seem to view her, because of it. Certainly, the thought of losing all that, in one fell swoop, makes her feel utterly at sea.

Who knows, though. Maybe it would be good for her to have a change.

Maybe Ryan Sieman, she thinks idly, would be good for her. They could form a foursome with Maeve and Conor, go on weekend road trips to Kerry and have one another round for dinner.

It's true that the excitement Ryan once brought into her life – for years, he really was such a welcome annual diversion – does seem to have faded a bit. It's true that he's never had much of a grip on her beyond their in-person encounters; she's never thought much about him when they weren't on the same land mass.

But is that really a problem?

As Fia runs and runs through the streets and avenues of Manhattan after work that Friday, faster and faster, the endorphins never seeming to kick in, she's inclined to think that maybe it's *not*.

She is perhaps entering the stage of life in which people begin (if they haven't already) to take a more mature view of things. They find someone nice, suitable, like-minded. They enjoy the practical and emotional benefits of simply being part of a pair.

Or – maybe even better, even smarter – they think *fuck it*, and opt out of the whole horrific business, absolutely and totally. No apps, no friends-with-benefits, no bullshit weekends in cabins.

Fia, of all people, should surely be able to commit herself to one of these logical options. She should surely be able to create for herself a life in which she is never again going to end up – let's say, for instance – sitting breathlessly on the front steps of somebody else's home, feeling utterly hollow and inadequate.

And yet, Fia's in precisely that position, the evening light fading over the Upper East Side, when another jogger slows to take her in. He looks down at her curiously, maybe a little worriedly, and she angles her face away. Seconds later, the guy is gone. If New Yorkers stopped for every young woman having a crisis on the street, they'd never get anywhere. Fia can hardly believe that she may be presenting, right now, like just such a young woman. Her breath is coming out ragged, no matter her furious attempts to suck in air. Her heart is pounding.

What is wrong with her? She's sure she's never felt anything like this in her life.

She makes herself walk back to her own apartment slowly, and when she gets in the front door, nobody's home. Either Annie or Kavita has left her post on the kitchen table, though. There is the usual collection of circulars, plus one large brown envelope.

Fia feels her stomach clench merely at the sight of it. She

rips it open, scanning the contents quickly, and then – it's like she's on autopilot – she walks into her bedroom, the document still clutched in her hand.

Out from under her bed comes a very particular box, and from that box comes a very particular leaflet.

Visit The Grand Canyon! it suggests, with that photograph of the helicopter hovering over the abyss. It's retained its colour surprisingly well, after all this time. When Fia turns it over, the writing in pen has faded a bit, but it's still readable, too.

What was it Benjamin jokingly called it, that first day in Susan Followill's office? Their break-up clause.

August 15, 2016 – get divorced, it says, with two signatures scrawled below.

Fia takes the leaflet in both hands now, tearing it in two, then four, then six. She tears it until it can't be torn any more, until all she can do is toss the shreds into the wastepaper bin.

Finally, *finally*, this task is off her to-do list. She glances down at her divorce decree once more, the document having fallen to the floor somewhere along the way, its black and white text staring back up at her.

And then – whether it's relief, or exhaustion, or something else altogether – for the first time all summer, Fia bursts right into tears.

WEEK TEN

Chapter Fifty-One

Exactly one week later, Fia sits on the steps of the Metropolitan Museum of Art, drinking from a takeaway coffee cup. It's 8.30 a.m., rush-hour traffic in full flow, the street vendors on 5th Avenue attracting a steady stream of customers.

On the steps, too, there are clusters of people dotted all around. NYPD cops and up-and-at-'em tourists, office workers, and kids from the various Upper East Side prep schools. This is a meeting place, a vantage point, distinct from the museum itself. There is so much activity that Fia doesn't notice Susan Followill until the other woman arrives right beside her, towering over her. Fia cranes her neck to look upwards, taking in Susan's tunic and trousers, the chunky wooden beads around her neck.

'Oh! Hi!'

'We have to stop meeting like this, huh?' Susan replies, with a grin. She shifts a little to take in the building behind Fia – the scale and beauty of it. 'I gotta say, this is definitely a first for me. No Benjamin?'

Fia just about manages a wan smile. 'Not so far,' she says.

Because the truth is, she hasn't ruled out the possibility – not altogether. The morning's meeting must surely have popped up on his calendar, just as it popped up on hers. It's Alyvia and Jonathan's big day – so to speak.

'I do think you guys might have mentioned a *little* earlier that you were also lawyers – and divorce lawyers, at that!' Susan continues, with remarkable good humour, all things considered. 'But then, I guess yours was a pretty unique situation. I can't remember ever having *less* contact with clients of mine! How does it feel to have everything done and dusted?'

Over the course of the past week, Fia somehow still hasn't entirely worked out the answer to that one. 'Well, we definitely really appreciate all your help with it,' she offers instead.

It seems to satisfy the other woman, at least. Susan nods towards the museum again.

'Guess I'd better head inside, get set up. You coming? Looks like it could take a minute to find where the hell we're meant to be. A Midtown deli it ain't, am I right?'

Fia musters another smile. 'I'll just finish this,' she says, gesturing with her coffee cup. 'I'll see you in a sec.'

And, as Susan takes off, she settles back down on the steps, absently scanning the surroundings once more. She looks out at all the bodies scurrying up and down 5th Avenue, letting herself imagine what lives they might be headed towards or coming from.

Five minutes later, she drains the last of her latte, but still she makes no move to leave.

It's not that she's *waiting* on Benjamin, she tells herself.

It's sure not that she's *hoping* he'll come. She's actually somewhat *dreading* the thought of seeing him.

Moreover, on his end, she can only imagine he feels similarly. She hasn't had so much as a 'hey, nice divorcing you' text from him this past week. On Wednesday, their paths crossed briefly in the lobby at ZOLA, and he practically looked *through* her, hurrying straight into a packed lift. He left her standing there, her heart pounding, her stomach churning, as though she were a stranger to him.

Fia does think Benjamin is invested in this case, though – invested, maybe more so than anything, in the little boy at the centre of it all. On that level alone, she hasn't been able to shake the suspicion that he might show this morning. The entire thing was his idea in the first place, after all.

8.40 a.m. becomes 8.45, though.

8.45 a.m. becomes 8.50.

Still, Fia sits on the steps, wondering how best to react to him if he appears. Cool indifference? A contemptuous tongue-lashing?

Her biggest fear is that, when it comes down to it, she might be able to pull off neither of those things. How can it be, that *he* was the one to behave badly, to mistreat and humiliate her – not just on the rooftop, that night, but every day since then . . .

And yet somehow, *she's* the one left feeling frozen, ashamed?

She doesn't know what that's about. It is bound to be the patriarchy, somehow.

'Fia!' someone shouts then, jolting her from her reverie.

On the kerb in front of the Met, a yellow cab has pulled to a stop. Stepping out of it – dressed to the nines – is Alyvia Chestnut. Despite the stilettos, she does an impressive job of dashing up the steps in double-quick time.

'Aren't you sweet to wait for me?' she says, before her eyes dart about a little. 'And where's that handsome intern of yours?'

Fia gets to her feet, brushing the crumbs from a blueberry muffin off her skirt and feeling like a wholly different species to the woman now before her.

'Not here,' she replies flatly. She's irritated – not at Alyvia but at herself. Suddenly, she can see clearly that Benjamin is not going to make an appearance this morning. She can't believe she even remotely imagined otherwise.

After all, on ZOLA's rooftop right now, a farewell breakfast is beginning in honour of the summer associates' last day. There will be Bloody Marys and mimosas, while the firm's lawyers pop in as and when they can to offer their thanks and best wishes. The summer associates will hold court until noon, enjoying the view and the sense of achievement, before they all head back to their Ivy League institutions.

Fia reminds herself that of the two Benjamins – the version she met at Camp Birchwood and the version with whom she's more lately become acquainted – only one is actually real.

And when has Fia ever known the real Benjamin Lowry to turn down anything approaching a party in favour of anything approaching work?

'Susan's at the helm today,' she tells Alyvia now, by way of reassurance. 'Even I'm just here for a little moral support. Same with Jonathan's lawyer.'

Alyvia seems remarkably unconcerned by any of this. 'I've had a *very* special morning,' she says instead, her eyes twinkling.

'Oh?' Fia replies mildly. She is aware, suddenly, of being very tired. She's been so incredibly tired all week.

Alyvia nods. 'Do you want to know a secret?'

It seems very much as though she is going to reveal one regardless, and Fia braces herself.

'I'm pregnant!' Alyvia exclaims. 'I literally *just* found out! Can you believe it?'

Fia lets out an exhale of disbelief. Caught unawares, she really *can't* believe this. Joy is very clearly radiating from Alyvia, though, so Fia rushes to offer her congratulations.

'Gussy is going to have a baby sister!' Alyvia continues delightedly. 'Or brother. But, like, hopefully a sister.'

Fia tries hard to keep her smile in place. Every time Alyvia edges towards likeability, she seems to slightly ruin it. And, on this occasion, she's not even done.

'I've already got a bunch of content lined up for when the baby gets here! I'm collab-ing with a diaper brand! Think about the longevity of that! Can you believe it?! With Gus taking a step back, it honestly just could not work out better.'

Again, Fia's smile stays fixed. '. . . Awesome!' she says. There is a reason Americans so love that word. It covers all manner of absurdities.

For a second, there's silence between them, as Alyvia beams.

'Uh, you probably shouldn't mention that in the mediation today,' Fia adds then, her professional brain kicking in. 'The new baby. If you're going to agree to stop featuring Gus on your page, you're going to want that to seem like a major concession – a huge loss of income – and you're taking the hit for Gus's happiness, and so on.'

Alyvia nods, tapping the side of her nose exaggeratedly. 'Gotcha. See? Who said you were just moral support?'

Suddenly, a new thought occurs to Fia. 'Alyvia, this baby, it's not . . .'

She trails off, unable – when it comes down to it – to make herself say Jonathan's name. The prospect doesn't seem out of the question, though. Yes, it is true that they are here today to more or less put the nails in the coffin of the Chestnut marriage. It's true that things between Alyvia and Jonathan have apparently been extremely unpleasant over recent months. But then, Fia knows better than most people that loathing and longing can sometimes sit fairly close together.

Suddenly, the adultery pops back into her head, too – the adultery that Jonathan had alleged at the start of this whole thing, and that Fia has, on Alyvia's behalf, very vociferously denied. Could Alyvia have had this new . . . *content partnership* lined up some time ago? It's an option. Really, there are a lot of options, Fia realizes, and none are any of her business. Alyvia's looking at her expectantly now, though. She's too far in – she has to find some diplomatic way of either asking the question or not asking it.

'What I mean is . . . well, whose is it?' she blurts.

Perhaps not a *roaring* success, as far as tact goes.

Alyvia, however, seems about as steady, as grounded as Fia has ever seen her. She just takes a breath in and out. The little smile that rises to her lips seems somehow calm and triumphant at once. 'Mine,' she replies.

And Fia can't argue with that.

For another moment or two, they stand there together, chatting idly about the traffic, the plan for the morning ahead, the huge television casting opportunities that are apparently available to newborn infants.

Then, just as they're about to make their way inside, Alyvia clutches at Fia's forearm.

'Oh, look. There's Jonathan now!' she exclaims. 'Not to mention his *new woman*.' A second later, though, her tone shifts into something more conciliatory. 'To be honest, I can't even say anything bad about her. She's been all right. Gus likes her.'

Fia turns slightly on the steps, following Alyvia's gaze – she recognizes the man striding towards them immediately: Jonathan Chestnut looks just like he does in the photos she's seen.

As for the woman beside him, Fia recognizes her immediately, too.

Jet-black hair, green eyes . . . every bit of her is as familiar to Fia as her own form.

The sight takes over, makes it hard for her to process anything else. Is this real?

It certainly seems to be.

The shock pulses through her like an electric current, even as Jonathan introduces himself and introduces his girlfriend to boot. His lawyer, he says, is running a little late.

'That's fine!' Fia hears herself splutter in response. 'Um . . . actually, Susan said she'd like to see just you and Alyvia to start with, anyway.'

Of course, it's a bare-faced lie, and she doesn't know where it comes from. The words just seem to spill out of her mouth.

Jonathan looks a little unsure about the idea, glancing over at his girlfriend. However, if it's permission he's seeking, she provides it fairly readily – a chirped 'Sure! That's totally fine!' that Fia recognizes as just a tad strained, even if Jonathan apparently does not.

He turns to face Alyvia, then, and for a second the two of them just regard each other, frosty but – perhaps – thawing. Alyvia's eyes flick over towards the entrance to the Met, and when she looks back, something silent seems to pass between her and Jonathan. Evidently, not all the layers of a long history can be erased. This *is* the place they brought their infant son, once upon a time, to welcome him into the world.

It occurs to Fia that maybe Susan Followill, though not half so glamorous or slick as the lawyers at ZOLA, might well beat most of them on a basic understanding of human nature.

The next thing Fia knows, she's nodding along as a quick flurry of practicalities are exchanged. She's watching as Alyvia and Jonathan head into the museum, side by side, braced for whatever lies ahead of them.

. . . And then there were two.

Still standing on the steps, amid the glorious sound and the technicolour of a Manhattan summer's morning, Fia looks across at George Ferarra.

Together again, at last.

Chapter Fifty-Two

'So . . . I mean, hi,' Fia manages. She hasn't massively thought this through.

'Hey!' George replies, a touch too brightly. 'It's been a while!'

Fia would call two years a while. George looks different now, she notes – not radically, but small changes have an impact: the thicker eyebrows, the new cut of her jeans, the flat shoes that have recently morphed, in popular opinion, from orthopaedic and elderly to simply *Scandinavian*. Fia wonders if she, too, looks different, if she's changed in ways she cannot see herself.

'Shall we . . . ?' Fia suggests then, gesturing with her hand.

Down the museum steps and past the fountain, there are some little tables and chairs shaded by linden trees. On the short walk over there, she and George cover the basics. Are they each still in the same jobs? Yes. The same apartments? Yes. So, George is dating Jonathan Chestnut now, huh? Indeed, she is. And Fia's firm was representing Alyvia, before this whole mediation thing? Also true.

Once all that's over with, though, they seem to run swiftly out of steam.

They're sitting down by now, sunshine glinting through the trees, and Fia thinks of the time George's tampon leaked in the New York Public Library. Fia rushed over there with a cardigan for George to tie round her waist and George was mortified to begin with. She was laughing like a drain by the time they left, though. Fia took one for the team, approaching the stern man at the borrowers' desk to explain how that chair ended up the way it did.

She thinks of how George taught her how to calculate a tip and explained what the word *copasetic* meant and told her that she really needed to throw out that one jacket; yes, it *was* quite cool that she'd had it since she was 17 years old, but still, it had to go.

How bewildering, for all that to be undeniably true, and at the same time, for the two of them – undeniably – to have nothing to say to one another right now.

'Well, I can't believe how long it's been,' George says, once the pause in conversation has officially tipped into discomfort. 'So fun to catch up a little bit. We should definitely grab a drink sometime.'

Fia looks George dead in the eye, letting the suggestion hover for a second. 'Sure,' she answers, and in a subtle way – she must still have some capacity to read the person in front of her – she knows that George can hear what she's not saying, loud and clear: *this is complete bullshit, and we both know it.*

After that, silence.

Of course, they could leave it there. Ordinarily, Fia would. A big emotional scene is not her style.

But, for the first time, it strikes her that once a person gets past the initial horror of such a thing, there is bound to be something liberating about it, too.

She thinks about Alyvia and Jonathan, their willingness to let a stranger root around in their most private business this morning, merely in the hope that something better might be possible on the other side.

She thinks, by contrast, about Benjamin Lowry, who hasn't even bothered to show up.

And, suddenly, Fia's just not content to linger in the subtext any longer. If this is the one chance she ever gets, with George, she wants to take it.

'. . . Did I hurt you?' she asks, into the silence, the question almost unbearably simple when uttered aloud. 'If I did, I'm sorry. And I'm listening. Now's the time to tell me about it.'

For another second, there's quiet. Fia feels like her heart stops inside her chest as she waits for what will come next.

Then, George lets out a self-conscious little chuckle. 'What? No! Oh my God! What are you talking about?'

On the opposite side of the table, Fia lets her breath release. Maybe she should be pleased to hear that – and maybe she is, in a way. Maybe it would have been hard to hear about some huge transgression on the part of her past self.

Mostly, though, Fia finds that she is not pleased. Instead, she is struck by sadness, by a profound sense of finality. You can't have a conversation with someone who is only going to act like you're crazy. If there exists any explanation as to why things fell apart between the two of them, she can see clearly now that George is not going to provide it – not today, not ever. That theory Fia had borrowed from Benjamin, back in the hospital in Dublin, is probably the best one she's ever going to get. Sometimes, a person just doesn't love you as much as you love them.

'You know, it's interesting,' she finds herself murmuring. 'You were actually the second person in my life who ghosted me. And now you're the second one who's turned back up again.' That Benjamin evidently never planned on hanging about for too long, even the second time around . . . she doesn't feel the need to mention that part. She just continues. 'You remember me telling you about Benjamin Lowry? The guy I married in Las Vegas?'

Fia waits for the other girl's nod.

'He joined my law firm this summer. So that's been . . . interesting.'

And if there's a slight sense, now, that George's curiosity is piqued . . . well, *good*, Fia finds herself thinking. *Let her wonder.*

She imagines she could capitalize on it – she would not be the first person to use the base human interest in gossip as a lever, as the means of cracking open an intimacy. She could rehash the whole saga right here and now on 5th Avenue, seek George's comfort or advice or comedy.

What Fia realizes, though – what she realizes this very second – is that she doesn't actually need any of that from the person before her. Whether out of habit or genuine desire, she's certainly wanted George's input at various points this summer. But she doesn't want it anymore.

'The thing is, with Ben, that should have been worse on paper, right?' she continues. 'I mean, he was my husband. You say that word, people take it seriously. That's a relationship that's supposed to be exclusive. Permanent. It has legal impact. But, actually, for me? It was so much worse when you disappeared.'

She pauses for breath, somewhat unable to believe she's

really admitting that out loud. In a certain way, the vulnerability feels good, though. Just as she'd begun to half-suspect it might, it feels like freedom.

'You've made me think I don't know what's real, or that nothing will ever last. I've driven myself crazy trying to figure out what went wrong, between us. I literally *dream* about you sometimes.' She halts again, offers a little shrug. 'And, look, maybe you'll go out for cocktails tonight and repackage all this. Maybe you'll say you bumped into this girl you used to know, and she was so intense and self-obsessed, or she was obsessed with *you*, or . . . whatever. That's your business. I'm sure you have your take on all this, and I can't make you share it with me. But I'm just telling you how it's been for me.'

Sitting across from her, George looks like a rabbit in the headlights now. 'I . . . I don't know what to say,' she replies uneasily.

And, honestly, Fi can't call it. She doesn't know if George's struggle is that she *has* taken in everything Fia's just said or that she *hasn't* – that, somehow, she simply isn't equipped to. It probably doesn't matter. As it turns out, Fia can give catharsis, some sort of closure, to *herself*. She's been doing that – slowly, slowly, at her own pace – even before today.

'Those first couple of years, living here in the city, I needed you,' Fia says softly, and the smile that rises to her lips is a genuine one. 'I'm so happy we were friends. We had *so much fun*.'

A flicker seems to pass over George's face – a spark of recognition – and it lets Fia know: that's true. She at least gets to keep that. She gets to know it wasn't all a lie, between the two of them. That's something.

'Even after I didn't need you anymore, I wanted you in my

life,' Fia continues. 'Obviously, that's not how it's worked out. Sometimes, things just aren't meant to be forever, I suppose. But, yeah . . .' Fia trails off. And this time, in the raise of her eyebrow, the tone of her voice, she knows it's perfectly clear that she's the one who doesn't mean it at all: 'We should grab a drink sometime.'

With that, Fia pushes back her chair. She gets up from the little table, turns on her heel, and she starts walking. Her high heels click against the concrete as she goes, and she's sure she can feel George's eyes on her retreating back all the while. With every step, her heart seems to beat faster, every inch of her like one big ball of nervous energy.

Already, she has to fight not to replay the interaction in her mind, not to think about how she could or should have handled it differently. She handled it how she handled it. And, though there are tinges of sadness in the mix, mostly – as Fia keeps walking, as she takes a few deep breaths in and out – what she feels is something close to euphoria. It rises and spreads, extending all the way to her fingers and toes.

It makes her want to *do* things.

And, suddenly, Fia knows, right as she passes the entrance to the Met, that she isn't going inside.

There's another conversation she needs to have right now instead.

Chapter Fifty-Three

'Is Benjamin Lowry here?' Fia asks someone, the moment she steps out of the lift and onto ZOLA's rooftop. She barely knows the guy she corners, and she can hear the intensity in her own voice – but so what? She goes from person to person, in fact, asking the very same thing of each one, then the next.

'Have you seen Benjamin Lowry?'

It's precisely the sort of undue interest, whether positive or negative, that she's tried so hard to conceal all summer. Now, though, adrenaline still coursing through her body, she is past caring.

She's circled the roof terrace twice to no avail, her mind increasingly frantic – where *is* he? – when she hears her name called.

'Fia,' comes the voice from behind her, and as Fia turns, she sees Celia Hannity standing there. Her boss appraises her for a moment, in a way that makes her squirm inside.

'Come talk to me for a second,' Celia says then, and Fia has no option but to abandon her existing mission and follow Celia into the lift vestibule – the very same place where she and Benjamin, all those weeks ago, had their first fight of the summer.

Once the glass door is closed behind them, Celia gets right to it.

'So, I received Benjamin's mentor evaluation this morning,' she starts, and Fia senses her whole body tense. As it turns out, though, there's no need. 'He had some very nice things to say about you,' Celia continues. '*Glowing*, in fact.'

Fia just blinks. In the circumstances, she can't quite tell how Celia wants her to feel about that. Caught on the hop, she's not sure how she *does* feel about it. She sets it aside to figure out later. For the moment, she just needs to get through this conversation. She needs to get back out there, find Benjamin, and stay focused on what she wants to say to him about how he's treated her. She can't be distracted by the vague mention of some flattery on a form.

'Well, I didn't put him up to it, if that's what you're thinking,' she replies then. 'I haven't even seen him since . . . that night.'

She's conscious it may not seem a hugely plausible claim, given what Celia has likely just witnessed on the terrace – namely, her desperate attempt to hunt down none other than the man in question. In fact, though, Celia doesn't mention it.

'Benjamin told me when he dropped off the evaluation that the divorce is . . . handled,' she says instead. 'And that his plans for after law school don't involve ZOLA.'

Fia nods. None of this is news to her.

'So, that's good news. You know one weird thing, though?' Celia says then, her voice rising in curiosity, as though this recollection is just returning to her. 'He spelled your name wrong the whole way through the evaluation! Like, every single time. I can't even remember how, exactly, but it was wild!'

And, as the other woman lets out a little chuckle, Fia can hardly help the way her breath seems to hitch in her chest.

Fiadh.

Why does the idea of him remembering that – reclaiming it, on her behalf – seem to make something ache inside her? Why does it strike her as ten times more meaningful than any other complimentary thing he might have written about her? She tries to push the questions aside. More confusion, she decides, to pull apart later.

On her end, Celia certainly doesn't seem inclined to spend any further time on the subject now. 'Anyhow,' she continues. 'I've given it a lot of thought and, all things considered, there's probably no need to report that little . . . incident to Human Resources. I've written a nice recommendation for Benjamin, so he can leave happy today, and once he's gone, you can just . . . carry on as normal.'

In response, Fia lets out a strangled little sound from the back of her throat. *Relief.* Immediately, the sensation floods through her like liquid. Should she end up going back to Dublin, it's not going to be in disgrace. She's not going to have to tell her parents she was fired and why – and ask them for a few quid to tide her over, to boot. The whole thing makes her feel almost dizzy, as if she's temporarily floating outside her own body.

But then, amid the relief, there seems to be something else, too. It takes a second to make itself fully known, like a whisper getting louder in her ears: does she *want* to just carry on as normal? Does she want to pretend as though this summer never happened? She cannot help thinking about *Fiadh* – the person she was before she ever set foot in America, the person she really is, at her core. If she is destined to stay at ZOLA's

New York office – if she's going to keep spending upwards of ten hours a day inside this building – it strikes her that she'd like to figure out how to be slightly more herself while she's at it.

'You know what? Maybe you *should* report me,' she hears herself say then.

Celia's eyebrows shoot up. 'What?'

'. . . I don't want to be here on a favour,' Fia replies, the truth of this fact solidifying in her brain even as she declares it. 'I don't want to owe anybody anything. Just, when you do tell HR, maybe say something about my work, too, will you?'

Celia offers nothing in response, apparently entirely unprepared for this turn of events. A large part of Fia can hardly believe it herself.

'I should have told you about the marriage right at the beginning,' she says. 'There's no getting around that. I just should have.'

'You're damn right you should have.'

'And I shouldn't have got . . . entangled with Benjamin, while he worked here. Everything I did or didn't do . . . that stuff didn't just *happen*, even though sometimes it felt that way. I chose it.'

Fia pauses, sucks in a breath. This is awful, every second of it – frightening and humbling and awful. Not for the first time today, though, she finds that there is a certain power, merely in admitting out loud what is true.

'But I'm good at my job,' she continues. And then, lest she be accused of outsized entitlement, 'I'm not saying I could run the place or that I'm some kind of special case. I know you could probably get fifty of me within the week. And I appreciate everything that people at ZOLA have done for me – you especially. But I *have* worked my arse off for this firm, for the guts of a decade. I *do* think I'm at the stage, now, where I'm contributing something. And, surely, there has to be some point where it starts to get even a tiny bit more like a two-way street – where you get *some* kind of loyalty back.'

This feels, in one way, like such a basic statement, such a very modest hope to claim. And yet, somehow, it also feels incredibly bold – by some, she's sure, it would be viewed as nothing less than *impertinent*.

Fia lets her eyes shift, gathering whatever courage she has left in her. Then she looks back up at Celia squarely. 'So, I suppose we'll see. I'm really not a snowflake – but I'm also not a machine. I've made some mistakes this summer . . . ones that have impacted absolutely nobody except me, but still. If it ends up that you need to fire me for them, then . . . I don't know. I suppose you need to fire me.'

And just like that, as Fia offers a little nod of conclusion and reaches for the handle of the vestibule door, Celia Hannity becomes the second person she's left speechless in her wake this morning. She's beginning to get a taste for it, she thinks. Even as heat blooms furiously in her cheeks, she's readier than she's ever been to make it a hat-trick.

Weaving her way through clusters of people on the patio, though, her eyes darting about, she does begin to feel a little less sure about the speech she's prepared for Benjamin.

There are no two ways about it – that name thing has rattled her. Maybe she's reading far too much into the addition of two extra letters, but it just . . . it seems suspiciously like the behaviour of someone who *knows* her, properly. Someone who *cares*.

She's passing by the makeshift bar area when Brett Sallinger stops her, a mimosa in an outstretched hand.

'Hey, Fia! I think you might need one of these, huh?'

As it happens, Fia suddenly feels like that's absolutely true, although she's not sure how Brett would know it.

'What do you mean?' she asks, accepting the proffered glass and taking a large gulp from it. The champagne to orange juice ratio is perhaps not as she would ideally wish it.

'What do I mean? Benjamin Lowry, that's what I mean!' Brett replies animatedly. 'Before he moved into my office, I thought *great guy*, you know? Smart, *obviously* going places, not to mention a Knicks fan. What's not to like? But honestly, these past two weeks? Talk about a sad sack! Tell me, how'd you get through two whole months of it? I feel like I might be depressed by osmosis or something.'

Fia frowns. 'You mean he's been . . .' She trails off, words failing her as she processes this latest information.

'Brooding?' Brett fills in. 'Miserable? A total downer? Yeah. All of the above. I mean, don't get me wrong, he's done the work I've asked him to – but, my God, I'm pretty sure the homeless guy on my block is in a better mood.'

Again, Fia's eyes scan the terrace urgently. It is as though, in her mind, puzzle pieces are slotting together. Or, very nearly, at least. The need to see Benjamin is every bit as great as it was when she marched away from George just an hour previously but suddenly it is altogether different, too. She can feel the frisson of the shift.

'Where is he now?' she asks Brett.

Brett takes a leisurely sip from his own drink. 'You just missed him – he took off about fifteen minutes ago. Get this, he wanted to go to the Natural History Museum! Or no, the Met!'

'. . . Benjamin's gone to the Met,' Fia repeats. It's more of a statement than a question, like something she's telling herself, trying to help her own brain absorb.

'I know, can you believe it?! I guess he's checked out completely by now, just feels like taking in some culture?' His voice lowers a little. 'These summer associates, am I right? And Benjamin's not even a Gen Z! Needless to say, I'm not expecting him back in the office today.'

Fia ignores most of this. 'Was he taking the subway? Or a cab?'

Brett frowns now, as though, for the first time, he might be noticing something a little irregular about Fia – some aspect of her behaviour or countenance that isn't quite as he normally sees it. Impassivity, self-possession, any attempt at sophistication . . . Fia herself would acknowledge that all those things are probably long gone.

'Uh . . . walking, I think,' Brett replies. 'Said something about clearing his head – I don't know.'

Fia takes that in for a moment, tries to calculate where Benjamin might be by now. She thinks about the bumper-to-bumper traffic heading Uptown, about the ever-delayed subway trains. Even if she started walking right this second, the likelihood is that Benjamin will soon arrive at the Met, and she won't be there.

And, if that's the case . . . maybe she's crazy, but somehow, she doesn't know if he'll hang around too long.

Then, in a flash, another thought occurs to her.

Downstairs, in her little office – on the very chair where Benjamin used to sit, actually – there is currently a plastic bag. In that bag, there are a range of items: an empty water bottle, a Tupperware lunchbox she hasn't cleaned out in days – and her running shoes.

Chapter Fifty-Four

Such an idiot, Fia thinks, as she sprints all the way up Madison Avenue, past 60th Street, 65th Street, 70th . . .

Really – she crosses onto 5th Avenue, pushing her way through swarms of other pedestrians – this has got to be one of the stupidest things she's ever done. And that's saying something.

Nonetheless, she can't seem to call a halt to the effort. Even amid the crowds and the humidity, even as her skirt and blouse pull restrictively against her skin, her feet seem practically to bounce along the pavement. It is as though, all summer, she's been in training for precisely this insanity.

Is she half-expecting to spot Benjamin along here somewhere? Maybe so. Her eyes scan the surroundings as she passes 80th Street, 81st, 82nd . . .

She doesn't see him anywhere, though.

She makes it all the way to the steps of the Met, to the exact place she'd started her day, and still Benjamin is nowhere in sight.

She slows her pace at last, tries to gather herself as she walks into the museum's cavernous entrance hall. It's all marble and limestone; vaulted ceilings and columns, and – again – no Benjamin.

Fia can hear her own breath coming out in pants now. Could he be upstairs already, in the Rose Room with Alyvia et al? Or maybe he hasn't even arrived yet? Maybe he's been and gone? As she races through all these possibilities, the ridiculousness of her own behaviour hits her anew. How on earth did she think this would go? Even in her own mind, she doesn't exactly know.

And then—

'Benjamin!'

She spots him, over by the information desk, his name tumbling instinctively out of her mouth. She feels almost as if he might be a figment of her imagination. But no – it's really him. As he turns around, his eyes widen a little at the sight of her.

'Hi,' she offers dumbly.

'Uh . . . hi,' he replies, walking closer to her.

And if he wonders why Fia is breathless or slightly sweaty or approaching from the direction of the street, he doesn't get a chance to ask. She gets in there first. 'What are you doing here?'

He bristles. 'It's my job to be here. I started this thing with Alyvia, every bit as much as you did. I realized I wanted to finish it.'

Fia absorbs that for a second. Maybe, in some other circumstances, it would feel like a triumph – the idea that she has mentored a feckless young summer associate for ten weeks, helped him arrive at a greater sense of his own professional responsibility. As things are, though, Fia just feels herself falter all over again.

'Is that . . . is that the only reason you're here?' she asks disjointedly.

For a moment, Benjamin says nothing.

'And I . . . might have wanted to see you,' he admits then, practically under his breath, as though the words are being dragged from him. Not quite a grand declaration of love or loyalty.

However, it's just about enough for Fia to voice the thing she's been wondering since she spoke to Brett, maybe even since she spoke to Celia.

'What you said on the roof, that night Celia found us . . . about us just being a casual hook-up or whatever . . . did you mean that?' she asks.

She's conscious, vaguely, of all sorts of other activity around them, all the hustle and bustle of a usual morning at one of the city's busiest tourist locations. But, at the same time, from their little patch near the perimeter of the entrance hall, it suddenly seems almost as though they are totally alone. Looking at Benjamin, she has the inescapable sense that his answer to this question could change the rest of her life.

Benjamin just looks back at her for a second. 'You know I didn't,' he mumbles, his dark eyes shifting uncomfortably. It is as if he thinks that her entire purpose here is somehow to humiliate him. Having just run for almost thirty blocks, that's . . . aggravating.

'I don't know that!' she snaps, in double-quick time.

'What?' he fires right back at her.

'How was I meant to figure that one out?'

This time, he pauses, as though forcing himself to really digest what she's saying. 'Oh my God, Fia, are you *serious?*' he asks. 'For a smart person, you can be unbelievably dumb, you know that?'

Once again, it doesn't exactly give her the warm fuzzies. If Celia was to be believed, he was much better at compliments via the written word. But the evaluation couldn't be further from Fia's mind right now. 'Well, you *have* been ignoring me for practically two solid weeks!' she exclaims.

'You've been ignoring *me*!' he all but explodes in return, drawing a few curious looks from people nearby.

Fia, too, is astonished. She's momentarily stunned into silence, in fact. That's . . . technically *true*, she realizes. Also, somewhere along the way, has she lost sight of the bigger picture here – of the *reason* she ran almost thirty blocks? She can hardly be blamed, though. Is it necessary, *always*, for him to rile her like this?

'And I get it! That's the thing, I totally get it,' Benjamin continues, a bit more quietly now. 'This whole summer, the stakes have always been so much higher for you than they were for me. Everything you've worked for . . . I wouldn't expect you to jeopardize that for . . . well, for me.'

As though in embarrassment, his eyes flick away from hers, lingering a moment on the pale, tiled floor. Then, he seems to force himself to meet her gaze again, letting out a heavy sigh. 'This past couple weeks, at the office, I've just been following your lead. Trying not make things worse. And that night on the roof, with Celia . . . same thing. I just said what I thought would help you the most. *Did* it help?'

For a few seconds, Fia offers no reply. Most of her brain – most of every single cell in her body – seems to be occupied by absorbing this new reality: the fear and the thrill of it. 'Mmm. Jury's out,' she manages vaguely. 'I'll explain later.'

In response, she watches Benjamin weigh up whether to press the matter, watches him decide against it. Instead, he glances down at her feet. 'Why are you wearing sneakers?' he asks.

And, all at once – out of absolutely nowhere, really – Fia can see herself in a white T-shirt on a Saturday morning, sitting opposite Benjamin at Sarge's Diner. She can see herself lying in the chipped bathtub up at the cabin, with him perched on the lid of the toilet seat, just there to talk to her – just there to irritate her, probably. It's astonishing, how these pictures seem to form totally of their own accord, like dreams she didn't know she had.

But, about her trainers. '. . . I'll explain that later, too,' she says.

This time, Benjamin lets out an irritated huff. 'Is there anything you *don't* want to explain later?'

And as Fia looks across at him, the answer is suddenly so simple. 'I think I'm in love with you,' she says.

It takes her own breath away, saying those words out loud, and hearing them seems to have much the same effect on Benjamin. For an agonizingly long moment, he just stares at her, his mouth falling open slightly.

And then, in a glorious split second, he's reaching for her, his mouth pressed to hers. Arms flying, lips parting, it's a desperate, perfect collision of a kiss. It makes every inch of Fia's skin prickle, her mind and body feeling finally – *finally* – in total alignment again. Inside this huge hall, there are people scurrying around them in all directions, and for the first time all summer, she doesn't care one bit who sees.

'I'm *completely* in love with you,' Benjamin returns, once they've pulled apart for air.

Fia can feel her face flushing. How impossible that seems.

And yet, gazing at him now, she knows for sure that it is true. His eyes seem darker and deeper than ever, his pupils slightly blown. She doesn't think she'll ever get sick of that look in his eyes – the wildness of it.

'I could end up being the absolute worst thing that ever happens to you,' she replies then. She's not being cute, not making a joke. She's deadly serious.

'Well, back at you,' he answers.

And that's also true. Doesn't Fia know it all too well? It is nothing short of terrifying, the degree to which Benjamin Lowry seems to be able to influence her emotional life. This summer has brought more fluctuation, in that regard, than she's ever known. And how abjectly awful she's felt, this past fortnight, when it seemed like he'd tossed her aside. The whole experience shocked her system completely. Heartbreak. She's ready to name it now, no matter her reluctance to do so before. It does seem a bit like insanity, to willingly submit to the potential, somewhere down the line, for *more* of that.

She doesn't entirely know if she can withstand it. But then, she thinks about George – about the fact that she's already had her heart slightly mutilated once. She's already known what it is to have to reshape her life in the demise of something. She's survived that. She's perhaps even seen the growth that can come from it. And, on balance, yeah – she thinks it was worth it. Given the choice, she'd do it all again.

So it is that she looks up at Benjamin, a droll expression on her face.

'Well, you know me,' she says. 'I like to take a risk every now and then.'

He just laughs, loud and hearty, leaning down towards her again. This time, they kiss more giddily, smiling against each other's lips, hands nudging playfully at each other. They stand there entwined for far longer than Fia cares to estimate.

'. . . So, you think we should go find Alyvia and Jonathan?' Benjamin asks eventually, glancing upwards to the Met's balcony.

'Honestly, I think Susan has it all under control,' Fia answers. 'Let's face it, we might even be the last two people on earth whose input she would want this morning.'

'Well, we *are* divorced now,' Benjamin says.

'We are,' Fia agrees quietly. It feels a little strange to talk about that, this late in the game. Benjamin still looks nothing but happy, though.

'And look how well we're getting along,' he replies. 'If you ask me, Susan Followill should be *begging* us to show the Chestnuts how it's done! I'm telling you, she'll want to put us on her website.'

Fia smiles along, but the question that follows is a sincere one. 'How did you feel, when the divorce came through?'

Benjamin shifts into seriousness too. 'I don't know. I can't describe it,' he says, as she nods in agreement. 'I think it's good, though,' he continues. 'No more baggage, you know? No more blame.'

And Fia finds she agrees with him there, as well. This ending – the same one that she has, whether consciously or unconsciously, probably spent most of her twenties waiting for – feels suddenly like a new beginning. In a flash, all the anxiety she's harboured about turning thirty seems to melt away. If anything, she finds herself almost excited by the number. She feels like she's earned it. She wouldn't, she realizes, go backwards for anything.

'Anyhow, are you saying you want to play hooky from work right now?' Benjamin asks then, a grin twitching at his lips.

434

Fia cocks an eyebrow. 'I mean, no, I'm saying maybe if we came back in an hour, that would be fi—'

'Because, if that's what you're telling me – as my superior – then, what can I do?' he continues, his voice rising in pure delight. 'Yes, Fia, I *will* go boating with you in the Central Park lake, if I absolutely must.'

She can't help it, she laughs out loud at that, letting her hand find his. '. . . So, just to be clear, you're not still hung up on Jessy?' she finds herself asking, a moment later, while they walk towards the exit.

For a second, Benjamin looks genuinely confused, the expression soon giving way to amusement. 'Jessy my girlfriend from college who broke up with me in a branch of American Eagle Outfitters seven years ago? That Jessy? No.'

'I'm just checking!' Fia squeaks in protest. And then, it's as though she's compelled to lay it all out on the table, everything that could possibly screw this thing up: 'Also, I have to tell you that I might not even want to stay in New York – like, long-term, I mean, no matter what happens with ZOLA. I might, but I don't know, it's just very complic—'

'So, you like New York when you're here, except for sometimes not so much,' Benjamin interjects, as they step out into the fresh air now. 'And then you like Dublin when you're there, except for sometimes not so much. That about cover it?'

Fia feels the wind somewhat taken out of her sails. '. . . Um, yeah.'

In fact, that's precisely it. Hasn't she seen before, more than once, how he seems to be able to distil things down to their simplest form?

He shrugs, with the very same casualness that would once have driven her almost to violence. 'That's just geography,' he says, and he stops still, turning to her at the top of the steps outside the museum. 'I'm going to lay this out for you, okay? I don't know how – or when – it happened that my idea of a perfect day started to look like you.' He pauses for breath, his cheeks pinkening slightly. 'And that's you in an office in Midtown, you in Dublin with your family, you up at the cabin in Greenport . . . You're the only person I fight with, but you're the only person – really, seriously, the *only* person – that I can sit in silence with. I literally just want to be where you are, Fia. I don't know how to say it any other way. You want to move to Ireland – hell, once I'm done with law school, I'll move to Ireland. We'll just . . . figure it out. If you want to.'

Something – everything – inside Fia whispers *yes*.

I do.

She must say it out loud, in fact, because she watches Benjamin's reaction spread across his face, like pure joy.

He loops his arm around her, the two of them perfectly in sync at last as they make their way down the steps, towards the entrance to Central Park. All around, it's people and yellow cabs, greenery and construction work, sunshine and the faint whiff of warm garbage. It's New York City in the last weeks of summer.

'Did you mean that about Dublin?' Fia can't help but ask, a few minutes later. They've made it into the park by now, and with the din of the city muted, she can hear how her own voice comes out sounding bashful. 'You would really consider living there?'

'Sure,' he replies easily. 'I'd try it out, at least. Obviously there's the whole immigration situation, though. I can't imagine your fine country lets just anyone in.' He pauses, a smile tugging at his lips anew. 'We may need to get remarried.'

Fia lets that notion register for a moment, raises an eyebrow slyly. 'What, purely for the visa?'

Benjamin holds her gaze, as undaunted as he has ever been. 'Purely for the visa,' he agrees then, all breeziness.

And, as Fia laughs, the sound rising like a song, something catches her eye.

Beside them, on the corner, there are a few pedicabs waiting for customers. There's a guy selling postcards and another offering caricatures and a little carousel of tourism brochures. *Visit the Statue of Liberty!* one of them reads, accompanied by a glossy photograph of a helicopter from which Fia can well imagine plummeting to her death.

She's not one bit keener to take this tour than she was to take a similar-ish one, long ago. But then, she thinks, such leaflets really are multipurpose. So very *useful* for all the big decisions in life, for any proposals a person might or might not eventually have for another. She reaches for one as they pass, slips it into her pocket.

Just in case.

Acknowledgements

Thank you, Lucy Stewart. It turns out that 'I basically just want my editor to enjoy this' can power a person through writing an entire novel. Your care and enthusiasm has been such a gift. I don't think I could have done it without you and that's really all there is to it.

Thank you also to the wider team at HarperFiction, each of whose contributions I wanted to specifically note in the credits to follow these acknowledgements. It takes a village, and I'm continually impressed by the talent and passion that all of you bring, in different ways, to the task of helping books reach readers.

Thank you to the team at Curtis Brown, especially Sheila Crowley, Sabhbh Curran and Anna Weguelin. I feel so fortunate to have such brilliant and dedicated people in my corner.

Thank you to my colleagues and clients at SD, all of whom make me sincerely grateful, on a daily basis, for my unique version of law firm life.

Thank you to the organisers of, and participants in, the Edinburgh Writers' Forum and the Scottish Book Trust's 'Debut Lab' 2022. So many authors talk about the problem of isolation, and I'm thrilled to have found a community amongst you all.

Similarly, thank you Marie Taylor, Lizzie Sparks, Clare Devlin, Sara McLaughlin, Fionnghuala Murphy-McEwan, Sarah McHugh, Mary-Jane Byrne, Heather Darwent and Kristin Cooper. I'm sure I've omitted people accidentally here. In short, if you are a woman and you are my friend, and you've ever let me hijack a perfectly nice lunch by talking at length about my novel (including, but not limited to, such subjects as: *what should it be called, how should it end, will anyone buy it, does this even make sense?*) then I appreciate every minute.

Thank you, Matthew, Caitlin and Daniel for being the smartest, coolest, best company (since birth). I love you.

Thank you, Charlie. You really haven't assisted at all with this book, and you don't know much about blue whales, but you've otherwise turned out to be a nice addition I'd say.

Thank you, Caitriona, Mum and Dad, for absolutely everything.

Credits

Together with the author, HarperFiction would like to thank the following staff and contributors for their involvement in making this book a reality:

Editorial
Lucy Stewart
Lynne Drew

Design
Ellie Game
Claire Ward

Sales
Alice Gomer
Harriet Williams
Bethan Moore
Ben Wright
Hannah Avery
Tony Purdue
Jacqueline Murphy
Laura Daley

Production
Sophie Waeland

Operations
Melissa Okusanya
Hannah Stamp

Copyedit
Katie Lumsden

Publicity
Sofia Saghir
Felicity Denham

Proofread
Penelope Isaac

Marketing
Emily Merrill
Sarah Shea

Finance
Natassa Hadjinicolaou
Fiona Cooper
Katrina Troy

Audio
Fionnuala Barrett
Ciara Briggs

Legal
Arthur Heard

If you loved *The Break-Up Clause*,
make sure you read Niamh's debut novel. . .

'Snap-crackling with wit and energy, ridiculously enjoyable'
MHAIRI MCFARLANE